Also by David Sheppard:

Oedipus on a Pale Horse
Journey through Greece in Search of a Personal Mythology

Novelsmithing
The Structural Foundation of Plot, Character, and Narration

The Mysteries
A Novel of Ancient Eleusis

THE ESCAPE OF BOBBY RAY HAMMER

A Novel of a '50s Family

by

David Sheppard

FOR

All the kids of Chowchilla.

Acknowledgements

A special thanks to Renate Wood in whose creative writing class this novel was initially conceived. She also read the first draft and provided much needed guidance. Renate passed away in 2007 from ALS. The novel was written with the criticism and support of a private novel writing group in Boulder, CO. Thanks to Amy and Sita for midwifing the first draft. I submitted a second draft to the Rocky Mountain Writers Guild's Advanced Novel Workshop under the direction of Dr. James Hutchinson, who provided support and critiquing.

Author's Note

This is actually my first novel and was written between the years 1988-93. It started out as a class assignment in my first creative writing class at the University of Colorado at Boulder, in which my instructor, the poet Renate Wood, suggested we write a short story about someone as different from ourselves as we could imagine. To satisfy the requirements of the assignment, I wrote and submitted what is now Chapter 2. The concept had its origin in my own childhood with the death of my older brother's best friend in an automobile accident. Later on, I became friends with the dead kid's younger brother. We played high school baseball and drank a lot of beer together. His family never really seemed to recover from the death. But his family was much different than that portrayed here, as is mine. The story had a momentum and direction of its own, and no one I knew actually shows up in the novel; however, anyone who went to Chowchilla Union High during the 1950s would certainly recognize the town, its people, and perhaps an element of themselves scattered about the various chapters.

Table of Contents

Table of Contents

Table of Contents

THE ESCAPE OF
BOBBY RAY HAMMER

A Novel of a '50s Family

Is not my word like as a fire?
saith the lord; and like a hammer
that breaketh the rock in pieces?
                    Jeremiah, 23:29

PART I

Charles Kunze's Gold Rush

CHAPTER 1: *Rascal at the Cemetery*

Memories of May 1952

Papa had a pistol. He hardly ever carried it, but I knew he had it on him that day. I saw that black metal barrel and the little round cylinder with the shiny gold bullets that turned when he fired it. I didn't see it sticking out of his back pocket which it sometimes did when he was going out in the field to target practice or maybe in his hand hanging down at his side when he was going out to shoot something that needed to be shot, like when a dog got its legs caught in the hay mower and was yelping and stumbling around on bleeding stubs and dangling pieces. I didn't see the pistol that way. That day it was more like the time he carried it inside his jacket when he was paying the hired hands for picking cotton, and they didn't like the way the weights were adding up. It was like he was expecting trouble. I didn't actually see the pistol, I just saw it in his eyes.

Not that Papa looked at me. He hadn't looked at me or said a word to me in three days. But he'd been thinking a lot about the police. He argued with them about how Lenny died. "It was no accident," Papa said. "Lenny was too good of a driver to make that kind of mistake." I thought he was going to hit Brock. Papa backed Brock up so that he had to get in his police car and leave.

I knew I'd done something wrong, but I just couldn't remember what. Maybe someone else was going to get blamed for it. And Papa kept on, so I knew he knew something.

It was all my fault.

Mama was grief stricken, so I didn't blame her for not keeping Papa from bringing his pistol, and I didn't blame her for what happened at the Chowchilla Cemetery. She was all torn up inside and kept Trish and Curt close. She just couldn't quit screaming. For three days after my older brother Lenny was killed, she'd been that way. It would be quiet in the house, quieter than usual because she wasn't working in the kitchen like she was most times, washing dishes or maybe banging pans baking chocolate meringue pies or just frying up a mess of fresh-caught perch. She was in her bedroom being real quiet, and then she would scream and just keep screaming like she'd forgotten that it happened and then remembered he was dead all over again.

That is the way it was with me. Every time I thought of it, it was like I had just found out all over again. While Mama was locked in her bedroom, I'd go into mine and sit on the bed with my head down. Sometimes little Curt would come in and sit on the floor at my feet. He was nine. Then Trish would come in. She was ten. She would sit by Curt on the floor, and we wouldn't say a word. Just listen to Mama scream. I felt like I should do something. I'd replaced Lenny as the oldest boy, but I didn't know what to do about things like he had.

Leroy was my best friend then but I didn't like him much. His daddy brought him over to see how I was doing. First he wanted to play catch, but I said no. Then he wanted to play with the dog, Lenny's dog, Rascal, and I said no again. So he sat on the bed beside me, and the two of us looked down at Trish and Curt as they looked up at us, Trish with those big blue eyes. With Mama letting out a scream once in a while, we didn't have to say anything.

"I don't want you here," I told Leroy after a little bit. "Go home." Leroy always irritated me, but I'd never been mean to him before.

And I was still mad at Lenny for hitting me with a baseball, even though he was dead. I was playing catch with him only the week before. He was throwing the ball really hard, and I got afraid because he'd hit me with the ball before. Charles was there too. He was Lenny's best friend. We were playing three way catch.

"Take it easy when you throw to Bobby," Charles told Lenny.

Lenny was almost five years older and always called me a sissy. He was a senior and I was in the eighth grade, even a little small for an eighth grader.

"Hold it, Lenny," said Charles, but it was already too late.

Lenny, he laughed because after it hit me in the head, the ball went straight up in the air like a pop fly and he caught it. "Funniest thing I've ever seen," he said. "A real high pop fly. When a ball hits a sissy in the head, the higher it goes, the bigger sissy he is. This one went a hundred feet high and I caught it."

Chapter 1: *Rascal at the Cemetery*

The ground floated on me, and it was hard to stand.

"You shouldn't have done it, Lenny," said Charles. Charles is the only one that ever took up for me. But he was mad at Lenny that day anyway. I didn't hear all it was about, but I thought they were going to start hitting each other over a couple of girls.

I was dizzy for days. Mama said that if the dizzy spells didn't quit, they'd have to take me to the doctor. She took my temperature, and even it was running a little high. Then Lenny got killed.

But after him hitting me, I decided that one day, one day when I got big enough, I was going to get Lenny. I had already started the countdown. The only thing I could hurt Lenny about was that he used to keep a little notebook where he wrote things. He didn't like me making fun of him for doing that. I used to sneak it out, read parts and then laugh. He hid it from me, hid it from everyone. So I would have to wait till later to get back at him. When I got to be a senior in high school, like he was then, I'd be big enough to kick his ass. But then I remembered that he laughed when Papa shot Tangi, so I didn't know if I could wait that long. You'd think that after he was dead, I wouldn't have had to be mad at him anymore. Him being dead didn't seem to help a bit.

But, Rascal triggered what happened at the Cemetery. Papa was primed for sure, but Rascal set him off. Lenny's dog was named Rascal. Rascal had the hots for Lenny's Block C jacket. Lenny had four white stripes on the left sleeve, one for each year he lettered in varsity baseball. Mama was always sewing a patch on it because Rascal liked to chew and that jacket was his favorite for chewing. He got mad when Lenny tried to take it away from him, and he'd growl and pull on a corner of it, or he'd stand on it with his front paws and bark in Lenny's face real loud. Lenny liked to tease him that way. Once I even saw Rascal try to mate it.

Aunt Loretta could see it coming. She kept telling me to stand back a little more from the coffin. Mama asked her to watch me because I had a bad case of the flu. I get nervous around Aunt Loretta. She always dresses weird. You'd think she could have worn something a little different for a funeral. Maybe it wasn't the way she was dressed so much as it was the fact she didn't have a bra on underneath. And she is so sloppy because she's just a turkey farmer. She hadn't even made sure she had all the buttons buttoned and a couple in the middle wasn't, so her blouse stood open a little. If you looked real close you could see inside. I mean, this was a funeral. At least her skirt was black.

So she was standing next to me, and I smelled a strange mixture of perfume and turkey shit as she patted me on the shoulder now and then and said, "Stand back a little, Ray." And Papa kept ignoring me to the point where I knew I'd done something wrong. For the life of me, I couldn't remember what it was. If he knew, why didn't he do something to me?

I could tell that Papa was irritated with Charles when he showed up late and had on those dark sunglasses. He could've at least been on time. Lenny and Charles played baseball at the high school together. Played a lot of things together for that matter. And one of them was Helen, Lenny's girl. She was one of the girls he was arguing with Charles over just before he got killed. She was there, right in the middle of things, all that red hair piled high up on her head so her long white neck and ears showed, and her face an absolute mess, as wet as it was, and her eyes still pouring tears. Her nose was so red I wondered if it was bleeding, and she kept rubbing on her face so hard that it seemed like her eyes, nose and that fat mouth of hers had all changed places. Didn't even look like a face and she wasn't usually that bad looking. Charles came over to say something to her, but she hit him before old Charles even got a word out. Slapped him hard in the face so that it echoed all over the Cemetery, almost knocked his sunglasses off. Even the preacher, Brother Hensen, turned to look, but he turned back real quick like he didn't want any part of it. Papa looked like he was going to help her for a second but then thought better of it. Helen kept at her nose so that it did start bleeding, and it was a while before she noticed. She had blood everywhere in no time. That side of Charles' face got real red like he was blushing, and he kept looking from side to side, turning his head like he was confused, and it was like "now he's blushing and now he's not." Then Charles noticed me, and came over and put his hand on my shoulder, but Papa shoved him back over by his father. Papa didn't want anybody feeling sorry for me.

"Karl," that's Karl Kunze, Charles' father, "you get that kid out of here," Papa told him, meaning he wanted Charles to leave. "And get the hell out of here yourself." Papa didn't want any of the Kunze's at Lenny's funeral for some reason. Karl's a short little fellow, wide as he is tall, and he didn't have a wife there with him because he didn't have one. She died in a car wreck four years before. He had on his overalls just like he had to stop milking cows to come to the funeral and was planning to go right back afterward.

10

Chapter 1: *Rascal at the Cemetery*

Since Papa was getting madder and madder at Charles, I got to thinking that maybe it was because Charles was still alive and Lenny wasn't. I know I sure felt like it wasn't right, me being alive and Lenny dead. Then Papa turned from Charles and looked at me, and I thought he was going to hit me. But then I saw that Papa was crying, and I'd never seen him cry before. I knew Papa didn't know what I'd done. But he acted so strange toward me that I even thought maybe I'd made a mistake, maybe I shouldn't be there at all. Maybe there was a thing that said kids shouldn't be at their brother's funerals. If there was, Mama and Papa wouldn't have thought to tell me because they weren't thinking straight. Trish and Curt were there, but they were little kids.

Papa was mad about something else, that something else was Charles. Charles stood tall and straight in his new pair of graduation pants and white shirt with his fists clenched, standing a good head taller than his father. He kept clenching and unclenching those fists and looking from side to side like if he got his chance he was going to straighten out something with Papa.

Then there was Gretta, Charles' younger sister. "Take that whore," Papa said, meaning Gretta, and there wasn't any doubt who he meant because he was pointing, "with you as you go," he told Karl. I didn't know what 'whore' meant then. I thought maybe she'd been chopping cotton for some farmer and that instead of 'whore' he was saying 'hoer' and Papa just called her that because he knew what she worked at but didn't know her name. Papa was mad, but I didn't think he could be mad at her. She was just standing off in the background, looking a little big around the middle for a girl her age. I remember hoping she'd get to stay because she had a big black hat shoved down on top of the fluffiest golden hair I'd ever seen. I really hated to hear that Gretta and Charles had to leave. She was the other girl Lenny and Charles were arguing about before Lenny got killed.

So Brother Hensen started his "ashes to ashes, and dust to dust" thing, and I was waiting for Charles and the rest of the Kunze's to leave like Papa told them, when up ran Rascal. Papa had left the pickup window part way down so Rascal could get some fresh air. But he got out through the window, and what he was dragging with him was why Mama started screaming again. It was Lenny's Block C jacket. Just before he was killed, Lenny had been looking for it. I heard him and Mama arguing. He accused Mama of hiding it because she didn't want to patch it anymore. The jacket had been lost for weeks. Rascal had found the jacket behind the seat in the pickup and was bringing it to Lenny for his final send off.

Now, Rascal hated Charles more than any dog has ever hated a human being. I don't know what Charles had done, but it must've been something bad. Charles was the only one Rascal ever bit, and he'd bite him every time he came over if Lenny didn't hold him off. Lenny was a little slow about it, and Charles always got mad. So Rascal came running into the Cemetery with Lenny's jacket like he'd just found the one thing to make this occasion perfect, and he looked like he was glad to get to do the last good thing anybody could do for Lenny. Then he saw Charles.

Papa'd quit harping on Charles being there and Brother Hensen was getting into all the fine words he brought that would put Lenny to rest, and Mama had quit screaming again and was just crying softly when Rascal ran up with Lenny's jacket, dropped it by the coffin and lit into Charles. "You mangy sonofabitch," is what Papa said when Mama screamed and I thought he was talking about Rascal but then realized that Rascal had just set him off on Charles being there again.

I'm still confused about what happened next. The pain in the back of my head started throbbing again, and I thought Lenny had just done something else to me. Aunt Loretta had me by the armpits and was pulling me off of the ground, and I didn't even know I fell. Mama, Trish and Curt were gone. People had scattered. There was a chase. Gun shots.

Aunt Loretta pulled me to her breast saying something about me fainting. "Don't look, Ray," she said. "They're all killing each other."

I heard Rascal yelping like he always did when Papa shot that pistol. I never liked to hear the pop of Papa's pistol because he always fired it fast and never knew what he was going to hit. Rascal didn't like that pistol either, so he ran and hid when he heard it. He didn't like it because Papa shot my dog, Tangi, with it when she was hurt so bad from the hay mower. I called her Tangerine because she was so small and round-like as a pup and so red. Peeking from just inside Loretta's hug, I caught a glimpse of Rascal running. He must've run forever because he never came back. And I thought Papa's pistol would never quit firing.

Aunt Loretta walked me through the short grass that had just been mowed to the far side of the Cemetery. I got to stumbling and couldn't stand again, so she was sitting and rocking me with my head in her lap, and she was all wet with my sweat that I had from listening to Mama's screaming and all the shouts and cusses and a couple more pistol shots. She was sweaty and I was sweaty and my hands were trembling and the side of my face all pushed up against her breast so I could hear her heart pounding. Then I heard more pistol shots, and Papa still shouting at Charles.

"Don't look, Ray. Don't look," Aunt Loretta said. And then "Oh, God, no. Oh Charles," as she covered my eyes again and this time, she started crying. Just before I went out again, I thought that the worst had happened. Papa had killed Charles, the only person with any sense that ever took up for me.

★

I had to stay in bed for days after that. Mama kept feeding me aspirin to get my fever down. And while I was lying there, I heard Mama and Papa whispering in their bedroom. They didn't make much sense. They said they buried him with Lenny. Not a whole lot of sense in that at all. They put Lenny's Block C jacket in there with them. I felt bad about the jacket too. Lying there in bed with the covers all pulled up over my head and the sweat pouring off of me from my fever, I wondered if they opened the coffin and put Charles inside with Lenny, one at the head and one at the foot like they were sleeping in a bunk bed, or if they just shoved him in on top of the casket. Either way, it didn't make much sense. Papa must have killed Karl too, I thought, or he would have stopped them from burying Charles like that. That night I didn't sleep good. I woke and saw a woman dressed in a red robe flying around the room. I think it was Jesus' mother, Mary. I kept looking at myself, putting my hand before my eyes. I was so hot, I thought maybe I was glowing in the dark.

A few days later, after I got better, I found out that Karl was still alive. Saw him crossing Robertson Boulevard in downtown Chowchilla. Then I thought maybe I'd misunderstood Mama and Papa about what they did with Charles. I thought maybe he'd be buried later. I read the Chowchilla News, in the place where they told about Lenny's death, to see about Charles. They never printed anything about it. I thought the police would come get Papa. I sort of held my breath on that one for days. Finally I asked Mama how they buried Charles.

"What's the matter with you," she said, and she was mad at me for asking. "Is your brain addled? He's not dead." If she hadn't been mad, I might've believed her. I didn't know why she didn't just tell the truth. I felt really bad for asking because she started crying and went to her bedroom

13

for the rest of the day. We had to fix dinner for ourselves that night. I knew better than to ask any more questions.

I didn't really believe what I thought I saw and heard that day, but it set in my mind like cement because I didn't have the truth to replace it. And in the four years since Lenny's death, I've come to know one thing. I want out of here. I heard Lenny talking about leaving before he got killed, talking about getting out of Chowchilla. He kept talking about how good things were on the outside. I've made up my mind to be free someday. Since Lenny died I've felt like I'm fenced in. I run in the fields sometimes, just run from one side of our farm to the other, from fence to fence. I watch cars on Highway 152 going to the coast, Oakland, San Francisco, Santa Cruz. I listen to baseball on my little Philco radio. I listen to the New York Yankees like Lenny used to do. I listen to football, the San Francisco 49ers. Maybe Lenny didn't make it, but I know I will. I know the world is different out there. I want out. But I need something, something to get me from where I am to where I want to go. It's as if a big canyon is keeping me from getting there. So I've been thinking about bridges. That's what people do to get over things they can't cross. They build bridges.

CHAPTER 2: *Fight!*

September 1956

I hear someone shout "Fight!" as our car pulls out from the high school parking lot, and then a trail of cars full of kids follows behind. So I get uneasy, feel a little wedged in like the car seat's too close, and I shuffle my legs a little, but it doesn't help none. Leroy's driving and laughing like hell, looks through the rear view mirror at them pulling in line behind us. He put the word out. He doesn't give a damn.

I'm talking to Leroy about how come we have to use the Berenda Slough because that's where my older brother, Lenny, got killed.

"Grow up, Bobby," he says. "He's been dead four years. You ever going to get over that?"

"I'm not fighting at the Berenda Slough, and that's that," I say.

So he heads out to Beacon Road, but I'm complaining about that too because me and old Bev been making it out there on Saturday nights.

"Tough shit," he says, so we follow Washington Road out of town to Beacon Road that hardly anybody uses except dirt farmers, and we stop, right in the middle of the beat up blacktop. God, it's quiet at first, except for a mess of blackbirds sitting off in some cattails. Some have blood red on their wings, screeching and raising hell, and I don't feel too good about that either.

Leroy comes out from behind the car stuffing his shirttail in his pants, and I'm thinking what's he got to be nervous about? Cars come from both sides now, stop so close Leroy has to tell them to back up a piece. Starting to look like a football game. Kids're cutting up, some shadow boxing. I'm going to hurt someone if it doesn't happen soon. I pull off my shirt, hearing them say how big I look. I feel good about that because old Melvin, he's not that big anyway.

Just about the time I think maybe he's not coming, here he is getting out of a brand new black '57 Chevy, and Bev just tagging along like a pup in heat with that tight skirt of hers and a fresh-lit cigarette. Melvin, he's pulling off his shirt, and coming toward me. I'm thinking how white he looks and with that blond hair, maybe he has albino blood. But he comes right over to me and spits at my feet looking like he owns the ground I stand on. I feel a little calmer now, and it's strange him being this mad at me, all the times we've been up to Snelling fishing those pot holes together. I wish I could feel madder at him. I'm just not quite ready for this anymore.

"Hear you say dairymen suck cows teats," he says. I hear someone snicker in the crowd. Melvin, his face turns red.

"I say a lot of things. So what's your problem?" I ask him.

He turns sideways, doubles up his fist. "Hear you say I got the brains of a cow."

Someone from the crowd butts in, "Just hit him, Melvin. He's not going to apologize. You took his girl, now take his head off."

"I wouldn't let on you had that much," I say, "but if you do, I'm easy about it."

He doesn't have an answer for that, just clears his throat and spits a lunger on my chest. He's helping me get ready for this real fast, so I shove him back a piece, feeling how soft and girl-like his shoulder is, and he takes a swing at me. We walk around in circles a minute with Leroy hollering at me to bust Melvin's head, and I'm thinking why can't Leroy shut his mouth.

We're coming in closer now, so I take a swing at him. I don't see it but feel his fist pop my eye and know the swelling is coming. That's when I hear someone holler for Melvin to cut me because I'm nothing but an asshole anyway, and I'm looking around to see who said that, wondering if Melvin has a knife, but here he comes again. I'm dodging and swinging and catch him on the ear. That makes him back off a little, and his ear turns blood red.

I go at him this time, feel my fist hard against the bones in his head and think maybe he'll go down. But he just steps back a little. I see it coming this time, but I'm not quick enough, and I hear the pop as my head goes back, and my feet are having trouble finding the ground. And then I feel it, a feeling I have sometimes that something real bad is about to happen. I can tell my nose is bleeding because I taste it, and it's dripping from my top lip. Leroy's still shouting for me to bust Melvin's head, and I'm thinking

16

maybe I'm going to kill Leroy.

I go at Melvin again now, feel my left in his teeth and have him in my sights for my right, and I know I've got him this time, just before I take another blow and go down. I'm looking up at him from my knees with two swelling eyes. He's fingering a chipped tooth which he sucks then spits a wad of blood. Leroy's pulling up on my arm, so I shove him back to stand and pinch my nose, wiping the blood on my Levis. I have to draw air through my mouth.

We walk circles again now, and I hunch over a little and move my right around in circles and then we throw a few. First my arms don't seem long enough, then seem too long, so I grab him around the waist and we roll around on the blacktop for a little with gravel digging into my skin. He smells like he just quit shoveling cowshit, and I don't like the feel of his warm skin much either. When we get up, my blood is all over his chest. We stand there for a second and off in the distance I think I hear an ambulance, then think maybe not.

Melvin looks at me from across the blacktop, breathing hard. I look down at my feet and up at him again through the tops of my eyes, and I hear the blackbirds screeching in the cattails again. He shakes his head a little. He starts forward this time with his hands at his side, and I go to meet him. I'm beginning to think he feels sorry for me. We stand there for a second, me looking down at his pale blue eyes, and he sticks out his flabby hand. My face is throbbing like it's going to burst. I don't think I want anymore, so I take the hand.

Kids scatter and I hear a couple of cars with glass packs rumble and then the screech of rubber. As I walk off, Leroy throws my shirt, and I look back to see Bev looking back at me, one foot in Melvin's black '57 Chevy and her skirt stretched tight. Her tits are heaving, and it looks for all the world like she's going to cry.

CHAPTER 3: *Leroy's Lies*

Leroy pulls up in front of my house with the lights and motor off, coasts in real slow so Mama and Papa won't know we're here. We've been in the bathroom at the Beacon station in Chowchilla trying to put me together again. It's getting dark, and I'm supposed to be in by sundown, but I'm putting off going inside because I don't know what might happen when they see my face. And then I wonder what Coach will say about me missing football practice. Being a senior has got to be the toughest job in the world. Everything I do now causes trouble. It started this summer and just won't let up. Last year wasn't like this.

"Don't tell them you were in a fight," Leroy tells me. "Give them a lie."

"Anybody can tell I've been in a fight."

"Well, tell them it was a fight by mistake. Tell 'em a bunch of Mexicans from Madera jumped you."

"Getting beat up by Mexicans is not something to be proud of either."

"Then tell them you killed a couple but got a little beat up in the process."

"And what did I do with the bodies, Leroy?"

"It's your lie, Bobby. You make up some of it."

"Not my style."

"Make it your style. Takes the edge off. Bigger the lie, the better. They don't have to believe it. Puts them on the defensive."

"I'm no good at it."

"A little practice is all you need. It might even help you out with your next girl."

"I don't want a next girl."

"Let someone else have a go at Bev."

"I don't have to let Melvin. He's taking his shot."

"Leave it to me. I'll find you one."

"Shut up and get a haircut. Would you?" I tell him. "Olin Davis could use the business."

"You always have to get personal, don't you." He's looking at my face out the corner of his eye with those thick eyebrows going clean across his head.

I light a Lucky and lean back, blowing smoke out the window. Have to keep it low in case Mama or Papa peeks out the window.

"I just feel bad. You don't understand. Melvin was my friend. Now I got another enemy. I don't know. It just bothers me."

Leroy just never stops moving. He's making like he's speed-shifting this old clunker, the steering column rattling like hell and the clutch going thud and then he's back in first gear again.

"I'm tired of all these Chowchilla people," I tell him. "I've lived here all my life and due for a change. You know that, Leroy? I've lived here all my life. I've got to get out of this place after I graduate. Maybe get a job in Madera or Merced. If I wait a year or two, I'll be here forever. This town is just like a jail. A jail, Leroy, and I don't need a life sentence."

"Now you've started picking on Chowchilla."

I have to go in. That's all there is to it. God I dread this, but I'm tired of Leroy's fidgeting. I throw my Lucky out the window, grab my schoolbooks and slam his rattling door behind me. Leroy's asking if I want him to take me in to school tomorrow, but I'm walking on in now.

CHAPTER 4: *Voices in the Dark*

Papa's sitting in front of that damn old yellow-screen Hoffman TV, cussing Milton Berle and eating dinner off a stool. Has the lights down low. He's ignoring me, knows he'll get his shot at me for being late. Good thing he hasn't seen my face. My little brother Curt's laid out on the couch, and I get this flash that maybe he's dead, but he's just sleeping. Mama comes in from the kitchen, wiping her hands on a washcloth, ready to crawl me. She stops dead in her tracks, voice crying before the tears come.

"Bobby Ray Hammer. What in Lord's name has happened to you?"

I'm thinking maybe I can just walk on past Papa. But he looks up from Milton Berle, "jesuschrist" coming out under his breath and then he comes at me. "Goddamn, would you look at this? You've been fighting again. Well, good enough for ya, good enough, I say," his voice sounding real strange, like maybe he isn't even Papa. Then he backs off, turns around and kicks over his stool, the plate, glass, milk and fried potatoes going everywhere.

Curt jumps like he's been shot.

"Come on over here in the light," says Papa. "Let's just see how bad you got your ass kicked." And then he's up in my face and me leaning back and putting my arm up. It's not like him getting that close to my face, his little eyes darting around. I don't know till now, he has to look up at me. "Dumb sonofabitch. Bet he put you out, didn't he? The way that eye looks."

Mama puts her head down and turns away like she's leaving the room, then turns back. "Hershel, do you think he needs a doctor? Oh Lord. Look at the swelling." Her voice starts out low but ends up in a high-pitched whine. She's crying real loud now.

"A doctor? Hell no! Shit!" he hollers, turns around and kicks a hole in the side of the leather couch. It even scoots a ways across the floor. I haven't seen him this mad in a while. "What he needs is a goddamn good whipping."

Curt's looking like he's going to run, and maybe he's going to cry some too. I'm looking for a way out, but they have me pinned against the wall.

And then Papa jerks off his belt, and I'm getting that sinking feeling again. I haven't had a whipping in four years. Then I feel it whiplash and the little metal tip, it hits me right square on the kneecap, and I'm bent over holding it there and dancing a little for him, big that I am, and feeling the new welts coming across my back and thanking God for Mama because she's quit crying and right in there trying to get him off and getting knocked around a little herself. Finally Papa, he backs off, puffing because he's so excited. I laugh a couple a times and have a strange smile on my face, like maybe this is the first fun we've had together in a long time.

The front door opens, and Trish comes in like she's in a hurry, and I guess she's heard what's happening from outside because she's mad as hell already.

Papa just ignores her and starts on Mama. "Goddamn, woman," and there's a little spit coming from his mouth, "here I am trying to teach him a lesson and you standing in there like you want some for yourself."

"You leave Mama alone, Papa!" It's Trish shouting and her eyes just puddles of tears. "God, why can't we be a normal family? Why do we have to fight all the time? Eugene's family doesn't. What's wrong with us?" She runs into the kitchen like there's an answer in there somewhere.

I look over at Curt and give him a quick wink to let him know not to take it all too seriously. God, you'd think by the look on his face that the kid was going to have a seizure.

"Oh, Hershel, he's already hurt so bad," Mama says. And she's up close too, with her head tilted back to get a better look through those bifocals and her hand on my chin pulling my head around. "I just can't stand to see him hit anymore." She starts whining and crying again.

"Now don't you go turning against me. I don't have a son anymore that's going to make much of a man. What Bobby Ray needs is something to remember this by." And then he turns back to me. "Didn't get any teeth, did he? That'd suit some of those little bitches you been running around town with just fine. A couple of holes in your mouth would be just right for you. Who was it anyway? Just who was it kicked your sweet ass?"

Since I don't say anything, he rears back with the belt again, but Trish is out of the kitchen in a flash with the broom, beating Papa across the head and gouging him with it till Papa grabs the handle and shoves her over in the corner. He tries to hang on to it, but she pulls it out of his hand. I wish he wouldn't shove her on the chest like that with those new tits just starting to show through.

"Don't hit him anymore, Papa. Can't you see? You dumb old goat. He's already beat up." Then she throws the broom at him, but he catches it by the handle, throws it at the TV.

Papa's still on me. "Tell me, Bobby Ray. Damn it! Who was it?"

"A bunch of Mexicans jumped me." Leroy's words just pop out of my mouth.

First he looks real serious, like this means big trouble, then looks puzzled. "If I thought you were telling the truth, I'd put my pistol to work, but you're telling me one. I know you are. There's a story behind this." And damn if Leroy isn't right. Papa has already changed. "Come on. Who was it? I've got to know."

I don't want to tell him, but it comes out in a little tiny sound anyway, "Melvin Swensen."

Trish is on her feet again, but she's still mad. "A bunch of damn animals, all we are," she says. "A pack of dogs, all with rabies." She heads down the hall to her bedroom.

"Melvin? Jack Swensen that's got that little dairy out on Road 7? His boy?" I think Papa even has a smile on his face now. "Little Melvin kicked your ass? That shit shoveler? God, this is getting better by the minute."

"I didn't do so bad, Papa. He didn't come out of it looking like he'd been shooting pool." Papa hasn't seen Melvin since he was twelve. Besides, I'm not so sure he's any smaller than me. I just keep going over that fight in my mind, seeing Melvin coming at me and wondering why I couldn't throw that right hand that was going to put him down. I had him in my sights, like when you get a deer in your sights and you squeeze the trigger and he goes down. Only with Melvin, I went down instead.

I hear the front door slam as Curt goes out into the dark. I feel sorry for poor old Curt. He must be feeling low. I'm walking into the kitchen, smelling fried chicken, thinking maybe I'll get something to eat. My face is beginning to throb again, so I better have a handful of aspirins. I go to the refrigerator for a glass of milk, Papa coming up behind explaining how tough Melvin has to be. He stands in the doorway, and I can still see his spit flying.

"Your big ass football buddies are going to think you're one tough sonofabitch. You'll have to tell me how they take it."

★

I'm in bed now in the dark. I'm on my side facing the window, listening to Trish cry in the next bedroom. God, Papa ought to put a sump pump in her bed with all the tears she sheds. Curt sleeps with me but against the wall. I hear him wrestling around over there now. I get kicked in the ribs a lot.

Before I go to sleep I always see bridges. I count bridges like other people count sheep. When I go to the library at school, sometimes I get the encyclopedia and look up bridges. I try to memorize where all the big ones are. My favorite is the Golden Gate Bridge in San Francisco. I've been looking through my new physics book for Mr. Wood's class. It has a chapter on bridges.

"You asleep yet, Bobby Ray?" Curt asks.

I thought he was asleep. I don't say anything at first, just listen to Stan's Private Line that comes out of Fresno on my little Philco radio. They've been reading dedications for Elvis' "Don't Be Cruel" for the last fifteen minutes. I'm listening for kids from Chowchilla and trying to remember how much homework I should've done for tomorrow.

"No, not yet," I say.

"You fight down at the high school?"

"No. Beacon Road."

"Anybody see it?"

"Just about half the school."

"You afraid to go to school in the morning?"

"Always afraid to go to school, Curt."

He has to laugh at that. "Me too," he says.

We lie here listening to the radio some more, and now I am worrying about how my face is going to look in the morning. Wonder what the girls are going to think.

Just when I'm sure Curt is asleep, he says, "You ever think about Lenny anymore?"

This really takes me by surprise because we don't talk about our dead brother. I wait a little before I can answer that. "Just all the time. Seems like I still follow him around asking questions, and he just keeps on answering back. Don't even seem like he's gone sometimes."

"You ever worry about dying?"

"No. I don't think so."

"You're almost as old as Lenny was when he got killed, you know."

I open my eyes. Look around the bedroom with the pale light coming through the window from the full moon outside. I've always thought of Lenny as being a lot older than me. But Curt's right. Lenny died in his senior year. And his best friend, Charles, got killed too. At least I think he did. I've always wondered if God would let me live to be older than Lenny was. I feel kind of strange now, like maybe I should be looking out for myself. I listen to the sounds of the house creaking, watch the darkness out in the hall. Try to see something that'll fill it up. Wish I'd closed our door.

"Yes, and you're the same age I was then," I tell him.

It's his turn to be quiet for a minute. "You think any of us 'll get out of here alive?"

"Yes. I will. And so will you and Trish. I'm going to see to it."

"That a promise?" He's starting to cry now.

"You bet it is. Just wait and see."

Then I hear Curt sniffling for a while. After I don't hear him anymore, I turn off the radio. Guess Trish quit crying too.

I remember how I found out that Lenny was dead. I think the way I found out was worse than him getting killed. Maybe not, but it seems like it. And after Lenny's funeral, Mama and Papa's whispering behind their closed bedroom door bothered me. First that policeman, Brock, came. Then Mama and Papa whispered. People dying is just a strange thing. And it happened to my big brother. I think maybe the whispering had something to do with God. God is a strange thing too. But I wish I could have understood the whispering. There's something else that bothers me about Lenny getting killed, something about me, but I can't remember what anymore.

I've been thinking about keeping a little notebook of things that go on inside my head, like Lenny used to do. But with the life I'm living, what's the use? A lot of things happen to me that I don't like. I don't like Papa hitting on me. I don't like anybody hitting on me. I hope I graduate. My grades are taking it hard too. If I don't graduate, there's no leaving this place.

CHAPTER 5: *The '48 Hudson*

Here comes big Thomas Powers walking across the courtyard, arms out from his body a little, stopping now and then to pinch a girl on the arm or tweak an ear, just bouncing along. He has on white pants and white bucks, and just because he's the big man on the football team, he thinks all the girls are in love with him. Claims he's going to be one of those big-city college boys after he graduates, talks a lot about USC.

It's noontime and we're parked in the vacant lot across the street from the high school, just leaning back in Leroy's old brown Ford. I'll be glad when I get my car out of the shop. I'm eating an orange.

"You've got to give it to him, Bobby," he says. "He's got style." Leroy has an opinion about everything.

"That's not style," I say, "it's show. Thomas has never made an honest move in his life," and I have to slow talking a little to swallow some orange. "That's what makes him a good running back. His whole life's a fake."

"Well, whatever it is, it works. He gets any girl he wants."

"They just put up with him. Don't want to hurt his feelings."

"Seems to me, they like him. Well, come to think of it, maybe it's just fat girls. Me and Wayne caught him and Brenda going at it this summer."

"Going at what?"

"What do you think? Bobby. I'll give you three guesses. Three guesses and a hint. We caught them in the backseat of his car up at Raymond." Raymond is this little town in the foothills about twenty miles west of Chowchilla where us kids go sometimes to get away from prying eyes.

"Couldn't have been her, Leroy," I tell him. What do you mean, "fat girls" anyway. I've known Brenda McCallum since seventh grade. She's not fat. Besides, she's just not like that."

I remember when Mr. Johns, the principal at Wilson School, brought Brenda into our seventh grade classroom one morning the second week of school. That was five years ago. I thought she had the prettiest blond hair I'd ever seen, it falling down in ringlets. Walked in like she belonged there. Just a short little thing. She was fat then, new to the town, new to the state even. Didn't matter to her. Just walked in and took over. Now she's the senior class president. Not anybody touching that girl. I throw some orange peal out the window, watch the kids sitting in the shade on that big lawn out front of the high school.

"Sure looked like her with Thomas to me."

"You can look again on that one," I tell him. "Wayne being there doesn't help your story any either." Wayne Hickman is the undertaker's son. He doesn't like anybody. "I don't know why you've started running around with him anyway."

I look over at the car next to us. My sister, Trish, is in the front seat cuddled up with her boyfriend, Eugene Waggoner. He's the first boyfriend she's ever had.

Eugene is a mousy little kid that keeps his head in a book all the time. He thinks he's an athlete too. I hear he's not bad at track. Trish went crazy the first time he asked her out. It was her first date ever. She was covered with little beads of sweat. I heard her talking to someone in her bedroom the night before, so I stood by her door to see if I could tell who it was. She was talking to herself, practicing conversations. It was like she was two people. Finally she came to me. "Ever kissed a girl?" she wanted to know. I looked her right straight in the face and laughed. She blushed but asked another question. "I've got to know this," she said and swallowed real deep. "What's a girl supposed to do with her tongue when she gets kissed?" She'd asked her girlfriends but they laughed and wouldn't tell her.

Mama doesn't like Eugene a whole lot. Papa, he thinks she could've picked worse. But he knows the Waggoner's. He's done some business with the old man.

Thomas crosses the road, comes by me.

"You tell your old man that the stalk cutter he's been asking about came in." Thomas' father owns one of the implement shops here in town.

"So what makes you think he'll buy it from you guys instead of going down the street?" I ask.

"Come on now, Bobby. Your dad knows he gets a better deal from us than anybody in town."

"Well, maybe he might want to go to Fresno," I say looking down at those white bucks. Isn't he something? "They've got some big implement

26

stores there. Got a good selection."

"But you've got to think about service. We're just a couple of miles away."

"Ya. If we buy from you, we'd better think about service."

"Come on, Bobby. Quit it, would you? You tell your old man to come into the shop."

"Lighten up, Thomas," I tell him. "You act like you're running your old man's business."

"I'm going to someday. And when you start farming on your own, you'll be one of my best customers."

"Well, we'll have to see about that," I say.

"By the way," he asks, "how is Pistoresi doing on your car."

"I haven't seen it, but Larry says it's supposed to be out next week."

He stands there for a minute like he's waiting on a train, brushing the blond hair out of his eyes, and he keeps looking down at me, his black eyes working their way around my face. "You coming to football practice?" he asks, walking on.

"Sure," I say.

He says, looking back, "Too bad you can't put that face in the shop while it's getting well."

The first bell rings and all the car doors open at once and everybody is putting cigarettes out in the dirt, but not me because if coach sees me sucking on a weed, that's it for football, so I just stick the last slice of orange in my mouth. I see Bev up by the school building, stepping into her shoes and brushing the grass off her blue skirt that flowers out, showing the edge of all those petticoats. We're all crossing the street now, and Leroy, he comes up behind, pokes me with his skinny elbow. But I've already seen Melvin out the corner of my eye. I wonder why he's not with Bev. His upper lip is still a little puffy, but he doesn't look so bad. If I'd hit him with that last right I had for him, he'd be hunkered over and walking sideways. I get a grin on real easy and look over at him.

"How you doing, Melvin?"

"Sore as hell," he says.

And then I see it, a car coming straight for me, but I'm not worried about that. I recognize the car. It's Lenny's. But it can't be because Lenny's car was totaled when he got killed. I stand at the edge of the road to get a close look at who's driving it. Sure enough, it's a '48 Hudson. Not many still around. The guy looks kind of familiar, I think, but just as he gets even with me, so I can get a good look at his face, he turns his head. For a second there, I thought I recognized him, and it scared me.

CHAPTER 6: *Expelled and No Football*

In the middle of my second afternoon class, here comes a mousy kid from the office with a note for fat old Mrs. Biggs, the history teacher. I'm listening close because I'm in trouble trying to learn this stuff. I'm trying hard to get Lenny's car out of my mind. I don't like that car being on the road again. These history dates just seem to come out of nowhere, and I don't have anyplace to put them. Mrs. Biggs doesn't quit talking, doesn't even slow down, just waddles over to my desk and lays the note in front of me without a word. Next thing I know, I'm opening the door to old man Sonnett's office. He's the new principal. I had typing from him last year. We all call him Clyde because that's his name. Just one step inside and I see Mama. That doesn't look good for me.

"Now, Mrs. Hammer, I'm sure we can work this out. But I've got to do something, considering the circumstances." Clyde doesn't even look at me. Mama doesn't act like I'm here either. She's too busy working on Clyde, and I think she has him on the run.

"If you'd just listen a minute you'd understand that Bobby Ray's not your problem down here. I know you've got a bunch of kids that you can't control, but Bobby Ray's not one of them. His papa will straighten him out if he doesn't mind his teachers. What do they say? They complaining?"

Old Clyde, he's just the picture of cool, sitting behind his big wood desk. He has his head shaved to get rid of those few wild hairs he had on top last year and that ring around the bottom that made his bald head look like a cap. But his head is still flat in back like somebody, maybe his mother, hit him in the back of the head with a baseball bat, and he's not going to do anything about that.

"Now Mrs. Hammer, I checked with his teachers just this morning. And quite honestly, he's becoming a distraction this year. His grades are reflecting it too. He received an F on his first test in civics. An F and we're not even through September."

I'm tired of standing and take the wood chair next to Mama, looking around at Clyde's office. He has all these square picture frames with nothing but papers in them that say what a big asshole he is.

"I don't see what his grades have to do with this problem. We're talking about the fight he had after school yesterday, not his grades." Mama's voice is getting higher and higher like she does before she jumps into the middle of me. I figure I'm about to see a good one.

"Grades are always an indication of what's going on inside a boy, Mrs. Hammer. He's not paying attention to his schoolwork. He's distracted and he's distracting others."

"Bobby Ray, you told me you didn't get into trouble anymore and that you're doing good in your classes. And now I find out this. What am I to think?"

"Ah, Mama, there wasn't any real trouble and I didn't flunk that test. Old lady Watson gave me an F cause I said something after the bell rang."

Old Clyde, he perks up to hear me talk. I think maybe his face is going to be red. I can't believe he has me in here for something that happened after school, off the school grounds even, and now he's pulling my grades into it. He has it in for me.

"That's Mrs. Watson to you, young man. She has a perfect right to adjust grades based on classroom behavior."

"The only other problem I have," I say, "is in physics and I've already talked to Mr. Wood about that. He knows I'm taking a chance by taking his class, but he's willing to work with me. It's important."

"That's another class I'm concerned about, Mrs. Hammer. Bobby shouldn't be in a class like that and I'm thinking of taking him out."

"You can't do that," I tell him. "Talk to Mr. Wood. He knows why I'm there."

"I intend to. You can depend on it." But Clyde doesn't look very satisfied. He better not screw that up. When he screws with physics, he's screwing with my life. I'm going to build bridges someday if it kills me. Besides, he isn't looking at me, and I'm beginning to think he isn't looking at Mama either. "Look, Mrs. Hammer, this is what I mean," he says. "We have a system here. Bobby received fourteen tardy slips in the last three months of last year, and we'll not tolerate that manner of behavior this year. But he's already started on the same track." He's looking just above Mama's head at the wall. So I turn to see what's so interesting up there. Mama

30

sure looks pretty in that light-blue, dress-up dress and her long hair pulled back tight in a big bun, and I'm thinking how proud I am of that woman standing up for me like this.

"Bobby Ray, how could you be late to class that much? You know better than that"

"Ah, Mama. I've never been late to class. They give me those for not having a pencil or saying something to the kid next to me. They've got a different rule for everything. Teachers don't have brains. All they have is rules." That ought to set him straight.

Clyde lowers his head then looks out the window.

"What you doing up here, Mr. Sonnett? You making rules to keep these kids in school or out?"

And now he's getting real patient with Mama too, so he talks real slow. "Mrs. Hammer, I told you that students who are a disruption will not be tolerated. They'll be expelled. If your son's one of them, and I think he is, he'll be dealt with accordingly. And now I'm making a decision on this case. There's no talking to either of you. He gets one week now, and if he doesn't straighten up, it's out the door, for keeps." And then he stands up, starts shuffling papers on his desk like this business with me is over. He hasn't even looked at me straight yet.

I'm thinking, hey, he didn't say anything about being suspended. "What you mean, I get one week? You kicking me out of school?"

"That's the verdict, young man."

"I've got some classes I can't afford to miss."

"You heard me, and it's final. You can come back to school a week from Monday." And he has that look like he's enjoying this, has a little smile on his face.

"What? A week and two days? That's too long. There's things I can't afford to miss. I'm still going to football practice. I know that." I'm leaning forward in my chair now, and he bends over his desk so I can smell his bad breath, but he's still looking just over my head.

"Not anymore, you're not."

I stand up because I'm going to hit that sonofabitch, but Mama has hold of my arm. He just can't do this to me. It's like he's taking away my future. Why's he trying to hurt me? I didn't do anything to him.

"You're not playing football this year, son. Football is a privilege and you just relinquished yours." And damn if he doesn't sound real sorry, like

31

there's just nothing he can do about it.

So I'm walking around his desk, trying to get to him, and he's walking to the far side. But Mama turns me around, pushes me toward the door, and she's not through talking to him yet either, and her finger is in his face. That gives Clyde something else to look at besides the wall over her head, so his eyes just bounce with the tip of her finger.

"'Dealt with accordingly,' huh. Let me tell you something, Mr. Sonnett. I'm going to the Board about you. You get this here kid out of school and he'll find other interests and before you know it, the last thing he'll want to do is go to school. You'll hear from me again about this."

CHAPTER 7: *Charles Resurrected*

Even Mama has her limitations. So Papa has me for work during the day, and he's just pleased as punch about that. If he works me for the next week like he has these last two days, I may not live to go back to school. He thinks this is the way it's going to be when I graduate. He keeps going on about it. I was thinking of talking to him about me going to Fresno to look for work after I graduate, but I don't think he'll take it very well. I'm ashamed to tell him I've been thinking about college a little lately. My grades don't say I'm cut out for it. He keeps talking about us having a partnership here on the farm. How can I turn him down on that? With me full-time, he can rent more ground, maybe buy another little piece of dirt. But I took this Iowa Test a couple of weeks ago. For the first time I really tried on that thing. I was just making believe I had an answer for everything, just like I was Mr. Wood. He does know everything. My homeroom teacher was mad at me when my scores came back, wanted to know who I copied off of.

I have a hay hook in each hand, staring across the flatbed at Papa. He hollers for Delbert, our hired hand, to stop the truck, and then he comes up close. "You've got to watch Delbert because he won't work if he's not watched. He likes to drive the truck because he's lazy." Papa is acting like I don't know anything about Delbert and him having worked for us almost ten years. Then Papa smiles like he's told me a secret.

But I can't concentrate on hauling hay. I want to know if that was really Lenny's car I saw the other day. I want to ask Papa about it, whether it was totaled or not, but I just don't have the nerve. And I'm thinking about my Chevy coming out of the shop today, since it's Friday, and wondering if Papa will let me go get it before they close. He knows I'm worried about it but won't tell me.

I jump down beside the truck in the hay stubble, stick a hook in each end of a bale and throw it up on the bed where Papa stacks it. God, it's hot.

The truck starts again, slow now, and I walk along to the next bale, boots crunching in the hay stubble, stick a hook in each end and throw it on the moving flatbed. Wipe a little salty sweat that's stinging my eye. We've been doing this all day, and as afternoon wears on, my arms tire, particularly when the stack gets tall and I have to lift the bales over my head. But that's okay because I've been doing this for years, ever since we lost Lenny. Before that, I used to drive the truck, and I'd hear Lenny and Papa talking and laughing. Usually, Lenny, he was making plans for the future. He talked a lot about college and playing baseball and how someday he'd play in the majors for the New York Yankees. I don't understand why Papa was always talking to Lenny about things he was going to do when he left home, and won't even listen to a word about me leaving. After getting kicked off the football team, no sense in me thinking about college or anything else except dirt farming. I always knew I could never play college football, but I was thinking about college anyway, thinking about just going to learn something.

Papa whistles for Delbert to stop the flatbed, and then we all stand beside it taking turns at the mason jar of ice tea Mama fixed for us. It still has a little ice on top but the tea's flavor is a little thin because she fills it with ice before she fills it with tea.

"When you going to let me take my turn at those hooks?" Delbert asks Papa. He's sucking on a piece of straw like it's a toothpick, chews the end of it into a brush. He stinks real bad like he doesn't take regular baths.

Papa studies him a minute. "How about tomorrow?" he says. "There'll be enough to go around through tomorrow. Bobby Ray and me've got a good system going, him on the ground, me stacking bales. How you doing, Bobby Ray?"

"I'm okay."

"He's better with his muscles than his fists, so let's give him another chance to be tough. He wasn't so tough the other day."

Delbert backs off a little, Papa saying that. Delbert gives me a wink. He's always wearing a cowboy hat. His wife is a Texan, and she likes cowboy hats, so he says. When he winked at me, he dipped his head a little so the brim would hide his eyes from Papa. He clears his throat, then spits off to the side. I'm wishing I didn't have to share the tea jar with him.

But I feel like I should say something back to Papa, him saying that in front of Delbert. But I can't think of anything that won't make Papa mad. That is the trick. Saying something to give me a little room without making Papa mad again. I'm just not smart enough to figure it all out. But then I haven't ever been too smart when it comes to talking. When I was in the fifth grade, I was having trouble paying attention in class and when the teacher would ask questions, she didn't always like my answers. And my grades were bad enough that they gave me this mentally retarded test. At first I didn't know if it was to see if I was a moron or if it was to make me a moron. I just knew the teacher was mad at me because I couldn't learn everything she was teaching. She used to beat me on the back with a ruler. I took the test with two other kids I knew were morons, so the sweat was pouring off me. She didn't seem too happy about the results. I heard the principal in her office scolding her. She took me out of the moron class and was real nice to me for two weeks. Seems like everything I do now is a struggle to keep from being a moron. Papa saying what he did and me not saying anything back doesn't help.

We go back to loading hay, and my arms are stiff from waiting around. I know Lenny didn't have any trouble with talking. He had an answer for everything. He didn't always worry about making Papa mad either. I bet he would have been okay in college too. He didn't worry about anything but baseball. He was tall and thin, must have been a foot taller than I am now, and no pitcher could keep him off the bases. He played third base, and the coach even let him play on the varsity when he was a freshman. He was that good. The coach used to brag that in four years, no one ever hit one past Lenny at third. I wasn't cut out for baseball. Not enough hand-to-eye coordination, Lenny used to say. So when I went to high school, I knew that football was the game for me, because the story was, hit and be hit. I figured I could handle that. But now Clyde has taken care of football.

The flatbed is full, so Papa grabs my hand and pulls me up to the top of the hay. We sit with our feet hanging off the edge, staring across the field into the distance as Delbert drives us back in. Papa looks over at me and laughs. "That damn black eye of yours may never go away. You know that?" He slaps me on the shoulder.

I just smile and look at my dangling feet, slap my thigh with my gloves.

"You've got to get madder than hell when you fight. You know that? I don't think a lot of fighting but when you've got to fight, you've got to get mad. What was it you fought over, anyway? Huh?"

I don't know why he asks me questions like that. He knows I don't want to answer before he asks. I wish I could be mad at him so he'd quit it, but instead, I get this big grin on my face that won't go away. It's like my mouth has feelings all its own, and I don't even have a say in what it does. So I sit here grinning and hating it, but I can control my voice so I don't say anything.

"Come on, tell me, Bobby Ray. A girl, wasn't it?"

Since my mouth is working on its own, I turn my head, look away toward Chowchilla, try to see the floodlight poles where the game will be played tonight. The game Papa won't let me go to; the game Clyde won't let me play in.

"Okay, let's just say it was a girl anyway. I can tell the cat's got your tongue like when you were a little kid. God, I didn't think you were ever going to learn to talk."

I know he's lying now because Mama always says I was an early talker.

"I've got a little experience on this one, because I had a fight over a girl once, once or twice. And don't you tell your mama either cause it wasn't over her. I wasn't old enough to be serious about girls, but I was old enough to get mad over them. It was back in Oklahoma, back before the dust bowl days. I know you don't want to hear about it, so I won't tell you, but listen to this, because it's true. If you're going to fight over anything, particularly a girl, you better be mad at the sonofabitch or you'll get your ass kicked every time."

Papa gets quiet a minute and if he would keep his mouth shut, I'd like it sitting high up here. I look out over the neighbor's farms through the haze in the distance that sometimes hides the mountains.

"You like this farming, don't you, huh?" he tells me.

"Ya. It's okay."

"Well, it won't be long now before you'll be with me full-time. I know schoolwork is a crock of shit, but a man needs it in the world today. Even the gin manager will look down his nose at you if you don't have that high school diploma. So I guess there's some use in you still trying to finish. If it was up to me, you'd been working full-time two years ago. You're looking forward to it too. I can tell. You want to, don't you? Huh?"

He's never asked me a straight question like that before and I think maybe this is my chance. "I was thinking about trying to get a job, maybe in Fresno or someplace."

"Shit. You want what? I don't know what pull big cities have for you young people." He takes off his hat, wipes sweat off the band. "You don't want that. You'll be working for wages. Nobody can have anything working for wages, always be doing somebody's dirty work. Getting laid off and looking for work." And he says it like it's a order. "I need you, barely holding this farm together as it is with you working after school and weekends. No telling what'll happen to all of us if you up and leave. I always thought I could depend on you."

I guess I never thought about the family needing me. "But, Papa," and I know I shouldn't say this, but it's something that's been eating on me a long time, "Lenny was going to leave and you never said no to him."

Now I see tears in his eyes. "Well, I never would've thought I'd live to see the day when you'd blame me for Lenny's mistakes." He shakes his head real slow. "I'm going to overlook it this time. You're young and don't know any better about some things."

We sit here for a while feeling the sway of the big hay load as the flatbed goes across the borders. When he starts talking again, it's real low at first. "I see old man Grissom's out watering that stub cotton he's raised again this year. You've got an opportunity here with me to learn good farming, not what that sorry sonofabitch does and calls farming. But I can teach you how to make it in this business." And now he's heating up again. "You go off somewhere else, I can't help you. If you do, don't come running back for help."

"I didn't say I was going to do it. I'm just thinking about it."

"You don't want to do that, Bobby Ray. Use your head, for christsake."

When we get back to the barn, instead of unloading the hay, Papa jumps off the stack, walks a ways, then turns back and says, "Come on. We better get to town if you're going to pick up that car of yours before Pistoresi closes shop."

We live only five miles out in the country, so it doesn't take long. Robertson Boulevard runs straight into town, lined with palm trees all the way. Chowchilla is like that. Lots of unusual things about this place. Almost everything in town is right on Main Street too. I guess that's to be expected for a little town of three thousand.

Papa drops me off at Pistoresi Chevrolet, on the corner of Fifth Street and Robertson. We call Robertson "Main Street" when it gets into town. Papa heads back to the farm, and I watch the backend of that old pickup drive away with the license plate hanging on with a piece of bailing wire, and I hear the sound of tools clanging inside Pistoresi's. The big doors are open to the service shop so I just walk on in, but then I back up a little because I see something that scares me. Someone actually. But I can't see too good because the sun's so bright out here. There's my car, standing like it's ready to roll out. But a tall blond kid is polishing a fender on my car. I know him and it scares me. I see a dead man.

I know I've been acting a little strange lately. I never fought a friend before and never been kicked out of school. Always had trouble but never been kicked out. My head starts throbbing, and I walk back up Robertson a block or two. Walk through the park.

I'm hearing things, like people shouting and off in the distance, gun shots. But it's just someone pounding a hammer. I stop at the park and watch kids ride a merry-go-round. I'm sweating again and notice how bad I smell from hauling hay all day. I stand in the shade of a tree for a minute, look up at the sun coming through green leaves. I feel some better. On the other side of the park, I see a bunch of people at a picnic table, but they've just finished so they're folding up their blankets and getting ready to go home. But I'm still afraid. That blond guy I saw was Charles Kunze rubbing down a fender on my '55 Chevy. I saw a dead man.

Finally I get up the courage to walk back. Hey, there's Larry Pistoresi standing talking to Charles. I feel good about that because Larry, he's a real person. Maybe it's not even Charles, just someone who looks like Charles. But that curly hair gives him away, and him being so tall. He's not as thin as he used to be. He was always making a fuss over me because we both liked football. They finished talking, so Larry walks off, giving me a wave hello. I'm hoping Charles won't recognize me. It's been a long time. I try to walk past him when he looks my way.

"Let me guess," he says. "I've got it. Bobby Hammer. That you? Never would have recognized you if you didn't look so much like your sister." Then he laughs and wants to shake my hand, even slaps me on the shoulder. "I'm kidding, Bobby. You really gave me a start," and now he looks serious. "I thought for sure you were Lenny. I guess four years hasn't been enough. Seems longer than that."

"Been four and a half but seems like a lifetime."

"How long you been out of school?" he wants to know.

I wipe a little sweat off my own upper lip. He seems familiar, just like he used to be. Seems stupid, me thinking he was dead.

Chapter 7: *Charles Resurrected*

"I graduate this year," I tell him, looking up. I don't have to look up at many people. I don't look him in the eyes. I know he's lying about me looking like Lenny. We didn't even look enough alike to be brothers.

"I would have guessed you've been out a couple of years. Damn. You really grew up, Bobby." And then he gets a real sad look in his eyes, shakes his head. "I don't know. Maybe I shouldn't have come back. I thought four years would be enough. Some people won't be too happy to see me. Do people talk about what happened anymore?"

"Never did. At least, not to me. I hadn't seen you in so long, I though you were dead."

"Me? Dead? I like that. People thinking I'm a dead man. But where did you get an idea like that?"

"I was little then. I didn't and still don't understand what happened to Lenny."

"Just as well. I know because I was there. I'm not surprised they won't talk. Some don't want the truth told. I don't talk about it either. But I might tell you someday, Bobby. You might understand."

"Since he was my brother, I figure somebody should tell me."

"Fair enough. Someday. We'll see about that. But now look at this." And he is pointing at my face. "You bought yourself a brand new shiner, looks like maybe two shiners. Out having yourself a hell of a good time, I bet, and had to pay a price for it." He's talking while working, using long strokes with a red cloth to finishing buffing my back fender.

"Having enough fun to get kicked out of school," I say.

"So they got you, did they? Well they're always after somebody. That brother of yours was the one who could get away with it. School wasn't much of a match for him. Your brother and I used to raise some real hell around here. No one raises hell like that anymore. Didn't matter what he did, whether it was playing baseball or playing with the girls, Lenny did it right. And him getting into an accident like that." He stops polishing for a second. "Hey, how do you like the candy apple finish on this Chevy? Doesn't it just frost your balls? Goddamn, with that white tuck and roll, straight out of Mexico. What're you here for anyway, Bobby?"

"Came to pick up my car," I tell him. "Where you been, Charles? You been gone a long time."

"Mountain View."

I guess I look a little confused.

39

"Bay area. South of San Francisco. Had a job for my uncle painting houses."

"That sounds like good work," I tell him. Now, I am real interested because I might be able to do something like that. A job painting houses could get me out of here.

"Sounds-like is about it. The money sounds good too."

"But what could be wrong with painting houses? Probably don't even need a lot of education to paint houses. And living on the coast is big- time stuff."

"Costs a lot to live there. I've walked under enough ladders to have four lifetimes of bad luck."

"But could you make it? Was it enough money to live on?"

"I did all right."

"Why'd you have to give up a good job like that and come back to Chowchilla?"

He laughs at me. "*Have* to come back to Chowchilla? I came back *for* Chowchilla, Bobby. That and a few people I missed. Still miss that brother of yours." He looks sad again for a minute. "Which machine is yours?"

"That candy apple you're polishing on," I shout over my shoulder as I walk off, heading for the office to pay my bill.

"Oh, mama! The kid got himself a pussy wagon."

★

God it feels good to get my car back and to know that Charles is really alive. I even feel better about Papa now. As I get in my Chevy to go, Charles opens and closes my door for me, bows.

"What'd you pay for a cherry like this?"

But I don't want to tell him, so I just say, "Pistoresi got it used somewhere on the coast."

"No shit? I knew a car like this. It was running a classy set of hubcaps though. Somebody could have lifted them. We could get some more just like them. Pistoresi didn't say who it was he got it from, did he?"

"Not to me." I was thinking about Charles living on the coast while I was paying my bill, so I ask him, "You ever see the Golden Gate Bridge while you lived in Mountain View?"

"Couple of times."

"They say it is the longest suspension bridge in the world."

"I'm not much on bridges, but I guess it's an okay bridge."

40

"How about the San Francisco-Oakland Bay Bridge You ever see that?"

"Sure, I've seen it. What's this thing about you and bridges? You got a hard-on for bridges?"

"I just like 'em, Charles. I'd like to build bridges some day." He's the first one I have ever told that.

"Painting houses is no way to start out if you plan on building bridges. You'll need some college. That sure leaves me out. I didn't get to graduate high school. All the trouble drove me out of town. That's another thing I'm pissed about. You've got to watch out for yourself in this life, Bobby. Nobody else will, that's for sure." Then he gets real serious as he comes up close, puts his arms on my door sill, almost whispers, "You got a steady girl?"

I hang my head a little. "Not anymore."

"Good. That's good, Bobby. You're a free man. Let's go raise some hell tonight. You want to go to the football game?"

"Mama doesn't like me to be out with older kids."

"Look, Bobby." And now I pull back from him because I see something in his eyes that scares me. "Don't ever let a woman, especially your mother, run your life. Women have a warped view of the world." Then he quiets a little. "Come on. Go to town with me tonight."

"Can't. Papa told me I won't be going to town while I'm not going to school. I would've been playing in the game, but the principal already canned that one too."

"God! You're a football player. Shit almighty, Bobby. That asshole must have it in for you too. Who's the principal now? Still old man Wade?"

"No. Clyde Sonnett. He's new this year."

"Sonnett? That bone-head typing teacher?"

"That's him."

"People like him will ruin your life. Playing football's important. I know because I played too."

I think maybe I'm going to cry if he doesn't shut up.

"Doesn't matter," he says, with a sweep of his arm, like he just brushed all the world's problems aside. "We don't have to go to town. Bring a .22 and we'll go to the country, shoot rabbits by spotlight. We could even shoot niggers if you'd rather. I know a couple of places where they're thick as grass in a spotlight. Rabbits, I mean, not niggers." Then he laughs, so I

41

know he's kidding. "In my jeep, we can go across country, raise a little hell like Lenny and I used to do. We've got to make up for what's happened to you."

"Not tonight. After I get back in school, Papa'll let me go. Besides, I'm tired, Charles. Papa's been working me like a dog."

"That old man of yours..." He straightens up, and for a second. I think he's going to walk off. "That sonofabitch..."

I don't like him talking about Papa like that.

"Don't tell him I'm back in town. Okay? I don't need that. Don't believe everything he says about me, either. Make up your own mind about things, things and people. That way you can live with the answers. Don't trust anybody. I was hoping you'd be grown up. You seem even older than I hoped. I've always liked you, Bobby. What a team we'll make. Chowchilla, lookout! Here we come!"

CHAPTER 8: *First Leroy and Then Bev*

It's late Sunday afternoon, and I'm sitting on the front porch tired as hell. I'm sorer today than yesterday. I think Papa is trying to kill me with all the work he's shoving at me. I get to go back to school tomorrow, and I'm glad about it. I've been up since four this morning driving the tractor. I think even Papa's starting to feel sorry for me. We've been broke down since early afternoon, and Papa has gone to Fresno to get the dealer to open his shop so he can get a generator for the flatbed. Papa's afraid it's going to rain and us this close to getting the hay in and the cotton picked. He took Curt with him instead of me. Papa doesn't ever want to be alone. He'll be talking to Curt about how much he hates the weatherman, how you can't trust him, and how he's going broke and how it was during the depression, working for fifty cents a day. Curt, he'll be looking out the window at the fields of cotton and corn as they go past and won't hear a word. They've been gone a long time, and I'm wondering want happened.

After seeing Charles, I've been thinking a lot about Lenny. I keep going over the week before it happened, and I can't account for all of my time. I remember Lenny hitting me in the head with the baseball, and that seemed to set everything in motion. Everyone was mad at him. Lenny hit me on Sunday. I remember it was a Sunday because Aunt Loretta always came over on Sunday. Still does. She's sitting in the kitchen talking to Mama right now. She didn't like Charles. When Charles showed up to see Lenny that day, he put a strain on things. I don't remember what happened the rest of the day after Lenny hit me. The time is just gone. The next thing I remember happened Monday afternoon. The school nurse sent me home because I was having dizzy spells. Strange thing is, Lenny was home too. It was like he hadn't even been to school. He and Papa weren't speaking. Mama was quiet for a change. She'd quit arguing with Lenny about his girl. But Mama and Papa were whispering. Lenny came home late Monday night and crawled into bed without saying a word. When I got up the next morning, he was already gone. Didn't even have breakfast with us. I went to school on Tuesday, but that's all I remember. Something bad happened that night. Lenny was home that evening because he'd been working in the field with Papa and they came in after dark and not talking. I don't think anybody said a word all the way through supper. During the night something strange happened. We'd all gone to bed except Papa, and he went back out to the field to drive the tractor but came in late while we were asleep and woke Lenny. Lenny slept in the same room with me and Curt in his own bed. It must have been after midnight. "Get out to Beacon Road," Papa said, like Lenny should've known he was supposed to be out there. "Something going on you should see." Then Papa stomped off to bed. Lenny never came back. Whatever it was took the rest of the night, I guess. I remember going to school the next day, the day Lenny got killed, but I don't remember what happened Wednesday until I was in the house and no one else there. What I did after the nurse sent me home is missing. The next thing I remember is that Lenny was dead.

I'm thinking about all this when Leroy drives up. Now he's sitting here on the porch with me, talking as usual, his old pencil arms and legs hardly holding open his clothes. He's always coming out to the farm making a nuisance of himself. Papa doesn't complain, but I know he doesn't like Leroy much. Leroy doesn't understand about working, him living in town. Papa says all Leroy knows about is going somewhere. Papa doesn't believe in going. He says, the more you go, the more you want to go till you never want to stay home. Says it's like a disease. Leroy piddles around in his daddy's auto repair shop a little, but that's it. And today, he's had the whole day off, had all his life off if you want to know the truth, and happy like it's his birthday, claiming he has good news for me too.

"Man, I've heard of so many girls that want to go out with you, you'll be busy till you graduate."

"Come on, Leroy, I'm in no mood for joking."

"It's the truth, I tell you. Word has traveled all over town. You get beat up, kicked out of school, kicked off the football team. Man, what luck. Every girl in the county wants a piece of your stuff."

"Come on, Leroy. You're making fun of me because I'm snakebit."

"No I'm not, no I'm not. I think you've found the secret to getting into every girl's drawers. I'm hoping some of your bad luck will rub off on me."

I try to take a swing at his head but my shoulder doesn't work too good because it hurts deep inside from lifting hay bales.

"I've got just the girl for you to start with, Bobby."

"Ya. This ought to be good. What have you got for me this time? Another harelip? Or is it another girl that wets the bed and don't take regular baths so she smells like pee, like those twins you fixed us up with two years ago?"

"Look, Bobby. I've grown up a lot since two years ago. No. I've got the right one for you this time. Trust me."

"Give me a name," I tell him.

"Brenda."

"Brenda McCallum? Get serious." She's the one he's been lying about Thomas nailing last summer. "Besides, you keep telling me how fat she is."

"I am serious. And maybe she is a little fat, but you've been wanting to go out with her ever since she kissed you in the eighth grade. And now, she's been asking about you, Bobby. Swear to god."

"Ah, come on, Leroy. She's not going for me. She's too smart."

"I agree, it's hard to believe," and I don't like the way he said that, "but I tell you, you're a celebrity. Shit, man. Nothing ever happens in this town. Everything that's happened since school started has happened to you."

"But not Brenda. She's in with all the teachers. Even Clyde likes Brenda."

"No. Listen to me," and here it comes. "If you get a date with Brenda, then she can get Phyllis Thompson to go out with me for a double date. Phyllis and Brenda are about as close as two girls get. You can get along with any girl on a double date. I'll do all the talking so you won't have to worry about it. See there? I'll do it for you, Bobby. Besides Phyllis isn't such a bad girl. I might even enjoy it."

He's been talking about Phyllis ever since school started this year. She's a nice girl, a little tall and skinny but definitely too good for Leroy. "Leroy," and now I'm shaking my head, and I don't know what to say because Brenda runs with a different group of kids from the ones I know.

"You're not asking her to marry you, Bobby. You're just asking for a date. Then ask her if Phyllis will go out with me so we can double date. It's going to be easy, Bobby. Shit. You're so good with the girls." And now here he comes at me from the other side. "To tell you the truth, I'm having trouble. I need some help getting a date. And all I'm asking for is

45

an opportunity. All I need is another start. I don't know why you can't help me out a little with Phyllis. Besides, I'm doing some work on my car starting this afternoon. It's going to be laid up for a while. Now your car's out of the shop and I need a little help. And Brenda's hot after your ass, I tell you. Shit! There's no way to ever get through to you. You're hopeless."

I hear a car on the road, hear it slow, so I look past Leroy, past the old peach tree on the corner of our driveway, and, oh shit! I see Bev driving up in her daddy's brand new Buick that has the four little holes on the side. Bev has never been out to our little shack before, and I am squirming and looking around to see what kind of state it's in. Lawn not mowed, chug hole in the drive that needs a little dirt, house could stand a little paint.

"Looks like it's already starting," Leroy says, "and they're coming for you instead of waiting for you to come after them. But this girl's trouble, Bobby. You know that. I hear she's been going out with a lot of other guys." And with that he gets up to leave like he's really in a hurry, already has his keys in his hand. "Brenda and Phyllis, neither of them like her. You've already had one fight over Bev. Brenda comes trouble free. Just think about it. Trouble free." I think maybe he's pushing a little too hard for some reason.

I'm tired of seeing people today and that goes double for Bev. Her daddy acts like he has a little money because he's had a big new house built on their dairy. I walk Leroy to his Ford, feeling the dirt on the tender balls of my feet. Leroy finally gets that old Ford started after grinding the starter a couple of times, and then black smoke boils out the tail pipe. I'm wishing it didn't sound so much like the exhaust comes straight out of the manifold, but he's raising a racket and squeaks a little rubber in second gear.

Now here Bev comes out of that black Buick.

"Bobby Ray," says Mama sticking her head out the front door. "Go get your Papa out of the Cotton Club. And do it now." Then she slams the door.

Bev has on those tight white shorts with a red blouse tucked in and black pointed-toe shoes, and out the corner of my eye, I see Mama peeking from behind the curtain. I wonder if Aunt Loretta is looking too? I wish Bev had on more clothes the first time Mama sees her. God, how many things can be wrong at once?

The first time I saw Bev was in kindergarten. I was standing outside on the classroom steps and she was on the other side of the schoolyard running from the swings to the teeter-totter. She had her black hair pulled back in a ponytail, and it bounced and swayed back and forth when she ran. Seems like she was always running back and forth trying to make up her mind, swings or teeter-totter, swings or teeter-totter. All through grammar school she was always sort of off in the distance. This summer was the first I really got to know her. But I can't get along with her. When she's around, I can't keep from looking at her. When I'm with her, I can't keep my hands off of her. That's what got me in trouble this summer. "Hands are serious business," she said. "At least where you want to put them. And I need to know how serious your are toward me before we do that." So I backed off, and that made her even madder.

"Bev, there's no sense in getting out." I'm walking toward her now, letting my arms dangle with my hands sticking out the pockets of my Levi's. I'm trying hard not to feel the pressure of Mama's eyes.

"Come on Bobby. Let's not fight anymore. I only want to see you for two minutes. That's all I want, just two minutes."

"What's two minutes going to solve? You already decided you don't want to go with me.

"Leroy tells me you've been dating girls from out of town. And I just think that we should consider what we mean to each other. I know now that Melvin is just a friend. And I've decided not to go out with him anymore, not on dates anyway. I hope you believe that. Melvin is your friend too, Bobby. Leroy caused the trouble between you and Melvin."

"The problem between me and Melvin is you. Not Leroy."

"Oh, really? Did you know he asked me out?"

"Leroy?" And I laugh a little but it doesn't feel too funny.

She laughs too and blushes a bright red to match her blouse.

"Forget I said that," she adds.

"Leroy asked you out? You mean, like for a date?"

"I said forget it!" And she acts like she's going to walk off and leave me standing here. "I've been thinking that maybe I've made a mistake about us," she says right quick. "Maybe you and me should try again. Talk about it anyway."

That goddamn Leroy is in trouble. No wonder he keeps talking Bev down to me.

"You don't sound too convinced about it yourself," I tell her. So why should I?" She has her hair down around her shoulders this time. She knows how much I like it like that.

"Bobby. You don't always have to be so bitter. Can't I stay a little while and talk to you over there on the porch?"

There is always a lot of flies on the porch.

"I can't talk to you now, Bev." I would like to talk to her but I have to get her out of here. I don't want her to see our little shack, and I can just hear Mama going on about those tight shorts. God, she does look good. "I'll call you sometime. I just can't talk to you now."

She starts to leave, then turns back.

"We lost the game Friday night, Bobby. Clovis beat us 33 to 13."

"So what? That doesn't make me feel any better."

I see Mama finally let go of the curtain. Guess she got her eye full.

Oh," and now she's whining again, "let me talk to you for just a minute."

This girl never listens to reason. Her voice is getting even smaller, and I guess I don't want her to feel too bad, but I got to get her out of here. I haven't had a shower in two days, my hair looks like a tumbleweed, and I got these smelly armpits. So I am feeling real bad about it, but I don't know another way to do it. Besides I'm still mad as hell about her going out with Melvin.

"I'm going to say this one more time, Bev. Get back in your daddy's big fat Buick and go back to cheerleading, praising the lord, or swatting flies. I don't care. I'm not talking to you. Not today. Not ever."

So she walks off, but, damn, she's not going back to her daddy's black Buick. It looks like she's going around to the side of the house, over by where Mama has her garden planted.

"Bev," I say. "Where are you going?"

But she won't answer. She just walks to the side of the house and motions for me to come to her.

So I have to go over. But I'm barefooted and I don't like it because of the stickers. When I'm standing right in front of her, she comes up close so our tummies are touching and her heat is coming through my Levis and this is killing me because I'm starting to swell up.

"Bobby," she starts in on me, barely talking above a whisper, "you could put your hands anywhere you want, if you would just tell me that we are going to be together after graduation. You don't have to tell me you'll marry me right away. But I need something. Just a little something. Then we can do it. And we can talk about getting married and having babies,

Chapter 8: *First Leroy and Then Bev*

Bobby. What could be wrong with having babies together?"

She pushing up against me, where I'm swelling, and I look out across the neighbor's field where a bunch of cows are grazing, and off in the distance I see cars on Highway 152 heading for San Francisco, the direction I'm headed after school. But how can I walk away from this girl? How can I stay in Chowchilla? How can she stand this close to me when I haven't had a bath?

"I don't know," I say.

She shakes her head and her face just forms into this gigantic pout. "Quit saying, 'I don't know.' Just say 'Yes' or just say 'No.'" But if you say 'I don't know' again I'm going to scream!"

"But I really don't know."

"You're impossible! You know that? You're just disgusting." And then she backs away from me, looks down at my pants and bare feet. Maybe she got a whiff. As she walks back to her daddy's Buick, I feel like I should say something but I just don't know what.

She doesn't slam the car door. She doesn't race the engine. She doesn't peal rubber. She just leaves.

So Leroy asked Bev for a date. I will fix his ass for that.

Mama is on the front porch glaring. "Bobby Ray. I told you to go get your papa."

"Oh, Mama."

She's never had me do this before.

CHAPTER 9: *Where Lenny died*

I'm standing just inside the door of the Cotton Club waiting for my eyes to adjust to the dark so I can find out if Papa is in here. Curt's sitting in Papa's pickup and mad as hell. My shadow is standing in a wedge of light that's falling on the wood floor, and that wedge gets slimmer and slimmer, and my eyes get better and better as the door slowly closes behind me.

"Hey, Hershel. Look at that." It's a man's voice, but I can't tell whose. "What the hell happened to you, Bobby?" the man asks, pulls back from the bar a little and I recognize him as Maxwell Gerald. He has a little place out on the Boulevard.

A girl in tight Levis steps away from the bar, away from Papa, I think, walks down to the far end, turns to look me over top to bottom. I see Papa get off a bar stool real slow, like he's going to get a whipping. He walks toward me putting his old beat up hat on.

"Time to go now, son?" he wants to know, like maybe I dropped him off and had something else to do, and now that I'm all through, it's time to go.

"Yeah. Mama is real worried, Papa," I say quiet like.

The corners of his mouth are both turned down real bad, so I think maybe he's going to cry. I wonder who's going to pay for this?

★

I'm standing at the edge of the ditch watching Curt cry. He's trying to set a siphon pipe in the tall grass. Sun is just about down now, and I look off into the horizon as I walk on down the ditch away from Curt. God, it seems like our family just can't get over feeling bad. Curt just took the worst beating from Papa I've ever seen him give out. I know that Curt is not the best kid in the world, but Papa just shouldn't hit him like that. I know what that belt feels like. And Trish just keeps egging Curt on because she knows Papa won't hit her, and all the stuff Papa should give her, he gives to Curt. So Curt gets his share and then he gets Trish's too. I think

Chapter 9: *Where Lenny Died*

Trish learned something this time though.

When we got home from the Cotton Club, Curt went on inside, but Papa and me stayed outside to check the pickup tires that he said weren't wearing right. Just trying to bide his time, if you ask me, before facing Mama. But finally I guess Papa figured he better go in and take his medicine. Just as we walked in the front door, Curt hollered at Mama. "You can go to hell too," is what Curt said. He was mad enough to say a lot more because he'd been sitting in that pickup a long time, with Papa in the Cotton Club, and he was ready to crawl anybody within reach. I figure he'd started with Trish as soon as he opened the front door, then Mama started on him. She'll correct Curt, but not when Papa is around. It sets Papa off. This time Mama hollered back before she knew Papa was in the house. "Watch your mouth when you're talking to me, young man. I'm your mother," is what she said. That was enough to convict Curt in Papa's eyes with the drinks in him. Curt was in the bedroom just off the living room when me and Papa came in, so he was trapped because there's not another way out. Papa didn't say anything, but I knew the belt was already hot from the hiss it made when Papa jerked it out of his pants.

Trish looked like the world just caved in on her. "It's okay, Papa. I started it," is what Trish said. But it didn't make Papa any difference. He'd already drawn his bead on Curt. "Papa," said Trish. "Whip me, Papa. It was my fault." And she started to cry. Trish ran at Papa screaming like she couldn't stand what was about to happen. "Please, Papa, please whip me, Papa. I deserve it not him. It was my fault, Papa." Papa hasn't ever whipped her, and I guess he never will. Mama whipped her when she was little, but never Papa. Seems like that's a load too hard for Trish to carry. Sometimes I think she hates Curt because of it.

I started to walk in and tell Papa he couldn't do that to Curt. But I figured he is our papa. Maybe he knows best. But he always buys belts with metal tips. I kept looking at little Curt cowering in the corner, and then I would turn away.

Trish walked into a corner of the living room and just stood there shaking and crying.

Curt took the belt on his arms first, till they hurt too bad, then rolled over on his stomach trying to spread the pain, but he couldn't take much of that either, so he stood and took the last few lashes that I saw face on, blinking and flinching every time the belt whacked him across the shoulders, but he still stood straight. Papa was using a forehand then a backhand. Papa never said a word, didn't even look mad. And Curt never cried. I've never seen a grown man look as brave as Curt. I had to walk off. Went to our bedroom, sat on the bed looking at the space between the boards in the hardwood floor like I did when Lenny died, listened to the silence in the whole house that followed Curt's beating.

I don't know what happened to Trish.

I'm looking out over the hay field that we've finally collected all the hay off of. We'll finish watering this field by morning. I can already tell the difference in the shade of green where we've watered. I see a couple of fresh gopher mounds in some of our borders and figure we'll soon be having trouble with our water getting out. Gopher holes make the water just disappear and reappear somewhere else. Like maybe out in Mr. Grissom's field.

I walk back to Curt, but he's still having trouble setting that siphon pipe at the high end of the ditch where the water is low, so I go over to help him, and he's mad and cussing the pipe and acting like that's the reason he's crying. When he's bent over, his old white T-shirt pulls out of his pants, and I see the welts Papa left on his back.

I know how Curt feels. Everything I do, I get into trouble. Right now I'm probably getting in trouble and don't even know it. Everywhere I go I get into trouble. If I go off and hide, I get into trouble. If I just talk to somebody, I get into trouble. If I don't talk to somebody, I get into trouble. Seems like I don't ever get a rest from this life. Sometimes I just want to shout, "Stop! Stop! for just a minute and let me think about some of this." Just let me not live for a minute, and maybe I can get caught up. But no. It just goes on and on and on. Seems like I am running about a week behind everybody else. By the time I find out what's going on so that I can do it right, I got something brand new to do, and already it's not working. It's just like somebody booby-trapped my life. All I have to do is show up and things are already going wrong.

"Come on, Curt, that siphon pipe got you by the ass?" I ask.

"I don't know. I just can't seem to get it started. Why doesn't Papa do this anyway? Why do we have to do his dirty work?"

"Hell, Curt," I tell him, "I saw him take a half hour to set one of the big ones the other day and sometimes he can't set 'em at all. It gets expensive when he does it. Once I saw him cuss the pipe first, then he beat it on the ground until it flew up and hit him in the face, then he took it over to a fence post and beat the pipe double, threw it across the fence into Mr. Grissom's junkyard. I think he sends us to change the water because he knows we'll do it right."

Curt laughs at that, sniffs but keeps on crying.

"Ya, those pipes are about as hard to get along with as Trish," I say. He doesn't laugh this time. I feel like I have to do something for him, but when I try to help set the pipe, he turns his back on me and walks on to the pickup. I notice how big his arms are getting. He's beginning to muscle up, just like me.

I get all the pipes set, watch the ditch to make sure the water level stays put. Then I walk real slow back to the pickup were Curt is, get in to drive and set there listening to him sniff and watching him wipe his nose on his shirt sleeve.

I drive past the house, go north a ways, then out east of the Boulevard on Avenue 23 1/2 with Curt asking me where I'm going, but I won't tell him. We go past the Cemetery where Lenny's buried, and when we come to the big dip where the Berenda Slough crosses the road, Curt quits crying because he knows this place. The concrete road is flat in the bottom of the slough bed that's about a hundred yards wide. Not a whole lot of water crosses the road, it being fall, and that only at the far east bank. I stop on the west bank, pull off onto the sand and get out. Curt's never stopped here before. Mama and Papa won't allow it. I've been by here a lot. Sometimes I come by when I go to the fairgrounds, but I've only stopped once myself. That was the day after Lenny died. I came with Papa to look for Lenny's baseball cap and wallet. I don't think Papa even knew I was with him.

Curt doesn't need me to tell him what happened here, but I tell him anyway. "Lenny was killed over there by that tree, about the same time of evening as now. Did you know that, Curt?"

He won't answer. The water never reaches up this high on the bank. Not unless it's a flood year. Lenny's blood is still soaked into the ground here. The rain just washes it a little deeper. The ground's still sacred.

"It was spring instead of fall, though," I tell him. "The sun was just set, and Lenny was coming home in his car."

"Lenny's car was broken down," he says like he thinks I'm lying.

"Lenny's car had been broken down until a couple of days before, that's right. Him and Papa put in a new transmission. He'd been taking his time with it, but something happened and he got it fixed in a hurry. Lenny had dropped the transmission dragging."

"How do you know he was dragging? You weren't there."

"I don't, but that's what I heard at school. It's not the story Lenny told Papa though. You can bet on that. I was helping him and Papa put in the new transmission. Papa was mad as hell. Chewed on Lenny all the time they were under the car. Thought he was going to use a wrench on him. Papa scared the hell out of me then."

"And I suppose he doesn't now?"

"Not really."

"Then how come you don't stand up to him?"

"Being afraid and not knowing what's the right thing to do are two different things, Curt."

I take Curt about ten yards off the road to the foot of an old cottonwood tree.

"That's where Lenny was lying when they found him," I say. "All wrapped up in that car of his, a piece of metal sticking through his head."

Curt flinches when I tell him that and starts crying again. "Stop it, Bobby Ray," he says.

But I figure he ought to hear it all. Feels good to say it out loud anyway. I go back to the pickup to get the lemonade thermos Mama fixed for us. "Sit down," I tell him, motioning to the foot of the tree. "We're going to stay a while."

"Papa's going to be mad," says Curt, and he's still sniffing a little.

I turn up the thermos. Like that sour sweetness. "Papa's not whipping you any more. I've made up my mind."

Curt laughs at me, sniffs again. "I made up my mind too when he was in the Cotton Club, but he did it anyway."

I hand him the thermos and he finishes it.

"Did you know somebody killed Lenny?" And now I'm just sort of trying the words out, not even sure what I am saying.

"It was an accident."

"Yeah, you're right," I tell him. "The police said Lenny just went off the road and hit the tree. But there's really two stories to him getting killed. The other one is Papa's story. I don't know all of it, but I do know a little."

"You're making this up, Bobby Ray." And he stands up. "I want to go home."

"No, you don't either. Sit down. I need to talk about this cause I've been thinking lately."

"Mama's going to be scared."

"Me thinking is not that scary. Besides, she's scared of everything."

He laughs again. "Ain't that the truth."

"Sit down."

"I don't want another whipping."

"Pull up your shirt, let me see your welts."

"You get a kick out of seeing where I hurt?"

"Oh shit," I say. "Put it back down. I changed my mind. Curt," and I must be feeling brave or I wouldn't ask even Curt this. "Do you remember Lenny's funeral?"

"A little." And he says it real quiet, like he's bracing himself for something.

"What was Papa shooting at?"

"At the funeral?"

"Yeah. You remember the gun shots?"

"Papa didn't shoot anything."

"Sure he did. He had his pistol with him. He shot something."

"That was someone else. Papa didn't have a gun. You were there."

"If he didn't, who did?"

"I don't know. Mama got me out of there real fast once the action started."

"Come on, Curt. This is important. I've got to know who it was and what they were shooting at."

"I was little then, Bobby Ray. Why don't you remember?"

"I was strange then Curt. Real strange. Sick. Besides Aunt Loretta kept me from seeing most of it. What do you think about her? Is she weird or what?"

"Not any weirder than you. You still should remember. All I remember is that some one shot my dog that I used to play with all the time."

"Rascal?"

"Ya. I think that was his name. He was my dog."

"No he wasn't. And I know this for sure. He was Lenny's dog."

"Well, I used to play with him all the time."

"You probably did. You didn't have to work then. So tell me who shot

Rascal."

"I don't know. You should remember the rest."

"But I don't. All I remember is that a few days later that policeman, Brock, came out to see Papa. I thought he was going to haul Papa off to jail for killing someone. I didn't know it was a dog. I thought somebody got shot. Brock and Papa stood right out there on the front porch and talked. Papa was saying it wasn't an accident. Brock said it was. And they were talking about Lenny getting killed."

"If you want to know about it, why don't you ask Papa?"

"You know better than that."

"So you're not afraid of Papa, huh?"

"Well, maybe about some things."

"Ask Mama."

"Mama's mean too, Curt. She won't answer a whole lot of questions about Lenny. The police were convinced it was an accident. Maybe Papa was wrong."

I quit talking, and Curt and I sit here feeling the dampness of the grass under us soaking into our bodies, it getting darker and darker and maybe even a little cool with fall coming on, everything around us dying, and Mama and Papa worrying about us not coming home from changing the water. When it comes sundown now, we have to all be home or Mama cries. I know we are getting in trouble again, at least I know they'll be all over my butt. But I'm feeling so close to Lenny, I don't want to even move. I get to feeling real strange about him dying here where we're sitting. Sacred ground. I just imagine I'm Lenny with that piece of metal sticking through my head and my blood and brains pouring out onto the ground and my body twisted into all that metal, try to feel him hurting, and think what a terrible time it was to die in the spring with high school almost over, graduation just around the corner, cotton and corn all planted, seeds sprouting and the County Fair coming up.

I suppose Papa favored Lenny because he was the only one of us born in Oklahoma. Papa used to talk about Mama changing Lenny's diapers while he watched the wind blow all his topsoil into Arkansas.

I look at little Curt, his old work shoes all muddy and split partway down the side, his Levis wet halfway up the knee, and him needing a haircut. Those welts are showing underneath his shirt again. Strange how Papa's belt leaves marks. It's like the edge on each side cuts into the skin, and the middle part must really pop because it just gets red and swells there. Where that tips hits, that's where the blue places are, blue with a little blood under the skin. That metal tip is wicked.

I didn't realize until now how Mama and Papa neglect Curt. They notice Trish because she works on them all the time. She's working on Curt's ass all the time too. Lenny was always on me because of the way I treated Trish, but he didn't understand about her. Maybe she's wised up. Mama and Papa are so lost in their own heartache, they don't even know they have Curt. It's almost like they are blind. So much they can't see. I wonder if there isn't some kind of sickness, a disease, that keeps you from seeing some things. It's almost like they have the flu, but instead of it affecting their body, it's affected their brain. Maybe someday doctors will give people a shot, and it'll get them over something like what Mama and Papa have. But a lot of it I know is my fault, them being sick and me giving them so much trouble.

I should help Curt too. I wonder what I can say to him now? Seems like I ought to be able to help. Sometimes it seems like it's just me and Curt against the rest of them.

"You remember Lenny's best friend?" I ask.

"I remember a tall skinny kid that used to come over sometimes."

"Curly, blond hair?"

"Maybe."

"That's him. Only he's not so skinny anymore. That's Charles Kunze. He's been gone ever since Lenny died. But now he's back in town."

"Why don't you ask him about the shooting, if you got to know. He must have been there."

"He was, Curt."

"Well, go look him up then, jees. Why you coming to me?"

"God. I've never seen anybody as mad as you."

"Everybody stays on my case all the time. Just get off my case."

"I have seen him."

"Then why didn't you ask him, moron?"

"Asking questions is not my strong point. Besides I'm afraid of him."

"Poor little Bobby Ray. He's not afraid of Papa but is afraid of Charles."

"Curt," and now I'm just about in a mood to kick his ass myself, "you're going to be so good at high school. That mouth will really go over big. I've been afraid of Charles for a long time, probably cause he used to run around with Lenny."

I finally get another laugh out of Curt. But it's not like he wants to. "So where'd you see him?" he says. "The suspense is killing me."

"You know the evening I picked up my car at Pistoresi's?"

"So what?"

"He was working there. He wants me to go out with him. He's going to show me all the things he used to do with Lenny."

"He was raised here. He's just another Chowchilla deadhead."

"He's a nice guy, Curt. No wonder Lenny liked to run around with him."

"So what are you going to do together?"

"Shoot rabbits. That's what he was talking about."

"I shoot rabbits. That's what the big boys do for big excitement?"

"One more thing. I saw Lenny's car the other day."

"You're lying."

"No I'm not."

"Really?" And now he sits up, even turns to look at me. "Where?"

"Crusing the school."

"Who was driving."

"I'm not sure."

"You're really a klutz. You can't even see good."

"I'm not sure, but I'll tell you who I think it was. I think it was Charles."

CHAPTER 10: *Sonnett Again*

"Hey, Bobby. Welcome back." It's Thomas Powers walking toward me through a crowd of high school kids. "You coming to football practice after school?" I don't know why he is asking that. The whole school knows I'm off the football team.

"I don't play anymore." I am in the towers building at school. Kids are fogging around and staring at me. I just want them to leave me alone. The clatter of all these footsteps down this wooden hall is enough to drive me nuts.

"What? You quitting football?"

"Come on, Thomas. Clyde kicked me off the team."

"Oh, yeah. I remember him doing that, but it couldn't have been permanent. Now that you're back in school, he'll let you play. Won't he?"

"I don't know. I'll have to check." Thomas has me thinking there may be some hope. I have an appointment to see Clyde right now, and I'm really sweating it.

"Hey, I hear your old man worked you till you begged for mercy."

"Who was telling you that?"

"My daddy saw your old man in town late yesterday."

"Hi, Bobby." It's Becky Wynsum, a little freshman I've had my eye on. She's the cutest thing I have ever seen.

Then Melvin comes up to me. "Good luck in there with Sonnett. Tell him what he wants to hear. Sweet-talk him, he loves it." Melvin's tooth will always be chipped. At least my face has healed, maybe just a little black under my left eye. I hear his mother got him back in school last week. He only missed two days. But he didn't play football so Clyde couldn't take that away from him.

"I hear Charles Kunze is back," he says coming up close.

"It's a fact. I saw him last week. I didn't know you knew him."

"Don't. But my brother, Johnny, does. He told me Charles was in town.

Johnny thinks something's going on, or Charles wouldn't be here."

Then somebody spins me around.

"Hey, Bobby." It's Leroy. Just the guy I want to see. "Loan me some lunch money," he says. Wayne, his new redheaded buddy, the undertaker's son, is with him. I hate that sonofabitch. "I'm flat broke," Leroy says. "Used the last of my lunch money for gas to come see you yesterday."

"Is that right? Well, I'm real glad you're hurting, Leroy, cause I hear you asked Bev for a date."

"Who would tell you a lie like that?"

I put my hand on his chest, shove him back a step. "She did, that's who."

"Bobby Hammer." I recognize that sour voice. It is old man Sonnett. "In my office. Right now."

So I am sitting in his old wood chair again while he stares at this folder full of papers he has on me. They don't put any of the good things I do in there, nothing about all the times I stayed out of trouble, all the fights I've walked away from. Just the bad stuff. Finally he decides he wants to talk.

"Were you going to fight Leroy Korenski right out there in front of my office?"

"What?"

"You and Leroy. Were you going to have it out right in front of my office?"

"Leroy is my best friend."

"I know that. And Melvin was your second best. Looks like you've just worked your way to the top of your stack."

"So that's it. What are you taking away from me this time? You kicking me out of school for good? You finally got me. Is that it? Or are you taking me out of physics?"

"No. I'm not suspending you permanently. I'm not suspending you at all. And I have talked to Mr. Wood. He stood by you, Bobby. And that surprises me. He really thinks you can make it in that class. So maybe you have an aptitude for something. I just can't believe it's physics. But I'm willing to let that one ride a while. And I was considering changing my mind about this football thing too. Some people think football does you some good. I had a tendency to want to believe them. But not after what I just witnessed out front."

I know Melvin is right, but I just can't sweet-talk this sonofabitch. The best I can do for now is to keep my mouth shut.

CHAPTER 11: *Lenny's Pistol*

We're in Charles' jeep now, going away from town on Robertson with nothing protecting us but the windshield. I've never been out in a jeep before, and it seems noisy and a little scary. I notice the dark a lot more with the half-moon in front of us heading for the horizon off to the right. Even the palm trees on both sides of the road seem darker than usual until they light up as we pass and then go dark again behind us. I've never gone out in the country at night to have fun, and with the faint lights of houses are far in the distance, seems a little lonely. Charles reaches back under a tarp and comes up with two Olys, motions for me to get the church key out of the glove box. The jeep whines so loud, it's hard to talk, but Charles hollers over it anyway.

"What are you planning to do when you get out of school?"

"Papa says I better dirt farm with him."

"I didn't ask what your papa wants. I know what he wants. What do you want?"

Now I'm in another fix. I don't know what to say to Charles. I know I should have a good plan for after graduation, but I don't. All I have are these dreams that don't mean anything to anybody but me.

"I'm not real sure," I say.

"Speak up. I can't hear you."

"All I know is, I want to get out of here."

He shakes his head like that's a big problem and starts to say something, but there's just too much noise. He's off on a dirt road now and the headlights bounce around on the ground, then up in the air like searchlights. He slows the jeep to a crawl, rolls down an old dry river bed, and when we come up the other side, he motions for me to get the .22s out of the back. He lays his across his lap and turns the spotlight on, moves it around until it falls on a small farmhouse in the distance.

I feel strange about that .22 of mine. I haven't had it out for a while.

I don't care much for hunting anymore. I don't believe I've shot it since Lenny died.

He starts talking again. "I don't understand why you would want to leave, Bobby. But I guess you don't know the potential of this place. You should stick around. I have a plan. It would work better with two than one. We might even recruit some others, if we can find the right kind of kids. This whole San Joaquin Valley's a gold mine. You can't believe the living you can make here without working."

We cut across country, bouncing around so bad I'm thinking I can't stay in my seat long. "I don't know, Charles. I kind of like working."

I see cottontails and maybe a jackrabbit or two scatter as we pull up to an old farmhouse. "Deserted," he says as he fires a shot into one of the windows, sending glass tinkling. I hope like hell he's right. The big dirt yard around it is really just part of the field. Through the dark I make out two cotton trailers, a big John Deere tractor and an outhouse.

"You sure it's okay for us to be here?" I ask.

He turns off the headlights and I punch holes in a couple more Oly's, then we start shooting cottontails.

"I'll shine the spotlight," he tells me, "and we'll see who can shoot the rabbit in the light first. Ready?" He balances his .22 on the top of the windshield, shooting with his right arm and working the light with his left. When the light hits the rabbits, some run, some stand still. The rabbits' eyes reflect like red coals from a campfire. Charles shoots a steady stream of bullets, knocking the heads off rabbits, and I'm just doing a lot of aiming, so I lower my .22 and watch. He stops and looks over at me, then laughs like hell.

"How long you been doing this?" I ask.

"All my life."

"You going to eat all those rabbits?"

"Nooo. You can't eat these rabbits. They have diseases."

He shines the light for me now, and I'm taking my time and get a couple, some take two or three shots. I get a jackrabbit with a gut shot and it sits quiet like on its hind legs with its big ears standing tall, glows white in the spotlight, its guts hanging out. Then I hear a woman scream.

"Where's that coming from?" I ask. Scares me.

"The rabbit," he says. "Shoot again."

"I mean the woman screaming."

"That's not a woman, Bobby. That's the rabbit you wounded. Kill it," he tells me.

I get really scared, start to run, then think better of it. Don't know what to do.

"Well, go ahead, Bobby," he says. "You going to take all night?"

I've never heard a rabbit scream like. Sounds pitiful. I look into the dark surrounding us. I just feel like somewhere out there a woman is hurt real bad. I try to finish off the rabbit, but I miss.

He brings his rifle to his shoulder. I see his .22 jerk a little when it fires, but I look the other way, off into the dark. I still hear the thud. "You're cruel," he says, like I've done something wrong. "You've got to be more humane." He stands around a little, like I've spoiled the hunting for him.

"Hunting is all right," I say, "but I don't like this much killing."

"Look. We're thinning them out. Okay? There's too many. When they're this thick they don't have enough to eat. Some starve to death. We're doing them a favor."

I don't have anything to say about that, but I know there's some truth to it.

"We're going to have to toughen you up about hurting things," he says. "Some night we'll have to get you some nigger pussy." Then he grabs a flashlight and a sawed-off shotgun out of the jeep, says, "Come on, let's do this Lenny's way. See what we can find inside that house."

He has to break the window with the butt of the shotgun to get to the lock on the door, and I look off in the darkness around us again for signs of somebody coming up. He still has to shove with his shoulder and the door rattles and shimmies a little when it pops open. Place looks a lot bigger inside than I thought. Only three rooms though, the living room we're in, the kitchen off to the left, and a dark bedroom that I can't see into. Stacked over in the far corner is a sofa, two easy chairs and a wrought-iron coffee table. On the floor to the right is a pile of junk, some of it kitchen trash, some of it cans of nails, and standing against the wall, two rolls of barbed wire. I spot a baby bed and that starts me to wondering about who used to live here. Probably a family. Maybe a young couple with a new baby. Looks like they struggled but couldn't make a go of it. I wonder if they stayed together, or if they had to split up?

I see something shiny on the floor and bend to pick up what looks like a toy train when I hear a blast that sounds like dynamite going off right by my ear. I get a flash like someone has caught us in here and has just shot Charles or maybe me, but I don't feel any bullet holes. I straighten up so fast Charles has to laugh at me.

"Take it easy, Bobby. Shooting windows is fun. Here. Try it yourself." And he's offering me the sawed-off shotgun.

I shake my head no and take a couple of steps back toward the door with the rich smell of gunpowder hanging in the air. That shotgun blast is still ricocheting around inside me. My hands are shaking. "I don't think we should be doing this, Charles."

"Look, Bobby, and listen close because I'm not going to say this again." And he puts his hand on my shoulder. "In this world, everybody has to take care of themselves. You do what you want. You can't judge what's right for somebody else. If they don't like what you do, let them stop you. You get to wondering what's right for everybody, you'll end up doing nothing. You get constipated, Bobby. Don't let that happen to you. You take care of yourself. Let others take care of themselves. They can do it better than you."

Charles shines the light over all this mess like he's looking for something, then picks up a claw hammer, shoves the handle down in his right front pocket. I back off a little more, and he walks toward the bedroom. I dig up some courage and follow him. It's been cleaned out except for an old bed with coil springs, and Charles shines that flashlight on a brown blood spot in the middle of the mattress. I turn to go back into the living room when another blast goes off followed by the sound of tinkling glass. Then another. He just took out both bedroom windows. Then he goes to the kitchen, lets out with a long whistle.

"This is it, Bobby."

I can hardly hear him because my ears are ringing so loud. There's no table in the kitchen but sitting in its place is a small water pump and a coil of two-inch rubber hose. About the time I get beside him, he shoots from the hip, takes out all three kitchen windows one at a time. This little house is so full of gun smoke, it's hard to breathe. He hands me the flashlight and the shotgun, then picks up the water pump all by himself.

"This is it," he says again.

"What do you mean?"

"The gold mine I was talking about. Go make room in the back of the jeep."

Chapter 11: *Lenny's Pistol*

He covers the water pump with the tarp and decides it's time to kill some more rabbits. We get in the jeep again, and he takes off across country, trying to run 'em down. Even though he's trying to pick flat ground, some of it's still plenty rough. Cottontails run ahead of us in the lights for a ways till we get close, then go sideways, and Charles, he tries to go sideways too, and he's sliding hookers and peeling out, and we're raising a dust storm that hangs invisible in the dark until the headlights hit it. Then he reaches under the seat, pulls out an automatic pistol wrapped in a rag, like he takes good care of it, hands it to me.

First I think I'm not going to take it from him. I don't like pistols. But then I think, Why not? What happens next, I don't rightly know. The jeep front wheel must have hit a hole. One second I'm reaching for that pistol and the next I'm flying through the air, then scooting along the ground on my back, then on my side, then head over heals rolling over bushes and down into a dry ditch where I come to a stop, spitting dirt.

I'm afraid to move. One thing for sure, I have to get the tumbleweeds out of my shirt, but then I find out I don't have much of a shirt on anymore, so I roll off the tumbleweed, and start trying my arms. By the time Charles gets to me, I'm trying to stand.

"What happened to you?" he asks.

"What happened to me? You mean, what happened to the jeep. One second I was in it, the next I wasn't."

"I hit a badger hole. Almost flipped. We were lucky. Both of us could have been killed. Where's the pistol?"

I ignore his ass for a minute and start trying to find out if I have any skin left. My left elbow is in bad shape but still works. Have a hole in my side where a bush almost went through but it's not bleeding much. My back doesn't have an inch of skin on it, one of my back pockets is hanging off my Levis, both knees have holes in them and doesn't matter if you're talking about pants or legs, both shoes are missing for now, and the left side of my face is solid scratches from my nose to my ear which isn't in too good a shape itself, at least that's what Charles is saying. I am surprise that I don't hurt anymore than I do.

*

Okay. Charles found his goddamn pistol. I found pieces of my shirt. Not enough to wear. I can walk sometimes but only for a short distance. The jeep has one front wheel bad out of alignment. I want to go home and

65

Charles has one more thing to do at the John Deere, the thing we came here for, according to him.

"Going to dig a little more gold," he says.

We pull up to the tractor, shine the lights on it. It's all green and looks taller than a house. He grabs a toolbox out of the back and runs up to the John Deere, starts to work on it. I'm still sitting in the jeep, shaking with cold and hurting. At first I didn't hurt much, but now I'm having a hard time hiding it from Charles.

"How do you know the tractor needs fixing?" I ask.

"Not fixing it," he says. "Taking the generator."

Then I know it was a stupid question, but I'm not feeling good and I want to go home real bad. He wants to know if I can siphon gas.

"Sure, but why?"

"Simple. We need to get out of here," he says.

I look at the gas gauge. Sure enough, I'm siphoning gas. Turns out, he's prepared for everything. Got a siphon hose? Sure, one right in the back, cut to length.

"Wonder whose tractor this is?" I ask.

"Better have another Oly," he says.

★

He knows a faster way home, by the freeway, so we head toward Highway 99. Charles, he's having a great time. "I haven't had so much fun since the last time I was out with Lenny," he says. "We're taking up where Lenny and I left off. I'll teach you everything Lenny and I taught each other." He looks real close at me, leans back like he's afraid of how I look. Then he laughs big, slaps his leg. "You're going to be all right. I can tell. You're a football player, Bobby. I used to be too. You are one tough sonofabitch."

I'm sitting here with the rags from what is left of my shirt wrapped around me, shaking like it's forty below. Just when we see lights from the cars on the highway, he slows at a farmhouse, and a German shepherd comes running out acting like he's going to tear the tires off the jeep. Charles brings out the pistol, takes two shots. The dog yelps and rolls once, then limps and staggers back toward the house. Charles goes like hell because here comes someone out of the house like he was waiting for us and then there's car lights on the road behind us. Charles has a big smile. Just before we get to the 99, there is a barricade with construction signs, warning signs, dead-end signs. I'm thinking we've had it now, but Charles goes off to the right around them and up a big dirt hill, the old jeep digging in and struggling in the soft earth that's to be a ramp for the new freeway overpass. Down the other side we go, like a roller coaster, through a gap in the Cyclone fence and we're on the 99, headed back to Chowchilla. He holds up the pistol so the headlights from the cars behind reflect off the shiny silver surface and hollers over the sound of the road and the whining motor.

"This pistol belonged to Lenny," he says. "Eureka!" and he fires it twice straight up into the air. "I've got a deal for you, Bobby. We've got to talk some more about you leaving Chowchilla. I don't think you want out of here as bad as you think. You'll have to hear me out on this. California is gold country. The gold rush is still on."

PART II

Everyone Has a Story

CHAPTER 12: *The Field Late at Night*

I'm looking up at the night sky, trying to pick out the North Star. I just realized, standing here in the dark the way I am and not being able to see much of anything, why I never seem to have my bearings around Chowchilla, why I never know which way I'm headed. The roads are all screwed up. In the country they're all laid out north-south, east-west, so that helps some, but Robertson Boulevard is off at an angle and doesn't quite fit. When Orlando A. Robertson first took his tractor into the empty field and broke the ground for the main street of Chowchilla, back in 1912, he plowed it perpendicular to Highway 99. But the 99 doesn't run north-south either. It's off at an angle. So the Boulevard runs in some strange direction, and that's the way the town lays, off at an angle. And then he lined all eleven miles of the Boulevard with palm trees like it's in Hawaii or something. But when I am driving home, coming out of town, as soon as I hit the city limits and start into the country, the Boulevard turns even more south, and there's just no reason for that. It's as if they didn't even think when they laid it out, or maybe they miss-figured it. They put another crook in it. Three miles out of town, the Boulevard hits Highway 152 at another strange angle because the 152, which goes to the coast, runs due east and west.

I'm listening to water gurgle from the valve at my feet, feel cold seep through these old rubber boots, and I find the north star just about the same time I hear something off in the weeds, probably an animal. I'm a little concerned about noises when I'm in the field alone at night because I think they might be somebody, but still I'm thinking about the other day when I got out my globe that Aunt Loretta gave me for my twelfth birthday. I spun that globe a few times and tried to figure some of this out. I couldn't then, but now I think I have it. The 99 is one of what they call the arteries of California, the artery that runs through the middle of the state, just following the lay of the land. And it's off at that strange angle, top turned toward the west. But that's not all of it. The state of California is turned at that same angle from the southern tip all the way up to Sacramento where it twists and goes north. When I turned the world about its axis so that Alaska was at the top of the earth, everything lined up vertical. From Alaska to California, even Mexico, down through Central and South America, they all lined up vertical. Then the 99 ran vertical and Robertson Boulevard ran horizontal. So what seems like is the real problem is that north and south are off. The earth is tilted on its axis and that puts Chowchilla out of whack. If there's something wrong with Chowchilla, there's something wrong with the rest of the world too. And here I was, hoping to find some place, some other town, where I would fit in better. Since other people seem to fit in wherever they are, seems more and more like what I thought at first is true. The problem is me.

That animal in the weeds growls again and I jump. I don't get along very well in the dark when I'm alone.

There's not anybody reliable I can talk to to get some of these things straight. Everybody is chewing on their own stuff and can't understand my problems. And now I'm thinking about a few days ago when I slipped and told Papa I've seen Charles. I was trying to talk to him about me working over on the coast after I get out of school, thinking maybe I could get a job like Charles had painting houses. Papa said you couldn't find steady work on the coast.

"Charles was over there for four years," I told him. "He had steady work." Then I felt my face flush. I knew I shouldn't have said it. I just don't always know what's coming out of my mouth. But lately I was thinking that maybe Papa had got over being mad at Charles.

"Charles? Charles who?" is how he answered. And all at once he was lit up.

"Charles Kunze."

"Godalmighty. That sonofabitch back? When you been talking to him?"

"I've just seen him around town."

Papa got up from his chair. "I ought to kill that sonofabitch," he said. "Him messing around with you." Then sat down. He got up twice more. Like he was going to get Charles. Sat down twice. Looked like he was even a little afraid.

"What's he done, Papa?" I asked.

Chapter 12: *The Field Late at Night*

Papa looked off and didn't say anything for a long time.

"That cock-sucking sonofabitch," he said. "I haven't ever got on to you about your friends, and you know that." Papa's face had turned red as a beet, and he even had a little spit flying. "But I'm telling you this and I mean it. Stay away from that asshole. He's nothing but trouble. Big trouble." Papa was so mad at me, he got up and walked out. Now if I want to see Charles, I'll have to go behind Papa's back. Good thing I didn't tell him and Mama that that was Charles' jeep I fell out of and got all skinned up. They were upset enough as it was. There won't be anymore hunting rabbits at night for me. Mama just screamed the next morning when I walked into the kitchen. She thought I had been in another fight.

Behind me in the dark, I hear the growl again. I turn on my flashlight and shine the beam in the weeds along the fence. Two red eyes shine back at me, eyes like the rabbit I gut-shot that night with Charles. Then it stands and I see that it's a dog or maybe a coyote. We stare at each other for a couple of minutes and it hobbles off slow into the dark. It's holding up a back leg that's hurt real bad and looks like it has other places where hair is missing. Probably got hit by a car on the 152. When it's gone, I stick my hand in the cold water and twist the valve handle until the water stops running. I've been having a bad dream, the same bad dream over and over. I dream that I've killed someone and buried the body out back of the house. When I have that dream, I keep the feeling all the next day. I know the police are still looking for me. It just bothers me. Chowchilla bothers me too. I never know which way is up. I've never heard anyone else talk about it, but it bothers me. Just like this whole area does. It bothers me and I was raised here. Born and raised here.

I'm walking back to the house now feeling a little guilty about seeing that injured dog and not doing anything for it. Feel a little like I felt about Tangi when the hay mower got her. I wanted to help her. I swear I did. But, you know, sometimes when you try to help an animal that's hurt, it'll turn on you. So Papa had to shoot her.

I don't know what to think about Charles after being out with him. It seems like he does a lot a bad things. But most kids out at night do things like that, maybe not so extreme. At least Charles is interested in what I want to do after graduation. He doesn't think anybody should run my life for me. Papa and Mama act like they know what I should do regardless of how I feel about. I know I shouldn't go out with Charles again, but I also

73

know I am. I can't resist the felling of freedom I had when I was with him.

Off in the distance toward Merced, in the faint glow of the night sky, I see the beams of two searchlights cross.

CHAPTER 13: *Aunt Loretta Has a Story to Tell*

The scraper's making a low growling noise on the hard ground behind the tractor. I'm scraping turkey manure into a pile for Aunt Loretta, and she's all over my ass for how I'm doing it. I'm wondering why Papa keeps sending me over here. Doesn't seem like I can ever please her. Maybe he can't either, but she's his sister. She lives alone out toward Dixieland on a piece of dry riverbed. When her no-account husband ran out on her seventeen years ago, she stayed on and took care of the turkey ranch. Some say she's pretty good with turkeys, some say she's not.

First she wants the manure scraped to this side of the pen, then that, and now I think she wants me to put it in the middle of her driveway. She's trying to scream over the noise of the tractor, and she's doing a pretty good job, the flashes of gold and spaces in her teeth showing with her jaw flapping, but I shut the tractor down to an idle, get off and stand so I can try to make some sense out of her. She pulls off that old orange duck-billed cap and uses it to point at the ground while she acts out what she wants done. She's squinting because now the sun is in her eyes. I feel sorry for her, that mind of hers trying so hard to come to some firm decision, but it's just not going to happen.

"Ray. Now wait a minute, Ray. If you put it over here..." She always calls me Ray because her husband was named Bobby, and she just won't call me that. "No, that won't do... Ray, cause when they come to pick it up... Did I tell you what they're picking it up in? Well, it doesn't matter anyway. They'll probably shovel it in. But they'll have to be able to swing the truck around, like this..." And she puts her cap back on, and using her palms about a foot a part, like that's how wide the truck is going to be, she traces an S-curve with them, like that's the motion of the truck as it backs in. "Or is it going to be like this..." And she comes at it from another angle, this time putting a little hip into it as she backs up, tracing her S-curve and moving her tiny feet in small rapid steps, almost like it's some strange dance and then she stops, bewildered.

"I just can't get it right, Ray. And it has to be right or they won't pick it up. They left it last year." She's starting to cry now like this is a matter of life and death. "They beat me up last year, Ray. They beat me up. I just can't stand to get beat up again."

Every time she says a loud word, the turkeys gobble, just adding their amen to her sermon. But her situation is serious. That's what makes it so pitiful. She'll get twenty, maybe thirty dollars for this pile of turkey shit, and Papa says that's half what it costs him in time and money for me to come over here. But she scrimps and saves every dime she can get and won't take money from anyone.

I get on my tractor and go to work. I put it where I think it belongs. I rev the motor as loud as it'll go, and I'm zipping around the yard boiling dust, and she's yelling at me sometimes and screaming at others, and I hear the gobble-gobble of those turkeys behind me and her old damn-near-dead dog leaves that piece of leathery cow afterbirth he's been chewing on, comes out to bark at me too. I don't pay her or him any mind even to the point of almost running over them, but I get to thinking that she doesn't have the brains to be boss, so before she knows it, I'm done.

Now. The only thing harder than working for her is trying to get away, and I'm trying to just drive on out of her yard and go home, but she's standing in front of the tractor with both arms up, and her palms pointing at me, knowing my mind and shaking her head no. She has a serious look on her face like sure enough, she's the boss. She's the only woman I know that always wears pants and long sleeve shirts.

"Ray. You're not getting away from me now. Come on in, Ray. I've got something for you in the kitchen."

Well, I think, if it's a piece of cake or pie or something good like that, maybe I could eat a little. As long as it's clean. I don't know why, but every time I'm alone with her in her house, my heart starts pounding real hard.

"Walk this way," she says, so I try.

On the other hand, I like to go into her house because she has this spare bedroom that she always keeps locked. Everybody wants to know what she has in there. The night Lenny got killed, Mama and Papa left Trish and Curt over here while they went to see what the trouble was. They didn't know Lenny was dead then, but they had a suspicion. Trish told me later that Aunt Loretta had death on her mind, so she must have known something. Trish said Aunt Loretta went into that spare bedroom and got out some coloring books. Trish followed her and got a peek inside. She said Aunt Loretta had it all set up like she still had a baby and it had been thirteen years since he died. They sat at the kitchen table and colored like they were little kids. Aunt Loretta couldn't stay in the lines.

★

Now I'm taking a pipe wrench from her, and her hand is dirty like it's never been washed but has bright red fingernails, and I'm bending down under the sink where there's been bad things happening for a long time. Then that mangy dog of hers comes lazing in the kitchen wanting to lick on me, and I stop. This is it. I've had it. "The dog's got to go," I tell her. "That afterbirth he's been chewing on smells like it came from an outhouse. It's me or him." And I am hoping she picks the dog.

"Come on, Twinkles," she says, taking him by the collar. "Ray's right. You're so old, I think you've already died on the inside, and it's coming out in your breath. But if you don't leave that fetal membrane alone, it'll cost you what little life you have left."

First, it's just the rot in the wall, and that's something I can't do anything about right now. But nothing seems to be leaking. Then here comes Loretta in with me where there's not even room for me. She's coming in under me and then over to the side with a screwdriver, and I'm wondering what she's going to do to a pipe with a screwdriver, and I can't help but laugh a little and feel ashamed of myself, and her turning that rotting-rabbit breath and skunk-armpits on me and then I see she also has a butcher knife, which I've got to be afraid of in her hand, and I squeeze over in the corner, try not to feel her warm body, but she has it all over me. I can't believe how much I sweat sometimes when I get in tight places. Strange thing is, she doesn't feel old or decrepit or weak like I imagined. She feels healthy, strong, probably stronger and more muscles than a sixteen year old girl. I can feel her little tits through that man's shirt she has on and then I think I hear something. Then I don't. It is almost like I hear thunder. I know one thing. I want out from under this sink. I feel like I can't get enough air, like there's something choking me. She has me hemmed in.

She runs that screwdriver in the round basket handle to the water shutoff valve, then turns it. First there's a screech as the handle turns, then water comes out in huge flat sprays through joints in the pipe and I'm fighting her to get it off again, and then she's on the hot water handle and the shit is coming at me so fast I'm going to be scalded. She goes to work with that butcher knife, trying to get the rotting wood out, and I guess she does accomplish something but very little, so she just quits, backs out from under there and lights a cigarette, starts talking and coughing.

I take a deep breath. And while she's smoking, I try to fix the leaks. She smokes cigarettes, one after another. Sometimes I think she's the reason I try it. The way she lips that cigarette, you would think it was candy.

But I don't know why she wants me over here all the time. She's always calling Mama and asking her to send me. She must have it in for me. The other day I came in from the field about eight o'clock at night and there was Aunt Loretta standing in the doorway to our kitchen talking to Mama. She turned around to see who it was and got a big ugly smile on her face.

"Oh, Ray, you're just in time," she said. "Come on in here. You've just got to hear what we've been talking about." She got me by the arm, led me into the kitchen, sat me down in the corner on the far side of the table when I really wanted to go wash up, pulled a chair right up in front of me, so she had me boxed in, started talking. She had on these faded blue shorts that were too big for her, her old varicose veins standing out like small rubber hoses, and long sleeves.

Mama was laughing so hard she had to leave the kitchen.

Loretta started in telling me a story. "When you were a baby," and she had her two hands in front of her, as if she was measuring how long I was then, and I was about six inches, "you were the orneriest little Billy goat that'd ever been born to two human beings. And with that bald head, you looked so innocent that everybody..." I could smell turkey shit all over her hands.

She just went on and on and on. She never shuts up about me. I guess she doesn't hurt anything. But jees. Enough is enough. And why me? Why not Trish? You would think she would want to talk about a girl.

After she left, I was talking to Mama and I asked her why Aunt Loretta had it in for me.

"Aunt Loretta had a lot of trouble when you were born, Bobby Ray," she said, like that had something to do with it. "Her baby died. The two of you were born a month apart. And she was really nervous. Her husband ran off and left her all alone."

But Mama fell silent after that and walked on in the other room like she forgot we were even talking.

Aunt Loretta puts her cigarette out before it's half smoked, then lights another, and I smell the lighter fluid down here, all the way under the sink.

"I hope you've been thinking about what we've been talking about for the last two years. You got to get to college, Ray. A bright boy like you can't let his life go to waste. Get an education, Ray. Nobody can take that away from you. Don't get yourself a girl here either. You do and you'll be stuck here for life. Wait till you get to college. You've only got one more year. Wait until then. You get a girl from somewhere else, you'll never come back. Least ways, not to stay."

She's too late for that. I've already asked Brenda out.

Damn if she doesn't start crying again. "You got to get out of here. You got to get out of here and tell people what's going on so somebody can stop it. We're dying, Ray. Do you know that? We're all dying."

I'm working on these pipes as fast as I can. Seems like all the joints are leaking. "Go outside and shut off the water at the main valve," I tell her, figuring I'll get some static about that for sure, but she jumps up and runs outside like God himself just pronounced a commandment. She lets the back screen door slap shut on the way out, and I hear it slap again on her way in and she's walking and talking.

"Ray, you're a pleasure to work with, Ray. I like working with you better than that brother of yours," she tells me.

"You mean Curt?"

"No! I don't mean Curt. I mean Lenny. Lenny was so sullen. Oh, good Lord, here I go talking about him to you and I promised Louise I wouldn't. Sometimes I think my mind is just completely gone."

"That's okay. I don't mind talking about Lenny."

"I bet you don't. Louise won't hear of it though. She's got her own idea about things. Don't get me wrong. I love Louise, Ray. If it wasn't for Louise I wouldn't be alive today. Hershel might even have me committed now. But Louise stands by me. She has to be the best woman God ever made. She's just so bullheaded about some things. And talking about Lenny's one of them."

"Well I been meaning to talk to you about Lenny. Me and Curt have been talking some about him. I need to know what happened to my brother. I don't think I know the truth."

"Oh, Lord of Mercy. Now you want to talk. This is just so hard on me, you coming over here."

79

"If you don't want me here, I can go. Papa's the one that asked me to come over."

"Oh, no, no, no. Hell no! That's not what I mean. No. Sometimes I can't wait until you come to see me again. And I want to talk to you about Lenny. There's so many things I need to talk to you about. Everybody tells me to keep my mouth shut. And I just can't do that. My mouth is just going all the time."

"I've always been confused about Lenny's funeral. And for a long time, I was willing to just not let it bother me. But now Charles Kunze is back in town. He's told me that people lie about what happened to Lenny. Seems to me it would be better to know the truth than worry about it the way I do."

"Okay, Ray. Okay. You've convinced me. But you should stay away from all the Kunze's. That's a piece of advice I can give you. Now just shut up a minute. Can you do that? Just shut up? I'm going to tell you what I know. It isn't much, but I'll tell you, if you'll just give me a little time. There's a reason I'm going to tell you, but I can't tell you what it is. Not yet anyway. Just promise me one thing. You won't tell Louise and Hershel that we've talked about Lenny. Particularly Hershel. God, I don't trust that brother of mine."

"What do you mean? What is it that you're not going to tell me? Why all this secret stuff?"

"Don't press me on it, Ray, or I'll run you off right now. Kick you completely off my place. Don't press me."

"Okay." I never thought I would hear her say that and me not run out the door.

"So here's what I know about Lenny, and I know it's the truth cause I saw him myself. And it's not much. All I know is that he was desperate. Before he got killed, the very day he got killed, he was desperate."

"You saw Lenny the day he died?"

"Don't you start jumping to conclusions. I didn't have anything to do with him getting killed. Everybody wants to know what happened to Lenny and what I did to him. Even the police were here. I could have shot that cop, Brock, myself. Him probing into my life like that. Why should everybody think I know? Sure. Lenny came over here. He was like an outlaw on the run. He was mad at your papa. Madder than I ever knew Lenny could be. I've never seen a boy so intent on disaster. He came asking

80

for advice. Can you imagine that? I know what I am, Ray. And he was desperate enough to come to me for advice. No one else he could turn to, he said. And me in the shape I'm in. I failed him, Ray.

"What did he need advice about?"

Her voice gets real quiet and raspy now, almost like a whisper, and she turns to look at the door like she thinks someone might hear her. "About killing someone. He wouldn't say who. He wanted to know if it was ever okay to kill someone. I never even told the police about this. Brock didn't need to know it cause Lenny never hurt anyone. But it's as true as me sitting here. Lenny wanted to kill somebody."

CHAPTER 14 *Trish Has Some Answers*

I'm standing in front of the mirror with my shirt off. First I flex one pec then the other. Curt is standing next to me giving me some serious shit about my hair, but I don't have time for his cutting up. I have Charles on my mind plus I have a date tonight. I put my comb in my back pocket and fold the very top of my new Levi's over one more time. Even with all the belt loops cut off, the little fold just won't stay down, but when it does, it surprises me how good it looks.

At school today, Bev was looking at me all through the pep rally. We were in the gym and I was sitting in the front row. She's leading the cheers and every time she came over in front of the senior section, she just stared daggers at me. She knows I'm going out with Brenda tonight.

Charles wants me to go out drinking with him sometime. "Do some serious drinking," he said. I have a little beer now and then, but I don't go in for drinking a whole lot. I don't want to come home drunk. I don't know what Papa would do to me if he caught me drunk. I don't know which would be worse, being out with Charles or drinking.

I bend down and feel the cuff of my pant leg where Mama ironed it flat for me. Just an inch folded under so that the crease scrapes my shoe top. I'm worried about the thick seams straightening back out. Sure enough, one is hanging down a little on the inside. Mama may have to iron them again. Curt's giving me the play-by-play treatment.

"There he is, reaching for his comb. Will he comb it again? You bet he will. Combs it one more time. Back on the sides now, back, back, back. Runs the comb straight down that duck's ass."

"Mama 'll have your butt if she catches you talking like that," I tell him.

He leans back a little, looks through the washroom to the kitchen. "Louise has her arm stuck up a dead chicken's ass. And she's talking to Aunt Loretta. She's not listening to what I say. Louise can't talk to Loretta and do anything else at the same time."

Aunt Loretta came over here wanting to talk my leg off again. She's really a cuckoo bird. I thought I was never going to get out of the kitchen in time to take my shower and get over to Brenda's. Mama may be occupied with Aunt Loretta right now, but Curt shouldn't be calling her by her first name anyway.

"You keep talking so much like a wise guy," I say, "they just might let you skip being a freshman next year. All you learn the first year is that you need a big mouth."

"Louise won't do anything to me, Bobby Ray."

"Well, you let Papa find out you've been calling Mama Louise, and Curt will end up getting Bobby in trouble. Cause I'm not just standing by while he beats you again."

"You're right. Hershel, he's another story. Not a very smart story, but another story."

"You keep selling him short, he just might surprise you." Then I remember something. "Hey. Listen to me, Curt. Come over here close."

Curt backs off like I'm going to pull a trick on him.

"Let me tell you what she said about Lenny."

"Get serious. Mama doesn't talk about Lenny."

"No. Aunt Loretta. I'm serious. This is important."

So he makes a move toward me, but he's still expecting to get popped by the towel I have in my hands.

"She told me that..." and now I know I've made a mistake. Curt's not ready to hear this. I've just had it running around in my head for a while and it needs to come out. But Curt's not the one to tell. I look at him a little strange. "I don't think you need to know this. Maybe now's not the time."

"You've got tell me now or I'll be wondering all night. I have to know about Lenny."

Just as he said that, Trish walked by the bathroom door. Curt said "Lenny" a little loud and I think she heard it.

"What you two jawing about?" she asks, coming through the door.

"This doesn't concern you," I say, "so just keep on walking."

"You said something about Lenny, and I want to know what."

"Why don't you just mind your own business," is what Curt throws in.

"He is my business. He was my brother too. What was it, Bobby Ray?"

"I have to know if you can keep that yap of yours shut about this." I shut the bathroom door that goes to the kitchen.

"I can keep my mouth shut just the same as Curt."

"No you can't. You're just like me. I wasn't even going to talk about this, but I can't keep my big mouth shut."

"So what's the difference if you tell me?"

She might have a point there. "Two people, that's the difference. Okay, but you've got to promise to keep your yap shut."

"Want it written in blood?"

"Not a bad idea. Go get a butcher knife, Curt."

He takes off like he thinks I mean it.

"Get back here," I tell him. Now I have both of them looking up at me like baby birds in a nest all ready for feeding, so I've got to deliver the goods. "Shut the door to the hall, Curt." Then I tell them. "Lenny wanted to kill someone the day he died."

"Really," says Curt, his eyes bugging out like big marbles.

Trish rolls her eyes, backs off like she's leaving. "No way, Bobby Ray. Your imagination has gone off the deep end."

"Come back here. There's more."

"Put on a shirt. I don't want to have to look at you."

I give her a biceps flex.

"Do that one flex she hates so much. The really ugly one," says Curt.

"Who told you that about Lenny?" asks Trish, like she's a little more concerned now.

"Aunt Loretta."

"Okay," and now she's laughing. "I believe that, and it explains everything. The two of you together are really something else."

"Tell her about Charles," says Curt.

"She already knows too much. I shouldn't have told her anything."

"Charles who?" Trish asks and when she asks, she reminds me of the way Papa asked, like she is already mad at me.

"Charles Kunze."

And now Trish is serious and she comes up close for me to tell her.

"Charles is back in town," I tell her. "He says people lie about the way he died."

"How does he know different?"

"He was there."

"So that's why you think Aunt Loretta is telling the truth?"

"Come on, Trish. She wouldn't know how to tell a lie."

"Do you remember who Charles is?" asks Trish.

"Sure. He was Lenny's best friend."

She laughs at me again. "He may have been, but do you remember what he did at Lenny's funeral?"

"No."

"He shot Lenny's dog."

"Charles did that?"

"Don't look so surprised, Bobby Ray. Surely you remember how Rascal hated Charles."

"But why would Charles have a gun? Why would he bring a gun to Lenny's funeral?"

"I don't know, but he had a pistol in his coat pocket. Rascal bit Charles twice, so he pulled out that pistol and started shooting. Papa started chasing him and cussing. I thought Charles was going to turn that pistol on Papa."

"So how did the funeral end?" I ask.

"With Papa and Karl shouting at each other. Papa told Karl that the next time he saw Charles he was going to kill him."

"Over him killing Rascal?"

"I don't know. Seems like they were shouting about a lot of things. I couldn't make any sense of it."

"It doesn't seem like that's enough to kill someone over."

"Tell her about the car," adds Curt.

"You want me to tell her everything?"

"All of it, Bobby Ray," says Trish.

"I saw Lenny's car passing in front of the high school during lunch hour a while back."

"How do you know it was Lenny's?"

"Cause it's the only '48 Hudson around here. Gray on top, blue on bottom. Always was the only one." I take a quick look at my watch. "You two get out of here. I'm late." And I throw the bathroom door open. "Go on. Get out of here."

"Come on, Bobby Ray," says Curt, "give her the hunchback. That'll get rid of her." Curt's talking about the way I can hunker over and flex my lats, pecs, biceps and abs at the same time. Kid at school showed me how to do it by bringing my arms in at my sides and hunching back a little to tighten my abs. I catch Trish just as she hits the door. She stops to look.

"Mama, you ought to come see this kid of yours in here. He's deformed. Needs surgery. Maybe brain surgery." She walks off, her words coming back from down the hall. "I think you should make him shave his armpits, Mama. At least make him wash them. Looks like he's growing moss under there."

"He already combs his underarms, Trish," says Curt. "I know cause he just did it."

"Shut up and get out of here, Curt." And I mean it because I'm tired of him.

"Got the comb stuck in there too. Now he'll have to go to the game with a comb stuck in his armpit. Brenda's going to really like it though."

"Shut up, you little shit," I say quiet as I can so Mama won't hear. But his mouth just keeps running. Then I hear Trish coming back again, like she forgot something.

"One thing Brenda really likes," says Curt, "is a guy with a comb in his armpit." Then he says something real low, like it is just for me. "That doesn't mean he'll get anything from her though."

I grab Curt, get him in a choke hold. He starts squirming on me and calling for Mama. Trish is back now and sticks her head in the door.

"If what I hear about Brenda is true," she says, "you won't have to worry about getting something from her. You'll just have to worry about how to get rid of it."

I tighten my hold a little so Curt can't say anything. He starts kicking me in the shins. I throw him, so he hits the door frame, ends up on the floor. I guess I was a little rougher than I meant to be. I see tears in his eyes.

"God, Bobby, you're going to kill him," says Trish acting real serious.

"Get out of here, Trish." And now I am mad. "Get out of here and shut up or I'll break your arms off and stick them down your throat."

I hear the telephone ringing off in the kitchen.

"That's Eugene," yells Trish. "I'll get it Mama."

"Bobby Ray," and now it's Mama on me with the rest of them. "You watch how you talk to your sister."

It always ends up that way. Everybody on me. I shut up, put my new shirt on that Mama just finished sewing for me, roll my sleeves halfway to my elbows, stand my collar up in the back, fold down the sides. Shirttail in my Levis. A profile shot. Elvis wishes he looked so good.

CHAPTER 15: *Leroy and His Uncle Jesse*

I'm a little early for picking up Brenda, so I stop off to see Leroy. Their house is at the corner of Alameda and Fourth Street. Has a wire fence around front grown up in weeds. Some old bald headed man with a mustache, some man I have never seen before, is sitting out on the front porch drinking a beer with Leroy's Uncle Jesse that lives with them. Jess is bare-chested. It's chilly out for no shirt. He has tattoos all over his arms that he had put on while he was busy getting his dishonorable discharge from the navy. His skin is so brown it looks like leather because he chops cotton and does other odd jobs for farmers around abouts. Always out in the sun. As I walk up, he says something to that old man and then laughs, something about me I think, but I can't hear him.

"Hi, Bobby," he says, when I get closer. "You and Leroy going to tear hell out of Chowchilla tonight?" He always shakes my hand like I'm a grownup. Makes me feel like I'm somebody. Kind of embarrasses me though.

"No," I tell him, "I've got a date tonight."

"Whoa," he says, and backs off like he's afraid of me, like he's going to run. "Now there's something I don't know anything about. Women. But if you keep your pants zipped, you'll be all right. You tell Leroy to keep his zipped too, ya hear." He has a tattoo just above the white bud of his nipple on the left side of his chest, a bright red heart with a crack down the middle and writing in dark blue just above that says "Loretta."

"If I can find him. He inside?"

"In the shower. Went in there some time last month. As soon as the State of California runs out of water, he'll be out." Then he turns to the old man. "This here's Jake, Shirley's brother." Shirley is Leroy's mother. "Might as well get to know him cause he got laid off at the Oil Mill and planning on staying with us for a spell."

Damn if Jake don't stand up and shake my hand too. Up close, he doesn't seem as old as I thought. I guess it was the bald head that fooled me. Jake looks embarrassed too and just sits back down on the porch, turns up that can of Colt 45. But then he asks me a question. "You Lenny Hammer's little brother?"

I haven't been called that in a long time and I don't like it so I don't answer him. But Jess does.

"Yes, but he's a better kid than Lenny."

"Oh, I don't know about that, Jess," says Jake. "I liked Lenny and that other kid, Charles, that he used to run around with. They were always hitting me up to buy a little liquor for 'em."

"You stay away from that drinking, Bobby," says Jess. "Don't get tied up in this stuff," he holds up the can of beer he's drinking.

"I liked Charles. When he was little, he was always going for broke," says Jake.

"He's back in town now," I say.

"That a fact? You see him, tell him to look me up."

Jess is standing there shaking his head no.

"What do you mean, Jess," says Jake. "There's nothing wrong with me seeing Charles."

I walk on in the house but I can still hear them talking.

"You'd lead the pope to a whorehouse."

"Ah, come on..."

It's dark inside because they don't have any lights on yet. Leroy has brothers all over the house. I've never stopped to count how many he has. Leon is the oldest. He quit school before graduation and has been out a while. He's over in the corner of the living room sitting on a foldaway that looks like it hasn't been made in a week. He's talking on the telephone and his girlfriend is sitting on his knee. She has a swelled up stomach like maybe there's a baby inside, and she's whispering something and nibbling on Leon's ear. Two other little ones are fighting over marbles spread out on an old coffee table. The littlest has on a dirty diaper and waddles up to me whining and holding up an empty milk bottle like I'm his daddy. I walk on through, down the hall, knock on the bathroom door.

"I told you," and Leroy's shouting, "I'll be out in a minute."

"No you didn't," I say, and he jerks the door open.

"Get in here and shut the door before Daddy sees you." All he has on is his Jockey shorts and there's so much steam I can't breathe real good. Leroy wipes the mirror with a towel.

"What's wrong with your daddy seeing me?" His daddy has always liked me. I'm taking shallow breaths because the steam has Leroy's smell all over it.

"I need five for tonight, Bobby. Can you loan me five?" He's trying to comb that straight black mop of his with this long rattail comb but can't see much in the mirror. I don't see any muscles on him, all he has is bones covered with skin and all this black hair starting to grow everywhere.

"You know I've got a date. No telling how much I'll need. I've never been out with Brenda before." I pull my comb out of my pocket, push him over a little to get a corner of the mirror, use the towel on it again.

"Where'd you get that shirt? Your mother been sewing for you again? Five don't mean much to you. Not like it does me. Daddy says things are slow at the auto shop just now. If you need something done to your car, take it to him. He could use the business."

"I need all the money I have. We might end up in Merced or somewhere. Who knows." I can see he has a problem though. And he didn't get that date he wanted with Phyllis either. The sonofabitch. It wasn't really Phyllis. It was Bev. "Why don't I just give you a couple of bucks? That's all I can spare."

"Come on, Bobby. Have some consideration." And he has to spit some toothpaste. "God, you got on new Levis too. You always have money."

I don't say anything. I'm not giving all my money away.

"Okay. Give it to me. That'll be enough for a six-pack. Maybe Wayne will have some."

"My money better not end up in Wayne's pocket."

"I'm talking about getting some from him, not giving it. Besides, he's not such a bad guy. I know he's just a time bomb waiting to go off. That's what makes it kind of fun to be around him. He's always ticking. I don't know why you don't like him." Then he puts his ear to the door. "You better scoot, Bobby. Daddy's been telling me I can't go out tonight. And this our homecoming game. Shoved me up against the wall. Accused me of stealing from him. Can you imagine that? Accusing his own kid of stealing from him. That isn't possible, is it? I mean, everything we have belongs to all of us in a family, doesn't it?"

I don't know why Leroy got so worried all at once. He has been stealing money from his daddy's wallet for years.

"Go on. Get out. Daddy sees you here, he'll know I'm going to the game."

I don't like loaning Leroy money. Feels like something has come between us now, like maybe he's mad at me. Besides, how will I get it back? I start to open the door.

"Wait a minute," he says. "I've been meaning to ask you. Charles Kunze's back in town? Uncle Jess says he's seen you with him."

"It was his jeep I fell out of a while back."

"No shit? Everything's a secret with you, isn't it? How come I have to find out from someone else?"

"We just hunted rabbits together when I was kicked out of school. I didn't know you were interested in Charles."

"Well I want to go next time. Shit, man. I'm always missing out on the big stuff."

"Besides, I don't run around with him anymore."

"Why's that? I hear he makes things happen. Why would you back off from a guy like that?"

"He's a bad influence."

"Since when did you get so self-righteous?"

"Leave it alone would you?"

"You don't have to get pissed. You and Brenda going to the dance after the game?"

"What do you think, Leroy? Is she a girl? You think she likes to dance?"

"Dumb question, huh. But I don't know that you can dance."

"Let me take care of that."

"Tell me something, Bobby. Really. Don't you think she's fat?"

"Leroy."

"Yes, I know. She does have a body. What an ass and she's got the best tits in town."

"Leroy..."

"Yeah?"

"How would you know?"

"Yeah. How would I know?"

"She's my girl anyway. I'll do the talking."

"Okay. I'll do the shutting up. But you know how long it's been since I had a date? I don't want to hear about it if you get some."

As I close the bathroom door, I smell black-eyed peas in the fresh air.

Chapter 15: *Leroy and His Uncle Jesse*

I peek in the kitchen, see Leroy's mother, still in this ragged nightgown, working over the stove. She has the baby in one arm, balanced on her hip and stirring the pot of peas with the other.

I hit the front door and make a run for my car. I'm going to be a late for sure. As I go past, Jess calls out after me. "Don't forget to keep your pants zipped."

CHAPTER 16: *Hot Night Out with Brenda*

Brenda has lost a few pounds. She's sitting close enough that I feel the warmth of her thigh coming through my Levis. She's been pushing me about what I'm going to do when we graduate. When I told her I was thinking about a junior college, she just screamed. "Bobby! You're coming, coming to college! Finally. Somebody cute's coming to college with me." She hasn't let up since. She keeps tickling me and rubbing up against me. "You've got to go to Fresno State. Why haven't we done it before? Gone out before, that is? We've gone to school together for years." I have on my red corduroy coat because it's a little cool, and she sticks her hand down inside to get to my ribs. "I was so glad to see you came back to school. I was afraid when you got kicked out that you'd quit. And now you're coming. Coming to college!"

The stadium lights are so bright I have to shade my eyes to see the crowd. I have the ragtop down on my candy-apple Chevy, and we're driving the dirt track around the football field. Phyllis Thompson, the senior candidate for homecoming queen, is sitting over the backseat of my Chevy, waving as I pull in front of the stands. Three other girls are in cars following us. They'll name the winner just as soon as they introduce the four girls to the crowd. Bev is running right in front of my bumper, her black hair pulled back in a big fluffy ponytail, and I have to let off the gas to keep from running over her. She and the other two cheerleaders are dressed in white with a red Indian chief on the front, covering up all those tits. They wave their pom-poms to pump up the crowd. When Bev jumps and twirls, I see her legs all the way up to her panties. Leroy is walking along in front of the stands waving to me with one hand and giving me the finger with the other down on his pant leg.

When Thomas Powers heard I was taking Brenda to the homecoming game, he looked me up special just to ask if I was studying up for her. Said she liked to talk about her honors classes. Acted a little like he was mad about something.

Brenda keeps throwing her long blond hair up over her shoulders. I didn't know her eyes were so big and brown until I picked her up. But I think she was scared of me, and disappointed. I held her hand when she walked me into her living room to introduce me to her father. Her hand was cold and the wettest thing this side of a fish. I hear she goes out with guys from college. Maybe I'm a little slower than the ones she usually introduces to her father.

I couldn't believe her old man. He's a carpenter, builds houses one at a time around town. He looked like a big kid with gray hair. Had on a striped T-shirt with the start of a beer belly hanging over his buckle. Set me down and started talking my leg off. He was watching the Friday night fights. Claims he actually saw Joe Lewis fight, in person. He used to be a golden gloves champion. I was so nervous about Brenda, I'd have rather stayed and talk to him. She's too pretty and too smart. Her mother was a sight to behold too. Had on a tight skirt with a low cut blouse. I can see where Brenda gets her tits. Her mother stayed and talked while Brenda was getting dressed. Kept smiling and looking me over like there was something she was expecting. I wonder what Brenda told her? She's good looking for an old lady.

Brenda turns to look back, both knees out from under her skirt punching me in the hip, and asks Phyllis if she's excited. Phyllis is about to wet her pants. Phyllis is the girl Leroy has been pining over, when he isn't pining over Bev. She doesn't say anything, just sits there over my backseat wringing sweat into her handkerchief and waving to the crowd when she needs to. Her old man's been dead two years. Got killed hooking a tractor up to a plow when his hired hand's foot slipped off the clutch. Squashed his head. She has been a pretty quiet girl since. Leroy was planning to ask her to the dance but Thomas beat him to the punch, started going with her about the time Leroy wanted to ask her out. Chasing Bev cost Leroy a little time with Phyllis. Thomas keeps telling everybody how skinny she is. She'll grow out of it though, he says. Tall as a bean pole. Should be Thomas driving her instead of me, but he's in the gym with the rest of the football team getting his ass chewed by the coach. At half-time we're down by fourteen. Brenda talked Phyllis into letting me drive her. Can't say Thomas was too pleased.

Across the field is a big wood tower where the PA announcer stays, and he's introducing the girls now. Cheerleaders sweep past my car because he's starting from the back. As Bev goes by she gives me a go-to-hell look. The crowd quiets a little, and I hear him announce Becky Wynsum. She's a sweet little kid, just a freshman, lives over on Defender Street. Her old man doesn't have anything. That's why they live on Defender Street. He works at the Oil Mill where they process cottonseed. Every dollar he makes at the Oil Mill, he drinks up in whiskey at the Cotton Club. Papa knows all about him.

This time the crowd is making a fuss over Billie Wade. She's our family doctor's daughter. We've been going to him ever since I can remember. Mama says he delivered me, Trish and Curt. She's a little too heavy to be pretty and not very smart either, but since her father is who he is, she gets around.

While we are waiting for the crowd to get quiet again, Brenda turns to Phyllis.

"Don't worry, Princess." Brenda has been calling her Princess all evening. "You're going to be queen."

"Oh, Brenda. I don't want to be. I just can't do it."

"Yes, you can. Don't worry about it."

"I just want it to be over."

"It's not going to be over, Princess. It's going to happen."

It's Cindy Brown's turn. She's sitting on top on a new Pontiac convertible right behind us. Now there's a girl for you, and the crowd goes crazy this time. Trish says she had hormone shots that caused her to pop out like that.

When the announcer introduces Phyllis, I feel the eyes of the crowd. Phyllis quits wringing her handkerchief long enough to stand with her feet in my seat and give them a good wave. But then the announcer is saying she won, so she *is* the queen. I can't hear anything for the crowd. Phyllis has started crying, so Brenda jumps in the back seat to hug her. I don't know what to do next, so I just sit here running my hands round and round the steering wheel. When Brenda sits back down, she hugs me too. With my face buried in all that fresh hair and the floodlights in my eyes, I'm feeling pretty good myself.

★

Washington beat us 33 to 6. We're in the gym now and the boards are still up for basketball with the little nets around the rims. Most of the lights

94

are off except for the ones back up over the seats. I'm in my stocking feet, like everyone else, and Brenda is trying to get me out on the floor just as Elvis starts on the phonograph.

"No," I say and I mean it, but she has both palms on my chest and every time I say no, she shoves me a little further out on the dance floor.

Then she comes up close, puts her arms around me, kisses me on the neck.

"You just take my hand and let me dance," she says.

God knows I want to dance to *Hound Dog* but I'm telling her I've never fast danced before.

"You'll have done a lot of things you've never done before, before this night's over. I have to teach every guy I go out with."

So I'm out here anyway, trying to keep up with Elvis' *Hound Dog*, and I have my arm out high for her to twirl under and then she's away from me and I pull her back again, kick my leg a little. So much for Leroy's nervousness. Brenda is laughing and talking to Phyllis who has just been crowned and is happier than I have ever seen her. She's dancing with Thomas right here beside us. Thomas hasn't said anything to me. I have the feeling he keeps sneaking a peak at Brenda.

Bev is dancing a little ways off and Phyllis is standing against the far wall looking tall and lonely. Bev has slipped out of that cheerleading outfit into another white dress and has that dark hair down on her shoulders. She's having trouble believing this is me, watching out the corner of her eye until she trips and almost falls. Last year she tried to get me to fast dance and I wouldn't. Strange thing is, she doesn't seem to have a date tonight. Melvin came in with some Mexican girl from Madera, and they're over in a corner and if he keeps loving on her, old man Sonnett will throw them out because Clyde, he's been eyeing them ever since they got here.

Since Brenda has gone to the bathroom, I talk to Leroy.

"I need a couple of bucks."

I smell something on him. "Where'd you get it?"

"What?" he asks.

"What you're drinking."

"Wayne. You owe me a couple of bucks."

"I owe you nothing."

"I asked you for five this evening and you only gave me two. I need the rest."

I turn away from Leroy, listening to that new song by Guy Mitchell, *Singing the Blues*, and here comes Trish with that pair of glasses she calls a boyfriend.

"Hey, Eugene," I say, pointing at Trish. "Where did you get this?"

Trish is quicker than Eugene. "Same place Brenda got that dog-meat she's out with," she says.

I can't take my eyes off Bev, remembering her thighs when she jumped and twirled. Leroy has asked her to dance three times now. Not that I am counting. Can't take no for an answer. What could Brenda be doing in the bathroom? Thomas is talking to Eugene about track so Trish turns her back on me. Eugene went to state in the mile his sophomore year and Powers wants to know if he'll make it back. Eugene is talking about training methods used by some guy in Australia named Herb Eliot, and all the time Trish is hanging on him like she's growed to his body.

Sure enough, Wayne has a mouse above his left eye. I keep trying to get a better look but can't see too good in the dark.

"Looks like you've got something hanging on your face there, Wayne," I say. "Piece of hamburger meat?"

"It's called a lump, Bobby. You get little ones in fights, unless it's you. Then they're like pumpkins."

It's real easy to get under his skin, and since he's drinking, I figure that's enough for now. He got the mouse in a fight he had just after the game with Brenda's little brother, Keith. Brenda found out about it as soon as we got in the dance. Wayne said some things about Becky that Keith didn't like. Keith has a temper. He's just a freshman, but I hear he was kicking Wayne's ass good when they broke it up. After the talk I had with Keith's old man this evening, I think Keith could be tougher than he looks. They had to break it off before the police got into it. Wayne isn't as tough as he thinks.

Wayne's father is the undertaker. He buried Lenny. Wayne is the one that shouted for Melvin to cut me when we were fighting out on Beacon Road. He thinks he's a baseball player and some say he is a pretty good catcher but the way he chews on the pitchers when they don't have good stuff pisses off the coach. Standing there next to Leroy, Wayne looks like a fat midget, short and stocky like he is, and Leroy is no giant next to me.

"No shit, Bobby," here's Leroy back begging, "I need three dollars if you can let me have it. I bet Melvin I could take his Chevy and he cleaned me out. I owe him a little."

"Come on, Leroy. You didn't really think you could take that new '57?"

"Close, the first time through," says Wayne. "That truck engine makes that Ford haul."

"Leroy," and now I'm trying to shame him. "Have you done something to your car?"

"Papa helped me soup it a little. That's why I'm short on cash. But Melvin's '57 Chevy is the fastest thing I've ever seen, Bobby. And you should see the new strip out on the Old 99. You're going to want to try it. A new quarter mile marked off south of Farnesi's."

"Try the strip against Leroy's '52," says Wayne with a grin.

Goddamn what an asshole Wayne is, him even suggesting that. Leroy's piece of junk against my machine. "Why?" I say, looking over at Leroy. "It's a Ford. No use wasting the rubber."

Wayne's grin gets bigger. "Another Bobbyism," he says to Leroy. "Lives in fantasyland."

Leroy laughs, backs off a step or two. He knows there ain't no sense in that. Wayne's trying to say my car is a piece of shit, but afraid to come out with it. And I'm thinking, I would like to screw Wayne up right here. Good thing I'm with Brenda. I'm beginning to think she skipped out on me.

Now Wayne starts on something else. "Heard you've been running around with Charles Kunze," he says.

"What's this," I say. "How does everyone know about me shooting rabbits with Charles? What the hell is so strange about that?"

"Charles likes to fight," and he's smiling at me now. "That doesn't seem like a guy that you'd buddy up to."

It's like everybody is looking at me. "So shut up, Wayne. He used to be good friends with Lenny. Leave it alone." And I turn to walk off. I'm tired of them and looking for Brenda. But Wayne won't let up on me, has me by the arm. I sling his hand off. "Don't touch me again. I'm warning you," I tell him. He still has that grin and I'm beginning to think I'm going to have to get rid of it. God, I get mad easy. It is like I carry this mad dog around with me. Might just jump out and bite anybody, anytime.

"I hear Lenny and Charles weren't as good friends as you say," he tells me. "Melvin's brother, Johnny, went to school with Charles. He's surprised you're running around with him. Says Lenny and Charles used to steal together, but argued all the time. Leroy's Uncle Jesse says he saw them fight once when he used to milk cows for Karl."

"Everybody has somebody that knows something about Charles." I face off against him. Put my hand on his chest, shove him back a step. Kids scatter. "Look, Wayne, stay out of my business. I know more about it than you think."

But here comes Clyde, so Wayne doesn't say anymore. That grin is still there but changed, like he's having trouble holding it. I hope his old man has a nice casket ready, cause he's not living a full life. Won't take a tall tree to make the box he's going to rest in.

Someone bumps into me from behind, and I jerk around, but it's just Brenda back from the bathroom cutting up with Phyllis about her crown that keeps falling off. Brenda is a little afraid of me at first. Wants to know what's wrong. "I get concerned about you," she says.

Leroy tugs on my sleeve.

"What's it this time?" I say.

"How about it, Bobby? I really need it." He has his head down, looking at the floor.

I don't want Brenda to see this, so I turn my back, feel bad about that. All I have in my wallet is a ten and a twenty, so I give him the ten.

"This is great, Bobby. It'll help pay back that other you owe me."

"Hey, come back here," but he's already gone.

Now Brenda has me out on the floor for a slow dance, Elvis crooning *I Want You, I Need You, I Love You*, and I have one arm around her waist and her hand cupped in mine on my chest and she's up against me so tight I feel her heat all the way down to my knees. Her mouth is up against my ear so close it tickles with her singing the words to the music real low. I love the smell of lipstick. She gets stuck on "I need you, I need you, I need you."

"What are you giggling about," she asks.

"You're tickling me again."

And she pulls that long hair blond hair back, puts her ear up to my mouth so she can hear because I'm not talking too loud. My lips touch her smooth skin. She raises her shoulder, squirms against me. She whispers she'd like to go now, so we head for the door.

We come out of the dance, put our shoes on out in the hall where we left them. Just as we leave the floor, I catch old tall Phyllis looking back at me. We're just about the first ones to leave, except for the guys that came stag and are leaving to get some beer. Lots a talk of going to Farnesi's.

"Let's *not* go to Farnesi's," Brenda says, "I'm tired of people."

Everyone is going to Farnesi's, so I'm disappointed, figure she's having a bad time. "Have to go home?"

"Oh no," she says coming up close. "Don't have to be in till one," she whispers and French kisses me in the ear. That settles that.

★

We have the ragtop up now. Lots of kids out that didn't go to the dance. I just turn right at Robertson and start dragging Main, honking at the cars I know, which is most of them. But I'm not sure what Brenda wants to do. I still think maybe she'll want to talk about school, like homework and stuff, so I get a little uneasy. I drive over by the show, the Sierra Theater, drive around the Sierra Drive-Inn right next to it. There's a new carhop the guys have been taking about. The place is crowded though, just one parking place left but when I start to pull in, Brenda says, "Don't stop here."

At the south end of town, at the corner of Robertson and Fifteenth, I make a circle through the dirt parking lot around the Palm Drive-In that serves those greasy rolled-up tacos I eat a ton of every now and then. Melvin jumps out of his car, flags me down.

"Hey, I've got a drag for you," he says when I get my window down.

"I don't need one tonight, Melvin," I tell him, feeling a little chill in the air. "I don't drag with girls in my car."

"Oh, Bobby, this guy's from Mountain View. Says he's heard about your car. Has a '55 just like this except it's blue, a rag top and everything."

"Tell him to look me up another night."

"Won't be another night. Get him while you can. Make a name for yourself."

"Not tonight, Melvin."

"How about, maybe later, Bobby? I'll try to keep him around. Say 'Maybe later,' for me, okay. Say that you'll look me up at Farnesi's. I can accept that." He starts to grin a little at how excited he is.

"Okay," I say grinning back. "I'll look you up. Maybe later."

So we are dragging Main again, and Brenda is quiet for minute, then she says, "Thank you, Bobby." And she kisses me on the neck, under my ear. Sort of comes out of the blue.

"What's that for?" I want to know.

99

"For not being like other guys. For being a gentleman."

As we pass in front of the park, she points. "There it is."

I see it too. A baby blue '55 Chevy with a ragtop. It's pulled up to Main from a side street, stopped at a stop sign, and as we pass, it pulls in behind us, blinks its lights once.

There are two sets of railroad tracks at the north edge of town. In between them, there's enough space to park in the gravel. They pull up beside me.

"I'll just get rid of them," I tell Brenda.

When I get the door open, she says, "Bobby. Are you sure? You can take me home, if you want." The interior light is on, shining highlights in her blond hair, *Love Me Tender* on the radio. I look at that white blouse she's filling up and the calf of her leg sticking out from under her skirt and a little gold chain around her ankle.

"It's not even close," I tell her.

Two guys in the car. The passenger talks first, and I just heard the driver call him Gordy.

"How about a go?" he asks. I look down, see a beer can between his legs. I can tell, he's tall and skinny. Has a flattop. Kind of reminds me of an old blond-headed Leroy.

"Na. Not tonight," I tell Gordy. "Got my girl with me." And for some reason, just calling her "my girl" sounds real good.

"What you got in it," the driver wants to know. He looks to be about twenty-five, heavy set, maybe a little fat, lost a little hair.

"Straight stock."

He smiles real big. "Ya, I heard about it when a kid in San Jose had it. I would sure like to make a run at it."

"Could be the same car. Maybe not. I don't know who had it the first year. Another time."

"You know Charles Kunze?"

So here we go again. The whole world has Charles on the brain. "Heard of him."

"You tell him," Herman says, "Mary still longs for him."

"First thing next time I see him."

"Make sure you get the name right. 'Mary.' You got it?" Then he laughs big. "Sure you don't want to try me? I don't get over here much. I hear you're Lenny Hammer's little brother."

"When he was a live."

"It's a sign of the times. They don't make a Hammer like they used to." I don't have much to say about that.

He shakes his head, looks away from me. "What a shame. Tell Charles that Lenny's going to haunt him to the grave."

"Jesuschrist, Herman. Do you see that girl?" It's Gordy interrupting, and he's looking at Brenda. Maybe I should've closed my car door. "Where did you find her?"

"She's just a friend." Don't like him prying into my business.

"We've got to come to Chowchilla more, Herman. It's like I was telling you. When it rains here, girls puddle up in the streets instead of water."

"I'm not hard to find," I tell him, walking off. "Another time."

"We'll see to it," says Herman.

I hear Gordy talking as I close my car door. "They grow 'em in the fields here, Herman. I tell you, they come out of the ground like potatoes. He probably pulled her off a cornstalk."

We head back up town. She moves over against me and asks if she can shift the gears for me. So when I have to slow going around the Palm Drive-in, she gears down while I work the clutch.

"Why you doing this?"

"So you can put your arm around me."

She pulls my coat open and gets inside it with me, gives me a squeeze.

"You've known Charles for a long time, haven't you?"

"He was my dead brother's best friend."

"I remember him. And I remember Lenny, too."

"You do?"

"Sure. He was my cousin's boyfriend."

Small town. "You mean..." and now I am hunting for a name, "Helen was your cousin?"

"Helen is my cousin. She's still alive, Bobby. Lives in Merced. They moved there after Lenny got killed, to get her out of Chowchilla. Her father worked at the Bank of America here. He just changed to the branch in Merced."

The next time I cross the tracks, as I start to turn right to drag around Farnesi's, she says, "Go left." So I go left, and we're heading out into the country, but just on the other side of the bridge over the Ash Slough, she tells me to turn right on a dirt road. Actually not much of a dirt road, just kind of a lane that goes a ways into a peach orchard and then quits in tall grass.

"This is good," she says.

"Were you at Lenny's funeral?"

"Yes. But let's not talk about that, okay? I've got you on my mind now."

I'm not quite sure what that means, except I feel the swelling in my pants. I don't remember her at the funeral. But I figure it can wait. I cut the lights and shut off the motor but leave the radio going and she adjusts it to make KMJ 560 come in better. I turn down the music a little, and when she turns her head around to look at me, I kiss her.

God, I never knew a girl could slobber so much.

I lean back toward my door, bringing her with me, turn a little so she's between me and the seatback, and we sort of lay down. I kiss her real slow like, and she moans. I put my hand on the front of her blouse. When I get my hand inside, she undoes her snap and I just get weak all over. Bev sure didn't have tits like this. And Bev had those tiny little girl kisses. I can't believe how easy this is. She just keeps moaning and groaning.

Just as I get going good, she stops right in midstream and I figure, Well that's all for tonight.

"Bobby," she whispers. "It's awfully crowded in the front seat."

"What should I do?" I whisper back.

"You are such a gentleman, aren't you?"

"I just don't want to stop."

"I don't either. I just want more room."

"Maybe I could put the seat back a little."

"No. I want to do it, Bobby. Do you want to do it?"

I can't get any words to come out.

"I want to do it in the backseat."

★

Now that I've taken Brenda home, I'm thinking about seeing if anything's going on over at Farnesi's before heading home, but first I stop at the Beacon station on the corner of Robertson and First Street just before the tracks. Ask old crippled Ben to fill my Chevy with that 100-octane premium and go to check myself out in the bathroom mirror. Got a little stuff on my shorts and I'm worried about that, so I throw them in the trash can, lock the door so no one comes in while I got my pants off. I wash the lipstick off my face and there's plenty of it, see only a little on my collar,

102

maybe Mama won't notice, then try to comb the calf-licks out of my hair. It's not like me, being out alone at night. Usually I at least have Leroy with me. Feels good to be alone. I just feel so free. Free and yet I have myself a girl. A serious girl this time.

Ben has just finished washing the back window. He's dragging that lame leg of his around like it's a suitcase. He's been pumping gas in Chowchilla as long as I can remember. Never seen him with a clean shave or a clean pair of pants.

"Where you headed, Bobby?" he asks. He's a nosy sucker.

"Farnesi's. I'm starving," I tell him.

★

The dirt parking lot at Farnesi's is still crowded. It's only a little after one. I walk away from my car, and just as my hand hits the door of the restaurant, I catch a look at a half-moon coming up through trees off to the east. It's a swinging door with glass squares that let a little light through, and as I push it open, Thomas sees me from his table in the middle of the room.

"Hey Bobby, we could've used you on the football field tonight," he shouts. Bev's sitting across from Phyllis and damn if that's not Leroy sitting next to her. Bev sees me and jumps up, heading for the bathroom. Phyllis is looking down into a Shirley Temple like it can talk back. Bev asks Phyllis to go with her. So Leroy jumps up like he didn't mean to be sitting with them, and walks across the room to sit with Wayne.

"Could've used some of your speed on defense," Thomas adds. He sticks his arm out to stop me as I go by.

"Looks to me like you got beat bad enough without the likes of me out there." I brush his arm aside to walk on past.

Thomas shouts after me, "Hey, Bobby, what the hell's wrong with your old man?"

I don't know quite what to say to that. But I go back and he gets up from the table. Thomas is the biggest kid in high school, so I have to look up at him, his freckled face. It's kind of hard to look around him too.

"Came into the shop a couple of days ago," he says, "chewed Daddy out about the tractor we just sold you guys."

"Hell, I don't know, Thomas. Why are you getting red in the face at me? I haven't heard anything about it."

"Came in to our showroom banging on the equipment like he wanted

103

to tear up the place. Threatened to give my daddy a whipping cause his tractor's using so much oil. What the hell does he expect?"

"Maybe just wants it to work like your daddy told him. Maybe he's pissed cause it drinks more oil than he can beer. That's a lot of oil, Thomas. Heard him say the other day it was matching him can for can."

Thomas shakes his head and sits back down.

"Glad you had a good game, Thomas," I throw over my shoulder.

Melvin, Wayne and Eugene are sitting in a booth across the room, where Leroy's joined them squirming in his new seat. Wayne is just sitting there with steam rising off him. I don't like the idea of sitting with him. Their booth is next to the door that leads into the bar and the bathroom where Bev's gone. Melvin has been kind of antagonistic lately too, but I guess I can get along with him. His home life is suffering. Melvin doesn't even have an old man, so he says. Has a stepfather, mean as hell and old enough to be his grandfather. Melvin stays with his brother Johnny most of the time. Had a fight with his stepfather not long ago, trying to keep him from beating his mother. Put the old man in the hospital. Broke the end of his nose off so that it was just hanging by a little flap. Melvin's not very big, but pound for pound they say he's the toughest kid in town. They had to sew the nose back on. I need to talk to Melvin after what Wayne told me, so I go on over.

"Ah, here he comes now, and with Brenda's pussy all over him. She sure is a juicy little girl. So how's your hammer hanging?" is the way Melvin starts in on me. Looks like he might've had a dentist filing on that chipped tooth.

"Not too bad I say." Even surprises me how convincing I sound. But I wish he wouldn't talk like that about Brenda. It wouldn't have been so bad except that here comes Bev and Phyllis back from the bathroom, Bev with fresh red lipstick and her hair pulled back over her ears, those ears just hearing everything. She gives Melvin one of her favorite eat-shit looks. She walks past me with a face blank as a rock. Phyllis picks up her Shirley Temple, giving me a cute smile.

I pull up a chair, sit at the end of the booth. Melvin and Leroy are sitting on the ends next to me.

"I don't want to hear about it," Leroy says. He looks sullen, like he's sobered up some too.

Melvin usually smokes Camels but tonight he's rolling his own. And he's not letting me off the hook. So while he's shaking the little cloth pouch to get a line of tobacco on that piece of brown paper, he looks up at Leroy. "I do want to hear about it," he says. "How was she, Bobby?" He's still looking straight at Leroy. "How big are those tits? How round is that ass? How much padding does she have in that bra?"

He is just shooting in the dark.

"Silence says a lot," he says. "Particularly with lipstick on your collar," then laughs.

"He didn't get any," says Wayne. "He wouldn't know how if she offered." He elbows Leroy. "That's a new Bobbyism. 'Can't use a piece of ass.'"

Leroy laughs but has to strain to get it out. "Why don't you shut up about it?" he says. "I don't need to hear anymore about Bobby's obsession with tits. Put a quarter in the jukebox, Bobby. I want to hear that *Green Door* song again. Trying to figure out what's behind that sucker. Flip the pages on that thing, Eugene. I think it's G9."

"I hate that song," I say. "'Green Door. Green Door.' You're not using my money." Leroy has a hangover. I stare Wayne down again. He looks over at Eugene. Eugene is looking at a menu.

"I want a cheeseburger and fries," says Eugene.

"Well, I'm glad you finally got some, anyway," says Melvin, still looking at Leroy. He's using big wood matches that he strikes on his pant leg to light that spit-soaked homemade cigarette. "I was beginning to worry about you."

I feel like I should deny something but he has me boxed in. Wish I hadn't thrown my shorts in the trash.

But Melvin is not leaving it there. "Lean in here, Bobby," he says quietly, tosses his head. "You ever punch Bev?"

"Ah, shit, Melvin," says Leroy. "Don't talk about it. I haven't had a date in six months. Have some consideration."

"Stick it, Leroy. I talk about what I want to." He's fumbling in his pocket for another match.

"You've got a girl," says Leroy. "You're not hurting. It's been a long dry spell."

"You've always lived in a desert," Melvin says, then he turns to Eugene. "Eugene didn't have Bobby's luck tonight. Didn't get any, so he says, Bobby. Your sister's still a virgin for one more night."

I might have to chip another tooth if he doesn't shut up.

"I'm really disappointed in you, Bobby" and he's talking loud again. He strikes the match, tries to light that cigarette. "I wanted to see a good drag race tonight. And you let me down, Bobby."

I look at him straight, smile a little. "I'm sure it won't be the last time I disappoint you."

"No doubt," he says. "It was those two from Mountain View. They left twenty minutes ago, thought you wouldn't make it back with Brenda having that noose around your neck."

I just shrug him off.

"Hey, there's your good buddy."

It's Charles, sticking his head through the door from the bar side and beckoning to me. Everybody turns to look at Charles. I've decided not to see him anymore but feel like I have to see what he wants.

"Hurry back," says Leroy. "I've got to get home, but I want to know what Charles wants. Daddy's going to kill me. I was supposed to be in an hour ago."

Everybody in the place watches me. I stand in the little hallway joining the bar with the restaurant. Four more years before I can go in the bar. I smell hard liquor on Charles' breath.

"Herman says, 'Mary still longs for you'," I tell him.

Charles looks real pleased. "Ah, sweet Mary," he says. "Well, we'll just have to do something for her."

There's a woman on a pay phone right next to us with lipstick smeared around her mouth, a Pall Mall in one hand and a drink in the other, the receiver caught between her ear and her shoulder, and I can hardly concentrate on what Charles is saying for listening to her. She keeps telling her daughter that she is twelve years old and that that is old enough to take care of herself and little sister. She doesn't care if the dogs are raising hell in the backyard. Charles is trying to get me to set up a stunt he saw pulled on a bunch of kids. Tells me about it but wants me to keep it secret. The woman on the phone keeps pulling at the red handkerchief she has wrapped around her hair for a scarf and tells her daughter over and over that her daddy isn't coming home because he's in Oklahoma and that's a long ways away and that she's looking for another daddy for her right now if she'll just be a big girl and let her stay a while longer. This stunt Charles is talking about isn't the kind of thing I like to do so I put him off. But I'm already starting to think about who I'd like to pull it on, and there's

106

old Thomas Powers sitting over there all propped back in his chair with his chest sticking out like he thinks he's a big wheel same as his old man. But it sounds to me like someone might get hurt during Charles' stunt. The woman starts to whine, stamps her foot twice and hangs up the phone, checks the change slot, pulls her car keys out of her purse as she hitches up her baggy slacks. She walks off and I realize where I have seen her before. When I went in the Cotton Club to get Papa, just before he beat Curt, she was the girl that walked away from Papa.

I go on back to Melvin and Eugene. They're both eating cheeseburgers with potato chips. Wayne and Leroy are gone. Guess Leroy ran out of time. Bev and Phyllis are both gone too. Place is beginning to clear out.

"What did Charles want?" asks Melvin.

"What does he ever want? More trouble."

Melvin hands me a check.

"I didn't have anything," I say, try to hand it back to him.

"It's Leroy's. Said you owe him money."

"Leroy said I owe *him* money?"

Melvin raises his arms like I just pulled a gun on him. "Leroy's not my problem."

Do I have a choice, I wonder? Do I have to pay Leroy's bill?

"Wayne was telling me you want to know about Charles," says Melvin.

"If you've got something, I want to hear it."

"Well I'm not sure I've got it straight. Maybe I shouldn't say anything. You two look like pretty good buddies."

"Suit yourself. Wayne's the one harping you knew something."

"Johnny was telling me sometime back, about a fight between Lenny and Charles." Johnny is Melvin's older brother that he lives with. "But it wasn't like a street fight. Not like they had something to prove in front of a crowd."

"But I never heard about a fight between them until tonight. Wayne said Leroy's Uncle Jesse saw them fight too. But it doesn't make sense. You know how word of a fight travels around Chowchilla."

Eugene tells the waitress to get him another cherry Coke and some French fries. When he eats, he keeps his cheeks full of food like a chipmunk. I ask her for some more coffee, fiddle with Leroy's check. I can't afford to eat and pay Leroy's bill too.

Melvin rolls another cigarette, like he wants the practice. Wets the seam with his tongue.

"It wasn't a street fight," he says, thinking real hard. "More like they really hated each other. Something they were carrying around and couldn't get rid of. Like maybe they were mad at each other all the time, like maybe they argued all the time over the same things."

"I don't know, Melvin. I can't remember a lot of what happened around that time."

"Oh, wait a minute. It had to do with the transmission in Lenny's car."

"So Lenny threw his transmission. I know that. I was helping him and Papa put in a new one."

He looks deflated for a minute, then perks up again. "Yes, but it wasn't Lenny that threw it. It was Charles. Now it's coming back. Johnny said Charles threw it dragging. He was driving instead of Lenny. But that was only part of it. There was something else galling them for a long time. Maybe it was a girl. I'll have to ask Johnny."

"That would be Helen," I say, thinking that now we're getting somewhere. I brush some sweat off my upper lip. The red haired girl with the bloody nose at the Cemetery is what I'm thinking about.

But Melvin is looking up and isn't even thinking about Charles and Lenny anymore.

"Jesus, Bobby. You know who that is standing in the door?"

I turn my head a little. "Those two guys from Mountain View," I say. "Looks like I get my first shot at the new drag strip."

"Hey, Waitress. Cancel those French fries," shouts Eugene.

★

The porch light is off. Trish always does that for me so Mama and Papa will think I'm home. I'm sneaking down the hall in the dark to my bedroom with my shoes off. Curt's in bed fast asleep. I shove him, tell him to go to the bathroom. He'll pee the bed if he don't. I grab some clean shorts out of the chest of drawers, feeling like I really should have my own bedroom. He's been lying in my spot and the covers are so warm I can tell how cold my feet are.

I'm just a little worried whether Mama will like Brenda or maybe if she'll like Mama. Sleeping with Curt seems strange tonight. Doesn't seem like I should have to sleep with my little brother.

Before I go to sleep, I go through it once more. First, it is Brenda on her back with her clothes off and me on top of her. Her moaning. Hard to believe. Then I'm in the right lane, revving my motor, pealing out. Three times Herman has to see it because he can't believe it. Three times he stays with me in low gear. Three times I get a half a car on him in second. Then he sees taillights. The first time he wanted to talk about it. Wanted some more. The last time, he didn't even slow. I let off and followed him out of town on Robertson with the full moon overhead. On my way home. They turned off west at the 152. Headed back to Mountain View. They're probably passing through Los Banos about now.

But the last thing I see, before my mind conks out, and maybe I hear it too, is Helen slapping Charles at the Cemetery.

CHAPTER 17: *Breaking Ground at Night*

"I can't stand it! Bobby. I can't stand it!"

"Well, I don't feel too good about it either."

"But how could you do this to me? Do you know what a predicament this puts me in? Do you know how I feel about you? Do you know what a deviate is, Bobby?"

"Yes. I know, Brenda. But it just doesn't even seem like I did anything."

"But the girls knew, Bobby! They knew for sure! Do you know how I can't stand that? I'm going to sue you. I'm going to sue your ass off. There's laws against people like you. You pervert. You weirdo."

"But I didn't do anything. I never told anybody."

"Somebody told Beverly Morrini! That's for sure! You could have told anybody but her! Anybody but her. I can't stand it! How can I live with it? Get some strange thrill out of it? Telling the guys and your ex-girlfriend give you a sexual thrill? Huh, Bobby, huh? Did it? You degenerate."

"I didn't tell Bev. I didn't tell anybody. Those bad words you're using don't apply to me. It just seemed like the guys in Farnesi's already knew what we'd done."

"My mother found out, Bobby! That's the worst part, the part I can't live with but have to. The part I'm going to sue you for." Her voice breaks and a few sobs come through. "Now I've got it at school and I've got it at home. No escaping it. And it's your fault. Do you know how I feel about you? How I feel about that thing you keep in your pants, that thing you carry around with you all the time? I'm going to sue that thing off you." Her words keep breaking off and coming through all those tears and snot sniffing. "You degenerate."

"I'm sorry, Brenda. I'm really sorry. Does this mean we're not going out tomorrow night?"

Clang!

Bet she broke the phone. I hope no one tells Mama.

Chapter 17: *Breaking Ground at Night*

★

I'm coming out of the old front door, through the screen that used to bang to but now just hangs off to the side on one hinge, going to do some custom work with the tractor for Mr. Grissom. I'm not feeling so good. That phone call from Brenda last night still has me shaking. Before I get to the tractor, here comes Papa home from town where he's been all afternoon. Mama's been worrying about him because he was only supposed to be gone an hour. I can tell he has been drinking by the way he's driving, the pickup kind of coasting in real slow, then the brakes lock and the wheels slide a ways on the sand driveway. I see through the windshield that he has a grin from ear to ear and when the door opens, he comes with it, hanging on and swinging from it like the tail end of a whip. When he turns loose, he takes three falling steps and hits the cottonwood tree and that holds him up. So he starts rubbing on it, bending up and down at the knees, scratching his back up between his shoulder blades like that was what he intended to do all along.

"If you were half the boy Lenny was, you'd kick my ass for coming home to your mama like this," he says.

I wince.

He gets a real strange look on his face with his eyes pointed up at that overcast sky like maybe there's an airplane, but then I notice a dark spot growing in the crotch of his pants and realize that he's peeing. But here he comes over to me, slinging his arms around like they are a couple of old ropes and damn if he doesn't take a swing at me then falls on the ground, and as I try to help him to his feet, he vomits on my boots.

Mama comes out of the house talking something about the Lord and what He's going to do to Papa, the way he acts. Papa's afraid of Mama when he's drunk, so he doesn't say anything more, just rolls over on his back, eyes going off in different directions like they are both made of glass.

But I hear the front door slam again and here's Trish. She goes crazy when Papa gets drunk.

"Mama, he's not worth it Mama," she says and stomps the ground with her left foot. "Just leave him there, let him rot. Dumb old goat. Better yet, let's just haul him out to the backyard and put him in the trash barrel. He's nothing but a piece of trash anyway. Light fire to him. Haul the ashes off to the junkyard."

Damn him. I can't be Lenny.

The Escape of Bobby Ray Hammer

★

It's cold. The sun's already down, the light fading and I'm about to start breaking ground over at Grissom's. I got the old tumble bug hooked up behind the little Ford tractor and as I pull back on the throttle, the old motor hums and I feel the vibration under my feet and in the steering wheel. The sun's just going down but since tomorrow is Saturday, I can work all night if I want. Papa lets me make a little money for myself like this and doesn't charge me anything for gas or the use of the little tractor. He just loves to keep me working, and sometimes it feels good to be out here all alone, sort of like I'm all grown up and with everyone else asleep late at night, feels like my troubles are not so big.

Just about the time I get the plow in the ground, here comes Johnny, Melvin's brother, driving up on a big John Deere tractor that I saw a few minutes ago working the next field over. I hop off and we walk toward each other, walking through the cornstalk stubble. He has on a long heavy coat and gloves. I wonder if I should have brought mine? Could be it's going to get even colder than I thought.

"Hi, Johnny," I say, but he's looking around at the ground like he lost something down there. He's wearing old city-slicker shoes that don't have strings in them. He gives me a nod, then hoiks and spits. Johnny's face is always redder than it should be.

"Melvin tells me you've been asking questions about Lenny and Charles." He gives me a quick glance. "That true?" His eyes look all bloodshot.

I give him a nod. His hair's coal black and sticks out in all directions.

"I've known Charles a long time and I'm going to give you some advice." Then his voice goes straight up in the air in this big whine and shout, even raises his chin like he's looking up in that overcast sky for a big V of geese. "Just shoot that sonofabitch!" he says, and he's turned his side to me so that he's not facing me anymore. "He's a rotten asshole and doesn't deserve to live."

"What's he done, Johnny? What's he done? I don't know Charles that good."

"Just lots of things!" And he keeps shouting. "I was always too old to still be in high school but he didn't have to say the things he did about me." He keeps pulling that heavy coat to and now I see that it's lost all its buttons down the front. He looks up at me so I see he's crying a little.

112

"Lenny was always good to me. I liked Lenny. He used to take me out with him once in a while when Charles wasn't around."

"Did you know about the two of them fighting?"

"Goddamn, Bobby, and this is the truth. They didn't even like each other. That's what people don't know. They hated each other." And now he's so mad I'm afraid he is going to throw a punch at me. "Charles wouldn't leave that girlfriend of Lenny's alone. I thought they were going to kill each other over her just before Lenny had his accident. And that was no accident, let me tell you. I told your papa and he believed me. But the police wouldn't. I bet it was over Lenny's girl. But I don't know for sure. Charles got to my girl too. Goddamn him. Got her pregnant. I just might kill that sonofabitch myself yet. My oldest kid is really his. But Charles killed Lenny, Bobby. I bet you he did."

And then he just turns around and walks off. Doesn't say good-by, just pulls that black wool coat up tight around his neck, pulls a stocking cap out of his pocket, slips it down low over his ears and walks off.

★

My right front wheel is off on the unplowed ground and the left is in the rut cut by my last pass. It's getting dark fast now, but by the backlight on the fender, I see the plow blade slice through the earth, laying it over like smooth chocolate. I can't get over Papa throwing it up to me that I don't stack up to Lenny. I'm trying to think what I can do to be better. Maybe if I could copy the way Lenny was, Papa would think more of me. But I don't know how Lenny was anymore. All I remember is how it was when he died. Still, I have a little time missing.

The cotton was early that year. I'd been out chopping with Delbert after school. Seems like I was a little late getting started chopping, but I can't remember why. I don't remember why Papa sent me out to chop anyway. But Papa caught me doing something, and he made me go chop cotton. So Delbert and me were in the field and Papa, he was supposed to pick me up at sundown, but he didn't show up and that was unusual because Papa was reliable then. So we chopped another round when it was almost too dark, and then we waited for him at the end of the field for a while and then in Delbert's pickup. Delbert talked some about the Fair coming up. His oldest boy had a heifer in the stock show that year. He talked about what a good man my papa was. How Papa had helped him when he first came from Oklahoma. They had relatives that knew each

113

other. But then Delbert got real quiet. I could tell he was worried too. Finally he had to take me home. It was out of his way, but he didn't mind. Delbert seemed to know that something was up, but he wasn't talking about it either.

No one was home. Even Mama was gone. It wasn't like her not having dinner ready for us when we come in from the field. Fried potatoes were still in the skillet full of grease and a pan of cornbread half cooked still in the oven and it turned off and the door open. The only thing that was done cooking was the beans. But there was raw meat laying out unwrapped. Mama never let meat lay out. And where were Trish and Curt? It just looked like something was wrong. I walked around inside the house calling for Mama, but when I didn't find her, I went outside in the dark and waited for them on the porch.

When they did show up it was late, about nine o'clock, and I was standing at the living room window watching the car lights go by on the road out front. I recognized the dim lights of Papa's pickup half a mile away. They looked like pale orange lanterns. I went out in the front yard to meet them. Mama walked right on past me crying real hard and telling Papa to tell me because she couldn't. Then Papa called me over to the side of the house.

"Get a hold on yourself," he said, cause what I'm going to tell you will kill you." He walked me back out of the light coming from the front window.

Right away I knew Curt had been killed, at least that was the thought that ran through my mind, and the thought choked me and my teeth just fell together. Curt was always with Mama.

Then Papa told me, standing there in the dark. "Lenny's been run over and killed," he said. He didn't just say "killed," he said "run over and killed."

I remember his words hitting me like bullets. Somehow I thought he said it like it was my fault. And I had a vision of Lenny being hit and knocked to the ground and then a car going over the top of him, banging his head on the oil pan, then the ground, then the back axle, maybe the rear end housing. That wasn't what really happened. I was just thinking. The only thing I can remember after that was that now I'm the oldest and right then I felt grown. I remember thinking that things were going to be different then. I'm ashamed to say it, but I thought maybe Papa would notice what I do more. I had a sense of satisfaction. I didn't realize that he'd want me to be like Lenny more than ever.

I couldn't see Papa's face because it was so dark, but I knew he'd been crying even though his voice was smooth and soft while he was telling me. When he finished, he didn't say anything for a while, but then he started to wail, almost like a siren off in the distance. I didn't even know he was making the sound at first. Then he walked off away from me a piece and wailed real loud like a wild animal. I took a couple of steps toward him and asked where Trish and Curt were. Papa never heard me, I don't guess. I went into the house but Mama was in her bedroom with the door locked, crying and scolding God like He was in there with her. I stood at her door listening and had an image of Jesus, all dressed in white with His long woman-like hair and the little white halo just over His head, standing in the room with Mama. His head was down like He knew He'd done something wrong.

The phone rang and it was Aunt Loretta asking when we were going to pick up Trish and Curt. Papa had told her that Lenny was in an accident, but Papa didn't know how bad it was then. Papa hadn't told Trish and Curt anything, just dropped them off like it was just the most normal thing in the world. Truth is, no one in their right mind would leave even a dog with Aunt Loretta. And they knew something was wrong all along. Now Curt was crying and asking for Mama in the background. Aunt Loretta asked how Lenny was. I told her he was dead. She didn't say anything for a long time. Then her voice shook a little as she asked if she should tell Trish and Curt. I told her no, I'd tell them when I got over there.

Poor old Curt was really crying by the time I drove the mile to her house on the tractor. Trish was just real quiet and standing off in the doorway to the kitchen like she was afraid of me.

"You better tell me what's wrong," little Curt said. "Cause I can't stand it any longer."

"Well it's not going to make it any easier, Curt, cause it's Lenny."

"Is he hurt?" Curt asked.

"He's more than hurt, Curt," but when I said it, I looked over at Trish. Her arms started moving in all kinds of strange ways like she'd lost control of them.

"You mean like dead?" And Curt seemed real puzzled.

I said, "Yes," and Trish, she was just nine and little too then. She looked away from me.

It was just the three of us standing in Aunt Loretta's living room feeling like we were carrying out grown people's business. Then Aunt Loretta said something strange. It was the only thing she said while I was there, and it was strange.

"Remember, Ray," she said, "you always have a place here with me if things get too tough for you over there."

I didn't know what to make of her.

So Curt quit crying and Trish started crying and the three of us went home alone on the old tractor in the dark, them sitting each on a fender with the one headlight shining in the front at the side of the road where we were going and the back light on the right fender shining a beam behind us on the road where we'd been. And everything in the world seemed real important.

I lost something that night riding that tractor home. I don't know what it was. But it wasn't like a pocketknife or a yo-yo or things like that that I kept in my pocket then. I have been looking for it ever since.

The next morning just before sunup, Papa got the claw hammer that he had used to build the little shed that he keeps the tractor in and beat the newborn bull that we were going to raise for beef to death.

★

It's midnight. Birds flying all around me in the dark now. They come in behind the tractor looking for the live things in the fresh earth after the tractor passes. It's a strange mixture, mostly blackbirds, killdeers and seagulls, a few sparrows. Seagulls and we are 150 miles from the coast. They're not afraid of the tractor at all as long as it's moving. I could kill all I wanted if I had a pistol. Wish I could remember what I was hunting with my .22 the day Lenny got killed. But I've been feeling strange about killing lately. Seems like Papa always taught me to kill anything that's wild. Particularly anything that's pretty or unusual. Like the only oriole I've ever seen. Papa shot it. And the fox we saw in the barn that time. Didn't kill it, but wasn't for the lack of trying. And him buying me my first BB gun to kill birds with when I was just eight years old. It's like, if you really like something, think it's special, you kill it. Same as when I was out with Charles rabbit hunting. I'm just needing to treat things different than I have been.

I also know that if I don't get some of this stuff settled, no matter how far away from here I get, I'll still not be rid of the pain that came with Lenny's death. Staying away from Charles hasn't helped any. I've stayed away lately, keep putting him off. He asked me to go to Fresno with him a couple of nights ago. Lately he's been talking about what we could do on Halloween night coming up soon. I don't think I should run around with him though. Nobody likes Charles. But nobody likes me either. And kids at school keep asking me about him. I wish I could tell them I've been out with him. He doesn't go by any rules. When we were out shooting rabbits and he was blowing out windows in that little shack, I realized for the first time in my life that all the laws and rules we live by are just made up. People make up the rules. You really can do anything you want to. Charles proved that to me. I always thought bad things started happening to you if you didn't go by the rules. But me and Charles did a lot of things we shouldn't have that night and nothing happened. And the thing is, Charles is right. You can't go by everybody else's rules because everybody has a different set. And then there's this thing about Lenny and what really happened to him. And Charles has all the answers. No one else is going to tell me what happened to Lenny, that's for sure. So why shouldn't I go out with him? Really, it's just up to me. It's like he has a pocket full of keys and each key opens a door to my life. Behind each door is an answer.

Brenda calling me the other night and chewing me out made me start thinking about the way I am. Here I was making plans about things I had no right to even think about, lots of things about her and me, and the future. Now she won't even talk to me. Trying to be good and pretending that I am good just doesn't cut it. Sometime I'm going to have to face up to who I really am. And I'm not all that good. So maybe I should admit some things, some things about myself. And I guess I'll start right here. It wasn't Papa who shot that oriole. It was me.

Part III

Taking Chances and Reaping the Consequences

CHAPTER 18: *Oklahoma Credit Card*

Charles is on his knees sucking on a hose. Leroy's holding one end in the tank of a Ford tractor, and the other end Charles sticks in a five gallon Army surplus can down on the ground. It's nighttime and we're out in the middle of Mr. Sloper's field getting a little gas for Charles' jeep. Charles sputters, spits. Walks away coughing.

"Don't let it run over," he tells me, trying to clear his throat.

I know the moon is up because I see a light spot in the clouds. A dog barks in Sloper's yard across the field. Charles has been asking about Trish and Curt. He asked tonight if Trish would want to come along. Said he realized Curt's a little young yet. He asked if Trish has a boyfriend. He was just talking. I wasn't talking back. I saw Trish and Eugene fighting the other day. I'm not sure what's going on between them. I get this uneasy feeling that Trish has been seeing Charles.

"It full yet, Bobby?" That dog's spooking him.

"Keep your pants on, Leroy," I tell him. I train my eyes in the direction of their house but can't quite make it out through the dark. Another dog, further away, answers Sloper's.

"Jerk it," says Charles. "He's coming."

Charles takes the hose from me and starts across the field toward the jeep. Leroy, he's already gone. I'm getting the lid on fast as I can, and then I'm running a ways behind Charles. I hear the jeep start, but the yap, yap, yap of that dog's coming up right behind me. When I get to the fence, I know I'm not going to make it through, so I drop the can and turn to meet this dog head on. He's almost on top of me when I hear a shot ring out from behind, and the dog yelps like he's hit, turns a circle growling and whimpering.

"No! Charles. No!" I tell him. I can just make out the dog in the dark, and I think I know him. "Skipper? Is that you, Skipper?"

The dog barks again, but now it's like he just wants to keep me away.

Charles's on me to get through the fence. I go over to Skipper and he crouches on the ground trembling like he's done something bad wrong. I hear a pickup in Sloper's yard start and see headlights come on. I know Skipper. Mr. Sloper got him for his wife when their son was killed in Korea a few years ago. No matter how much she went to church, she just couldn't seem to get over him being dead until she got the dog. I reach down, pet him and he rolls over on his back and then it's just wet tongue everywhere. I call him "pup" even though he's a grown dog. I figure every dog is just a puppy at heart. Charles is not going to kill this dog.

"Bring the dog," says Leroy. "Maybe we can sell him."

Leroy is in a bad way. Ever since I brought him along when me and Charles went to Fresno to pickup some hubcaps, he wants to steal everything that doesn't move. This dog is his first moving object. But it's because he has stole everything else. He goes into the 5 & Dime on Robertson, makes off with his pants and shirt stuffed full. Came out to the field the other day where I was plowing-in a ditch we don't need anymore since our cotton is all laid by, wanted me to see what all he got. It looked like he'd won the Halloween jackpot. He had a package of jack-o'-lantern masks, two packages of orange balloons, one package of Halloween candy, a left tennis shoe, three bubblegum balls he pounded out of the penny machine, and two sex magazines he got from the drug store over by the Cotton Club. Brenda sure puts those girls to shame in the tit department. And get this. He had a real nice protractor that you use in geometry. Sole it from the stationery store. Had it all in a brown paper bag. I laughed at him a little, and he didn't like it.

"What're you going to do with all that crap?" I asked. "It's kid's stuff. One tennis shoe?"

"Throw it away before Mother asks where I got it."

"Why don't you quit stealing, Leroy? You're going to get caught."

"I can't, Bobby," he said, and he looked real concerned. "I've tried. You don't know what Charles is doing to me."

And I think he started crying because he turned around without saying he was leaving and walked real slow back through the field to his old brown Ford. The other day, during civics, I caught him making a list of things he was planning to steal after school. He hid it from me. And I know he's going out with Charles when I'm busy. But he won't talk to me about what they do together. Charles hasn't said anything either.

122

Chapter 18: *Oklahoma Credit Card*

As I head for the jeep with the Army can in my hand, I hear Mrs. Sloper calling for her dog. I dreamed the other night that I was standing on our back porch calling for Tangi, and she came to me. She was all rotting and smelled real bad, so I couldn't get close to her. I tried to see how she was walking with two of her legs cut off. She wasn't mad at me anymore.

CHAPTER 19: *Halloween and a Little Dynamite*

Mama's just a hard case. She doesn't understand a whole lot. I'm on my way to town on Wednesday, Halloween night and damn if Trish isn't sitting in the front seat with me, and Curt's in the backseat. Damn I can't stand that! Mama said I had to bring them. Curt's not so bad because I can get rid of him, but Trish? I'm supposed to show her a good time. So here I am sitting under the steering wheel, all puffed up and wondering how I'm going to get rid of her. I'm trying to be better to Trish, but I just can't seem to get the knack. When I told Leroy I had to bring her, he decided to take his own car. And Trish, she's fighting with Eugene and doesn't have a way to get around anymore. Eugene called me last Friday night. Said he had a date with Trish, but she didn't show up at the Palm Drive-in where they were supposed to meet. Wanted to know where she was. Later that night she came home on time, but I didn't see who brought her.

"Where can I drop you off?" I ask her.

"You're not dropping me off. You heard Mama."

"Curt," I ask, "did you take a bath?" I smell something and it's coming from the backseat.

"What's it to you?"

"Curt, what have you got?," asks Trish. "That smell's about to gag me." And then she leans over the backseat to take a look.

"You two are always picking on me," says Curt.

"Let me see in the paper bag. Curtis!" And she slaps him but he blocks it with his arm. "Let me see."

"Bobby Ray, get her off me."

"Oh, good Lord. You should see this, Bobby Ray. He has one of Mama's pillow cases with four white candles, two bars of soap he stole from the bathroom cupboard, a cardboard mask of Count Dracula, a plastic jack-o'-lantern, a book of matches, and a turd in a paper bag."

"Where did you get the dodo, Curt?" I ask.

"It's mine and it's fresh. I didn't steal it from anybody."

I take a glance back and see him guarding all that stuff like an old hen protecting eggs.

"Where you headed anyway?"

I shouldn't have to baby-sit Trish tonight, but after what happened last night, I can't take up for myself. I couldn't help what happened. I was sitting at the kitchen table watching Mama and Trish do the dinner dishes. Papa was in the living room cleaning his pistol. I heard him spin the chamber, then the click, click, click as he dry-fired it. He always likes to shoot three times, for the Father, the Son and the Holy Ghost, is what Mama says. He keeps it in her cedar chest. She doesn't like it there but puts up with it. Makes him keep his bullets in the dresser drawer with his underclothes. When Mama took a bowl of garbage out to the trash barrel, Trish started in on me. She asked when I was going to call Beverly. I told her to just stay out of my life. I don't need her meddling. "Bev's the nicest girl I've been out with," so she said. Can't figure out why Trish, a freshman, has taken up with Bev anyway.

And then Trish started on Charles. She told me she knows he's a thief and that I'm no better. It's like she's following me. Somehow she has some firsthand knowledge about Charles. We started to shout at each other, but I had to watch my voice because Papa was listening. I told her to stay away from Charles, quit playing with dynamite. I was thinking about telling Mama to keep better track of her. We were talking real quiet like, through clenched teeth. And then she started in on me about what Brenda says about me. That was my last straw. I went up to the sink and had her by the arm when Mama came back in from taking out the garbage. Mama jumped on me too, claimed she'd warned me about squeezing Trish's arm before because I leave blue marks. Threatened me with Papa. And then I made my big mistake. "Her mouth's awful big, Mama, to be hooked to such a little body," is what I said. "If her mouth was the same size as her bra, she wouldn't get into so much trouble." And all at once, I wished I hadn't said it. That was when Trish hit me in the face with the dishrag full of soapy water and pounded on me with both fists. I was already feeling sorry, but I knew there was no use trying to take it back. Mama finally got Trish pulled off of me and while I was drying with a dishtowel, Trish got quiet. Mama, she got real quiet too, and I didn't know what was happening. Trish walked out crying. Then Mama turned on me. "I don't think I've ever known anyone as mean as you," she said. "Trish worships the ground you walk on and you treat her like dirt. Here she is just becoming a woman and feeling so uncertain of herself. I'm ashamed to have raised you."

But this thing about Bev is what really worries me. Eugene even called the other night, asked if I'd be interested in double dating with him and Trish. He was trying to get me to ask Bev out too. He sounded worried, not about Bev, but about Trish.

What Mama said about wishing she hadn't raised me, still hurts. And she said it while we were alone. Somehow it's the being alone that hurts the most. So that's the reason I have Trish with me tonight, the reason I can't take up for myself anymore.

I drop Curt off at the Palm Drive-In where a crowd of eighth graders is gathered.

"I'll pick you up at the Bowling Alley at eight o'clock," I tell him. "And you better be there."

"Yes, Papa," he says back.

We make a drag back up main street toward the Palm Drive-In, but before we get to the edge of town, Trish tells me to pull off into the half-circle driveway in front of Wilson School where a bunch of high school kids are parked. That's the bad thing about having Trish with me. She's always giving orders. First thing I see is Thomas Powers standing tall above them all with his girl, Phyllis. He has that big colored kid, Chelsey, with him. Chelsey plays football with Thomas. He's a pretty good guy but still, it's strange to see a white guy and a colored kid running around together. Then I see Leroy's Ford, so I guess I will pull over. Oh! Shit. There's Brenda's car. And there she is, behind Thomas.

Melvin's new '57 Chevy is here too, and that Mexican girl from Madera he loves on all the time and he's loving on her now. The other girl I don't recognize, but she gets out of his car when she sees us. It's Bev with a new hairdo. Got it all puffed up on top of her head. Now ain't she something. She's cinched her belt on that fluffy dress so tight her waist is about the size of my arm.

Before I get stopped good, Trish gets out, runs over to Bev. Maybe Trish will go with them. I walk over to Leroy. Wayne is here too, but even arguing with Wayne is better than being with Trish. I glance over at Brenda. Wish she would talk about what happened between us, but there's

126

not much chance of that. She has a Halloween mask pushed up on top of her head, a rubber band pulled down under her chin. Every time I look toward her, she turns towards Thomas. I can't stand to be this close to her and not say something, so I turn toward her anyway.

"Brenda, I need to talk to you." I just kind of throw the words at her.

"Not a chance, Bozo," she says.

"Hey, Bobby," and it's Thomas calling me now. "Tell your old man to come get his tractor out of our shop." Thomas pokes Chelsey in the ribs and laughs a little. Chelsey is really quiet for a colored.

"Ya? Well, you tell your old man to fix it first," I say.

Then I turn back to Brenda. "I need to ask your cousin something."

"Too dumb to use a phone?" But she looks concerned anyway. Yanks at that big old pullover sweater she has on. It's big enough for two people so I can't see much but I know what she has inside.

"I don't know Helen," I tell her. "I'd like for you to ask her a question for me."

Then damn if she doesn't walk toward me. "Make it quick and stand away from me," she says. "I don't want to smell you."

I take a step back, but I've had a shower. "I want to know about Helen and Charles."

Brenda takes a step closer.

I take a step back.

"They were friends," she says.

I have to keep checking myself to see if her eyes are knocking holes in me.

"I want to know why she slapped him at Lenny's funeral."

She rolls her eyes then turns her head, looks back at Thomas. Takes another step toward me. "What does that have to do with you? You're naive, Bobby. You know that? Really naive."

"I guess that's true, cause I think I need the answer, and I'll never be able to figure it out by myself."

"What difference will it make?"

"Could change a lot of things."

"You're a strange one," she says, and walks away, scoots up against Thomas, puts her arm around him. I wonder what Phyllis thinks about that? Brenda pulls that mask down over her face and looks straight at me. It's a skull, like she is a dead person with all the flesh rotted away.

127

They're leaning back against Thomas' '56 Ford pickup. He has it all fixed up, painted black with pin striping and chrome tailpipes but it's still just a farm wagon. Front end is lowered and with that bed sticking up in the air, looks like a giant stink bug.

"Hey, Thomas," I say.

He turns toward me but doesn't say anything.

"Tell your old man, that oil guzzling sonofabitch of a tractor belongs to him," I say, looking over at Chelsey. Chelsey is the best football player on the team. Some kids are afraid of him. They say he has one hell of a temper, but he seems quiet all the time. God, it's strange to see a colored guy running around with a bunch of white guys.

"You tell your old man he better come up with some money to pay for fixing it or we'll take a piece of ground."

"You tell your old man he better find a piece of backbone before he comes claiming Papa's land." Then I feel like I want to add something. "Chelsey, if I were you I'd watch who I run around with."

Phyllis is talking to Leroy and Wayne. Now that's a switch too. They're standing by Leroy's junk heap. So I go over.

"Hey, Bobby. I've got a deal for you," Leroy tells me.

"Ya, what's that?"

"I want to buy your car."

Now I know Leroy's mind has finally snapped. "And here I thought you were having a hard time with money," I tell him.

"No kidding, Bobby. I can make you a good deal."

"But that's like wanting to buy one of my arms, Leroy. I don't want to sell an arm."

"Ya, but with what I could give you for it, you could put a little with it and get yourself one of those new '57s. Your daddy's got money. You could swing it."

"Keep your car, Leroy," says Phyllis. "I like it." I guess she has weird tastes in cars.

"Don't need a new car," I say. "You have so much money, buy yourself a '57."

"Just think about it. That's all I'm asking. Just think about it."

Then Wayne butts in. "Bobby thinks smalltime, Leroy. You've got to remember that. Just small-time potatoes. Another Bobbyism."

"Where's your car?" I ask Wayne. "Your daddy got the hearse tonight?"

That shuts him up because he doesn't have a real car. I think his face turns a little red to match his hair.

"Okay, I've thought about it," I tell Leroy. "I still won't sell it."

"Does your car slide hookers, Leroy?" asks Phyllis. "I've never turned a hooker."

I don't know that I've ever seen Leroy smile before. Not a real smile anyway.

"I like sliding hookers and pealing out," Phyllis says.

"Come on," says Leroy. "I'll show you."

"Phyllis, you be careful," says Brenda.

I hear someone behind me, then feel some arms go around my waist, this hand go inside my shirt. That warm hand feels good against my skin, Bev's hand.

"Let me go with you and Trish," she asks from behind.

Brenda just went into shock.

★

I put ol' hitchhiking Bev in the backseat. Don't want to follow Leroy so we go on uptown, hit a few back streets, over by the show. Little kids everywhere in the dark. I stop for a minute, go in the Bowling Alley. No Curt. But it's not quite eight o'clock yet. Then we go over by the park along Kings Avenue, a police car spotlights some of the bushes, then turns left toward Main Street. I see something there in the dark. It moves out from behind a bush all humped over, running toward the road, maybe toward us. It's a man. I have to hit my brakes because I almost run over him. Trish screams. He crosses the road in front of my Chevy then comes up beside the passenger door. It's Charles.

I hear Trish catch her breath.

Trish jumps in the backseat with Bev. Charles gets in the front. Has a small box.

"It's the fuzz after me, Bobby," he says. "Get this Chevy moving." He's all dressed in black.

"What's in the box?" I ask.

"Something Leroy picked up for me," he says.

I laugh a little. "You mean it's a box of bubble gum? Or did he get you some rubber bands."

"Don't be so critical, Bobby. Leroy has potential. He did all right. He's my right hand man."

129

"Why are the police after you?" asks Trish.

"Who's the broad?" he asks not even looking back.

"You might remember my little sister, Trish."

"I know her," says Charles.

"Damn it, Bobby Ray. I'm not your little sister. You haven't got the brains of a Billy goat."

"Trish is all grown up," says Charles. "At least she thinks she is." He has this big smile on his face. "And just as pretty... No. No. Take that back, take that back." And he has turned around, looking at her real close now. "Even prettier than ever."

Jesus, Charles.

"I'm Beverly Morrini, Bobby's ex-girlfriend that he doesn't think enough of to even introduce anymore." And when she says it she hits me on the shoulder with her fist.

"Why, Bobby," Charles says, looking over at me. "You like girls with spunk. There may be hope for you yet. You've got a girl in this car, maybe two girls in this car, that hate your guts. And you haven't even kicked them out. Maybe there is some fight left in you after all."

"What are the cops after you for?" Trish asks again.

"Up to my old tricks. Lenny's tricks."

"What?" she asks.

"Just a little fireworks."

"We're looking for Curt. Got to take him home."

"No need worrying about him," says Charles. "I picked him up fifteen minutes ago. Took him home for you. The police were chasing him. Someone called the cops because he and a bunch of other kids were waxing windows. Lit a sack a shit on a doorstep."

We head over to Ventura Street, which runs all along the west side of town. The girls are whispering and giggling in the back. By the hospital where the rich people live, I turn right because Charles wants me to go by the Danish Creamery. What for, he doesn't say. I end up on First Street but just before I get to the Creamery, he says, "Pull over and cut the lights."

I roll down the window and listen to the clanging of milk cans ringing through the cold night air. I see the Creamery through the trees, even see some cane growing tall and green out back on the bank of the Ash Slough. Charles is sitting over there fooling with something in the dark, can't tell what and can barely see him because he's dressed in black, just see that blond curly hair. I get a sinking feeling that maybe he's playing with himself. But then he tells me to pull out and to leave my lights off. Then he rolls down his window and strikes a match like he's lighting a cigarette. Sparks fly and I think he just lit a sparkler. He dumps something out the window though, holding his arm down beside the car before he lets it go.

"Down the alley," he says.

I'm wanting to turn on at least the park lights, so I can see where I'm going.

"Keep the goddamn lights off," he says.

Then I hear an explosion, except it's so close it rocks the car, hear sand blast the rear end.

Trish screams again.

"Did the Creamery blow up?" I ask.

"Hell no," says Charles.

"Was that us? Did we do that?"

Charles, he isn't saying anything.

"What do you have up there?" asks Bev and she sounds like she aims to get an answer.

"Dynamite," says Charles.

"Oh, good god," says Trish.

★

We're over by the little league diamond, and I'm watching the Police Station over on Second Street but it looks deserted. One police car parallel parked out front. That and the front door with the lit up "Police" sign is all I see. Trish leans over the backseat to watch Charles light the fuse to the second stick of dynamite. He's showing her how to put the fuse on the cap and insert it in the waxy stick.

"Careful, careful, Charles," she squeals.

Bev is up close behind me trying to see what he's doing. She's so close that I feel her breath on my neck, smell Juicyfruit. I turn my head to see what Trish is up to and feel Bev's soft hair on me just as she kisses me lightly on the cheek.

"What did you do to him?" Trish asks real quick, and I wish Bev hadn't done that. "Did you kiss him?" she asks again and laughs like it's the biggest thrill she's ever had. "Bobby Ray got kissed. Whoopee!"

"Lean back, Bev," I say, "and shut your mouth, Trish."

We're two blocks away when the dynamite goes off, but it's so loud

131

that it sounds like it's inside the car. Must be breaking windows out of people's homes. Hope nobody gets hurt.

*

Now I'm standing beside my car with both hands on the cold metal roof and my legs spread, feet are firmly planted in the dirt and gravel of Farnesi's parking lot. Red light is reflecting off my white tuck 'n roll. Looks like blood everywhere. Brock, the policeman that graduated from CUHS ten years ago and played halfback on the football team, keeps running his hands up and down my legs from my shoes all the way to my balls. He's spending so much time up there I am beginning to wonder about him. Charles is spread-eagled on the ground on the other side of my car. He jumped out when the fuzz pulled us over, and they put a gun on him, told him to hit the ground. He hasn't been up since. I don't know if they're going to let him up. They've searched him three times and keep asking for his pistol. Two other policemen drove up a few minutes after they stopped us and started searching my car for dynamite. They have the front and back seats out on the ground now.

Every time a carload of kids makes the U here at Farnesi's, they give us a long stare. Melvin and Eugene parked a little ways from us a couple of minutes ago but haven't gone inside. They're leaning up against Eugene's car watching the action. Trish and Bev are standing over by the police car. Bev has the last few sticks of dynamite up that big fluffy dress of hers. Trish looks like a little angel.

*

So the cops couldn't find anything and had to let us go. Charles says he's going to kill Brock. Says Brock doesn't know who he's screwing with. It's late and we are at the graveyard now, out on the corner of Avenue 23 1/2 and Road 14 1/2. This is where Lenny is buried. It's turned cold and the wind is kicking up a little. Thomas has a crew of kids unloading a mess of stolen pumpkins from the back of his pickup. When Charles saw that Thomas had Chelsey, a colored kid, with him, he got real quiet. Smiled like he was thinking a long ways off. Then he got real serious. "No. We better not," he said. "The dynamite is enough excitement for tonight." But then when he saw that the colored kid was Chelsey, Charles' attitude changed completely. He walked over and shook hands with him. Started asking him about his sister. They must have talked for ten minutes. I tell you, Charles knows Chelsey. Must of known him a long time.

132

I have my car lights shining on them so they can see to unload the pumpkins. Trish is with Charles. He's doing the watching this time, and Trish is putting the firing cap in the stick of dynamite. Bev's standing next to me not talking, but something heavy is worrying her mind. Thomas is standing at the backend of his pickup telling them how to unload, like the big asshole he is. Brenda's standing next to him with her arm on his shoulder.

I can't stand to see her touch him. I walk up beside them.

"Brenda," I say.

She turns around.

"God, don't you ever quit? What is it this time?"

Thomas looks around and sees that it's me, so he ignores me like I'm a little kid.

"I still need to know."

"Know what? I can't believe I have to put up with this, after all you've done to me. We're not friends, Bobby."

"I need to know why Helen slapped Charles at Lenny's funeral. I'm serious, Brenda."

I guess she can tell that this really means something to me because she walks a ways away from Thomas with me. "Why don't you ask Charles? He's just standing right over there."

"He's the reason I want to know. I don't trust him, Brenda. Not interested in his answer. Not yet. Helen's the only one who can tell me that I can trust."

She shakes her head, watches them unload pumpkins. "Alright. If I see her again, maybe I'll ask. Okay? I could call her, I guess. But I'm not making any promises."

"I sure appreciate it."

"You're not my friend, so don't bother me anymore." When she walks back to Thomas, she casts a worried glance at Bev.

They're stacking pumpkins on the blacktop just inside the cemetery gate. Since the gate is closed and locked, the pickup is pulled up real close to it. Leroy and Wayne are in the pickup throwing them down to Melvin and Eugene, who're on the ground just inside the gate. They throw them so fast some smash. Leroy throws some so hard, they don't even try to catch them. Charles and Trish are inside the graveyard placing the dynamite. Brenda puts her arm around Thomas' waist, lays her head on his shoulder.

I'm going to have to do something about that.

Charles stands next to the stack of pumpkins that's almost as tall as him. "After this, everybody heads home. You kids got that?"

I don't hear any objections.

★

When the dynamite goes off, we are watching on Avenue 23 1/2 from inside my car with the motor running. I see a flash, feel the concussion and the car rock just before we catch a few seeds and a string of pumpkin slop on a side window. I move on out toward the Boulevard, figuring I'll take Charles back to town to get his jeep.

"Take me home first, I don't want to go back to town," Trish says. "I've got to get home."

"You can wait till I go home," I tell her. She's not running this show.

"You worthless piece of pumpkin guts," she says. "Just can't stand not having it your way."

"Don't bother taking me back to town," Charles says. "Take me home. If I go near my jeep tonight the fuzz 'll get me. My father 'll take me to get it tomorrow."

So I make a U, go the other way on 23 1/2. We cross the Berenda Slough at the place where Lenny died.

"X marks the spot," he says.

I wonder what he means by that? More and more, I just question everything about Charles.

I pull into the dirt yard in the front of Charles' place with his little shack off to the right, a barn on the left where his father milks cows. The ground is all uneven and the barn looks like it's a hundred years old. The right end of the barn, just to the right of a haystack, Charles uses as a garage. There's a car in there and my lights reflect off of its bumper. It's Lenny's car. I would recognize it anywhere. Charles opens the door, steps out. I nod for Trish to look at the barn. "See the Hudson?" I whisper to her."

"Oh, God, Bobby Ray," she says. "It is Lenny's."

"Come on, Trish," says Charles. "I'll take you home."

"Oh no you won't," I say.

But Trish is out the door in a flash.

"Trish!" I say. "Get back here."

"I need to get home."

"I'll take you. Right now."

134

"You take Bev home. I'm going with Charles." She slams the door.

Ah shit! Not only do I have to take Bev home alone, like they've planned all evening, I finally realize, but I have to leave Trish alone with Charles. And I can't do anything about it.

"Okay if I get up front?" asks Bev.

"Sure," I say. "Might as well play it all the way to the end."

Coming out of Charles' place, I go out County Road and head toward Highway 152. Bev's sitting all pushed up against the door like she's afraid of me. I look over at her.

"You two had this set up, didn't you?" I ask.

"Don't know what you're talking about."

"Do too."

"It was good being with you again."

"You weren't with me."

"I don't mean it like that. It just felt good being around you."

I make a left on Robertson, head out further into the country. We don't talk until I see her house.

"You've changed, Bobby. Brenda's come between us?"

"Can't expect things to be like they were."

"She doesn't want you, Bobby. I do."

When I pull up in her driveway, I notice the milk barn off to the left of the yard, the shed straight ahead with the little Ford tractor parked inside, and the yard all flat and covered with gravel. Everything looks like it has a place. Everything with a fresh coat of paint. Even the tree trunks are straight and have whitewash up to where the limbs start. I stop and leave the motor running, the lights on, so she'll know to get out and that I'm not coming with her to the door. I have to get home to make sure Trish is alright.

But Bev is not opening the door. She scoots over beside me.

"Bobby," she says. And damn if she doesn't reach up and shut off my ignition. Punches off my headlights. "I'm betting my life on you. You know that?" And then she takes my hand in hers, rubs my palm against her cheek then sticks my thumb in her mouth. Her tongue is slick as a snake's belly. "I'm betting on you and me. Some people are meant to be together. That's the way I see it." And now she is unbuttoning her blouse part way. "That's the way I see us. So I don't mind what you do to me anymore," she says as slips my hand inside her bra.

More in there than I thought.

"As a matter of fact, I want to do everything with you. If you can think of it, I want to do it." Then she slips my other hand under her dress, inside her panties. "I want your hands everywhere on me. I don't want anyplace on my body where you haven't touched." She spreads her legs a little and it's wet down there. "You are the only one that has ever done this to me, Bobby." Then she unbuttons a couple of my buttons and sticks her hand down inside my pants, inside my shorts. When she has a good hold on me she says, "You are the only one I have done this to. Now we are one. There's no escaping it. But we're not making love till you come to me."

I button my pants while she buttons her blouse.

"I'll be waiting for you."

She opens the door and slides out, waits for a minute standing there with the door open. Starts crying.

Wouldn't you know it?

Just before she slams the door shut, she says, "I love you, Bobby."

First time in my entire life anyone ever said that to me.

★

I'm home now but standing outside in the dark. Been standing here for an hour and a half watching the stars turn overhead. Must be about two-thirty. I just couldn't bring myself to go to bed because Trish isn't home yet. I turned off the porch light so Papa and Mama would think we're home. Then I went to Trish's bedroom, but sure enough, she wasn't there. So I checked on Curt. I guess Charles really did bring him home. He was sound asleep. At least Charles did something right. But what could Charles be doing with Trish? She's just fourteen. Maybe I should see if I can find them. How could I let him take her? He was supposed to bring her straight home. Maybe he couldn't get his jeep started. He has Lenny's car too. I've got to talk to him about that car. I don't like him having it. I've let Papa and Mama down again. They depend on me to watch after Trish. Why would Trish do this? This is crazy. Maybe... He better not hurt her.

I keep thinking about where Bev put my hands on her body. I can't believe I just sat there. I want to go back to her house, sneak in a window or something. I can't imagine how good lying in bed next to her would feel. I bet she's warm all over and wrapped up in quilts right now, and here I am, standing outside freezing.

Finally, I see some lights turn off the Boulevard onto our Avenue. The

136

lights are close together, so I imagine it's that old Plymouth Charles' father uses as a work car. I step back behind the oak tree when he gets close. They're in Lenny's Hudson. He cuts the lights before he pulls in, but I still see the faint glow of the dash lights on their faces. Trish looks around inside for some of her stuff. He's looking around with her. Oh shit! I can't believe where he's putting his hands. She kisses him. I pull back behind the tree. Can't watch anymore. She is only fourteen. I walk around behind the house a ways. I'm still glad she's home. At least she's not dead.

I hear dogs barking in the distance and a compressor's hum. I know the neighbors are starting to milk cows. Charles drives off, and I wait a little before I go back around front. I figure she's inside by now but when I get close to the front door, she's still standing in the shadows straightening herself up, buttoning a couple of buttons on her blouse. I figure she must have noticed me standing here so I call to her, quiet like.

"Trish," I say.

But she jumps like she's been shot. Then she sees it's me. "Goddamn you," she says, and her teeth are clenched. "What are you doing out here, spying on me?"

"I was worried." And I walk a couple of steps closer.

"Keep away from me," she says and I notice that she's trembling, but it's not just her hands or maybe her lips shaking like they sometimes do when she's real mad, but her whole body. It's like a tremor running through her over and over.

"I just want to make sure you're alright."

"I'm not. I'm real sick. Just keep away from me."

I get an image, like from the Bible, of a leper talking to me. But I take another step toward her anyway.

She spits on me.

"Keep back or I'll hurt you," she says.

CHAPTER 20: *Swapping Lies with Charles*

I t's midnight and I'm sitting under a bridge with Charles. A train's going by overhead, and the clatter is so loud we can't talk right now. We have a case of Pabst Blue Ribbon, and when we finish a bottle, we throw it into the cement embankment so that it shatters. Charles has his pistol, the shiny one he says belonged to Lenny. He tries to shoot the bottles before they hit the cement. The road's not far away, so I'm afraid someone in a passing car will hear the shots, and we'll get into trouble. He missed the last one I threw, just made a thud on the cement and fell into the stream. The bullet ricocheted and hit just to my right. I hear a bullfrog with what sounds like a rubber throat start croaking. I look in the dark shadows of some tules, but I don't see him. I sit back down. The caboose rattles off the bridge, so Charles starts in on me again about him and Trish not being any of my business.

"Look, Bobby, I like Trish. What I do with her is my business. What Trish does with me is her business. She is not you. If she has a problem, she can come to me or she can go to her parents, to you or anybody else. I may not like it but she can do it. She's free to do whatever she wants." He throws an empty bottle awkward like with his left hand and shoots it with that pistol before it gets to the embankment. Dark ripples spread from all the pieces of glass that hit the water.

"But she's under age."

"Here you sit drinking beer I bought and paid for with my own hard-earned money, you who live at home with everything paid for and don't know the value of a dollar, you only seventeen when the drinking age is twenty-one, you getting all the benefits of running around with someone that's a little older and you sit here telling me why it's wrong for someone else to do the same thing."

"But she's a kid, Charles. Damn!" I would have stopped myself if I could, but I've already jumped up off the ground. "And she's a girl. Charles, she's so plain and skinny like a broom handle. Just a freshman. Just fourteen."

"Ya? Well, sit down, Bobby. I didn't say I punched her. We had a good conversation the other night. I know you like those girls with all the makeup and tight skirts. But some girls have something that shows through clothes, no matter what they have on.

"You better stay away from her, Charles. I'm warning you."

"What?" And now I've got his interest. "What did you say? I want to make sure I heard you right. You're doing what to me?"

I didn't notice the bullfrog had quit but now he starts up again.

"Don't mess around with her. She's too young."

"Now you're coming back to your senses. And I suppose there's some truth to what you're saying. She's more grownup in a lot of ways than you. Look, if you're jealous, I can understand. Some boys have a thing for their sister."

"Ah, shutup, Charles. You're warped."

"What!" And he gets up and kicks me on the leg and it hurts. "Wait a minute," he says and walks away from me. "Goddamn wait a minute! I don't talk to you like that. Why are you talking to me like that? That's not something you get away with." Him and his words are going away from me, and then he turns around, comes back, grabs me by the shirt collar, stands me up.

He's going to hit me.

"Goddamn, you're going to be so good at what I've got planned." He turns me loose so that I fall to the ground. "Oh, christ!" And he turns his back on me, walks away again. "Come on bullfrog. Come to Charlie." It's as if he's a little kid now. "Come to Charlie, little bullfrog," and then he starts shooting that pistol into the tules. I count five, maybe six shots into the dark water, him just slinging bullets out the end of that pistol barrel, every shot spitting a little fire. "Ah-ha. Ah-ha," he says, staring into that dark water like it's a deep well. Then he takes a long stick, starts raking in the water. When he comes back out of the darkness, he's holding up that bullfrog by a toe, it spread-eagled against the stars, a little quiver running through it.

"You like frog legs?" he asks. "When you peel the green skin off, they look like a baby's legs. Put a little salt on them and they'll be nervous all night." Then he sits down, starts talking about the stunt we're setting up to scare a bunch of kids. It's like we never argued.

"Have a seat, over here," says Charles, patting the ground beside him. He tells me about an old house he's staked out not far from here, vacated recently so it still looks lived in. I'm supposed to tell the kids at school that there's a woman living there who'll give it to anybody. She's young and the most beautiful thing anyone has ever seen, blond hair, blue eyes, big tits. The works. She had an old man but he ran off and left her, so there's no one else home, nothing to be afraid of. To make it believable, we need two groups of kids. One group that knows that it's a joke, and one that wants to get laid. The group that knows is to say they got laid last weekend, and she was the best they ever had. Her name will be Mary.

I have on my heavy coat. Even though it's cold and getting a little foggy, I lay back on the grassy bank and use the church key to pop the top on another Pabst Blue Ribbon. I wipe the moisture from the cold bottle on my pant leg. I have this image of Mary wearing a white blouse and yellow skirt with a black belt cinched tight around her waist. Even though Charles didn't say so, I know her long blond hair is parted in the middle and hangs down around her shoulders in big curls. I think she smiles a lot too. The only problems she has are caused by her no-account husband leaving her. I'm wishing she was for real because she sure sounds good to me. Charles keeps telling me to emphasize that there's nothing to be afraid of.

He stops talking for a while. "Do you like to lie, Bobby?"

"Don't guess so," I answer real quick. "Sometimes it's hard enough trying to tell the truth without making things up."

"Well, I like to lie," he says.

Now I feel a little silly because I didn't understand what he was talking about.

"I like to make up lies, sort of storytelling really. That's what this stunt is we're pulling, just a lie being acted out. It's almost like a play except that the actors don't know it's just a play. But nobody gets hurt, and you won't believe the thrill. You're going to talk about this till the day you die. But the others, the ones that don't know that it's a trick, they'll get the biggest thrill. This is really for them. They're going to see people die all around them. They'll know they're going to die too. And after it's over, all the kids that died will come back to life. Just like you would want it to be."

I'm thinking that seeing people die is not exactly my kind of thrill, but after him explaining it that way, it doesn't seem so bad.

Charles starts telling lies.

"I'm the reincarnation of William H. Bonney, alias Billy the Kid."

I feel a chill go up my spine, and it's not the cold ground either.

"I've killed twenty-one men, one for every year since I was born. Rustled more cattle than they have in the state of Texas. This time I've come to Chowchilla because it's a place to hide. I came to kidnap and rape women. Came looking for niggers and Fairmead is close by. I've changed from killing white men to niggers. From rustling cows to rustling nigger women. I really like niggers. They're just like toy people. You can fight them. You can shoot them. They'll work for you for damn near nothing. You can cuss them right to their face. Niggers don't have a soul. I like what you can do with niggers. Take a nigger girl for instance." Then he stops for a minute. "Your turn, Bobby. Keep the story going."

"But I don't know anything about Billy the Kid."

"This is a lie. Just speak like him. Everyone has voices inside them. You can speak with the voice of anyone who's ever lived. Adolph Hitler, if you want. Maybe even people yet to be born. Lenny was really good at this."

So I try to think some mean thoughts while I down the rest of my beer and open another bottle, lean back and stare up at the stars overhead. After a little bit, I feel the sweat pop out on my forehead.

"I'm sitting on a grave," and then I have to stop to take another swig of beer because my throat is dry. "Nothing but sage brush and tombstones as far as I can see. I killed all the men in this cemetery. My personal cemetery. I killed the man that's six feet under me. Only he wasn't really a man yet. Wasn't twenty-one. The only one I feel bad about." I saw a picture of Billy the Kid once, still remember that rumpled hat and the rifle standing at his side, so this is getting easier. "He did something to me. I don't even remember what. But I got him. Killed his parents, maybe. He was leaving the bunk house. Just got on his horse and was riding away. I shot him in the back. Oh, shit!" And I jump and run a little bit. Before I know it I've taken two steps out in the river.

"What the hell are you doing?" Charles wants to know.

"I saw something."

"Well quit crying and get out of the water."

"I'm not crying."

"You are too." And he has to laugh at a little. "Get a hold on yourself. What was it?"

141

"I shot somebody. I've really shot someone."

"God. You have the highest guilt level of anybody I know. You haven't shot anybody. You just met Billy the Kid. Now get back over here."

So now he has me calmed down a little but my feet are all wet and getting real cold.

"Billy the Kid is powerful stuff for you. Maybe we better back off a little, pick another subject. How about Jack the Ripper. That one ought to carry you a ways. You might jump all the way to Sacramento."

"Come on, Charles. Quit laughing at me. I'm through lying."

"Tell me some lies about all the girls you've laid," he says.

So here I go again. I tell a couple of lies about some girls I've seen but don't even know and throw Brenda in the middle. He tells me that all those girls are ugly.

"I like to screw virgins," says Charles. "They're my specialty. You always get a little blood. How about Bev?" he wants to know because I left her out. I was impressed with her on Halloween night," he says. "She has spunk."

I can tell my face is flushing here in the dark and I hope the moon isn't so bright that he can see, but I'm going to tell the truth about her. Well, maybe not the whole truth.

"No," I say, "Not that I didn't try. But I don't even think she's physically equipped for it." And I try to laugh a little about it, but it doesn't sound right.

Charles doesn't have any trouble laughing. "Physically equipped? Where did you get words like that? You respond well under pressure. You just doubled your vocabulary with one sentence." He laughs again. "You can always tell when a guy's lying," he says. "I bet you got her every night you went with her."

"So tell me about you and Trish." I figure as long as we're by a stream, I might as well fish a little.

"Goddamn, you are really pushy, aren't you? Why can't you leave that alone? We're going to come to blows over her yet. I told you, Trish is a good-looking girl. Brothers never know what their sisters look like. I never thought Lenny would have gone for my sister, Gretta, the way he did either."

"What are you talking about, Charles?" This is really getting disgusting.

"Didn't you know? Gretta and Lenny had a thing for each other."

"But he already had a girlfriend. Helen."

142

He's real quiet for bit and I think maybe he's had enough of this lying. "You know about Helen, do you," he says finally.

"I know about the two of them. She's Brenda McCallum's cousin."

"Well, that's another one of the lies people tell. Helen wasn't Lenny's girl. She was mine."

I don't know quite what to say about that.

"I hate to tell you this," he says, "but Lenny had a mean streak. Some of the things he liked belonged to other people. Helen was my girl before she was Lenny's."

"So what's this about Gretta?"

"He fucked my sister. Got her pregnant."

"What?"

"That daughter she's got? Belongs to Lenny."

"You're making this up. This is just a lie."

"Of course, I'm lying. But it's a good lie. Cause everybody knows it's true. Everybody but you."

I throw my bottle up against the cement so quick Charles can't shoot and grab another one while he's talking. I can't even see him now, it's so dark with the moon behind a cloud.

"Lenny wasn't all some people think he was," Charles says. "You don't remember how he treated you, do you? It's been long enough you forgot."

I just get quiet and start choking down my beer. "What's the little girl's name?" I ask.

"Samantha Blake. Four years old. Just started kindergarten at Stephens School."

"That's the same kindergarten I went to. But if she's just four, she's not old enough to be in kindergarten."

"He was always bragging about having laid Gretta. Lenny was an antagonistic sonofabitch," he adds. "Claimed there wasn't a girl in the world he couldn't screw."

I'm thinking that sounds like Lenny all right.

"After that, I guess I came to believe him myself." Charles sounds far away like he's talking to himself.

"I don't believe this, Charles. And I don't like you talking about Lenny that way."

"Lies hurt as much as the truth, don't they? But that's why I kicked his ass. He wasn't as tough as everyone thought either. But he was mean. So I put him in the ground."

"You've gone plumb crazy."

"Something else you don't know." And now his tone has changed, like he's having fun again. "Your mama's not your real mama. And she's a killer. That woman you think is your mama had my mother killed."

"Come on, Charles. Get off it." He doesn't have any reason to start talking about Mama.

He laughs. "Sure. It's true, Bobby. The woman you think is your mother, is your father's second wife. Your fake mother is a murderer. Actually, I even heard once that you're adopted."

"Damn you." I figure two can play this game. I change the subject. "You think that's something. You got shot and killed at Lenny's funeral."

"I what?" he says.

"You're a dead man, Charles. Papa shot you right there by Lenny's casket. I don't know exactly what happened. Aunt Loretta told me Papa shot you right out there on the Cemetery grass and they buried you with Lenny to cut expenses."

"Good god, Bobby. How did you come up with something like that?" But he's tickled to death about it.

"You're not the only one that can tell good lies."

"But they buried me with Lenny?"

"Sure. They opened that casket right up, put Lenny at the head and you at the foot. Just like it was a bunk bed. I tell you, you're a dead man, Charles. No sense talking to you cause you're just a ghost."

"Well you've got part of it right anyway. Lenny's funeral was something else."

"But now I hear that you did all the shooting. You shot Lenny's dog?"

"Rascal? Sure, I shot Rascal. That mangy sonofabitch. But I didn't intend to use the pistol on him. He wasn't to blame for everything."

"Who did you take the pistol for?"

"I'm not telling you that. You're not ready for that one."

"Another thing, I could never figure out why Helen slapped you."

He turns toward me and his face has changed, points his pistol at me this time. The full moon shining off that barrel.

"You shut the hell up. You're asking too many questions," he says.

It gets real quiet for a minute except for another bullfrog that's started sending out its message. I guess I've gone too far. But I turn up my beer, as if him pointing the pistol at me doesn't mean anything.

"I'm not talking about Helen anymore," he says, then lowers the pistol. His face is all scrunched up like it's going to burst and he just shudders all. Then it passes, as if he just had a bad chill. And then he does the strangest thing, like something out of a storybook. And after he has done it, I think maybe it didn't even happen. Like somehow I just dreamed it. But he grabs me and kisses me on the cheek. A quick hard kiss like he's trying to hurt me and doesn't know how. Then he walks away. He stands with his back to me. Takes a pee.

I wipe his slobbers off my face. "This isn't funny anymore, Charles. Let's quit." I wish I could wash my face. I don't like his stuff on me.

"You ever play Russian roulette?"

"What!"

"Don't worry. Jesus, Bobby. It doesn't work with an automatic pistol. You need a revolver."

He's real quiet now, and a long time before he says anything. "You're right, Bobby." And his voice has changed again. "We've got to quit this. Sometimes I get started lying and just can't stop. Just want to tear apart the entire world." He takes a big breath, sighs. "But I like you, Bobby. You know that? You are a challenge. I like being out with you." Then he changes the subject. "Let's go look at that vacant house."

★

We pull up to a stucco house out in the middle of nowhere. Off to the right is a new barbed wire fence that stands about shoulder high. The wires shine like silver in the moonlight. On the other side of the fence is a peach orchard that looks like it goes on forever. The railroad track is only a hundred yards away and I hear the rhythm of another train on it.

On the way over, I asked Charles about the plan, the one about mining California's gold. "If I'm not leaving Chowchilla after I graduate, I need to know what you have in mind."

"I've put you on hold for a while," he says. "I'm not as sure as I was about you. But it's still gathering steam. You can depend on that."

Charles works the latch on the door with his pocket knife then pushes it open. I look past him as he shines the flashlight around the empty living room. I smell garbage. The linoleum creaks under our feet, and now I hear an owl hooting in the trees. Seems even colder in the house than outside.

"You'll leave the other kids in the car and come in by yourself first," he tells me. "I'll be in here with a flashlight shining on a curtain because the electricity is off." An old refrigerator with the door open stands against the wall in the kitchen. "You and I'll talk for ten minutes, then you go back outside and tell the others that the coast is clear." I see a short hall and the open doors to two bedrooms. "Tell them that you already had your turn and that Mary was even tighter than you remembered."

I feel like we're planning a murder.

He walks into one of the bedrooms. He backs up against me and points with the flashlight. "Look at that," he says, sighting down his arm. And here it's again. Another strange thing from him that I don't know what to do about. He's pointing at the only thing in the room, an old pogo stick standing in the corner, but he has backed up against me and put his hand on my crotch. "I'd like to make some use of that thing," he says.

I back away from him. Feel a chill run all over my body. Is this guy queer?

"Then you bring the kids to the front door and knock." And it's as if whatever he did to me, he did by accident. "I'll open the door and you look surprised. Ask if Mary's home. I'll say, 'So you've come back to fuck my wife again, have you? I'll fix all of you worthless bastards.' Then you tell 'em all to run for it and run like hell yourself. I want two others that know it's a joke. Pick kids you can trust and tell them to keep their mouths shut. Leroy'd be a good choice. When they start screaming and dropping, it'll add a touch of realism."

Just before we leave, Charles steals all that was left in the kitchen. Two old dish towels that he says he can use as oil rags.

On my way home, I'm thinking that this is supposed to be a joke. But the way Charles keeps feeling of me, looks like the joke is on me. I can still feel his hand down there between my legs. And this joke about Mary doesn't seem funny anymore. But then, I've been against this from the start.

★

I don't sleep very good when I've been drinking, and sometime during the night I wake and wonder if Charles was trying to kill me the way he was bouncing those bullets off that embankment. And then it hits me. Charles told me he killed Lenny. I raise straight up in bed. I've got to tell Papa. We have to do something. But I know how Papa likes to get his sleep. It can wait till morning. So I lay back down. Then I don't know whether I dreamed it, or if Charles really said it. And if he said it, I don't know if he

146

was serious or if he was lying. And he said that I'm adopted.

★

It's morning and as I crawl out of bed, I feel hot and puffy all over. Think I have a fever. I'm not so sure I should tell Papa about Charles. Once Papa gets going, there's no stopping him. I better be sure. I half believe Charles now. But this thing about Mama not being my mama...

I'm sitting here at the breakfast table with Mama and Papa talking peaceful about the price of cotton and how they hope it doesn't rain before we get it all picked. Seems like as long as I keep my mouth shut everybody gets along fine. And I'm thinking, no wonder things are so bad around here. I cause the trouble. I don't even belong to them. If I was with my natural family, wouldn't be any fussing and fighting. My papa would care as much for me as Papa cared about Lenny. And my mama wouldn't say she was ashamed of raising me.

I eat a bowl of cornflakes real quick and while they're still in the kitchen, I go into their bedroom and open the lid on Mama's big old cedar chest. I haven't been in here in a long time because she doesn't like people messing in it. She keeps all her sewing stuff in here too, so I have to dig down under that. And then there's a couple of flat cardboard boxes, and one of them has Papa's black pistol laying on it. I move it off to the side, but sure would like to pull that hammer back, aim and fire it. Papa never gets it out for target practice anymore. Then I raise the lid on one of the boxes, and it's full of pictures. Right on top is a picture of all four of us kids with Indian Chief headdresses, full feathers except for Trish and she has just one feather in the back. Lenny is about a head taller than me and damn if Trish isn't almost as tall as I am. Curt's a little thing. Looks like he just got out of diapers. Lenny has his thumbs in his front pockets with his fingers all spread real awkward like. He's trying to smile but has the sun in his eyes.

I go into the other box and after a bit I come up with Lenny, Trish and Curt's birth certificates. Lenny's is different from Trish and Curt's because his is from Oklahoma. Theirs are from California and in the left corner, the state seal. In the right corner, there's the mark of a paper crimper and words saying it's official. Mine should be like theirs because I was born in Merced too, but it's not here. I wonder where it is? I think I hear Mama, so I better get out. I put the boxes where they were and put the black pistol back on top, place the sewing like it was and close the lid. I know Charles lied. I just can't prove it right now. Walking out of their bedroom, I can't

147

keep my face up.

★

It's afternoon now, and I'm in the field alone sitting high above the gray stalks, which are full of big fluffy cotton, driving the picker. The sun's shining in my eyes bad, and I wish I had Lenny's baseball cap. I wear it sometimes when I'm in the field. When the picker blows the cotton into that big basket behind me, it dumps cotton stalks, dead leaves, twigs and dirt, all over my head and back, stuff falls down my neck. I feel like a trash pile sitting up here. Sometimes I blow trash out of my nose for two days after driving the picker.

I'm wondering if the real Bobby Ray Hammer died soon after birth, and they adopted me to take his place. If someone is adopted, what happens to their birth certificate? Maybe Mama and Papa don't even know the truth about where I came from. Maybe they found me somewhere. Mama always seemed to like to read me that story from the Bible of baby Moses being found in a basket floating down a river. Maybe that's how I ended up in Chowchilla. I came floating down the Ash Slough. Then I wouldn't have a birth certificate. Or, maybe this is all wrong thinking. Maybe my certificate just got put in another box for some reason.

And what's this about Mama having Charles' mother killed? Heidi Kunze died in an automobile accident, eight years ago.

148

CHAPTER 21: *Mary Has a Little Something for Everyone*

Word spread like wildfire. I didn't have to tell anyone. Leroy did. Now I have six kids with me in my Chevy, and we're driving through fog so thick I have the windshield wipers going, and since there's no white line, I have to use the side of the road to guide me. We're a half hour late and I have a bunch more kids than Charles wanted. Would have been even more, but I told them no. Never underestimate the ability of Leroy to con every kid in town into something. Some kid's parents found out about Mary and were looking for her house so they could run her out of the county. I have three cars and at least fifteen kids. Who's in the last car, I'm not sure. We even had a colored kid that wanted to come. I told Charles.

"Oh, bring him, Bobby," he said. "Please. We'll put him out of his misery. That'll add a touch of realism to the whole thing. We can bury his body under a peach tree. The peaches will be the sweetest a white man ever ate."

I told Chelsey it would be best if he found something else to do.

Leroy said that Phyllis kept asking questions about Mary. Wanted to know how many guys were coming. Acted like she might want to come too.

Bev knows about it. She came to me all puffed up. "You do this and I'll go out with Leroy Korenski. So help me God. He's asked me out twice in the last week."

And then there was Brenda. She heard about her little brother, Keith, coming. She had a lot of smart things to say about what she called my "sexual orientation."

Thomas Powers and Wayne Hickman are two of the four assholes I have in the backseat. Thomas and Eugene, Trish's boyfriend, are not really assholes, but they're back there anyway. Keith McCallum, Brenda's little brother, is sitting between me and Leroy. Here I am, trying to drive in the fog, and Keith won't shut his mouth.

"Tell me again what she's like, Bobby," he asks. "Help me keep my courage up."

"Well, she's really nice and she'll talk to you and run her fingers through your hair while you're doing it to her. Everybody better be good. No cutting up."

"Why does she want to do it with so many guys?"

I don't have an answer for that question. "You ever had any before?" I ask.

"No," he says.

I wonder why that's so easy for him to say when I've lied about it the last four years? Then I get to thinking about it being his sister that I did it with first, and I'm wishing that this was real for him. I know how bad he wants it. And Brenda. I wish I wasn't even here with this herd of kids and that I was off on a country road somewhere with her in the backseat of my Chevy. I just can't seem to shake that feeling I had with her. In the back of my mind I keep hoping Charles won't be there, that this whole thing falls through. I don't trust him with all these kids. I keep wondering if he really did something to cause Lenny's death.

The kids in the backseat are all drinking whiskey. Me and Leroy are not drinking and I won't let Keith touch it either. Before I picked 'em up, I had a fifth of Jim Beam someone left in my car a couple of weeks ago. It was only half full and didn't seem like enough to get these guys going.

"We need some more, Leroy," I said. "But I don't have the money."

"No problem," and Leroy pulled out his pecker and brought the bottle up just below full. Then he shook it but it didn't fizz.

"This ought to blow 'em off," he said. "They may not even need Mary after a shot of this."

We put the bottle in the floorboard in back and let them find it. "Stay away from it cause I don't know where it came from," is what I told them.

"I know where it came from," said Wayne after he turned on the dome light. "Says here, Kentucky Straight Bourbon Whiskey. Eighty-six proof. It comes from Kentucky."

Every time Thomas turns up that bottle, I think I'm going to puke. I remember Leroy wiping his dribble off the side of the bottle against his pant leg and how warm it felt when he handed it to me. I feel kind of sorry for Thomas, the big dumb bastard that he is. But Wayne, I hope he gets hepatitis.

150

"Tastes a little weak," says Thomas.

"Or maybe a little strong depending on how you look at it," Wayne says. "Strange whiskey." He has to clear his throat.

I told Leroy that if he let Wayne in on this being a trick, I would tell his mother about his stealing.

"So it's blackmail is it?" he said.

"I'm not looking at it quite that way," I said.

"Doesn't matter how you look at it. It's still blackmail."

"I'd just say, it's added security."

"Against what?"

"Against Wayne."

"So it's come down to that."

"Down to what?"

"Blackmail."

"It's not blackmail, I told you."

"Then you don't trust me."

"Sure I trust you. I trust you now."

He felt better after he pissed in the whiskey.

The only other kid that knows that Mary is a hoax is Eugene. He's still Trish's ex-boyfriend. They were about to get back together again, but she's mad as hell after finding out he was coming with me. Eugene will have some tall talking to do. He has more balls than I ever thought. He sure wants Trish back too.

"Whoa," says Leroy. "Damn. You just missed the turnoff. Just ran a stop sign too."

"I'm going to get everybody killed in this fog," I tell him. I slow to a stop, the other cars coming up close behind.

"That must have been Road 22," he says. "It's the first road after the railroad tracks."

So I have three cars turning around in the middle of the road. Hope no one is coming. They'll never see us.

I'm back on the right track now and turn off Road 22 down the short dirt drive to Mary's place, going slow through the mud puddles from the rain we had last night. Can't see the house until we are almost on top of it. Looks a lot darker than I thought, and I have to look real close to see that there's a light on at all. I feel like this whole thing could just be my imagination. What if someone has moved in there, and Charles didn't know? The car doors slam behind us. I get out quick and tell them to get back in because I have to make sure the coast is clear. Their interior lights glow in the fog around us. Feels like fine rain on my face. I tell 'em to keep quiet because Mary has a baby, and if we wake the baby she'll make us leave.

It's dark around the front of the house, which faces away from the road and toward the railroad tracks. I try the door and it's locked, so I knock and Charles pulls it open, has a shotgun through his left arm, pointed at the floor. This one's not sawed off. I feel heat coming from inside, but Charles has on a big leather coat made of sheep hide and, with his hat pulled down low on his face, I hardly recognize him. Seems real solemn. I step inside and it's even hotter than I thought. He has a couple of candles burning and at first I think I see a shadow move but then realize it's someone else in the room. An electric shock runs down into the pit of my stomach. It's Herman, the guy from Mountain View that I beat in a drag race. Hope he's not mad at me for my car outrunning his. Herman looks like an old bald-headed man. Doesn't say anything to me, acts like he doesn't know me. I don't like that at all. He's pacing like a mountain lion and banging a rifle butt on the floor as he walks. Doesn't look like a shotgun. I think it's a lever action 30.06. This was just suppose to be just a bunch of kids having fun, and now Charles has men mixed up in it. Red shotgun shells are scattered all over the counter. I'm hoping he's dumped the shot, so I go over and start fidgeting with them.

"Get away from there," says Herman.

"Who you got in the cars?" Charles asks. "I see three. I thought you were going to keep this small."

"It's all kids from school. I tried to keep it small, but Leroy wouldn't keep his mouth shut. Word just spread. I couldn't help it, Charles." I hear something moving around in the back bedroom.

"Jesuschrist," he says. Shakes his head and walks away from me. "What do you think, Herman?"

"She doesn't like crowds, usually no more than five or six."

"I don't see what difference the number of kids makes," I say. "This is just a trick."

"I've got some news for you," says Charles.

I hear snickers, sounds like a girl's voice. "Who's back there?" I ask.

"We got a girl. You want a quick piece of ass? We're doing this straight

152

up."

What little light there is in this place dims, and I swallow hard.

"We have a real girl, Bobby. This is called the Flip-Flop. All those who think this is supposed to be a trick are about to get their balls tested. All those who thought it was the real thing are about to get their wish. Their wish and a little more."

"You mean there really is a Mary, and she's going to screw all these kids?"

"She always was real. She lives for fucking. But now you've got too many guys."

"I couldn't help it. Once word got out, everybody wanted a piece. I turned away two car loads."

Charles, he snickers, and Herman, he laughs, coughs a little.

"With that kind of publicity, the next car that pulls up 'll be police. What do you think, Herman? Can she handle them?" asks Charles.

"Bring 'em on. Once she gets going, she stays hot for a week. Keep 'em quiet though."

"Okay then. Nothing's changed. Just tell the last carload that they have to stay in the back and take their chances. Mary may not want all of them. She's never had so many stiff peters."

"Bring her in here now," says Herman. "See what she thinks of this young punk. You ready to dip your wick, boy?" His voice is real gruff and sassy.

I don't have an answer for him.

"Get the guns out of sight," says Charles as he goes into the bedroom door.

It's hard for me to believe they're telling the truth. And the image I had before of Mary being pretty and nice has all changed. If she was to walk out of the bedroom now, I would see her as tough as leather and worn as an old saddle. Charles comes back with Gordy and following along behind, sure enough, he has a naked girl by the arm and pulling her into the living room. The girl is giggling and has a drink in her hand. She smiles and sashays up to me.

I've never seen a naked girl before. Even Brenda never took all her clothes off. So that's what all the fuss over tits is about. This girl has the most beautiful body I've ever seen. I never knew girls had so much skin on them. She smiles at me and starts to put her arms around my neck. Then

153

she stops like there's something wrong with me. Her face looks like she just saw the devil. She turns, puts her head on Charles chest, cuddles up to him.

"Not this one, Hon," she says. "I can't do this one."

"What's wrong, Grace? He's not that ugly, is he?"

"I know his papa."

I don't want any part of this anymore. I know this girl. I wonder how I can kill this whole thing?

"Oh shit," says Charles. "Gordy, get her back in the bedroom." And when her naked butt has waddled out, he turns to Herman. "You go in the spare bedroom. We better get this going quick. If she gets on one of her crying jags, this could blow up in our face." Then he turns to me. "Bobby, this is getting tough. We wanted you to be the one to introduce the guys to her, one at a time. It would've worked nice if you'd been the first to crawl on her. She's like that. The first one always sets the tone. But she's not going for you. So she'll be alone in the bedroom for the first guy. Now this is the tricky part. I want the nicest kid you've got to go first. Someone gentle and understanding. You pick him. For sure, don't choose Leroy cause he's a little rusty with girls. She's always a little wild at first. This guy 'll have to tame her and take care of her while the others get their ride."

I know right away, I have a special guy for this job.

"Herman, Gordy and me will be hiding in the spare bedroom. We've got a little surprise for everyone."

"What are you going to do now? I thought it was the real thing. Just a Flip-Flop."

"The show is still on. You're still in charge. Don't forget to scream when we start shooting. Scream like you're hit and fall to the ground."

I feel like screaming right now. "Does she know what this is all about?" I ask.

"She knows about the kids. That's all she's interested in. She loves kids. The surprise will do her good."

"How far are you going to let it go?"

"We'll play it by ear. If they all make it through the bedroom action, we'll call it the Long-and-Hard. But I bet the Flip-Flop is more like it."

And then I realize where I have seen Grace before, and I've seen her twice. The first time was when I got Papa out of the Cotton Club. She was the one that walked away from Papa and looked me over good. The second time was when I was talking to Charles in Farnesi's. She was the woman on the phone with the kids at home alone. I wonder where her kids are now?

Herman sticks his head out the bedroom door. "Get 'em in here," he says. "Shit. Don't take all night."

I go outside into the cold, and my legs are shaking so hard I feel like I'm dancing. Grace knowing Papa and not wanting any part of me because of it, is really bothering me. What has Papa been doing with her? I go from car to car telling them to stick together and be quiet. Melvin is in the second car and he wants to know what I was doing in there so long. I tell him I already had my turn, that she was even better than I remembered. Tits were the size of balloons. "How would you know what a good piece is like?" he laughs. "If you got some, it was your first." I just brush it off and tell him he'll find out for himself. I go on to the last car. I don't know how these kids made it here. When the driver rolls down the window to talk to me, the smell of beer is as thick as the fog. I see Eugene in the backseat. His eye lids are drooping and he's trying to talk to the kid next to him about how he ain't ever had a "pieces-of-ass" before and he's real scared. His words come out all stuck together. I tell them that there are too many kids, and that everybody may not get a turn, but they can stay to the back of the pack and see how Mary is feeling. They're all real disappointed. I tell them not to worry. We'll just have to see.

So now we're all in a pack walking toward the house with half of them lighting up a fresh cigarette and I'm in the lead, knowing that I've never been in charge of anything before. Then I hear a car, so I look back. Sure enough, the other two cars just showed up. Damn! They found us. Well, it's too late to do anything about them now so I just go on, hearing the car doors slam and the pitter-patter of running feet coming up fast behind us.

"Wayne," I say catching a glimpse of him out of the corner of my eye. "Come up here."

"What you want?" he asks sounding real suspicious.

"Got a job for you." Charles wanted somebody special. Well, Wayne is special to me.

"Oh no you don't. You're not cutting me out of this."

"Course not. You go first," I say. "But you've got to help me with Mary."

"What?"

"The girl. I need some help with her."

"Sure. But why me?" he asks, stammering through his words. "Why not Leroy or Thomas?"

"Leroy? With a woman? Get serious, Wayne. Just stay close and I'll tell you what to do."

"Bobby?" And I don't know that Wayne has ever called me by my first name.

"What's your problem? I told you that you get to be first."

"Leroy said..." And then I realize what his problem is. Leroy has told him that this is a joke, that there really isn't a girl. Leroy just can't keep his word.

"The girl is real, Wayne. Trust me on this one."

Keith is walking on the other side of me. "I sure do appreciate this, Bobby," he says.

"You can tell me how much when it's over," I say.

I tell them before they go inside to be sure and wipe their feet because Mary is real neat and doesn't want anyone messing up her floor. I look back out the corner of my eye and see Eugene lagging behind and staggering a little. I'm still worried about Herman and Gordy being inside. They're old men, but I guess they can't be any worse than Charles. It's so dark on the front side of the house that I'm a little scared too. I tell them to put out their cigarettes because she doesn't allow smoking. When I go to knock on the door, my hands are shaking. Then I turn back toward them and whisper real loud, "One last thing. She's got an old man, her father, that lives in the spare bedroom. But don't worry about him."

"Oh, shit," says Thomas. "Oh shit no." He sounds real downhearted and has quit whispering.

"What are you concerned about, Thomas?" asks Melvin. "Don't you have to fight for a piece of ass from Brenda?"

"When I bark, she fucks alright, but it's not in front of her old man."

That is the last straw. Someday Thomas will pay for saying that about Brenda.

"Don't worry the old man," I say. "He's an invalid. Stays drunk all the time. Don't be loud and he won't wake up. It'll be alright."

After I knock, nothing happens. I wait a minute wondering where Charles is, then knock again. Still nothing. Then I remember. I'm not supposed to knock now. "Nobody home," someone says from the back of the pack, and then gives a little nervous laugh. I open the door.

The living room looks like I just stepped into a different house. There's a sofa and two easy chairs that weren't here ten minutes ago. Must be ten candles burning in a thing that looks like silver deer antlers sitting on a coffee table beside a big fluffy teddy bear. I've slowed so much guys are starting to push past me. I walk across the creaking floor to the hall.

"Wayne? Where are you?" I whisper.

He comes out of the crowd, pale like he has a bad case of the flu.

"You go first," I say.

He's looking up at me, eyes real watery in that candlelight like I just gave him a death sentence.

"She's in there alone. Just be nice and she'll do anything you want. She'll even pull your pants off for you. She likes to do that."

He takes a deep breath, but he hasn't gone anywhere yet. "The girl is real," he says to himself.

"The first one is always special to her. So you have to stay with her and introduce all the other guys. You got that?"

"How about you? Don't you want to be first?"

"I've already had my turn."

"So I'm not really first."

"She's not a virgin, Wayne."

"Ya, but you could stay with her instead of me."

"I've got to pick the guys. The order is important. Besides, you don't want all these other guy's juices inside her when it comes your turn. Do you? Right now it's just mine."

I just hear a squeak from him.

"Don't worry, Wayne. She'll help you get it hard."

Just as he's about to try the doorknob, I say, "Don't worry about the clap. She's clean."

So Wayne is inside and I'm standing at the bedroom door trying to hear what's happening. Wayne is about as subtle as a spit in the face. The guys are making themselves to home. Leroy has tried to bum a cigarette off of two kids already. Thomas is telling Leroy and Eugene a dirty joke about a farmer's daughter that had three tits, and Keith is looking for the bathroom.

"Don't sit on the arm of the sofa, Melvin" I say. "She doesn't like that."

"Well, what the hell *does* she like?" he asks.

I hear the bed squeaking through the door and the sounds of hard breathing. Then a loud "Ouch." It wasn't a girls voice either. "Don't do that," says Wayne. Then silence.

And now Leroy comes to me. "Is there a real girl in there?" He has the teddy bear in his arms.

"Sure is."

"Why didn't you tell me it was going to be this way?"

"Why did you tell Wayne? And how about you asking Bev out?"

"So it's come down to this, has it?"

"To tell you the truth, I didn't know it till I got here either."

"You're a goddamn liar, Bobby Hammer." And Leroy shoves me up against the wall. "You and Charles are messing with my head."

And then there's a shout from the bedroom. It's Wayne again.

And now shouting from the girl. "You pencil peckered little shit!"

"Goddamn you bitch!" says Wayne. "My face, my face. I'm marked for life." Sounds like Wayne is working his magic on Grace.

Then the spare bedroom door bursts open. Herman has turned into a wild man. I've never heard a voice boom so loud. "Get out of my house, you worthless assholes!"

"Run for it everybody!" I shout. But I push open the bedroom door to see how the girl is making it. Charles' pogo stick he had the other night is still standing in the corner. Grace looks up over Wayne's shoulder just as the first blast from a shotgun goes off behind me and she lets out a blood clabbering scream. Herman puts the next blast through the ceiling, plaster, sheetrock and shit going everywhere. Leroy screams and falls against the far wall, then hits the floor with a thud and the teddy bear fall on top of him.

I hear Charles shooting out the windows in the spare bedroom.

Wayne, I can't help but feel sorry for him, his red ass just went crashing through a closed window. He didn't have anything on below the waist.

It's time for me to get out of here too. "Oh, god no!" I scream, and turn to run, and when I do I'm so scared it's just like this is real and I'm afraid one of them will shoot me in the back. I break through the logjam at the door. Charles is shooting the living room windows out now. The world has turned to glass.

It takes a second for the ones still outside to turn and run. They still don't believe this is happening, and I'm running through the pack, bumping into kids, push a couple down, when another blast goes off. "Oh, god, I'm hit," I shout and feel my knees hit the soft earth. Every time that girl screams, I scream.

Someone stops to help me, I don't know for sure but I think it's Thomas, then a blast goes off and he splits, looking back like he sure would like to stop but just can't bring himself to do it. I'm rolling on the ground now. Someone else is screaming in pain a ways in front of me, then I hear Charles.

"Shoot 'em! Shoot 'em! Get 'em all."

And shotgun blast sound like machine guns, and I hear that 30.06 doing full duty. Some kids stop and come back to help others for a second and then another blast goes off and maybe they'll drop too or leave their friends and run for their lives. Kids falling all over and begging for help. Not many still standing.

I start crying and screaming. "I'm dying. I'm dying." I think I'm faking but real tears come from my eyes. The sound of my own voice scares me. Maybe these kids are really being killed, maybe I'm really hit. I know I'm wet but I thought it was just water off the ground. I look up just in time to see Thomas go over that shoulder high barbed wire fence without breaking stride. I hear kids crying in the distance, shouts in the orchard muffled by the heavy fog. Cusses. Groans. Another scream. Silence.

At the far side of the house, I hear a motorcycle. Then another. Doors slam. I roll over and sit up because they sound close. A car starts. The girl screams again. I'm blinded by a headlight which lunges toward me and I'm afraid I'm going to get run over so I hit the ground again, lay flat. They roar by, and boom! I am hit. A motor cycle ran straight across my leg. I know I'm hurt this time and probably real bad. They roar on, looking as big as buffalo, digging in and slinging gravel and after they go by I have trash all over my clothes. I drag myself out of the way of the car that comes on the heels of the motorcycles. As it goes past, I see Charles making the front end of his cycle rear up, the headlight shining up into the fog like a searchlight, that back wheel still digging dirt, and with the shotgun in one hand, he fires both barrels into the sky.

★

"Goddamn you, Bobby. You are a wise ass. You know that? You are a conniving, self-righteous little shit." That's what Charles thinks of me for siccing Wayne on Grace. Charles found me later that evening at the pool hall. He wasn't too pleased. But everything turned out okay after the fog cleared. My leg wasn't hurt as bad as I thought. Wayne only had to have a few stitches on one thigh where he got cut going through the window. He did the real damage when he ran full steam into the barbed wire fence. The girl's scratch marks on his face cost him a little pride, but then he had a lot so he could spare a little. He wants to be around me all the time now. Two weeks later he had to tell me all about what was running out the end of his pecker and his penicillin shots. Said the nurse forgot to tell him not to stand up right away, so he fell over but he didn't pass out. Says my bills are still come in, wants to get the full tally before he comes to collect. One kid had to have some buckshot removed from his butt, but his father thought he deserved it. I have a new reputation with the mothers of Chowchilla. Mama doesn't know about it yet, praise the Lord, at least if she does, she's not talking. Papa has been more agreeable than usual.

Mary is doing better too, says Charles. And just the other day I saw Amazing Grace crossing Robertson Boulevard on the arm of Brother Hensen.

CHAPTER 22: *Another Fight, Sort of*

I'm sitting in my algebra class. Got a teacher that's tall with hair that's blond. He wears plaid shirts and has glasses because his eyes cross real bad. He's writing this equation on the board about "y = mx + b" or something like that. After he puts the "x" down, he just quits talking like he can't remember anymore or maybe he forgot what he's doing. Some kids keep telling him what the rest of the equation is, but he walks back and sits on the edge of his desk facing us like he's through. His eyes are glassy and he hums to himself real low-like. "Beautiful Dreamer" is the name of the song. Then he lets a fart that starts low and turns into a real zinger. It turns real quiet and I feel like running.

Cute little Becky Wynsum leaves the room for a minute and comes back with Clyde Sonnett. I would have gone myself, but my left leg is still sore. We sit here looking up, like we're studying until our teacher gets up like he just remember something important, goes to the board and puts the "+ b" on the end of the equation. He smiles like it's the smartest thing he's ever done.

Wayne's sitting in the next desk over. He turns to Eugene who sits right behind him. "That's a perfect Bobbyism," he tells Eugene. "When the chips are down, his brain turns to beans and just farts. Otherwise, when Thomas took Brenda away from him, he'd have done something about it."

I wish I could shut Wayne up. I'm going to do something about Thomas but wan't to do it in my own time.

Other kids claim they have strange teachers too. But this teacher is something special. It's like his mind got a kink in it. I could almost hear it pop. I know he's a nice guy, and sometimes I think he knows algebra real well, but now I can't concentrate because his mind might pop any second. He's kinda like Papa. I don't know what he might do. Mr. Wood's physics class is different. The man is a genius. Thomas is in there with me and he's struggling too. Mr. Wood called me aside one day after class. Said he thought my algebra was a little weak. Liked to scared me to death. I thought he was going to kick me out. I told him that I was taking the first semester of algebra and that I was studying real hard. But he said I needed something specific, and that he could teach me enough algebra in five minutes to get me through physics. And he did. Right then. And showed me how to work a physics problem with it. The thing is, I understood everything he said. I'm even doing better in algebra now. I've never felt smart before. I even feel a little guilty about how smart I felt. Right then, I felt like I could learn anything in the world, so I went to the library and got the biggest book I could find on bridges. There's enough equations in that book to solve all the world's problems.

★

The Powers' have this little ranch out in Dixieland. They don't live there, but that's where they keep a small herd of cattle. Since I'm on my way to Madera for Papa, I think I'll stop by and see if Thomas might be out there, see what that asshole is up to, not knowing quite what I have in mind. On the way, I'm thinking about Brenda and getting madder and madder, thinking about what Thomas said Brenda does when he barks.

A strange thing has happened too. Brenda called me the other night. It was late and I was about to go to bed. Everybody else was already asleep when the phone rang. I was afraid it'd wake Papa. I know how he doesn't sleep too good. I thought Brenda was going to chew on me some more about taking Keith to see Mary.

"I talked to Helen a few days ago," Brenda said, then stopped because her voice was shaking. "I asked her why she slapped Charles at Lenny's funeral. She didn't answer, Bobby. She just cried. Then she asked about you. Asked how you are. She remembers you. She didn't know that Charles is back in town either. But she wouldn't answer the question."

"Oh," I said. "Well, thanks for asking anyway. I appreciate it."

"You're welcome, Bobby," Brenda said. "Sorry it took so long. Sorry I couldn't get an answer for you."

"That's okay."

"But Helen wanted to make sure I asked if you knew anything about Lenny's journal. She would like to see it."

"I don't know anything about Lenny having a journal." What does she mean, I wonder? Does she mean like a journal bearing that goes on an axle?

162

"Okay. She was afraid you wouldn't know."

And then the line got quiet but she didn't hang up.

"Bobby?" she said finally.

"Yes."

"I've made a mistake."

"What about?" I ask.

"I just can't bring myself to talk about it yet."

"Okay."

"Good-bye," she said right quick and hung up. I swear, she was crying.

I'm still worrying about this when I pull into Thomas' place. I see Thomas out by the corrals dumping feed for their cows. I'd recognize him from a hundred miles with that big brimmed hat and cowboy boots he works in. So I pull over, jump out and head toward him pulling off my coat. He comes for me, smiling, acting like he's glad to see me.

"Hey Bobby, what you doing out in this neck of the woods?" he wants to know. I don't say anything, so he puts a real puzzled look on his face. When he gets close enough, I drop my coat and take a swing at him, hit him on the lip but he flinches, blocks part of it, backs up.

"What the hell are you doing, Bobby?" he says, throwing his hat off to the side. Guess he doesn't want me to mess up his hat. "What the hell's wrong with you?" he wants to know when I keep coming at him. "You gone crazy?"

I figure I don't need to give him an explanation. He's just trying to make a fool out of me, so I keep coming and he's damn near running backwards to keep away from me. I can see that he's bleeding a little out of the corner of his mouth and think that a couple more shots is probably all he can take.

"Come on, Bobby. You keep coming, I'm going to have to take you apart. I don't want to hurt you because you're my friend."

"We're sure as hell are not friends. Come on. Just come on. Try to take me apart, if you think you can."

"A little fellow like you, Bobby? I'm out of your league. You trying to make a name for yourself? Come on. Tell me what the hell's the problem. We're friends, Bobby. We played football together. Still would be playing together if Sonnett hadn't found out you kicked Melvin's ass. I'm not saying you're not tough. God knows I've been tackled by you enough times to know how hard you can hit."

163

I know he's not the smartest kid to ever pass through CUHS, so I guess maybe he needs telling. "It's what you're saying about Brenda."

"What?" And then he laughs that little laugh of his that says he's better than me. And he relaxes like, well if that's all that it is. And so, while he is not ready, I hit him again. This time I catch him good on the top of the head, up there where his flattop is real flat and it hurts my knuckles.

"Ow! Damn you!" And he clenches his teeth and puckers his mouth and he's after me now but I'm quicker than he is. I step inside with his wild left going over my head, and I remember that rabbit I gut shot when I was out with Charles so I hit him just below his breast bone, and damn if it doesn't work and he's out of breath right now, and I can take him if I want him. But seeing him like that, him usually acting like a big shot and now being so pitiful, I don't want to mess him up too bad so I back off. Somehow, knowing I can take him is scary.

He puffs a couple of times and I can tell that he's still suffering, but here he comes so I throw that right that I never threw at Melvin, the one where I know I'm going to put him down except this time, I miss. He hits me in the side of the head and I don't know what with but it hurts worse than anything I have ever felt before. And my leg that Charles ran over is throbbing again. Lenny used to hit me when we were playing and it really hurt and Papa used to whip me when it would hurt pretty bad, but this hurts so bad I'm really afraid of Thomas. But then he stops.

"Bobby, you're a whole lot tougher than I thought. I've had enough. If you're through, I'm through."

I'm staggering a little and walking around him in circles but it doesn't even seem like we've started good. I put my guard down though while he's talking to me.

"Now what's this about Brenda."

"You've been talking about her. Ruining her good name."

"God, Bobby. She's my girl. Now why would I want to give her a bad name? But I'll tell you what. I'll take it like you're doing me a favor, watch my mouth from now on. Okay? What do you say?"

I guess I was hoping he would still be mad about it.

"My God, what are two men like you and me fighting for anyway?" he asks. "All that we've been through together. You even took me out to see Mary. I told my daddy about it and I thought it was going to kill him, he laughed so hard. There's no reason for you and me to be fighting. High school will be over here before you know it. Brenda? Hell I know you may still be a little soft on her, but Brenda and I've been going together since summer. We broke up a couple of times, but I bet we get married someday. We're alike, Bobby. I hope you're not still thinking about her for yourself. You're not like her."

"How would you know?" I ask and he has to laugh that little laugh again.

"Bobby, I always hated to see you and Bev breakup. God, you two were just made for each other."

"You don't know anything about me and Bev."

"Hell, Bobby, she still talks about you all the time. Everybody's raising a fuss about her hiding that dynamite for you. Always suspected she had dynamite up her dress. I know she's been seeing Leroy lately, but she doesn't want him. Just wait and see. Women always get their way with a man if they really want him. We can't be fighting like this and being mad at each other anymore. You and me are going to be in business for ourselves before too long. We're going to show this country what farming is all about. My dad and yours? They don't know how to make money. They're small time. My daddy knows the implement business but not farming. We're a new breed, Bobby, you and me. We're going to be rich, richer than rich. We're going to own all this land. We're going to own land that stretches from here all the way to the Sierra Madre. I've been planning. You must be planning too. I see you out there looking over people's ground. If you're like me, you want it for yourself."

I'm really confused now. I've hated him all this time and seems like he can think up better things for me than I can. And what's this shit about us being men.

"You're a tough bucket of bolts. God, I'm glad we had this fight. It was a good fight too, Bobby. I haven't had a fight since I was in the seventh grade and an eighth grader tried to take my marbles. I hope we don't have to do it again though." And then he grabs my hand and shakes it. "But I've got to go back to work now or I'm going to be letting my daddy down. Come and see me again sometime. And get over being so mad. I don't like it. Remember, we're friends."

And then he just turns his back on me and walks off like we just had a normal conversation. I don't quite know what I have done or why I did it.

CHAPTER 23: *Leroy Bites the Big One*

It's midnight, Saturday night. I'm in my Chevy revving the engine and the front bumper is even with the white line of the marked-off quarter mile. This is the new strip, just down the road from Farnesi's on the old 99. I pump the clutch a little, make this old Chevy lurch and buck like a wild bronco. I'm in the left lane feeling a little uneasy about being on the wrong side of the road. Melvin's going to the other end of the strip to see the finish. He just left with a couple of other guys. I see his red taillights brighten then he pulls off to the right. Leroy pulls up beside me in the right lane, revving the engine in that old clunker. Charles steps in between us, a couple of yards in front. He'll do the flagging. Wayne got Leroy into this mess. Leroy is a wonder. He has Bev with him. Trying to impress his girl tonight. God, she's turned into a wild one. She's had him dragging everything in town. This is his fourth race tonight. She said it's better than a roller coaster.

Charles raises his right arm overhead with a finger pointing to the sky, the other, he points at me. I nod. Then to Leroy. Then his left arm goes up over his head like his right arm, then both come down.

I jerk the clutch and hear my tires squalling. Leroy gets the jump on me but I expected that. This Chevy doesn't have much traction when all that horsepower under the hood is turned loose. He goes to second before I do, but when I hear my lifters floating, I make the shift and hear a new squall of rubber, and start pounding the seat because I know he'll be coming to me now. But he's right beside me so I wait for high gear because all those horses have to make a difference, and then the lifters float so I'm in high gear and lunging forward in my seat, but nothing makes a difference. Something is wrong. I see his red taillights. This Chevy isn't moving right. He's just moving on. My car just doesn't seem to have it tonight and I'm wondering if someone didn't do something to it. If I find out someone screwed with my car I'll kill them because nobody screws with my car.

Chapter 23: *Leroy Bites the Big One*

Now I'm starting to pull on him, all I need is a little more time. Ah, shit! He just hit his brakes. I didn't see no white line. What's he stopping for? That chickenshit sonofabitch just quit early so he can say he won.

I pull over behind him in his lane, let off the gas, but I'm still moving up on him like I wanted to before he let off. God, he's coming to me fast. Whoa! He's on me before I know it and I squall rubber and work at the wheel but his car is moving so odd, I think maybe I catch his bumper. I can't believe what has just happened. Looked like Leroy's car just went over on its side. I look in the rear view mirror and see a world of dust and Leroy's Ford on its top and still rolling and I catch a flash of something, like maybe it's Leroy. Oh, no, no. It's like Leroy's car is flying through the air. Now all I see in the rear view mirror is black.

I coast to a stop. I don't want to go back but I have to. I make a slow turn and brace myself as my headlights swing around and hit the road again. All I see is Melvin's car at the side of the road and then it pulls out in a hurry and his lights come on, shining in my eyes. I can't see Leroy's car, but there's a big cloud of dust drifting across the road. I just hope I was imagining things, and then I see Leroy's car on its back, laying over beside the railroad track. I swear to God, it looks just like a big dead animal with its feet in the air and smoke rising from it. No fire yet.

Melvin pulls off before he gets to Leroy's car and shines his lights on something in the bar ditch. The doors to his Chevy open and three guys jump out, run over and stare down at something lying there in the dark.

I stop at Leroy's car. But I'm afraid to get out. I keep imagining Bev all mashed up with blood pouring out of her body. Finally, I open my door and walk through the weeds in the bar ditch. Leroy's radio is still going and I hear Fats Domino singing *Blueberry Hill*. I'm scared of what might be inside but I bend down anyway and first see the upside-down steering wheel and nobody behind it. Then I see Bev sitting on the inside of the roof. She's sitting on the dome light weaving from side to side, humming along with Fats. I lean in, stare up at the seats. No Leroy. I smell motor oil.

"Where's Leroy?" I ask.

"I don't know, Bobby. He's a hard one to find." There's a blue knot on her forehead. She's smiling and talking like a little girl. Starts humming again.

There's a little light because the dome light is on, but Bev's sitting on it. "Are you hurt?"

167

"I gots a hurt, but I can still play."

It's as if she thinks we're playing hide'n-go-seek. Even through her sweater, I can tell that her left arm is broken.

I talk to her straight, but try not to scare her. She doesn't know where she is yet. "Don't try to stand," I tell her, putting my hand on the top of her head. "Crawl toward me."

She keeps trying to use that left arm. "My arm hurts," she says.

"I'll have to help you with your arm."

She looks up at me with wide eyes. She suddenly realizes something's wrong. "I need help, Bobby," she says, starting to whimper. "Leroy's gone. Where did he go?" And she said it like she's disgusted with him.

"You and me are going to get in my car and I want you to sit real still. We'll find Leroy." She's starting to shake all over like she's real cold.

When she steps out on the ground, she finally comes to. "Oh, my God! Bobby, what's happened?" She turns to look at Leroy's car. "We've had an accident! What were we doing in Leroy's car?"

"Come on, Bev. You need a doctor."

I get in and drive the short piece to where Melvin, Eugene and Thomas are standing. Bev has her head back on the seat and is starting to groan. I see some blood from the corner of her mouth. Melvin squats over something, then gets down on his knees, turns his head down low to the ground like he listening for something. I don't want to think about what it might be. I park at the side of the road in front of them. Melvin shouts for me to kill my lights. Sure enough it's somebody. I pull up next to them, roll down my window.

"How's Bev?" someone asks.

"I've got to get her to the hospital."

"She pretty bad?"

"Broken arm."

"How come you wouldn't let up," someone else wants to know.

"Who? Me?" I say.

I tell Bev that Leroy's okay. Just shaken up pretty good. I use my handkerchief to get the blood off her mouth. "Is your mouth okay inside?" I ask as I pull out toward town.

★

Nobody is blaming me for what happened to Leroy. Nobody. Well, maybe Wayne. I checked the front of my car but couldn't find a mark on it.

168

Melvin sat in the backseat while I drove Bev to the hospital. We passed the ambulance on the way. Charles had gone for it as soon as he saw the dust fly. They almost beat us to the hospital with Leroy.

At 3 AM, I went back to the scene of the accident. Melvin went with me. We stood there at the side of the road, his hand on my shoulder, said no way did I clip Leroy's bumper. He claims he saw space between my car and Leroy's just before he went off the road. I don't know what the truth is. The police kept going over and over it with me. Took me from the hospital to the police station. They know it all now.

Papa, he came down too. "Get that cocksucker out of here," is what he said when he saw Charles giving his statement.

"Calm down and have a seat," is what Brock said back. "Everyone will get a chance to have their say."

"He's the cause of this. I should have killed him years ago."

"I'll put some cuffs on you, if you don't shut your mouth," was Brock's answer.

Papa calmed a little, told me to tell the truth. He talked to Brock for a long time after they sent me out. Beats me what they could have been saying. I just sat in Papa's pickup with the radio off. Played with the doorknobs, the cigarette lighter and wiped a lot of dust off the dash. Charles came out and talked to me for a bit, but he had to leave because I didn't want Papa to see him talking to me. Charles said he knew it wasn't my fault, said not to worry, that he'd straightened it out with the police. But I don't know what the police are going to do about me. I don't know what the truth is about what I have done.

★

Today is Sunday morning. I'm riding around town with Melvin in his new '57 Chevy. This thing really scoots. We drive past the hospital on Ventura a couple of times, then stop and go inside. Melvin goes first. There's just a little square entry way with a couple of benches and then the hall. Three of Leroy's brothers are sitting there, one older, two younger than Leroy. Leon is the oldest. He looks at me.

"How you doing, Bobby?" he asks. First time I've seen him without his girlfriend.

"Okay, I guess. How's Leroy?"

"Same."

His Uncle Jesse is sitting on a bench by himself. He doesn't have on a

169

coat, just a T-shirt, and his tattoos show all down his arms. First time I've seen him sober. And this is a strange thing from him. He gets up, but he doesn't shake my hand like he usually does. He hugs me. He's clean but he smells of garlic.

Melvin takes a seat in the only chair in the room, but I walk on through the open doors into a hall. The whole place looks deserted. On the other side is a large room and out in the middle, on what looks to me like a tall rollaway bed on wheels, is Leroy. I would've thought they could've done something better for him. I can tell it's Leroy because of the shaggy hair and the eyebrows. He's lying on his back covered with a sheet and blanket. His mother's standing beside the bed like she's just about to do something, and his daddy's sitting on a stool over in a corner with his head down and his hat in his hands looking like Leroy is already dead. Like he's just wasting time. Dr. Wade's standing up by Leroy's head fiddling with something then walks over to the medicine cabinet as if he has all the time in the world. He's hurt me so many times I don't know if he can help Leroy. I don't like the smell of alcohol. He takes a look at me but it's as if he's seeing through me.

I wonder where Bev is? I look around for a nurse. Leroy's mother sees me when she turns around and even though it didn't show when she had her back turned, now I can tell she's been crying for a long time. I wonder if she's going to be mad at me but she comes over and hugs me.

"Thank God you're okay," she says.

"How's Leroy?" I ask.

"Doesn't look good, Bobby. Not at all. They won't let me see the right side of his head."

"Do you know where Bev is?"

"Down the hall."

I peek in a couple of empty rooms. Finally see a nurse coming up the hall.

"Can I see Beverly Morrini?"

"Sure. She's sedated though, can't talk because her tongue is swelled. She bit it."

Bev looks to be asleep but when she hears me, raises her hand.

"Are you sure you're okay?" she asks. I don't know how she knows it's me because she didn't open her eyes.

"I'm fine. I'm just worried about you. You and Leroy. Do you hurt

170

much?"

She shakes her head no but starts crying. "Take my hand, Bobby. Hold it real tight, till my mother gets back."

"They put your arm in a cast?"

She tries to pull her left arm out from under the covers but I stop her.

"Don't," I say. "That's okay. I just want to make sure you're alright."

Mrs. Morrini walks in carrying a purse the size of a grocery basket. I feel like I've been caught doing something wrong but she seems glad I'm here. Bev is already asleep.

"Oh, Bobby. It's so good of you to come. She's been asking for you. She has a concussion. Sometimes she thinks you were killed. For some reason she believes she was driving and that it was her fault. She'll be a lot better by tomorrow, Dr. Wade says. If Leroy doesn't make it, it'll be very hard."

I walk back out front, sit across from Melvin, between Jess and one of Leroy's brothers. Ken, the one just younger than Leroy, asks me if I was dragging against Leroy.

"Yep. I was," I say. Too late to lie about that.

"How did Leroy do?" he wants to know.

"Kicked butt the whole quarter mile," says Melvin, pointing his finger at me, then pulls back and starts searching for his little pouch of roll-your-own cigarettes. "Bobby never had a chance."

I can't help but laugh a little. "Put me to shame."

Ken laughs almost like a cough, turns his head to the side, laughs again. "Nobody'd believe that old Ford hauls."

"Chewed me up."

"Leroy's always working on that old Ford. Won't touch the body, and won't tell anybody what he has under the hood, not anymore." That's all he says and then we just sit for a long time.

Leroy's six-year-old brother is named Cletis. He pulls a little screwdriver with a clear orange handle out of his coat pocket like he's going to fix something. He turns to Ken with a mean look on his face, points that screw driver at him, turns it first one way then the other like he's working on him. Ken tells him to stop it. "Just stop it," he says.

From inside, I hear their mother crying real low, then a little louder. She comes out front crying hard. Leon asks how he's doing. She says that the doctor just told her Leroy's not going to make it. Cletis starts crying. I go on outside, stand and wait for Melvin to take me home.

The Escape of Bobby Ray Hammer

★

It's nighttime now, and I'm lying in bed staring up at the dark. Bev called me earlier this evening from her hospital bed. She gave me the exact time like they do when a baby is born. Leroy died at 8:05 PM.

CHAPTER 24: *Another Funeral*

I just can't stand myself knowing what I did to Leroy. Look at all these people in black standing out here at the cemetery. Brother Hensen just finished saying all the right words for Leroy, the words Lenny never got. Grace Magdalena's staying so close to her preacher you would think there's a hit man after her. And everyone's milling around except for the Korenski's and they're in what looks like a football huddle over to the side with all their kids and several people I've never seen before. One old woman is in a wheel chair. Heard someone say that she's Leroy's great grandmother. Leroy's Uncle Jesse called me over so she could see me. She didn't say anything, just looked me over good. I don't know what that was all about. My mama and papa are standing next to the coffin but they didn't know Leroy much, so there wasn't any reason for them to come. Trish and Eugene are together again. So they're here. Curt stayed home to shred cotton stalks. Said he didn't need another funeral.

All the women have on hats and all the men don't. Aunt Loretta is standing with Mama and Papa. She looks like a woman today. She's in a red dress and a little white frill hat with a blue ribbon hanging down the back. She gets her clothes from the Salvation Army. First dress I've seen her in since Lenny died.

I wish it would rain or something, but it's like it can't. Can't even make a decent cloud. This little fog just hangs off in the distance around trees and houses. Can't even get good and foggy anymore. And the sun won't come out bright either. Can't throw a good shade. I didn't know how to dress with this weather. Funerals confuse me anyway. Seems like you shouldn't dress up for bad things. What's the point in trying to look good at a funeral? I don't know. I just put on my pair of dress pants and this shirt everyone says looks so nice and wore my same old jacket I wear to school. Don't know if I should have my zipper up or down.

Charles is standing over there looking down at Lenny's grave just like I am standing here in front of Leroy's casket. He's been standing there ever since he got here. I don't like him being over there but I guess I'm not doing anything about it. Papa started walking toward him but Mama stopped him. I don't know about all these flowers stacked around on this hill of dirt either. Just doesn't seem right for a boy. Wish somebody would take them the hell out of here. I'm looking down below the casket at the dark hole in the ground, move up a little closer. Want to see what six-foot-down looks like. See what is ahead for me someday. So long Leroy.

Why doesn't somebody do something? I just want something to happen. Brother Hensen said some fine words, and I think they did help a little. Mama goes to his church, but he doesn't like me, says if I mess around in girl's pants, I'll go to hell. It's like nothing has really happened. Seems like somebody should do something to make it alright when somebody dies. I just can't figure out what would do it. Maybe I should say I'm sorry to someone.

Leroy's mother, over in that huddle, is just crying softly and going from person to person to get hugged. She asks each one of them, "Is it true? Can it be true?" Each time they shake their head yes. And then she says, "Tell me it's not true."

She goes over to her brother, bald-headed Jake, and she's leaning on him so hard I think she's going to bring him down. They both stagger a little. "Is it true, Jake? Can it possibly be true? How could this be? Not Leroy. Not my boy, Leroy." Mr. Korenski is just standing off to the side with his brother Jesse, looking like he's the loneliest man that ever lived. Then Jess leaves him, walks over to Aunt Loretta, says something. They both look over at me. Now that's a strange pair of people.

Mama and Papa come over, stand by me. Papa starts talking about wishing he hadn't got the transmission in Lenny's car fixed so soon then Lenny would have been home working instead of out gallivanting around when he got killed. He catches a shuddering breath. Then he turns his back on me and Mama, walks to the car. Mama says she wished she'd prayed harder for Lenny, like she prays for me now. Maybe I should tell them about Charles. What he said he did to Lenny. But I don't know if it's true. I just seem to make a mess of everything. Look at all these people here because of me.

Brenda is standing off to the side with her mother and father. Phyllis is with them too. Phyllis is all humped over like an old lady. Brenda goes over to Leroy's mother and gives her a hug, then starts toward me, goes back. That's the fourth time she's done that. Maybe she wants to let me know that this proves she was right about me being such a creep. But it's hard for her to be mean to people. Or maybe she wants to tell me she's sorry my friend is dead, but then remembers what I did to her.

Wayne's standing off out of the way with his daddy. They're both dressed in black. Sure makes that light red hair of his stand out. Wayne is the only one that didn't mind telling me what I had done. He came to me Monday at school, first thing. "Leroy was my only friend," he said. "I know how everyone is trying to make you feel like you didn't play a part in him dying. I can't prove anything, but I just want you to know that I hold you personally responsible." He was so business-like that he reminded me of his father.

I keep thinking about that night. When I looked inside Leroy's upside down car, the dome light was on. I could see Bev's legs through her skirt because the dome light shined through it. Bev had wet her pants. I also noticed that the glove compartment had popped open. There, scattered all over the inside of that car top, was the stuff Leroy stole and said he'd thrown away. Bev was sitting in the middle of it, that arm of hers just dangling.

They're supposed to say words of rest and peace at funerals like Brother Hensen just did for Leroy. I can't stand it that the words never got said for Lenny. He hasn't had a moment's peace since they shoveled the dirt in on him. And that's the way he still is lying over there now in his grave. He's never going to rest in peace. Trish loved Lenny more than anyone in the world because he was her biggest big brother. When me, her and Curt were sitting in our bedroom listening to Mama scream, the two of them kept looking up at me. And I always thought there was something strange about that. But now I know. They were looking up at me for an answer. And I didn't have one. Trish would look up at me with those big baby blue eyes of hers, a little bloodshot from crying, and it would just break my heart.

Charles is standing behind me now. I turn around and look him in the eyes. I didn't know that they were so pale, a pale blue. They have puddles in them and I see a reflection in those puddles. Each one of them is a small picture of me. Charles took up for me again, and this time with the police.

Brock says that since Charles was at the scene of the accident, he's helped a lot to get me off. Charles starts to say something to me, but it's as if he can't find the right words. He stutters. "You didn't kill Leroy," he says finally. "I know you feel like you did, but you didn't. I know that for a fact. You may never know it." He walks off in the direction of Trish and Eugene, stops and stares for a second. I think I see Trish shake her head no. Then Charles walks on to his jeep.

Eugene glares at Trish.

I'm still watching Leroy's mother. I remember when I met Leroy in the first grade. It was the first day of school and we had to share a desk because they didn't have one for everybody. The teacher paired us together because someone had lied to her and said we were cousins. He was on the left side next to the window. I didn't like it because we had to put our papers in the same drawer. It seems like he really is gone now. And I'm getting the message that anybody can go at anytime. There ain't no telling. I just wish I could've told Leroy one thing. I wish I could have told him that I'm sorry for being mad at him all the time. If there's something you want to say to someone, better get it done quick. When they're dead and gone, you'll have a lot of time for not saying things.

Aunt Loretta comes over to me, brings Leroy's Uncle Jesse with her, puts her hand on my shoulder just like she did at Lenny's funeral. "I buried Twinkles the other day, Ray" she says. "Dug the hole myself with a shovel."

God. Why did she have to bring up her damned old stinking dog? Jess just kind of hangs off behind her.

"You just be careful from now on," she says. "I don't want to be putting you in the ground."

Jess comes up beside me. "We're all going to miss Leroy," he says. "But I know you'll miss him most. You knew him better than any of us. If you need to talk, come see me. I'm going to miss him too." He hugs me across the shoulders.

"You listen to Jess, here, Ray. Go talk to him sometime. He's a good man. But you need to come see me again, too, Ray. I have something more I need to tell you. You and me, we have so much talking to do."

I remember her at Lenny's funeral, her hugging me, the sound of Papa's pistol firing. Only now I know it wasn't Papa doing the shooting. It was Charles. I keep forgetting that. I don't know why but I thought Papa wanted to kill me.

Oh, no! I just remembered something. And now I know what scared me that night in the tules when me and Charles were doing the Billy the Kid stuff. That night, for just a second, I knew I'd killed someone. Now I know why I felt that way, and I've found the time that was missing from the day Lenny got killed. I remember coming home early from school that day. I was still having dizzy spells, and the nurse sent me home. But Papa caught me out in the field hunting with my .22, so he made me chop cotton with Delbert. "If you're feeling good enough to hunt, you're feeling good enough to chop," is what Papa said. But I hadn't been hunting, not for rabbits like Papa thought. I had been hunting for Lenny. And I'd found him. He came out of the house, got in his car and drove off. And as he was driving off, I pulled a fine bead with my .22 and put a bullet in the back of that '48 Hudson. After that I walked to the far side of the field till Papa caught me. So I've always known, somewhere inside, that I must've shot Lenny. He must have been injured and having trouble driving when he came to that dip at the Ash Slough. Must've passed out and went off the road. I killed my own brother.

I feel so bad. I need somebody to help take away the pain. I turn around and over by a small maple tree are Phyllis, Bev and Bev's parents, Bev with a cast on her arm, standing around like she's waiting on someone, looking off into the crowd of people. I thought she was still in the hospital. I walk over and see tears rolling down her cheeks, carrying that black stuff she uses on her eyes with it. Bev's mom smiles at me. I don't say anything, just put one of my hands on each of Bev's cheeks, pull her face up to mine and kiss her on the red lipstick in the corner of her mouth. And then I hug her right there in front of Mama and Papa and the preacher and anybody else who cares to see that Bobby Hammer really likes this girl.

PART IV

Coming to Terms with Charles

CHAPTER 25: *Waking and Worrying*

Sometimes I wake in the middle of the night and I don't feel so good. I get to thinking I hear doors slam, like maybe somebody is leaving. I don't worry too much about Curt because he sleeps right here beside me. But when I wake all at once, I think maybe it's because a door slammed. Sometimes it's just Trish flushing the toilet. Then I hear her cry and cuss a little before she goes back to sleep. Sometimes it's Papa. I'll hear him walk the hall, his old boots gritting on the hardwood floor and the floor snapping and popping. I won't know but what he's going to wake me to go to the field. If it's almost sun up, if I can see a little light starting in through the bedroom window, I know he's going to get me up. But if it's still dark, I won't know if he's going to the field and maybe want me to go with him or if he'll just walk the kitchen floor for a while then go back to bed. If he goes back to bed, then I hear his door slam.

I get to thinking that maybe when a door slams, whoever's inside of that room just disappears. I know it's not true but I can't help the way I think. Sometimes I get up and walk the old cold floor to Mama and Papa's bedroom and stand by the door listening for him snoring. I feel better if I can hear him. Then I know they are still there. If I can't hear a sound, maybe I'll open their door a crack. I don't want to because I'd hate to see him on top of her. I know how she doesn't like him on her. I don't want to wake them either because Papa, he doesn't get much sleep anyway. But I have to know if they're okay, and the old door is warped so if I don't pull against it as I turn the knob, it pops open a little and the hinges squeak. One time I did that and Papa was lying there awake. The light from the moon was shining through the window on him and him all pale. Mama was lying on her side, turned away from him with her mouth open like she was dead. He asked me calm like what I wanted, called me "son" like he does when he's just real worried. I said that I wondered if it was time to go to work. I had the strangest feeling he was doing something while he was lying awake. Like maybe he was thinking things that shouldn't be thought.

Sometimes I dream that I hear a knock at the door during the night, and I go see who's there. It's always Lenny and he has earth caked all over him and he's been lost in the field and trying real hard to get home. He has a bullet wound on the side of his head. I worry that that's the way he really is, lost and injured and lonely. He wants to come back home. I have the feeling I should be doing something to help him. I always wake up shaking after I have a dream like that. Used to be it was just Lenny alone. Last night he had Leroy with him and they argue all the time.

Lately, I've heard Mama and Papa arguing about me. I think I heard Mama say they should get rid of me. She said something about juvenile hall. I don't know if that was the words she said because she was whispering to Papa in their bedroom. I know some of the kids at school have been put there. Melvin has been in and out of there twice. I don't want to believe that Mama and Papa don't want me anymore. I spend a lot of time thinking about Charles and what I should do about him. I don't really believe he killed Lenny. I just keep blaming what I do on other people. Charles even stopped the police from putting me in jail. He said he was sorry he ran over my leg out at Mary's.

When I lie awake, I think about going out with Bev again, how I must be leading her on. We've been talking about having a farm here in Chowchilla. I keep getting in deeper and deeper with that girl. A good life here isn't possible for me. Sometimes I get down Mama's *Bible*, she doesn't mind if I ask first, and I read the story of Cain and Abel. Maybe that's why I feel that I have to leave Chowchilla. Here's what God said to Cain:

> And now art thou cursed from
> the earth, which hath opened her
> mouth to receive thy brother's blood
> from thy hand;
> When thou tillest the ground, it
> shall not henceforth yield unto thee
> her strength; a fugitive and a vagabond
> shall thou be in the earth.

Always before I can get back to sleep, I have to say something Mama taught me years ago. "Our Father who art in heaven…"

CHAPTER 26: *Digging Post Holes*

I don't know if I should feel real good or real bad. I'm working with Papa on a fence we're putting in over on the Gerald place on Robertson Boulevard, between our place and town. I didn't sleep much last night after being out with Bev, so I'm still drowsy. The sight of blood was what bothered me. I've been a little shaky about blood ever since Leroy died. Papa's driving the pickup along the edge of the field with me in the back, pickup bed bumping up and down so I can hardly stand. When Papa hollers, I kick out a fence post. I have my work coat on because the fog hasn't lifted yet. My clothes are getting damp but I've been hot inside ever since last night. Once in a while, someone I know will come by on the Boulevard and honk, so I wave. Just a minute ago it was Eugene. What a time he's having with Trish. I still know she is mixed up with Charles somehow. Now, it's Brother Hensen driving by, has Grace with him. Wonder if he's been out to see Mama again? Glad he didn't stop here. Papa's usually in a good mood when we're working where he can see people, but I've never seen him grin as much as he has this morning.

I didn't know that doing it to a girl could be so scary. I thought it was suppose to be fun. First, seemed like she wanted it, then seemed like she didn't. We'd neck for a while and she'd say, "Bobby!" like she was mad at me, get back on her side of the car for a while, then come back for more. When I tried to get my hands in her blouse, she was hitting me and holding me at the same time. When it was over, I wished we hadn't done it. Now I feel better about it, I think.

Papa has two posthole diggers, one for me and one for him. He has his and he grins and walks away from me, counting the steps he wants between posts. His old hat looks like it's made from canvas, like maybe it was cut from a tarp. Looks like he's been sitting on it. Whenever he finds the next place he wants to put a post, he sticks the digger in the ground holding both handles together, actually kind of throws it in the ground, then brings the handles apart taking out a bite to mark the spot. Then he walks away through the weeds measuring the distance to the next one. I'm just standing here watching him, but I better get to work.

Bev was in a strange mood last night when I picked her up. Acted like she wanted to fight with me, scooted over next to me, closer than usual. Told me we were *not* going to park after the movie. Put her hand on my thigh while we were driving to town. Her hand sweated through my pant leg. Then she wanted to make out right there in the movie. I heard these two guys up behind us snickering. Embarrassing is what it was. The whole school will be talking about it Monday. Still, I'm beginning to get a taste for Juicyfruit.

I'm tired. Papa's been working on the hole right next to mine, just finished and stands watching me. We've been digging post holes all morning and my arms are give out. Once in a while I have to chop my way through a decayed tree root. Papa says a cherry orchard grew on this spot years ago. I'm just about deep enough on this post hole. After I break through the damp pasture grass, there's this thick brown topsoil that's wet and makes everything grow so good, at least it grows good in some places on this patchy piece of farm ground. Sometimes I run across a lost penny or one time even an old key. About a foot down the topsoil turns to clay, which won't grow anything. Then there's this grainy sand, and below that, gravel that the diggers grind in all the way down until I stop. I guess this used to be an old riverbed maybe thousands of years ago. I'm hoping I'll find an Indian arrowhead or something. I lay my diggers down and stand the post up in the hole. We have a whole row of posts leaning one way or the other. Next we will pack in the dirt so they stand straight up.

Papa says, "Let's eat lunch," so we're walking to the pickup to go home. I wonder what Mama'll have for us.

I knew Bev was mad at me as soon as I saw her. I was standing in her kitchen talking to her mother about us having more rain than normal and some people getting concerned about a flood, and then her father came in and we talked dairy farming for a little, him being worried about an old cow that had to have an operation to remove a piece of wire from one of her stomachs. Her little brother, Steven, was sitting at the table eating dinner by himself. "What do you think about the flood, Bobby?" Steve asked. "I don't know that there's going to be one," I answered. "There is," he said. "I just know it."

Chapter 26: *Digging Post Holes*

Then Bev came in from her bedroom, didn't say hi, just walked to the door and said "We're leaving, Daddy." Interrupted what he was saying to me. I can still see her standing there, turned slightly with her hand on the door knob, all that dark brown hair falling around her face and on her shoulders. Had on a white blouse, a red skirt and black belt pulled tight. I could hardly believe she was going with me. She looked so grown-up. But when it was over and I kissed her good night with her porch light shining down bright on us, she was shaking like a scared little kid.

I have my elbow hanging out the window and the wind's cold but feels good drying my sweat. I'm watching the fields go by. Herb Coleman is out breaking ground on that little red tractor of his and the ground just splits, rolls over and lays there, all upside down like. A flock of birds follow him. Some fields still have bare cotton stalks standing. Used to, Leroy might be on the front porch waiting to tell me something that was going on up town. But that won't happen anymore.

As soon as I hit the door, I know Mama has pinto beans on. That and fried potatoes and cornbread. Curt's off tending water with Delbert, and Trish is in the washroom folding clothes and claiming she's not hungry. It's not like her not eating lunch with us. If she'd been out in the field with us she'd sure be hungry. But while I'm washing my face and hands, I notice something in the mirror I didn't see this morning. The left side of my face has welts on it. I think maybe I see two fingers of a handprint. And even a little bruise on my right cheekbone. Tender to the touch. So I'm eating lunch across the table from Papa with my hand over the left side of my face so Mama won't see. She hasn't said much of anything. I notice she has out her big black Bible on the coffee table in the living room. She's usually talking to Papa about how the work's going or some bill come in the mail. Just seems real quiet for us to be having lunch. And now I know what Papa's been grinning about, and he knows I know. I shovel in the food and get out to my car to make sure the old blanket I put on the front seat hides the whole blood stain. Have to pull it over a little. Then on the way back out to the field, I wonder if I remembered to lock my car door.

Bev said she knew a better place we could park. We were walking out of the show after seeing "Forbidden Planet" where this invisible thing came out of this guys mind and killed people. English teacher told us to go see it because the story comes from some famous play. We usually go get a cherry Coke at the Sierra Drive Inn before we park. But not last night.

We've only been out a couple of times since we started going together again, and we've been going out to Beacon Road where we used to go. There's a little wood tower out there at the side of the road and it has a pale yellow flashing light. Usually a couple of other cars out there too. Last time it was Melvin. He'd picked up some eighth grade girl walking home. A friend of Curt's, as a matter of fact. But last night we were out at the far end of Robertson Boulevard, about ten miles from town, off the side of the road parked in some weeds. I was hoping I wouldn't get stuck. Nobody was going to see us because the fog rolled in.

Well, at least Papa's quit grinning. I'm packing the rest of the dirt in around the last few posts. It has to pack tight or the post will start to lean after a while. I have the metal end of the shovel in the air and stick the sharp wood end of the handle into the soft earth around the post. I poke holes around it till I have to add more dirt. Then poke again. The barbed wire comes in these rolls of one hundred yards each. Papa has one now, rolling it in front of him with his gloved hands, and the shiny wire laying out behind in the weeds. I can tell Papa's tired by the way he walks. His seat wants to drag the ground.

I'd just raised up and looking at Bev's blood all over me when she slapped me, not hard the first time but it took me by surprise. The second time hurt real bad. Then she conked me with her cast. I had to hold her hands after that. If I'd thought about it, I'd known she hadn't done it before. I could've taken it easy. I thought it wasn't working because of me. When I stopped her from hitting me, it was like she remembered something.

"Look, Bobby," she said, "I got hurt down there." Started crying like a baby.

Papa has the wire stretcher now. It's just a mess of ropes and pulleys with a hook on each end. I walk to the far end of the field and wrap the wire around the last fence post then twist it back around itself. Drive a big staple in to hold it. Sun must be going down because it's starting to get dark but we have a little light left. It's looking more and more like rain. By the time I get back, Papa has the stretcher untangled. One end is wrapped around the post and hooked back onto the rope. It holds tight to the post. The other end is wrapped around the wire a couple of times then the hook grabs the wire like a claw. This new wire is stiff. Barbs are so sharp they keep sticking through my leather gloves. Papa starts pulling, that wire starts stretching. I'm walking along holding the wire off the ground in places so it won't get caught. It keeps snaking its way toward Papa. When the wire gets all the way off the ground with a lot of tension in it, when it's stretched real tight, I go along pounding staples into the posts with a claw hammer to hold the wire in place. That's the way it's going be from now on, stretched tight and nailed to the post.

It's raining hard when we pull up at the house. I've been worrying all afternoon that Bev may be hurt real bad. I got to thinking maybe something really was wrong with her. Maybe she couldn't take what I did to her and bled to death after she went inside. I need to call her. First thing I do is look down inside my car and, sure enough, the blanket's gone and that blood spot on my white tuck and roll glaring up at me. I'm just hoping real hard it was Trish who took it instead of Mama.

As we go inside, I walk behind Papa. Trish is ironing clothes and has shirts, pants and dresses on hangers hanging off everything in the house, doorknobs, window sills, and even off the edge of the china closet. I see Mama in the kitchen washing off the table, getting ready to set it for dinner. Trish gives me a beware kind of look. Mama looks up at Papa and her eyes are red so I know she's been crying. I make the turn and go down the hall to my bedroom.

"I want to talk to you, young man," she says.

I know what "young man" means. My back starts tingling all over knowing she's coming up fast behind. I walk into my bedroom, flip on the light, and whoa! There's my bloody shorts I put in the burn barrel out back last night after I came home. They're laying on the corner of my bed, still have some ashes on them and a little wet, laid out like they're all ready to wear again.

"Listen to me," is the way she starts in. She's bent over and using a forced whisper. "I know what you were doing last night with that little black haired slut that wears shorts and red lipstick. And I know about you taking kids to visit that whore. You're playing the devil's game. The Lord's going to take you like He did Lenny if you keep this up. How do you think I'm ever going to get to heaven with you pulling stunts like this? What do you think Jesus thinks about you?" Then she storms out.

I wish she had just said God. Why did she have to say Jesus? Everything I have, seems like somebody wants to take it away from me. I've always felt that if no one else was on my side, at least Jesus was.

CHAPTER 27: *The Slap in the Library*

Yesterday I went to the library during study hall and got out a book on bridges. Soon we'll be studying bridges in Mr. Wood's class. Physics is the most amazing thing. Now we're studying about subatomic particles that come from space. Mr. Wood even made a cloud chamber so we could witness particles from outer space hitting the earth. While I was in the library, I also took a look at a dictionary. This is what it said about the word "journal":

1 a: a record of current transaction: as (1) : DAYBOOK 2 (2) a book of original entry in double-entry bookkeeping b: an account of day-to-day events c: a record of experiences, ideas, or reflections kept regularly for private use d: a record of transactions kept by a deliberative or legislative body e: LOG 3, 4 2 a: a daily newspaper b: a periodical dealing esp. with matters of current interest 3: the part of a rotating shaft, axle, roll, or spindle that turns in a bearing

When I was twelve, I used to read the Hardy Boys books written by Franklin W. Dixon. The books were about these kids that solved mysteries. Joe, was always getting his older brother, Frank, in trouble. Seems like every story had a chapter where the kids ran up against a code they had to figure out before they could solve the mystery. Sometimes the stories started out with a note written in code and when they broke it, it just caused them a lot of trouble, and the rest of the story was about how they got out of the trouble that breaking that code caused. Now dictionaries are all written in code. I've known that for a long time, but since I don't read a lot and don't have much need for big words or unusual meanings, I haven't bothered to break it.

So I was sitting in the library with this dictionary open, and I must've had a real puzzled look on my face because after reading about the word "journal" I realized that Helen wasn't asking if I knew where Lenny's "journal bearing" was. She was asking about the little notebook where Lenny kept all his thoughts. He always called it a notebook but after reading the dictionary, I realized it could also be called a journal. I was almost sure that was what she meant because of the part of the definition that read "a record of experiences, ideas, or reflections kept regularly for private use." "Private" fits because he sure as hell didn't want anyone reading it. The part about "a daily newspaper" didn't apply even though he used to cut out parts of the Fresno Bee sports page that told about Joe DiMaggio. And the part about a deliberating or legislating body could also apply to the way he was always planning his life and telling me what to do, but I knew that wasn't it. Sometimes I think too much, and I thought too much again right then. I thought that Helen might've just been interested in Lenny's clippings out of the Chowchilla News about the good things he did on the high school baseball team. Sort of like the folder Clyde Sonnett keeps about me but in reverse. I was still a little confused about what she was after. I couldn't figure out why anyone would be interested in someone else's thoughts.

So I was sitting there at a table in the library when I felt something behind me, up close to my head, felt hair against the back of my neck and then I smelled Juicyfruit.

"What's bothering you so much, Bobby? You still puzzling over bridges," she asked, taking a look at the book on bridges I had open.

Bev works in the library during study hall. I didn't want to talk to her about this journal business, so I should've lied and talked some about bridges. "The word 'journal' is bothering me," is what came out.

"I keep one," she said. Then she smiled at me with those red lips like she wanted to take her words back. "A lot of girls do it."

"Lenny's girlfriend, Helen, that he was going with just before he died, wants to know if I have his journal."

"Do you?"

"I'm not sure what she means by journal. Does she mean his clippings that were in the paper about what he did in baseball? I think Mama has them."

"That sounds more like an album than a journal."

"He kept a notebook of his thoughts about things, but why would she want to read that?"

"What girl could resist? When were you talking to Helen?"

"I haven't. She lives in Merced. I had Helen's cousin asked her a question for me, but her cousin didn't get an answer back."

"So Helen thought the answer might be in his journal?"

"No. She knew the answer. I guess it was too personal. She wouldn't tell me."

"Gosh, Bobby. What did you ask?"

"I just wanted to know why she slapped Charles at Lenny's funeral."

"I can understand why she wouldn't answer that. And you can make a good guess at why she wants to read his journal."

"I can?"

"Sure. She did something wrong. She wants that journal so she can see if he said anything about what she'd done."

"Why would you think something like that?"

"Cause she slapped Charles."

"She wouldn't slap Charles because she did something wrong. She'd hit him because he did something wrong."

"You've got a lot to learn about romance, dear. But they probably did something together, something she feels guilty about."

"And Lenny found out?"

"Yes. And now she wants to know if he wrote about it in his journal. How long has it been since the funeral?"

"Four years and... eight months."

"She's probably been stewing over the whereabouts of that journal all this time. Now she has a way to get that journal. That way is you."

"What would Helen and Charles have done that worried her so much?"

That brings a blush from Bev but no answer.

"So the journal has the answer?" I ask.

"She's probably afraid it does. And she probably knows where the journal is, but can't get to it."

"Why would you think that?"

"Because girls know everything about their boyfriends."

I don't like the sound of that.

"Girls know everything. She knew about the journal. Right? So she probably knows where he used to hide it but she can't get to it or she'd already have it."

"But I'll have to tell her that I don't know where Lenny hid his journal."

"I wouldn't approach it quite like that. Are you interested in what's in his journal?"

"I don't think I should read it. Lenny never liked for me to pry in his business."

"But you did when he was alive."

"How do you know?" And right then I felt like I could hit her.

"You just told me. How would you know he didn't like for you to pry into his business if you didn't do it? You were probably jealous of your older brother. Why else would you want to read about his private life?"

I'm really beginning to sweat now. "Why are you saying these bad things about me, Bev. I don't like it."

"Because they are true, sweetheart." And then she puts her hand on mine. She has tiny bright red fingernails. "Your reasons for wanting the journal now are probably decent enough. That's why you won't look further. People are motivated by corruption, Bobby. Chances are, you have a good reason for wanting that journal now."

"Well, the police never really determined how Lenny died. At least Papa was never satisfied and Charles says people lie about it. I even think I might have caused his accident. I know Charles was mixed up in it."

"You feel guilty about something you did before he died, but you also think someone else could have caused his accident. So you want to find the guilty person and clear yourself in your own eyes. God! Bobby. What could be more reasonable than that? See? And you're ashamed of it. That proves it's a good reason."

"How do you know how to figure out all this stuff?"

"My mother has a degree in psychology, but now she's a full-time housewife. She says that you just find the right motive and start backtracking. It's like unraveling a sweater. Just find the right emotional thread and pull. You've had the right thread but you wouldn't pull it. Daddy doesn't like this way of thinking. He calls it gossip. You should hear him when she tries to psychoanalyze him. He says all that degree means is that she's a educated mess. I don't have the education. It just comes natural to me."

"So what do I ask Helen?"

"Since you're asking questions about things that happened at the funeral, questions that she won't answer, she's probably worried that either you just found the journal or are looking for it. You know she's looking for it, and chances are, Charles is too." And then she gets real wide eyed.

"That's it! There's the answer."

"The answer to what?"

"Your question! Helen slapped Charles at Lenny's funeral because he asked her if she knew where Lenny's journal was. Now, she probably still feels guilty and thinks there's more behind your question than there is."

"I don't know. All this sounds far fetched to me. But, you know, Papa was mad at Charles during the funeral too. He tried to run Charles and the rest of the Kunze's off."

"Wow! So your papa knows more than he's telling too."

"More about what?"

"More about what went on between Helen and Charles."

"Well, maybe so. He had to have a reason for being mad at Charles."

"So ask him."

I just shake my head. "I tried that. Papa doesn't answer questions about Charles. Every time I mention Charles, Papa says something about wishing he'd killed him."

"Gosh, Bobby. This does sound serious."

"So, what should I do?"

"Helen's waiting for your next move. Trust me, Bobby, she'd love for you to say you don't know where the journal is. Even if you say that you have it, she'd really feel good because that'd mean you've known what was in the journal all these years and nothing happened, so she'd know nothing was in it, nothing damaging to her at any rate."

"Things were happening fast just before Lenny got killed. Helen and Lenny must've had a falling out. Otherwise she would know what's in it. Sounds like she's afraid of what I might know."

"Now you're starting to think. My guess is she's terrified, but not about what you know, about what you might find out. She's terrified that you're going to ask if she knows where you might look for it. Then she'll know that the hunt is on. That's our next step. If she's anything like the rest of us girls, she won't come back with an answer. She'll come back with another question. And that question will tell you where the journal's hidden."

"Okay. I'll have to tell Helen's cousin to ask her. I'll call her tonight." And I thought that would be the end of it. I even closed the dictionary, walked back over and put it on the shelf. But she came with me. There's never an end to anything with Bev.

"I need to study bridges now," I said.

"Let's do it now, Bobby. Let's call her cousin now. We can use the telephone here in the library."

And then I knew that I'd been right. Talking to Bev about this at all was another mistake. I'd trapped myself. "Brenda is Helen's cousin," is all I said.

Her face just exploded with something. I don't know what to call it, but it scared me and for good reason. One thing about Bev. She is predictable. But she did it before I could catch her. And it rang all over the library. Talk about thinking everyone is looking at you. The high school library is a crowded place. And it had never been as quiet as it was following the splat when she slapped me.

)

CHAPTER 28: *Aunt Loretta Knows More and She's Talking*

Bev has been sending me a lot of notes about betrayal, stuff out of the dictionary and encyclopedia. Brenda was more than glad to talk to Helen again.

"There's a skeleton in the attic that needs flushing," is the way Aunt Loretta put it.

Right now, I'm in Aunt Loretta's attic when I thought I'd be sitting at her kitchen table eating a piece of chocolate cake that she made because she knew I was coming over. I like hot chocolate frosting on chocolate cake. Something always stands between me and the goodies. Since Twinkles died, she got herself a grown cat and another dog, a puppy. That sounds okay on the surface, but it doesn't work so good when it rains and her having such a small place. The problem is that it's been raining all the time lately. Her place doesn't usually leak much but today the place is a sieve. And that German shepherd puppy won't leave that tomcat alone.

I'm up here in her attic trying to stop leaks. There's this door in the ceiling that you pull down by one end with a short rope so that a ladder folds out. I climbed up and went to work. I should be on the outside with a bucket of hot tar, but I'd drown with all the rain. I just heard a clap of thunder. Aunt Loretta's passed half her kitchen up here for me to stop the leaks with. She's handed me a can of putty, a putty knife, a butcher knife, a hammer, three sacks of different size nails, a tube of caulking, a bunch of fence slats she found down there somewhere, an old jar stuffed with bee's wax, and a box of matches. I have everything except what I need. The place is musty. A light socket dangles from the beams so I have light, but with all the wires running around up here, I could get electrocuted.

Just about the time I'm ready to climb down, I helped some but not a whole lot, she tells me to look underneath the tarp. Well, let me tell you, there's nothing up here but tarp with puddles in it where it sags. And it covers all these old cardboard boxes that look like they're full to the top with dust.

"I want 'em, Ray. We need 'em all."

So I'm passing them down to her through that hole in the ceiling.

"I've got it. I've got it. I've got it." She says. But when I turn it loose, she drops it, and the box breaks open, and she has a new mess of books and papers all over the floor. I bet I've passed down fifteen boxes. It's cold up here. I wish I'd brought my heavy jacket. If I'd known I was going to be working, I would have put on some work clothes. We don't work when it rains.

When I finally get out of the attic, she says, "Me and Louise have been fighting." And that brings another thunderclap. I don't know why but the older I get, the younger she looks. The other day I asked Mama how old Aunt Loretta is and she said, "Almost thirty-two. Fifteen years older than you." A couple of years ago, I thought she was probably sixty.

So her kitchen looks like she's moving out with all the boxes here on the floor. Or maybe like she's moving in because she's going through those boxes dumping stuff like hell won't have it, has her sleeves rolled to her elbows. "I found it," she says, and she has a picture in her hands. "Look at this." She holds up a photograph in one hand and a beat-up deck of cards in the other. But I'm not looking at the picture or the cards. This is the first time I've ever seen her forearms and the scars all over the insides of both arms that run from her wrists almost to her elbows. Now I know why she always wears long sleeve shirts. Never seen anything so ugly. Who could have done that to her? And then I notice that her left hand doesn't work as good as the right, won't straighten out all the way. I used to think that that was kind of a cute way she had of working her hand. Now I know it's because she can't help it.

"Hershel's been over here complaining that you've been running around with Charles Kunze. If you are, you need to know some things about Charles and the rest of us. Charles knows, so he has an unfair advantage. Louise and Hershel used to be friends with Heidi and Karl. They used to play pinochle together. I kept score for them. If you ask Louise, she'll deny it, but it's true. Here. Look at this." But then she sticks it behind her back. "Promise you won't tell her I showed you this?" And then she shows me a picture of a young Mama and Papa and, sure enough, there's Karl and I guess that's Heidi Kunze but I don't remember her. They're all standing around what looks to be a '36 Ford. Heidi looks kind of pretty.

195

That's when I hear a loud knock and the image I get is that Mama's at the back door and has caught us doing something nasty. That half-grown dog just bristles and lets out with a "Woof." The tomcat spits at him.

Aunt Loretta has to pull three times to get the door open and there's Bev, coming through the back door with a big smile on her face like that smile will make up for something she's done wrong. "I couldn't figure out where the front of this place is. Bobby here?" She knows the answer because she's looking past Aunt Loretta and sees me plain as day. She comes in soaked to the skin and dripping rainwater off her eyelashes.

"How did you find me?" I ask.

"Your mama. I think she'd have said anything to get me off her front porch."

Aunt Loretta first looks like she's mad then gets a hand towel for Bev to dry off with and runs to her bedroom with the sniffles.

Bev looks at me like, what's wrong with her? "Introduce me," she says. But when Aunt Loretta comes back in, Bev beats me to the punch. "I'm Bobby's girlfriend, Bev."

Aunt Loretta acts like she didn't hear anything. She holds up another picture, this one in a frame, and she's rolled her sleeves back down and buttoned them.

"This is me and my sweetheart eighteen years ago," she says, smiling with her lips closed. And then she puts it down, turns her back because her face is the brightest shade of red humanly possible.

But Bev won't let it alone. She goes over to her and takes the picture from her. "Why, Aunt Loretta, you were absolutely gorgeous. And who is the young man?"

But she is not answering that. She jerks the picture back, holds it tight to her chest, and with her head down, walks back in the bedroom.

"Is she okay?" Bev asks.

I shake my head no. "Never has been," I whisper.

"I've seen that old boyfriend of hers before, but I can't remember where," says Bev.

"She didn't let me get a good look at it."

Aunt Loretta comes back in, goes straight to the cupboard, gets out three plates. Then she jerks open a drawer and dumps the awfulest mess of forks, spoons, and knives on the table. She turns to Bev. "Bobby and I were about to have a party. Will you join us?" And the 'Will you join us?' has the strangest formal sound coming out of her mouth.

"Can I make the coffee?" asks Bev.

So while the pot's perking, Aunt Loretta rummages through another box and comes up with another picture. She just loves pictures. And since Bev came in, she's hardly said a word, as if she's turned into a deaf-mute. But now she's showing Bev a picture of a little girl.

"How old were you?" asks Bev.

Aunt Loretta holds up three fingers on her good right hand.

"It was taken on your birthday, wasn't it?"

And she shakes her head yes but looks down at the floor, then takes the picture from Bev and goes into her bedroom again.

"Do you realize what the occasion is, Bobby?" asks Bev.

"What occasion?"

"This one. What we are celebrating."

"This isn't an occasion. This is just Aunt Loretta. She's just strange like this."

"God! You are the most insensitive human being on earth. Men! The cake's not for you, dummy. It's her birthday. This is a birthday party."

Just before we eat cake, Bev sings happy birthday to Aunt Loretta, with me humming a word or two every now and then. I don't know why she didn't bring her pom-poms. I'm beginning to think there's more tears from Aunt Loretta than rain outside. After a couple of courses of 'For she's a jolly good lady,' Bev asks her how long it's been since she had a birthday party, but can't get an answer.

Bev finally answers for her. "You haven't had one since you were three, have you?"

She just shakes her head no.

We are on our third pot of coffee and the cake is cold but still good. My hands are trembling and my armpits could match some of the bigger puddles outside.

"Charles is a little funny in his drawers, too." Is what Aunt Loretta has just said, as another thunderclap rocks the house.

"What?" I ask

"He likes guys, Bobby," says Bev, "sexually."

"What do you mean, sexually? You mean like queer stuff?" Then I start sweating when I remember what Charles did to me when we were casing Mary's house. He put his hand between my legs, and I didn't say anything about it. Charles probably thinks I liked it.

"Lenny wasn't like that," says Aunt Loretta. "But Charles has a little streak of it in him. When Lenny found out, he laughed till he split his sides. And he used to taunt Charles with it. They used to come over here to help me before you got old enough, Ray. Wasn't a word out of Lenny's mouth that didn't kick Charles down a little lower. People'll say things around me they won't say around anyone else. It's like I'm not even there."

"That casts a new light on what happened between Helen and Charles," says Bev. "Lenny's journal is starting to sound more and more interesting all the time." Then she gives me a mean look. "You talk to Brenda again about it and I'll strangle you." Then she loosens up a little. "Leroy had a problem too, Bobby. Or maybe Charles made him feel like he did. I knew there was something going on with him. Leroy was reckless."

"What do you mean, reckless?" I ask.

Bev thinks for a minute. "Charles must have been doing something sexual to Leroy. I've had guys work their stuff on me, but Leroy was desperate. I've never had anyone beg. Tried to talk to me about his problem but couldn't find the words. He kept saying, 'You don't know what Charles is doing to me.' Charles had a lot to do with Leroy getting killed."

"I always kinda figured that I was responsible."

"You think you're responsible for everything bad that happens, don't you?"

Aunt Loretta butts in again. "Charles blames Louise for his mother getting killed. Charles believes Louise drove Heidi to suicide."

"What was the trouble between Mama and Mrs. Kunze?"

"You better brace yourself for this one, Ray." She gets out of the chair she's sitting in and walks to the kitchen sink real slow. She has her back to us so I can hardly hear her voice. "It was Hershel, that brother of mine. Hershel had an affair of the heart with Heidi."

"Oh, Jesus," says Bev. Then she gets up and goes to stand beside Aunt Loretta. "That's not a very easy thing to say about your brother, is it?"

"Karl Kunze is a very forgiving man. Louise isn't. And she didn't blame Hershel for what happened between him and Heidi. She blamed Heidi. And some of the Kunze's say what Louise did was the cause of Heidi's death. And I'm not going to say what that was. Cause I've already said too much."

"I think Charles is mad at all us Hammers. He's after Trish. She was baby-sitting for Grant Pierson's kids the other night while they went bowling. I drove by their place, and sure enough, there was Charles' Jeep parked out front. I've tried to talk to him but he won't leave her alone."

"I've never mentioned it to you," says Bev, "but I've talked to her about it too. She won't listen to me either."

"If your Papa finds out about him seeing, Patricia," says Aunt Loretta, "he'll kill Charles for sure."

One last picture. Or maybe I should say three pictures in a bunch. This time Aunt Loretta won't let me see them. Bev is just really impressed at first, and then I hear something about a baby and a lot of ooing and aaing. I just realized something while those two are gooing at each other. And I never would've believed it if I hadn't seen it with my own eyes because Bev is a beautiful girl. But I realized how much Bev looks like Aunt Loretta. And then Bev, now get this mind you, Bev hugs Aunt Loretta, like she just realized she was her best friend. And now it's Bev who's crying.

It's dark and me and Bev are sitting in her daddy's Buick just outside Aunt Loretta's house. I keep seeing Aunt Loretta's shadow move back and forth on her kitchen curtain. Bev has the radio on and Tab Hunter is singing "Young Love." This Buick still smells new, and Bev tells me how much she likes making out to the sound of rain on a car roof.

"When did she try to commit suicide?" she asks.

"You saw her arms."

"Hard to miss that."

"Why'd you hunt me down today?" I ask. "Why'd you come over here?"

She smiles at me, bites her bottom lip. Her eyes are dark but I can still see a sparkle. "Guilt," is all she says, and then gives me a slurpy tongue kiss.

★

I'm laying in bed beside Curt, thinking about all the things that happened at Aunt Loretta's and staring off into the dark down the hall. The thing that bothers me the most is how deep I'm getting involved with Bev. She just keeps pushing on everything where I'm concerned. She's the stickiest person I've ever seen. Now she knows Aunt Loretta, and by all appearances, they really like each other. At least Mama still won't have anything to do with her.

"Bobby?" asks Curt. "You've sure been quiet lately."

He always startles me when I think he's asleep. "Have a lot on my mind."

"You still running around with Charles?"

"I don't know. After what I learned over at Aunt Loretta's today, I think I'm getting in over my head with him."

"He was nice to me when he brought me home on Halloween night."

"I bet he was. He seems that way at first. But stay away from him. You can't trust him. You can't trust yourself around him. I think he's after all of us."

"You're going to stay away from him?"

"No. I have business with him. And I do mean business. It's sure not fun."

The things that Aunt Loretta told me today are really bothering me. I don't know what to think about my papa. I sure can't talk to Curt about that. So here I am starting it too. I have to keep things from Curt, the same as Mama and Papa have kept all this from me. Sounds like trouble's been brewing in this family for a long time. Maybe Charles has some reason to not like Mama and Papa. Still, none of it answers the question of what really happened to Lenny. I've been thinking about what Bev said about finding the right thread and pulling on it. The problem is, if you pull long enough, you destroy the sweater.

CHAPTER 29: *Fighting Niggers*

Charles' milk barn is lit like a jack-o-lantern. It stands a few yards from his little shack. I was hoping to get here before sundown, but it's already dark. He's standing at the far end of the barn, has one cow still milking, a huge Holstein, and he's with her now, patting her on the side and rubbing on her. A stainless-steel milker with four black-rubber suction cups heaves on her udder. Just as I walk into the barn, he winks at me. I hear a bunch of calves bawling in a holding pen out back.

I feel like I shouldn't be here. I was hoping to see Charles alone. Thomas Powers has a flat-ended shovel and pushing manure into the gutter. Wayne Hickman follows Thomas with a stiff-bristled shop broom, and Eugene Waggoner hoses the place down. The pale light from two naked bulbs overhead makes Wayne's red hair glow, casts shadows. Looks like they're trying to get this cow milking over with so they can go somewhere. Melvin Swensen steps out of the little brick milk house that sits beside the barn. He has an empty milker in his hand. He just nodded at me, but when he first saw me, he frowned. I came to see Charles because I have some bones to pick with him. But all these kids are here. Feel like I'm crashing a party. How come all my friends are here, and nobody told me anything about it? I wish I had a date with Bev.

When Charles hits the barn lights that jack-o-lantern winks out and we walk in the dark toward his shack, all of us in a crowd. Charles comes to me.

"How you doing tonight, Bobby?"

"I need to talk to you, Charles."

We walk on to his shack without talking. He stops just outside his front door. The rest stand looking at us.

"You got a problem, I'd like to help."

"I mean there's some things we need to get straight. I need some questions answered."

"Sounds serious, alright. Come inside while I get dressed." He turns to the others. "Soon as I wash up, we'll be right out." Charles stands his boots to the left of the steps and pulls the screen door open for me. "Go on in. Make yourself to home. It's not much but at least it's mine." He lets the screen door bang to, closes the wood door, has to shove it. The little window in it rattles.

Charles doesn't have a kitchen or a bedroom separate. Everything's in his living room except the bathroom, and it's just off the kitchen. Actually the whole room looks like one big kitchen because the stove and sink are on the left wall and the refrigerator is in the corner on the right wall. He must have a cleaning lady. It hits me right then what it would be like for me to have my own place. I haven't even thought of it before. My own place. I could come and go as I please. If I had problems, I'd just walk away from them. Charles' life always seems so free, nobody to tell him what to do.

"You want to grab a quick beer? One in the icebox. Don't let the others see it because I don't have enough for everybody." He jerks off his shirt, throws it in a corner, grabs another one out of a small chest of drawers. His bed is pushed up against the far wall, made up with square corners.

"What do you know about our parents being friends years ago?" I ask.

"A little. But god, Bobby, this is heavy stuff to start out a five minute conversation. I don't know that this is the time." He's at the kitchen sink, talking through the water splashing on his face. "Besides, you're mad at me."

"I'm not mad, Charles. I just need to get things straight."

He comes at me drying his face on a towel. "Then why're you all puffed up? Loosen up a little, Bobby. Come with us tonight. We're just going to Fresno. You and me need to have this talk. But another time."

"I don't feel quite right about going because I wasn't invited."

"Well, I don't know. Maybe we made a mistake. Come with us anyway." He walks over to me and slaps me on the back. "I know there's problems between our families. Always has been. Problems between you and me, too. But what the hell, life is full of trouble."

When he says things like this, the way I feel about him seems silly. I turn away from him though. "It's about you and Trish," I say, but don't have enough force behind it.

202

He follows me, sticks out his hand. "Later. Come on. Give me some meat."

"No, Charles." And I walk away from him, stand by his old white refrigerator. "You're not brushing me off like that. And I <u>am</u> mad at you. You're messing around her again. You were with her when she was baby-sitting the Pearson's kids the other night. I want you to stay away from my sister. And this business about Leroy. I want to know what you were doing to him just before he got killed."

"Jesuschrist, Bobby. How many times are we going to have this conversation? This is old stuff. I wish you'd shutup about me and Trish. But now I can tell, I'm not going to get that wish. You're going to keep on and keep on, just drive it in the ground. Okay, I'll talk to you about our family and about Trish. We can have it out about her if you want. But we're going to do it on my terms. And now you're adding Leroy getting killed to our problems. I though you were carrying the guilt. But come with us tonight and I promise, we'll get something straight between you and me before the night's over."

We're back outside now. I wish I hadn't let Charles talk me into it. We're all standing around a mud puddle. The only light we have comes from Charles porch light. I'm using the side of my shoe sole to cut little ditches so that water from the big puddle runs over into a little puddle. Thomas leans against his daddy's new Olds on the other side of the puddle. Charles is talking to him.

"We need a fast car tonight. One with a good top end."

"My daddy checks the odometer," says Thomas. "He doesn't like me going out of town. I know how he feels about his Olds. It's our family car, Charles. Besides it's low on gas, and it's new. Not a car to be going to fight niggers in."

Maybe I should second-guess this trip to Fresno. Sounds like a mess of trouble to me. I'm not sure taking to Charles is going to be worth it. Eugene comes over, stands beside me.

"We'll disconnect the odometer," says Charles. "You're just making excuses."

"Let's take the old Hudson over there," says Thomas pointing to the garage where Lenny's car is parked. "We never take yours anywhere. You foot the bill for a change."

Charles smiles a little. "I like your attitude, Thomas. Maybe I haven't been holding up my end of this. And that Hudson. If there's one thing that a Hudson's good for, it's fighting niggers."

"If we'll be fighting niggers, we won't need any wimps along either." It's Wayne putting his two cents in. He's off to my left sitting on the hood of his dad's Plymouth with his feet on the bumper. I can just barely see Wayne's eyes in the dark. The porch light is shinning on the right side of his face. He peals splinters off a piece of wood with a pocketknife, throws them out in the middle of the puddle. He looks at me while he talks, but think he must be talking about Eugene.

"I don't know about this fighting colored people," says Eugene. "I didn't sign up for that."

"You don't know for sure that we'll be fighting coloreds," is what Thomas says. "There's lots of things to do in Fresno. We may meet a car load of girls at Stan's Drive-In and end up all getting laid."

"Shit. I can get laid here in Chowchilla," and now it's Melvin working on Thomas. He's standing next to Thomas, leaning against Thomas' car. Stands about to his shoulder. He takes a drag and flips a glowing cigarette into the middle of the puddle. It goes out with a spit. "That's why we're going to Fresno. To fight niggers. If anybody here's chickenshit, he better go home now." He has his hands in his pockets, just looking at the ground, kicking mud in the puddle. "I don't give a shit how big or little he is, if he's not willing to fight, he's not going with us."

"We'll be fighting niggers alright," says Charles. "But there's no need to worry, Eugene. We can take care of you. My Hudson doesn't have any gas in it either, Thomas. But gas is just not a problem. There's little pockets of natural gas all over the countryside. And we've got an Oklahoma credit card."

"How come we're going to fight colored people, Charles?" I ask. "I thought you and Thomas liked coloreds the way you buddy up to Chelsey."

"Chelsey's a special nigger," Charles tells me. "He's a white nigger. I'll have to educate you on Chelsey. He's not a nigger you want to fight either, unless you have suicidal tendencies."

I look over at Eugene. Ask him real quiet like, "How'd you get mixed up in this?"

He leans over close to me. "Easy," he says. "I thought we were going rabbit hunting."

"Sometime I'll have to tell you about rabbit hunting with Charles."

Chapter 29: *Fighting Niggers*

"You'll get a kick out of this, Bobby," says Charles. "Lenny was the best nigger fighter in the state."

"You asking him along?" says Wayne. "Goddamn, Charles. I'm not concerned about Eugene. But, Bobby? He can't hold up his end of his own dick."

★

We siphoned a little gas out of Herb Coleman's red tractor for Charles' Hudson, and Charles has just pulled onto the main street of Fresno's colored district, moving slow. "Okay, this is it," he says. "Let's make it good. We won't get another chance." Up ahead are these low flat-top buildings like I've seen in western movies, all looking like they could use a bucket of paint. Not many cars parked on the street. One car doesn't have any tires and the hood is hanging off a fender.

"Niggers keep coming in and out of those buildings like bees at a hive," says Melvin. He's leaning up over the backseat, and I feel his breath on the back of my neck. "Come on, Charles. Let's get 'em."

I'm sitting in the front seat between Charles, who's driving this Hudson, and Thomas riding shotgun. Eugene's in the backseat sitting between Melvin and Wayne.

"Wait'll the street clears a little," Charles says. "Good god! Niggers everywhere. Don't you just hate those sonsabitches? They multiply just like rabbits. Okay, let's do it. I'll go slow." He hits the horn so the street clears a little. "We don't want to kill any of 'em out here in public. Everybody pick out a nigger and chew on him. You'll have to piss 'em off if you want a fight. Watch for cops, Eugene."

I don't know what to do. I'm looking for something to be busy at, sitting here in the middle. Glad I'm not by a window.

"Lean on over in front of Thomas," Charles tells me. "Pick out a big buck for yourself."

I guess I'll get my chance. And here we go. Charles sounds the horn again and a few of them scatter. One old man with a bad leg jerks into a run for a few steps till he clears the road. Just as we get to the crowd that's separating for us, Charles slows.

"Hey, motherfucker, how about a fight?" Charles asks this big black colored man with bushy hair and a little gray at the temples. A surprised look is all Charles gets back.

Oh shit! I think, I can't believe it. That black sonofabitch is a grown

205

man. And huge. Charles can't want to fight him. But the colored guy just backs up, walks to the curb like he's afraid. "What you got, boy? Knives and chains?" he shouts at Charles.

Thomas looks at this fat colored kid. He's big but couldn't be over twelve. "Hey, asshole. You want to fight?" asks Thomas.

"Na, sah. I surely don't," he says back, just like Thomas asked him for the time and he didn't have a wrist watch.

I see one that's tall and thin, about my age. He's good looking, has his hair parted on the left and enough brown grease to pack a set of wheel bearings. He has the best-looking colored girl I've ever seen following about a half step behind him. She has on a red silk dress so tight she has to shimmy to get any walking motion and enough loose jewelry to out rattle a snake. Seeing her, I get my courage up, so I lean over in front of Thomas.

"Hey, mister, you want to fight." I didn't mean it like that, but it just comes out sort of respectful. I hear Eugene laughing in the backseat and Charles cusses.

"Hell yes, I want a fight," says that good-looking colored guy. "I got a girl here too. You want a piece of ass? Ten bucks, baby face. The best ass in town. The best a honky ever had. I'll bust your face while she busts your balls."

I sort of sit back not knowing what else to say. I know I'm going to catch it for what I just said, but I can't take my eyes off all that chocolate skin in a red dress.

Then Wayne jumps into it. "You can keep the girl cause she's got the clap. I want you, motherfucker. I want to bust up your face just because you think you're such a hot looking piece of stinking shit. Come on, asshole, get a car, out in the country, right now, you and me, pretty boy. You and me and all the rest of the niggers you can round up."

"Hey, Clorisa. Look. It's Tom Sawyer. What a trick you could turn on him, honey. Look at the red hair and freckles. He's already hot for you, baby."

I'm aiming to keep my mouth shut since I'm already in so much trouble, so I turn around to look at Melvin who has a live one on his side. Charles has slowed a little, so this colored guy makes a run for Melvin. Melvin sticks his head out the window, then stands up so, above the waist, he's outside the car.

"Slow down, Charles. This nigger wants some action right now and I have just what he needs. Come to me, nigger, I want you real bad. Slow down, goddamnit. Let him catch up."

Charles slows some more so he gets close enough that they take a wild swing at each other but only crack knuckles. Another one runs up behind and pounds his fist in the middle of the trunk, makes a big thud, even rings a little.

"Hit the gas," says Thomas. "They're everywhere. Let's get out of here."

Charles hits the breaks instead, and Melvin almost falls the rest of the way out the window. "Whoa," he says, still hanging onto the door handle. Eugene has hold of his belt loops, pulling hard. Charles has us going about thirty in reverse and the coloreds are scattering like a flock of chickens.

"Come on, you black sonofabitches, get a car. We'll wait on you," shouts Melvin, then he crawls back in. "Pull over, Charles. This nigger's coming back. He wants to fight as bad as I do. I can see it in his eyes."

"We'll get swarmed," says Charles He slows a little further on when we reach some trees and houses. "We've got to get them to chase us. I don't like the odds right now."

"Damn it, Charles, I said stop. I tell you, that one's coming back."

"I know he's coming back, but he's not in a car."

"I don't think so," says Thomas, looking through the back window. "He just walked into a bar."

"He went into the bar to get some more niggers. I tell you he's coming."

"He went into a bar to get a shotgun. When he comes back out we won't want any part of him." Two more blocks down the street, Charles pulls over, gets out to check the trunk lid. Starts cussing, gets back in, strange thing is, he has a smile on his face. "Niggers are more fun than a funeral. They're not afraid of anything. Maybe we should go back, take a chance on getting shot at."

"I don't think so," says Thomas. "I'm not voting for chancing it. I'm through with this colored stuff. Let's go to Stan's and see if we can find some girls."

"What do you think, Eugene?" Charles asks. "You want a fight or a piece of ass?"

"Oh, goddamn," says Wayne. "Why ask Eugene. The second biggest chickenshit in the car?"

Melvin is boiling too. "You mean that's it?" he says. "That's all there's going to be? You drag me all the way down here to fight niggers, I got one

207

in the street waiting for me right now and we back off. That's it? Now you want to go to a goddamn drive-in to get a piece of ass?"

Eugene gives a little nervous laugh. "I don't know if I could handle a fight, and I don't think there's much chance of me getting a piece of ass at Stan's. I've never seen a car hop serve one on a tray, but I sure could eat a cheeseburger."

Even Melvin has to laugh at that. "Ah shit. Let's go get a piece of ass and a cheeseburger," he says. I can tell. Melvin feels better already.

"There's more niggers in Fresno. They're not all here in nigger town," says Charles. "We'll get another chance to fight. But as a consolation prize, we'll make a run through Fairmead on the way home."

I'm wondering what he means by that. Fairmead is a little town of colored people just outside Chowchilla.

"Who called that nigger, mister?" Melvin wants to know.

"It was a new Bobbyism," says Wayne. "Who in the hell else would be dumb enough to call a pimp mister?"

"You have to admit, it worked though. The pimp offered him the jackpot, a fight and a piece of ass for ten bucks."

"Bobby won it but sure wouldn't claim it."

"That's an old Bobbyism. 'Can't use a piece of ass.'"

"He was playing hard to get, holding out for that pimp to throw in a pack of cigarettes and a fifth of Jim Beam."

"Do you think he would have done it, if the nigger'd thrown in a load of watermelon?"

"How about a pint of brown hair grease?"

"A shoe shine?"

"What would it take, Bobby?"

"Bobby?"

★

We're sitting in the car at Stan's Drive-in with the radio tuned to Stan's Private Line, listening to dedications for the next song. The carhop just took my dedication to Bev. I hope she's home listening to KMJ 560. This place is big time. I've never seen so many lights in one place. It's laid out in a circle and cars are piled up three deep around it. Takes a while to get out if you're up front. We are in the middle.

"We could have used Leroy with the niggers," says Wayne. "He could have conned them into fighting us."

208

"Ya," says Melvin. "He'd a stole the black skin right off their back."

There's four girls in the car next to us on the right, and Melvin's been talking to them. Wayne's not much with the girls.

"Where you guys from?" this fat girl in the backseat wants to know.

"Santa Cruz," says Melvin, without even thinking. "We're in Fresno because we're going to Fresno State next year. Thomas here's got a full academic scholarship in astronomy. He's going to be an astronomer. He's got brains pouring out his ears. But what we all like to do most is surfing. We just mostly surf all the time."

"Where does he get stuff like that?" I ask Thomas.

"Lies come easier to him than the truth."

"So what are you good at," the driver asks Melvin, and the girls in the backseat start laughing.

"I've been waiting for you to ask me about that," says Melvin, and he pops the back door open, steps out and, sure enough, he's peaking in the window of their car, talking about things that I can't hear. Thomas pops his door open.

Melvin comes back, sticks his head a window. "Come on, you guys. These girls are eager."

Charles turns to Eugene and Wayne. "Bobby and I have something planned. So we're going to be leaving you for a while. Aren't we, Bobby? You guys go with these girls."

"Let me go too, Charles," says Wayne. "I don't want a girl. I'm up for anything you can throw at me."

"There's no place for three," Charles tells Wayne. "Could be a little dangerous."

"First I've heard of it," I say. "What the hell is this?"

"I promised you earlier we'd settle the problems between us. You game?"

"Where're we going?"

"How about it? It's either you or Wayne. We'll get something straight between us, like you were talking about earlier. Get a little action on the side maybe. You ready for it?" He gives me a gentle elbow.

I'm thinking about the time we were casing Mary's house and Charles put his hand on my crotch. He better not pull something like that again. Maybe I should let Wayne try him out.

"He's a dud," says Wayne. "I'm on my way, Charles. You catch up." And he scoots over into the middle of backseat like he was set for life.

"Okay. Let's do it," I finally manage.

"Meet us back here in three hours," says Charles. "Hop out, Wayne."

"That'll be midnight," says Wayne, crawling out the door like a beat dog. "What the hell is going on. You bring us out here and dump us. I though we were going to fight niggers."

"Find your own fight, if you want one. I'm no baby sitter. Any kid in these cars here will either fight or fuck you."

"No, Charles," says Wayne. "Bobby's just doing it because I want to go so bad. I'll go, I tell you. Hammer, you sonofabitch. Feed him to the dogs, Charles." He walks over and kicks a tire. "Damn!"

CHAPTER 30: *With Charles in Nigger Town*

We're ten miles out of town on this little dirt road, just pulled off the blacktop a hundred yards back. I've never seen a place so dark. Three grown colored me were standing in the road back where we turned. I see plowed fields and a peach orchard nearby. Maybe an orange grove, too dark to tell. Charles pulls into a yard with a big house and lots of little houses around it. No lights on inside. Almost like a tiny town. A country store just down the lane.

Charles stops at the big house with a flock of colored kids chasing each other in the dark. Two dogs, one a big black bear-like dog, the other small and rat-like, come out like they want to eat the car. Around back, I see a fire burning. Charles kills the lights, turns off the motor.

"Wait here," he says as he gets out and walks toward the front of the house.

Those dogs don't pay any attention to Charles. It's like they don't even see him. But that big bear is up on my window, so much I pull back from it, even lock the door. He has his snout all over the window spreading spit and snot so that it runs down into the sill, his teeth clinking against the glass. That rat-like dog hits all the tires with his leg raised.

Charles comes back. Looks like bad news. "She's moved," he says.

"I thought you said we were coming out here to talk about family problems," I say.

Charles just ignores me, starts the car, and we pull a little deeper into the neighborhood with the lights off. A little drizzle starts to build on the windshield. Seems like every house here either has a fire in front or out back. The black dog stays with us, madder than ever now that he sees we're staying. Charles pulls up at a little shack, only this isn't a little shack like my home with stucco and a tile roof. This place is made of wood and as far as I can tell, doesn't have windows. The wood has never been painted. The front porch is as wide as the front, stands on legs two feet off the ground except for one corner that's propped up on cinder blocks and a used tire. No steps going up. Out comes this skinny colored woman in a thin summer dress, acts like she was expecting us.

"It's okay to get out now," says Charles. "The dogs don't bite."

"Oh, Charlie, Charlie," she says. "I knew you'd be back."

I wait a second before I pop the door open and wish I hadn't hesitated because now Charles is a ways ahead of me and that black sonofabitch has gone crazy. He's backed off but keeps making runs at me. Almost knocked me down. He has every dog in the village barking at me. I hear some from three blocks down the lane. So I just ignore his ass, won't even look at him, walk toward Charles and that colored woman that he's now kissing on as if she's his wife. But that goddamn dog won't leave me alone. He's barking and wheeling around like he'll tear my legs off. He comes at me from behind. I feel him nip the back of my shoe first, then he nudges me between the legs with his nose.

"He's mouthing me, Charles. Can you get him off of me?" The dog has his nose up my butt, and then I feel this gigantic pinch on the inside of my thigh. "He bit me, Charles, I tell you. He bit me."

"Git away from 'im, shoo," that colored woman says. I think she's talking to me. "Well, Charlie, you finely done what Prissy ast and brought her a white boy."

So now I'm out back of that wood shack warming my hands on the fire. Charles disappeared ten minutes ago with the woman. So have all the kids. They left me with this girl that keeps stacking wood on the fire and laughing like there's something funny about a big fire. "This fire's yourn, Bobby Ray," is the way she put it. She has on a pair of tight Levis and an old shirt tied in front around her middle. Leaves a little brown skin between her shirt and pants. First she wants to play catch, has this old tetherball that is too soft to bounce. So we pass it back and forth a little. Then she holds it, comes to me, teases me about the ball then starts to run from me. I chase her a little, but she lets me catch her. She bounces that ball off my knee real quick, picks it up again. The next time she starts to throw at me from close range, I put my hands up to catch it.

"No, Bobby Ray," she says. "Jus let me bounce it off you."

So I stand here and she comes up close, bounces it off my chest, each shoulder, one at a time, top of my head. I catch it when she throws it at my stomach.

"Use to live outside a Chowchilla," she says. "Ma brother still does. Lives with his pappy." So she comes up close, takes my hand. "What you want do now, Bobby Ray?"

It's like she fell in love with my name. I don't know why Charles introduced me to her using my full name. So she starts swinging me by the arms, us moving around in a circle. Part of the time she has that fire on her face and then she's black again. We get going so fast, feels like she's going to pull my arms out of my shoulder sockets. "Wheee!" she says. I get a little dizzy, have trouble standing straight. Her hands are like soft leather, smooth like the Naugahyde on my car seats. We stand side by side looking into the fire, the flames licking at the wood, glowing coals down inside. They have a pot on with water for coffee. Has some ashes floating on top. She runs her hand along the back of my shoulders, down my arm. Still feel a little light rain. She got rid of the dogs, but I still can't keep from watching for them.

"Come on. Show you where I stay."

I have my arm around her waist as we walk to a building that's about the size of an outhouse. It doesn't have a door, just an open space. Some naked bedsprings sit on cinder blocks with a sheet of plywood on top. Two tattered quilts laid on that. Inside is not as big as I thought.

I don't want my hands on her, but they just find her skin by themselves. They want the swoops her body makes. I shouldn't be in this town. I don't know how old she is either. But this time I can't stop myself. I've never wanted anyone so bad.

"Don't have a bra, Bobby Ray. I'm not like a white girl." Her mouth tastes like vinegar. A little later, she says, "Don't have panties either."

I smell the wood fire burning. Hear the popping just outside the door, see the flickers on the wall inside. Smell hot coffee.

"All I need is for you to member," she says. "Bobby Ray, Bobby Ray. Jus member me."

Everywhere she touches me, I burn. I feel like a blacksmith pounding hot metal. She feels like hot coals inside.

I don't know if I fell asleep, but the next thing I hear is a shout. I didn't catch the words. The dogs start barking again. As I go back out through that hole she has for a door, I see a colored boy coming out of the dark toward me, moving fast.

"What you doin in there, white boy? What you doing with my lil sister off to yourself?" He's taller than I am and a lot thinner.

I try to move on around him back to the Hudson. I hear shouts from the other side of the house, hear Charles. I don't need a fight here, that's for sure. But he won't let me past.

"Chelsey," and now it's the colored girl from behind me, "leave 'im alone. He's my business."

Oh, shit! I think. I hope this isn't the Chelsey I know. I think it is, but it's just a little too dark to see for sure. Chelsey is standing off against me. I walk around him, head for the front of the house with her walking between him and me, keeps pushing him back. I get a good look at him in the fire. Sure enough, it's the Chelsey I go to school with. I shouldn't be here. This is a place for colored folks, not white kids.

Prissy comes up from behind, pushes me to the side.

"Go on," she says to me. "You be leaving now."

"You shamin yourself with a white boy," says Chelsey. And then it's like he just recognized me, and he looks real puzzled. "Bobby Hammer? Is that you?"

"How you doing, Chelsey?" I ask, but the words don't seem like the ones I should be using.

"Git out, Chelsey. I don't need you fussin at us." Prissy sounds a lot older now than I thought she was.

"Can't let him git away with it, Prissy."

"You talkin crazy, Chelsey."

Charles and three colored men are leaning on the Hudson with their arms up on the roof, shooting the breeze. Charles is on the opposite side of the car from the coloreds. They turn to look when they hear us coming. Charles' colored girl is inside behind the wheel. Charles is petting that big black dog.

"Chel's flushed out the second honky," is what the tallest one says when he sees me coming. "He always has had a nose for white trash. Where's old Zulu? He'll make a meal out of this one."

"Bobby," and it's Chelsey calling me from behind. "I thought you were my friend. My little sister's not too smart. You're gonna have to pay for this one."

"Git off the car, Homer," says Prissy. "These boys are leaving."

"Thirteen and already bossin the men folk," is what Homer says back. "Zulu! Get over here. You dumb old mutt." That bear-like sonofabitch Charles is petting on comes running to Homer.

214

"Sic'em," says Homer and he's pointing at me.

But a pistol fires and old Zulu yelps. It sounds so close, I figure someone has shot me, but then I see it was Charles firing over the hood of that Hudson with Lenny's little silver pistol.

"Get the dog away from Bobby or I'll kill him," says Charles.

But the coloreds don't have to do anything because that pistol has already taken the fight out of old Zulu.

"Get in the car," Charles tells me. "You calm down, Chelsey. Nobody's been hurt here." Doesn't look like he's wanting to stay here though.

"Charles," and now it's Chelsey talking, "you shouldn't a brought him out here. I'll see you at school, Bobby.

Prissy is pushing me around to the driver's side of the car, and when I reach for the back door handle, she gets there first and slides to the far side of the backseat, rolls down the window, starts chewing on Chelsey again. Charles is in the front seat and has pushed his colored girl over, started the car and already has it rolling.

"You better leave my sister here," says Chelsey as we pull away. "Maggie, you get back here too." Then he bounces a clod off the top of the Hudson.

Charles drives a couple of miles before he stops in the dark, and it gets real quiet. I hear the old Hudson creaking, settling down. Charles and his colored girl whisper up front for a couple of minutes, then disappear below the front seat. In a little bit I smell the awlfulest smell two human beings ever made.

Now that I know Prissy's just thirteen, I don't feel about her quite like I did. Curt's thirteen. I cuddle up with her again, but something is missing. And Chelsey is mad as hell at me. I can't say I blame him. Me and Prissy just lay down in the backseat for a while waiting for them to get through. Prissy is as warm as a slept-in bed, has sour armpits. I feel her breasts rising and falling against my chest, feel her heart beat on my lips against her neck. Then I hear a little low-level crying up front. They whisper a little. Maybe some whimpering.

"You want to switch, Bobby?" asks Charles.

"Switch what?"

"Switch girls."

That's what I though he meant. "I don't think so."

Prissy is shaking her head no about forty miles an hour.

"Come on. Let's switch." And he raises up off his colored girl.

215

"No, Charlie," Maggie says.

"Get in the back."

I hear them pulling on their clothes and she's crying.

I raise up off of Prissy.

He reaches back where we are, grabs Prissy's arm. "Come on over the seat," he tells her.

"She doesn't want to," I say.

"It's not her decision."

"I'm saying no, too," I tell him.

He pops open his door and grabs his girl by the arm, drags her out of the car. "Jesuschrist. What am I going to have to do to keep this going?" He jerks my back door open.

I step out in the cold air facing him. His colored girl walks around behind me to get in the backseat. I hear the back door on the other side pop open.

"This isn't right and I'm not doing it," I tell him.

"Bobby," he says, and he has both hands raised like he just gave up. He's searching for words. "You're on my territory now. Quit fucking with me, if you know what's good for you."

"Listen, goddamn you, Charles. Stop it! Will you? I'm going to hit you, you sonofabitch. You can't do this to me." And I wish I'd said he couldn't do it to Prissy, but I made a mistake.

"But, Bobby," and me being mad seems to have calmed him. "Look. It's already settled. The girls have decided."

I look inside and sure enough. Prissy is already sitting in the front seat. Now why did she want to go and do that?

"Get back in the car before we have real trouble," Charles tells me. "I've never seen such a trouble maker as you."

So I'm sitting on one side of the backseat and Charles' colored girl is sitting on the other. She just told me her name is Maggie. Charles is kissing on Prissy up front but she's not helping him any. In a little bit their heads disappear below the seat. He keeps whispering to her. She keeps whispering "no" back. Then I hear a slap and I don't know who hit who but she's crying.

Maggie scoots over next to me. "You want to take a walk?" she asks.

We're out in the cold walking the gravel road, but I can't keep my mind off of what's going on in the car. A short ways off through the dark,

216

I see an old barn and a little shack. I think it's a shack but I can't see it too good through the dark. See a little light in a window, I think.

"You got a white girl back in Chowchilla?" Maggie asks.

"Yeah, I have a girl. I like her a lot too." And right now I think Bev is about the best girl in the entire world. "But I sure wish Charles would leave Prissy alone. This isn't right." I hear crickets off in the grass and a hoot owl flaps by overhead.

"I be Charlie's girl going on six years now. Why you come out here when you already have a girl?"

"Cause I'm stupid. I'm dumb as a rock, if you want to know the truth. I didn't know why Charles was bring me here, but I should have. He's always up to no good." I keep hearing a ruckus from the car but can't tell what it means.

"So why don't you stay home from now on. You dragged Prissy into this."

That's when the car door pops open again, and I see Charles holding one of Prissy's arms and slapping her. Every time he slaps her, she hits him in the face with her fist.

I run over there.

"Charles. Damn you. You sonofabitch." And when I get there I pound him right in the middle of the back. Thud is how it sounds. And then I back off. I see Prissy has a bloody nose and a puffy place over her left eye.

Charles turns loose of her and climbs out of the car real slow.

"Okay, Bobby Hammer. This one is between you and me."

I see his face in the light from inside the car. Looks like he has a bloody nose too, maybe a split lip.

"You girls," he says over his shoulder, "go on back to your nigger camp."

"It's too far to walk," I say.

"Two miles isn't far for a nigger." And then he comes toward me.

I go straight at him, stick out a left jab that goes wide and then throw a right that goes over his head. He's down low, grabs me around the waist with both arms and raises me over his head. He starts running with me up there. While I'm pounding him in the back with both fists, I look off in the distance and see the two colored girls disappearing in the dark. They're walking fast and looking back at us. Then Charles throws me into the bar ditch on my back among a bunch of wet weeds. While I'm trying to get

217

up and get the crap off of my back, Charles gets in that Hudson and drives off, slinging a little gravel toward me. That doesn't look too good for me. I stand in the road watching those red taillights moving on away when he hits the brakes, and I think maybe he changed his mind about leaving me here, but then he turns off to the west on another road, heads for that old barn with the little shack close by.

By the time I get to the barn, I'm soaking wet from the rain. The light has gone off in that little shack, but now I see that it's just a piece of a shack, has two sides missing so that the roof slumps to the ground. I must've been mistaken about the light. The Hudson's parked in front of the barn, barn door swung out a little. When I stick my head inside, I think I hear a hog grunt. I smell something sour.

"Charles," I say. "You in here, Charles?" I go on in but I don't like it a whole lot. Sure enough, I hear a hog over in the corner. I wait a little, then I see some pens. Don't see a hog. Too dark. I walk to the middle of the barn, then to the left, looking for that hog. "Charles. You in here?"

I hear a voice that comes from behind me. "I'll make you a proposition, Bobby."

I wheel around, look close, think maybe I can see him leaning up against the top rail of that hog pen with his side to me. It's too dark to be sure. He sounds out of breath. I don't say anything, hear a grunt again and now I see that hog sticking his nose through the boards trying to get a smell of Charles.

"I'll give you what you're after if you give me what I'm after."

"No deal," I say.

"Maybe you don't have a choice."

"I'll walk back to Fresno."

"I don't doubt that, but getting back to Fresno, or Chowchilla even, is not what you're after. Is it?"

"You raped her. I'd like to break your head open."

"I did not, sonofabitch!"

I see a little movement out of him and something hits me in the stomach, felt like a fist, but he was too far away for that. A big whish of air comes out of me. I'm bent over trying to suck air. It's slow going. While I'm bent over, I feel around in the straw on the ground, find the lump he hit me in the stomach with. Feels like a big pulley.

"You forced Prissy," I say, finally. "I saw you. You held her down. You hit her. Jesus, Charles. You raped her."

"She got in the front seat by herself, spread her legs by herself. I didn't get a chance to do it. She gave me and her both bloody noses butting heads. Damn near knocked me out. Hard-headed goddamn nigger. Got a loose front tooth."

"You raped her, Charles."

"She's just a hot little woman, a little too wild but then all broncs have to be broke if you want to ride."

"She's just a kid."

"You sound like you never touched her yourself."

"Charles! Goddamn it. I didn't rape her."

"I didn't do anything to her, Bobby. You fucked her. Not me."

"I didn't force her."

"I didn't do anything. You're just like your papa. Sit down over there in the hay." He shines a flashlight into the corner across from him, and the light hits my eyes like the full sun. "Your ears are still virgins, so they may bleed a little, but I'm going to tell you what you've been wanting to hear. I'm going to tell you the truth about your family and mine. So sit your ass down on those ropes and listen to me, if you can stand to hear the truth. I'll tell you how Lenny died, if I can get this hog to shut up." And he kicks the old hog on the snout that's sticking through the boards. Hog oinks and takes a walk around the pen, rooting the ground with that stub nose and snorting.

I figure I'll try Charles out on this one. May be worth taking a chance. The hay's a little damp, so I sit on some ropes hanging down from wooden supports and coiling around in the hay. Charles leaves the flashlight on, sets it on its end, leaning it against the barn wall so the beam lights part of the sloping roof. He sits on some ropes too.

"Start the night before Lenny got killed," I tell him. "He got out of bed in the middle of the night and never came home. I didn't see him until the next day. Where'd he go?"

"Pushy, pushy. Okay, have it your way, but it's going to cost you extra. It was two o'clock in the morning on the day he died, and he caught us out on Beacon Road. Helen had all her clothes off and I was on top of her when Lenny jerked open the car door and pointed his pistol at us. She even had her socks off cause she liked to have the bottom of her feet rubbed. This is the pistol he used," he says bringing it out of his back pocket.

219

I still have that pulley in my hand, and I figure I can break open his skull if I have to, but it isn't much compared to his pistol. The hog is back again, but Charles doesn't notice.

"Lenny wanted Helen out of the car and wouldn't even let her get her clothes first. He just wanted me the hell out of there. But when I drove off he put a couple of bullets in the back of my dad's car. Helen was screaming. 'Just my panties, Lenny, please. Just my panties.'" Lenny had no mercy. 'No panties for the pitiful,' he said. Helen was my girl, not Lenny's. But she was just a whore anyway. I kept telling him that, tried to tell him that no girl was worth what he was doing, but he wouldn't listen. 'It's Helen's turn now. I'll come kill you later,' he said. But he sounded a little undecided about me. Then he shot up my dad's car as I was driving off. He sure had a bad case of wanting to kill me. Put a bullet an inch from my head. I really thought he would kill Helen. I would have gone to the police, but then I didn't have a lot to do with them if I could help it. Wouldn't have saved her life anyway, if he'd really decided to kill her. At first I couldn't figure out how Lenny knew we were out there. It was two o'clock in the morning for christ's sake. But then I remembered. Before Lenny came, a pickup drove by. It had its lights off and came by slow so we didn't even know it was there until it had gone past. Helen heard something, so I raised up and saw the tail end of a pickup. Didn't recognize it then, but later, I realized it was that goddamn papa of yours. He sneaks around at night spying on people. Peeks in parked cars. That's the only way Lenny could have found out."

"But you were messing around with Lenny's girl. I saw 'em together. She was his girl."

"She was my girl. We had some trouble and he stepped in behind my back. He could have stayed away from her, and she would have stayed mine. But that was just the way Lenny operated. He always wanted whatever his friends had. I had Helen, so he wanted her. Just like your papa. He saw my mother with my dad and so he wanted her. If he'd left her alone everything would have been okay, but he wouldn't leave her alone."

"How could you know this stuff about our parents? It happened before you were born. This is just another of your lies."

"Let's get one thing straight right now. I don't lie. I never have. That's one thing you can depend on about me."

"That's a lie in itself. You lied the night we played Billy the Kid."

"You are really something else, Bobby. You know that? You're just too cute to be real. But you're partially right. I was less than a year old when your papa fucked my mother."

"So how did you find out?"

"I heard about it at school, a big stink about it started twelve years afterward. I was in the eighth grade at Wilson School when it happened. *Why* it got started again, I don't know. But I know *who* started it. That goddamn mama of yours. My mother killed herself over it. Your mama told my mother something and she killed herself. She hit a semi head on at ninety miles an hour out at the Red Top intersection on Highway 152. Took them a week to get all her pieces out of the car. There wasn't anything left of her bigger than your fist. My dad told me this. He still thinks it was all his fault. But I know it was your mama and papa."

"Come on, Charles. Your mother didn't have to do what she did. She could have said no. Who knows. Maybe she came to Papa."

"Goddamn, you! You are a sonofabitch, but you are dead right. You know that, Bobby? You are dead right. I've had a little experience with women. You saw a couple tonight. They're trash. All of them are nothing but trash. They can't stop themselves from doing the things they do. They're like kids. They do what you tell 'em."

"The ones you pick are like that for sure." I'm thinking, my mama's not like that and he hasn't ever run across anyone like Bev or Brenda either.

"Your mama is the worst of the lot. So then there's Lenny. My best friend, and my sister's boyfriend."

"So what you said about Gretta and Lenny when we were telling lies under the bridge is true."

"A lot of truth to it. Some, just rumors. But the truth is, Lenny and Gretta went together until I latched onto Helen. Your mother had a fit when she found out that Lenny was going with Gretta. She absolutely forbid it. She hates all us Kunze's. She thinks your family is better than ours. So Gretta and Lenny had to sneak around. But then when I started going with Helen, Lenny decided he wanted her too. He took her and she wouldn't see me anymore, for a while. Then Helen and I started sneaking around on Lenny."

"So Helen was Lenny's girl! You just didn't like it a whole lot."

"Shut up. You can interpret this any way you want. So your papa caught me with Helen at two o'clock in the morning and he told Lenny, and

Lenny brought his pistol out to Beacon road, ran me off, and kept Helen out there naked. Helen left her clothes in my car and I still have 'em. Those precious panties that she would have given her life for, I still have them. Keep them hanging on a nail in my living room. That's what happened the night before Lenny died."

"Come on, Charles. Tell me the rest. I want it all."

"You'll get it all. Just hold your horses. I left Lenny and Helen out on Beacon Road, went home. I should have gone to the police, but I couldn't. I went home and set in my room waiting for the sun to come up. Didn't seem like any sense going to bed, so I didn't. I heard dad get up to milk the cows, heard the door bang when he went outside. Just about the time I heard the compressor come on out at the milk barn, there was this peck, peck, peck on my window. It was Lenny. I went over to the window and cracked it a little. I asked him where his pistol was because I was afraid he would use it on me. He said he was through trying to kill me. I opened the window and climbed out. I took my .22 with me though. I didn't trust him that much. We walked along in the dark just before sunrise to the little shack I live in now. We had a hired hand living in it then. The sun was just about to come up. He smiled at me. 'I just wanted you to know that I'm still going to kill you over this,' he said. I reminded him that he just said he was through trying to kill me. 'Besides,' I said, 'she's just a girl, Lenny. Keep some perspective, for christ's sake. She's just a goddamn girl.' And that sorry sonofabitch. You know what he said? Said it like it was a joke. 'I am through *trying*,' he said. 'I *am* going to kill you. I just wanted you to know, it's for sure now.' And he walked off and left me standing there. I asked him if he killed Helen. He didn't even bother turning around. 'What do you think?' he asked. 'She was just a whore.' I thought he had killed her. I pointed my .22 right in the center of his back. He knew I was probably going to shoot him. But he didn't even look back."

Charles stops to catch his breath and starts poking at the hog again, and I'm afraid he'll quit there. And this last part is what I have to know about. But Charles takes the butt of that pistol and whacks that hog across the nose with it. I guess that hog doesn't have a whole lot of feeling in its nose because it doesn't seem too concerned. So Charles turns around a little and bends over like he's looking real close at that hog's snout and, oh shit, I can't believe even Charles did this. Now that hog is squealing and running around like bloody murder. I turn my head, look the other way. Even

222

though I couldn't see much in the dark, it was too much. What Charles did was bend down so he could get that pistol barrel lined up with one of the holes in that hog's snout, the flat end of the snout pointing around in different directions like it had eyes that could see in the dark, and Charles shot a bullet up in it. So the hog is squealing and running around with all the pain of having that bullet stuck somewhere in his head, and he hurts so bad he wants out of that pen. He's trying to climb the fence, first on this side and then on the far side. Charles shines the light on him, and I see blood bubbles coming out his nose. I hear a loud squeal and then six grunts, one for each step while he lumbers toward another spot to try the fence, and when he hits the fence and bounces back, he squeals again. It's as if he knows that if he can get out of that pen the pain will stop.

Charles has to talk louder for me to hear him over the hog.

"I went on to school, watching around every corner for Lenny and hoping he would cool down about me. I kept waiting for someone to say that they heard Helen was dead, but they didn't. Lenny didn't come to school. I don't know what he did, but I bet he was off writing in that notebook of his like he was doing all the time. I would sure like to find that notebook. I think Lenny knew what your mama told my mother that made her go crazy. I think maybe he knew. He always acted like he did. I even went to the junkyard after I came back to Chowchilla and bought this old clunker Hudson of his because I thought maybe he hid the notebook somewhere in it. I bought it and went to work at Pistoresi's because that was the only way I could afford to fix it up. I know he used to hide the notebook in the Hudson, up under the dash. I saw him do it many times when we were out together. 'Whoa!' he'd say, 'Time to pull over and write a little about that.' And then he'd reach under the dash and pull out that little blue book. 'I'm a crazy sonofabitch, Charles,' he'd say. 'You just sit over there and watch me be crazy.' But I have stripped this car, and it's just not there. I won't quit looking. I'll find it someday."

The hog is squealing too loud, so Charles turns around and shoots the suffering sucker in the side. That brings the hog down and I figure he's dead. Must have hit his stomach because it popped like sticking a pin in a balloon. And now it starts to stink like a garbage dump. At least I won't have to listen to all the squealing. But I'm thinking about what Aunt Loretta told me about Lenny coming to her wanting to know if it was okay to kill someone. Sounds like what I've been thinking all along was

223

true. Lenny wanted to kill Charles.

"That evening after school, just as I was going out in the field to bring the cows in for milking, here comes Lenny."

"Okay, stop right there." I can tell he's surprised I'm stopping him like this because I haven't said much of anything for a while. "What time was it when you saw him?"

"It was a little past five. What are you getting at?"

"Was he hurt?"

"Let me tell my story and you might find out."

"Okay. But hurry cause I got to know."

"Lenny wasn't one to let things go by without dishing out vengeance. But Lenny looked as if the weight of the world had just lifted from his shoulders. Even though he'd been up for thirty-six hours, he didn't even look tired. 'I've been talking to my mama and now I understand everything. You have a good life,' he told me, and he shook my hand. And then he hit me in the side of the head with his fist, the hardest I've ever been hit and then he hit me in the other side of the head, so I went down, maybe even went out for a second. Then he pulled his pistol out of his back pocket and tossed it onto my lap. 'It's been nice knowing you,' he said. 'Go shoot yourself.' And then he walked off. It was like he was planning a trip, maybe to play baseball for the New York Yankees like he used to always talk about. I really thought he'd made up his mind to go to New York."

"I don't believe you, Charles. That's just not Lenny." I hear a little grunt out of that hog and he flops a little.

"I don't even believe it myself. But that's what happened. I was there. I lived it that way. I was still milking cows when Brock pulled up at the barn. I figured he came because they'd finally found Helen's body. "I hate to do this," he told me, he still liked me some then, "but I've got to take you down to the station." I thought right then that Lenny'd told the police that I had killed Helen, and then he took off for New York. I asked why he wanted me, and he said, "For questioning concerning the death of Lenny Hammer."

"You don't know what happened to Lenny. Do you?"

"Not really. I didn't see it happen. He had an accident not far from my place and was killed. The policed held me for two days. I knew if I could find Lenny's notebook, it would clear me. But the police let me out just before the funeral because they didn't have enough to hold me on."

"Lenny wasn't injured when you saw him last?"

"I don't understand why you think he was."

"Cause I took a shot at him with my .22 when he left the house after talking to Mama and Papa. I know that when I pulled that fine bead on Lenny's '48 Hudson, my aim was good. I was always a crack shot with that .22. I was aiming to shoot out the license plate light. Scare Lenny a little. I always figured that the bullet had ricocheted and hit Lenny. This is the first time I know for sure that that is not true. At least it's not if you're telling the truth."

"You didn't shoot him. He couldn't have put me out with two punches if he'd had a bullet hole in him."

"That night under the bridge," I say, "you told me you put Lenny in the ground."

"I figure his dying was over Helen. I keep coming and going on this one. If I'd let him have Helen, he probably would have lived. I think he might have... I think he would have..." Now he's up fumbling around with those ropes he was sitting on.

All at once, while I'm sitting here being so glad about knowing that I didn't kill Lenny, Charles throws all those ropes at me.

"What the hell," I say. And then he's all over me. He has his elbow in my throat, and I think he just busted my lip. I'm struggling with him but he has these ropes around a couple of posts and before I know it, has my hands tied up over my head.

"Did I ever tell you about all the fun I used to have bulldogging steers?" he wants to know.

I hear that old hog grunt and come to its feet. Squeals real loud three times. I think my heart is going to jump out of my chest. I hear the hog breathing through the hole in his chest.

"Well, now," he says to me. "You got what you wanted from me and now it is my turn with you."

"Stop it, Charles. Stop it." He has me spread-eagled against the wall. He's up close, hunching, rubbing himself on me like he's having a seizure, bends down over my neck, bites me on the throat like a vampire.

"Oh, shit, you're going to take out a chunk."

"That's right. I would like to eat you."

I feel the buttons down the front of my pants popping loose one at a time. Feel cold air when he pulls down my shorts. I try to kick but I can't fight him off. That old hog tries to come to his feet again. New smells come from him. Then he falls, sucks air, grunts, pants, just trying to get his dying over with.

I start to swell, feel the warmth inside Charles's mouth, feel his spit running down my balls. "I'll kill you if you don't quit it, Charles."

I see the hog's sides heaving, his mouth opening and closing, sucking more air. Every breath comes with a groan until he quivers, goes into this straight-legged convulsion, lies still.

I hear the barn door squeak and then someone asks, "Hey, who the hell's in here?" I see a light beam hit the far wall.

"Untie me, Charles," I say. "Untie me."

"Shut the fuck up," whispers Charles, getting his flashlight off the ground and killing the light. "That nigger 'll kill both of us."

"Hey, mister. Over here. I need some help."

"Who's at?"

Charles has his hand over my mouth. That's my smell on his breath. He just shakes his head and backs off. Then he comes toward me again, starts untying me. When he gets the ropes loose, he leaves me to get free and walks on around to the old colored man that's walking toward us real slow. Shines his light on Charles.

"Pinky? You okay? You here, girl? You guys been messing with my girl? Grunt fer me, Pinky."

"Hello, there Mr. Nigger," is what Charles is saying to the old man. "How are you?"

But the old man doesn't like that so he points a little skinny shotgun at Charles, looks like maybe it's a single shot .410.

"Back off a lil, son. Don't like white fok in ma barn."

"We just had a little car trouble, but we got it fixed now so we'll be on our way. You about ready, Bobby?"

"Back up a little, son. Don't get me wrong. Juss don't want you close to me. Want a look at my hog and then we can talk a lil if you like."

Charles has worked his way around the old man. I can see now that he's crippled, has to scoot his feet instead of taking steps. His lips are moving with this weird motion over and over. Slobber runs down one side of his chin and from the looks of the top to those coveralls, I'd say he's been doing it for about a month. And here I was hoping to get some help from him.

"Come on, Bobby. Let's get the hell out of here."

"Oh, jesus. That my hog? Pinky, that you?" His voice doesn't ever change, just that same singsong voice.

"Bobby, if we don't get out of here, I'm going to have to kill him over that goddamn hog. Either that or let him kill you."

"Oh, godamighty. You done my hog in."

So here I'm going out of that barn door after Charles. I put a fist in the middle of his back as that .410 rakes the barn wall. I have to let up or that colored'll kill both of us. Then I'm getting in the car with Charles. Charles starts laughing as little buckshot rakes the car. I hit him with my fist, pound on his shoulder and even get one blow to the side of his head. None of it seems to faze him. He just keeps on laughing. And it's going to be just like nothing happened. I can already see it coming. It's just like nothing happened. How can I ever tell anybody what he did to me tonight?

CHAPTER 31: *Shooting Roof Tops*

I'm sitting in the backseat of Lenny's Hudson, hunkered over in the corner trying to keep from touching Wayne sitting next to me. I don't want his freckles on me. I've been into it with him because he won't leave Eugene alone. Keeps picking on him. It's been raining hard ever since we left Fresno. Melvin's sitting on the other side of Wayne, and he won't keep his mouth shut either. They keep talking about these white girls they were messing around with, and I keep thinking that all I had was a colored girl, no telling what I caught from her, and then what Charles did to me. Charles had Thomas drive and said he wanted me by a window because he has something special for me when we get to Fairmead. And he keeps talking like we had a great time at the colored village. I keep wanting to hit him in the back of the head with a club.

Thomas takes the turnoff toward Fairmead, the little colored town just outside of Chowchilla.

"Why are we going through here?" I ask. I don't get an answer. "I've had all the niggers I need tonight," I say.

Fairmead is southeast of Chowchilla, just across the 99. The only time I've ever been here was when I was ten and Papa took me to see a crop duster that crashed into a house and burned. The pilot and a little colored girl died in it and the bones were still laying there in the ashes and her mama screaming and crying.

It's dark inside the car except for the dash lights up front that I see reflecting off of Charles' sour face. Charles told Melvin that he got that puffy lip in a fight with a nigger. Melvin didn't feel too good about missing out on the action. I told Melvin that it was a colored girl that hit Charles, but that didn't help him much. Helped Wayne out a little though. He couldn't quit laughing. It's raining hard outside, so the windshield wipers keep slapping. This old country road is full of large puddles, sometimes so deep they slow the car and send out spray on both sides. I need a good soaking in the bathtub.

Thomas slows a little as we come into Fairmead. Place is actually not a town, just a few houses and a store, and I hear a clicking sound from up front that I've heard before. I look up and see the shiny metal barrel of Lenny's pistol. Charles has just filled the clip.

Melvin's raising hell because Charles is rolling down the window letting rain come through in big drops. I don't know what Charles is shooting at so close to those houses, but I hear the crack of the pistol and see it jump, forcing his arm upward.

"What the hell are you shooting at?" I ask.

"Rooftops."

"Oh, shit. Here we go again."

And then he fires and I hear the thud over the sound of the road as the bullet hits the roof.

"Hey, you black bastards!" he shouts. "Get your black asses back to Africa!"

And then Melvin has to put his stuff in. "Eat shit, niggeerrrs!" he screams.

"You're going to kill someone, Charles," I tell him.

"That's no big matter, Bobby. They're just like dogs, dogs and baby dogs." At the other end of town, Charles says, "Turn around, Thomas." And Thomas is taking orders without question and driving real slow. Charles turns toward me as he rolls up his window. He's holding the pistol up over the backseat in his left hand. "Here, Bobby. It's your turn."

"I don't want to shoot a roof, Charles," I tell him.

"I'll take it," says Melvin.

"Give it to me, Charles, I'll do it," says Wayne. "Give it to me. Bobby's wimping out again. Hurry, Charles. Give it to me." And Wayne's reaching for Lenny's pistol.

I'm just not taking any more shit from him, so this time I use my elbow, knock the breath out of him. Maybe hit him a little harder than I intended. While he's bent over sucking air, I take the pistol from Charles, feel the warm metal handle. Only it doesn't feel like it's the warmth from Charles' hand. It feels like Lenny's heat. This is the first time I've held his gun. I feel like I could turn that pistol on Charles real easy. Anyone in the car for that matter. I don't like anybody anymore. Right now I feel like there isn't anything in the world that I wouldn't do. And I know there's nothing worse than a nigger unless it's a white man who runs with niggers. I have this stinking nigger smell all over me. The window is down, cold rain coming in in big wet drops as the pistol turns toward the first house. So much water, I can't see too good. Just as I shoot, I see a light come on in a bedroom window. Fire shoots out the end of the barrel and the pistol jumps so bad, I almost drop it. Then I put a thud into another rooftop that already has a light on in the living room. Seems easy once I get started. I shoot again, then take out a window in the little store with an Oly sign on the front door. The sound of breaking glass is like music, so I put a couple more in that window. That brings me back to my senses or maybe it's that I know Wayne's about to hit me. I take the blow aimed for my head with my shoulder. Then I have my hand on his throat with my arm straight to hold him away from me and push that red head of his down to the floorboard, him with his knee in my chest. I've taken a blow to the left side of my head and I'm worried that my eye might be cut. I tighten my hand on his throat and feel this big round hose-like thing in his throat that his Adam's apple sits on. Think I will just rip it out, hope it kills him, but Charles pulls me. Wayne hits me again on the same side of the face, on the cheek this time.

Then Charles slaps me. That stops me and I take another blow from Wayne to my right eye this time before Melvin can get between me and him. I can't feel anything Wayne has done to me anymore. I just feel the burn on my cheek where Charles slapped me.

I'm staring at Charles and he's staring back. I take a swing at him but the punch doesn't go anywhere because Melvin catches my arm.

"Nobody slaps me and lives," I say to Charles.

"Punk," says Thomas. "You going to try to whip everybody in the car?"

"If I have to."

"Somebody's got to bring you back to your senses," says Charles.

"No man slaps me and lives."

Melvin's sitting between Wayne and me now.

"If you guys don't stop it, I'm going to have to kick all your asses," he says.

I stare Melvin down too. "You'd have more trouble with me tonight than you did out on Beacon Road," I tell him.

He laughs at me. "I don't doubt that. But lighten up a little, anyway." he says.

Wayne's sitting over there trying to talk but has this really hoarse voice that can only say a couple of words at a time. He's calling me Hammer now instead of Bobby and saying over and over that my time is coming and that I'm going to pay for what happened to Leroy and it's going to be just me and him. He's saying all that, two words at a time, so it takes a while.

My face still stings from where Charles slapped me. If he'd hit me with his fist, I could have handled it. But he didn't. He slapped me like I'm a little kid.

But what I just did with Lenny's pistol starts working on me. I don't even know where the pistol is so I look around a little and find it in the floorboard. While I'm sticking it in my coat pocket, I think about pointing it at each kid in the car and pulling the trigger. Feels good to think about killing each one of them.

I sulk for a couple of minutes, start to change back inside. I just can't believe I really did it. I shot Lenny's pistol into a house that had real people in it. While Thomas drives us over to our cars, I remember how I could see lights in that one house, see through its windows, see people inside. I keep seeing this scene. Maybe I didn't see everything that I think I did now and maybe I keep adding things to it, but I could see them inside, as if it was some man sitting there eating a late dinner at the table and it being real late at night, like maybe he'd been out working in some man's field all day and into the night and just got off work and was eating dinner or even breakfast, now it's so late, that his wife had to get up from sleeping to fix for him, his legs feeling real tired with his wet boots still on, his clothes all wet from the rain, and then he hears this gunshot and the bullet ripping through his attic and I imagine that he runs to check on the kids to make sure they didn't get hurt because it's me out there shooting at his roof and he runs up into a hall and has to go up a ladder to get into the attic where his kids sleep and his head disappears up into the darkness and he's looking around to see if his kids are okay and it's so dark I can't tell what he sees. Then another shot rips through the shingles.

When I start to get into my Chevy with the raining beating down hard on me, car exhaust fogging around me, fumes clogging my nose, Charles comes to me.

"I want the pistol back, Bobby."

I've had all of Charles that I'm good for this evening. "I don't know that you need it, Charles," I tell him. "Besides, it doesn't belong to you. It belongs to Lenny."

We're both ignoring the rain and it already has him soaking wet and it's starting to drip off of my nose and making my left eye sting.

"But he gave it to me. And now, he's dead."

I look at him straight, say nothing for a minute. "All the more reason. It's just cause I want it. It's mine." And I take a step toward him. "Mine just because I say it's mine." I have the pistol in my coat pocket. It feels cold against my hand. I have it pointed at him.

Charles stands there looking down at me for a minute, real straight faced. "I still can't believe you would fight me over a nigger girl. God, she's a dog, Bobby."

"Stay away from my family," I say. I could just squeeze that trigger and solve so many of my problems right now.

He laughs at me a little. "We had a fun time tonight, Bobby. Think about it. There's a lot more were that came from."

"That's what I'm afraid of."

"Okay. I guess the pistol belongs to you."

CHAPTER 32: *Flood a Coming*

It's early morning and I'm standing at the front window staring off through the cold rain toward town. We won't be working today. There's been more talk of a flood. Serious this time. Mama is in the kitchen banging skillets and what not. She always listens to the radio in the morning, this little station out of Merced that has the farm report. Papa's in the bathroom shaving. I just keep going back to last night, feeling Charles mouth on me, hearing that hog die, seeing inside that roof I shot, see this little baby dark boy, and I don't want to call him a nigger, and he's lying up in that attic and has this bullet hole in his body somewhere and he can't figure out why he woke up and hurts so bad and he doesn't know that he didn't wet his bed but that that's his blood he's laying in so he's crying and thinking that it's pee that's stinging him so bad and his daddy's trying to get to him but he can't find him in the dark.

I have decided to kill Charles. I walk down the dark hall listening to the hardwood floor creak, go back to my bedroom where Curt's still lying in bed asleep. I push the closet door back real quiet like, look at my red corduroy coat here in the dark. I don't know where I'm going to carry Lenny's pistol tonight when I go to town. Maybe I can just carry the pistol in my car, maybe under the seat like where Charles kept it all the time. But I might have to keep it on me if the only way I can get to him is inside some building, like maybe Farnesi's. I might shoot him in Farnesi's. My coat pocket may not be big enough for it. I'll have to try the pistol in my pants pocket. What's the use in waiting? Maybe I should go see Charles at his little shack. I listen to the rain against the window. That's what woke me early this morning. The rain.

Curt rolls over and looks at me through half-closed eyes, then rolls back. Looks like he's pissed off.

"You've been in another fight, Bobby Ray," he tells me.

But my eye is not swelled much this morning and it's not cut as bad as

I thought it might be.

I go back in the kitchen. Mama says that a lot of rain fell in the mountains over night, then asks what I want for breakfast. But I'm just thinking about eating something light. I'm wondering what Charles is having for breakfast. His last breakfast. Most of the time Mama's just like a short order cook. She'll fix a different breakfast for each of us.

"You better not let your papa see that eye," she says.

Trish comes in yawning, still in her nightgown. She's in the refrigerator getting a glass of milk, and Mama wants to know what she wants to eat.

"What are you going to eat, Bobby Ray?" Trish's asking me.

I don't know if I'm usually mad at her, but I don't feel mad now and that's different. "I'm just thinking about a bowl of Cheerios," I tell her.

"Can I fix it for you?" she asks me.

"What do you want, baby girl?" Mama asks.

"That's okay, Mama," says Trish. "I'll eat a bowl of cereal too. There's not any use in you cooking a big breakfast unless Papa's got to have one. He'll be wanting one though. You can depend on that. Nothing ever changes in his life. Not if he can help it."

Maybe I'm just imagining all this stuff about her and Charles. She looks like she doesn't have a problem in the world.

Now I start thinking about consequences. If I do this to Charles, it won't just change my life. My life is over. As far as the police are concerned, Charles is innocent. He's never been caught for any of the things he does. If I do this, I'm going to jail or maybe I'll be on the run the rest of my life. That's it. Maybe after I kill Charles, I'll skip the country, go to Texas or some place like that where there's lot of outlaws and open space. And here I have Bev for a girlfriend again. If I stay around here it'll be jail for a while and then the Gas Chamber. Or is it the Electric Chair for us here in California?

Papa comes in rolling up his sleeves.

"Where'd you get the pants, Papa?" Trish wants to know.

He's wearing fresh clean clothes. A new pair of khakis.

"They've been in the closet a while. No sense in wearing a new pair to the field the first time."

"Why, hell no. Wouldn't want to look good out in the field, would you?"

Trish is always cussing in front of Papa. I sure won't do it. She embarrasses me. Strange thing is, he won't cuss much around her. He'll even cuss around Mama, particularly around Mama, depending on the circumstances. But not Trish. He quit it a few years ago when he found out she could out cuss him.

"Farmers are just damn hoboes anyway," she adds, taking a look over at him out of the corner of her eye. "Isn't that right, Papa?"

Papa knows better than to get into it with her.

Trish pours the milk in my bowl for me, over all those little round O's.

"Two spoons of sugar for me," I tell her.

I try to imagine the way he's going to look when I shoot him. Between spoonfuls of Cheerios, I think about Charles' back being turned. I shoot him right between the shoulder blades so that it shatters part of his spine as it goes in, him lurching backwards.

Mama tells Trish to be quiet because the radio's talking about the Ash Slough again. I'm watching Mama roll out the dough for biscuits. Radio says the next big swell in the Slough will be around midnight. Papa tells Mama to flip on the light so he can read a little of yesterday's Fresno Bee. Guess he'll be reading about me in tomorrow's paper. Mama's cutting out little round patties of dough with an empty Campbell's soup can then sops both sides in a thin layer of what Trish calls snake oil she has poured in the pan. That makes the biscuits crispy. I get to thinking about Charles, his father Karl. Little Karl. Just another dairy farmer. Has a few acres of cotton. Charles has two sisters. Gretta, the one that Lenny liked, was one year younger than him. I don't know where she lives now. The other one's older than Charles. How much older and what her name is, I don't know. But she's off somewhere married. Charles is the baby boy, the only boy. I wonder what they're going to think about me shooting their only brother? They probably don't know anything about how mean he is. This time I think about shooting him with him turned sideways so the bullet goes in his temple leaving a small red dot and brains and bone blow out the other side, maybe a little blond hair and blood stick to the wall behind him as he goes down.

Curt comes in. He's in one hell of a bad mood. Got calf licks all over his hair that's wet in spots. He gave up on it. He has hair like Lenny's. Brown and straight as a stick.

"What do you want to eat, Curt?" Mama wants to know, as she puts strips of bacon into a skillet that's hot enough to make them sizzle.

"Biscuits," is all Curt says, but he's looking at Trish and just waiting for her to say something. She's not looking at him for anything. I wonder what they have cooking?

I can see myself in a striped suit already. It's going to be prison for me from now on. Bread and water. Feels like I'm saying good-bye to everyone here at the breakfast table. I didn't know how good I have it.

"Go to town with me, Bobby Ray," Papa says through the paper. "You must be getting better with your fists. This time it's only one eye. I won't mind being seen with you."

I'm thinking about going with him, but I have to look up Charles. I have to get this over with while I still want to do it. I look out the window at the wind and rain twisting the old willow tree out back. But what the hell. I haven't been to town with Papa in a couple of months. Besides, this'll be the last time we'll be together. The last time I'll be out on the street.

"You going to leave him out in the pickup while you go in and talk for a week?" asks Curt. He has this look in his eyes, like he would really like to take Papa's head off. But Papa doesn't treat me like that since I got grown.

"What kind of a burr got in your shorts during the night?" Papa asks Curt.

"It's going to flood tonight," says Trish.

"Stay out of it," Curt says back.

★

Me and Papa are standing on the bank of the Ash Slough, over by the Danish Creamery. It's just past noon, but dark enough to be sundown. I can see the spot where me and Brenda parked the night after the dance. We're standing next to the bridge where the railroad track and old Highway 99 cross the Slough side by side. A crew of volunteers are bagging sand and a couple of tractors pushing dirt up where they can get to it. We're talking to Mr. Grissom about how strong the bank is. Or Papa's talking to him and I'm listening. Mr. Grissom has an unlit cigar in his mouth, looks like he's been chewing on it for a week. He's given me a couple of strange looks. He's saying that the bank's strong enough but that they're expecting another three or four feet of water sometime after midnight. It's going to be touch and go. People in town better get prepared, he says. Then damn if he doesn't turn on me. Takes that cigar out of his mouth and points it at me.

236

"Hey, Bobby, you little chickenshit. The next time you use one of my shacks to gang-bang a girl, you better leave your shotguns at home. Otherwise, you're going to spend a couple of nights in the county jail. You'll foot the repair bill too."

Then he turns back to talking to Papa about the possibility of a flood like nothing happened. Papa doesn't act like anything happened either. Except he blushes a deep red. I walk away from them. I've never seen anyone so sure enough of himself as Mr. Grissom. He chewed me up like a dog with a rabbit and Papa just standing there.

Here comes Leroy's Uncle Jess strolling up. He walks on past, down the Slough bank without saying anything, waves for me to follow. He has on a long sleeve flannel shirt so I don't get to see his tattoos. His skin's so dark, he looks a little like a colored himself. It's a little cold for no coat. "How you been making it without Leroy?" he wants to know when I catch up to him. "You two were close as brothers."

I don't know why he thinks that. "I get a little lonely now and then, but I'm doing pretty good."

"A little lonely, huh?"

"A little."

"Who you running around with now?"

"Different kids. Have a girlfriend."

"A girl named Bev and a friend named Charles Kunze."

I don't know how he knows about Bev. "Ya. I see Charles once in a while."

"Leroy saw him once in a while too. Can't say it did him much good." He pulls off his hat and the rain makes little drops in his greasy black hair.

"I got him into that. Took him out with me and Charles stealing hubcaps once." I look down at the ground, toe a muddy clod.

"I wouldn't think you'd do something like that."

"I've done some things I'm not too proud of recently."

"Haven't we all, Bobby. Haven't we all. I know Leroy had his problems before he died. He talked to me a little. He was interested in that girl you're going with. Bev."

"He always was interested in her, I guess, but wouldn't say anything. He was always trying to date her behind my back."

"He talked about you a lot. Always talked about all the stuff you had that he didn't."

"Seemed to me like he was always trying to con me out of everything I had."

"Leroy tried to push everybody around. He's the only one of my nephews that would bum cigarettes off me."

I have to laugh at that. "He beat me out of a few cigarettes, and a few more things, too. I probably shouldn't tell you this, but before he died, Leroy learned stealing. That's another thing I got him into."

"You mean he would steal from you?"

"No. Not Leroy. He wouldn't steal from me but he would con me."

A light drizzle falls and the water in the Slough is just a few feet from the top of the bank now. Looks like a slow moving lake.

"I've never seen the Slough look like this, Jess."

"It's been this way a couple of times in the twenty-five years I've been here."

"To me it's always been just a few mud puddles full of grass and cane. When we were little, me and Leroy used to come here in the summertime after school to hide in the grass and smoke cigarettes. Maybe shoot a few birds with a BB gun or a .22. Look, Jess. There's an old armchair out in the middle. At first I thought it was a drowning man." It floats slowly along in the muddy water, rolls, then hits a tree and stops until it can swing around, then gets going again.

"So you only miss Leroy a little, huh."

I don't say anything.

"I have some cousins in Arizona that I go see from time to time. They're the best friends I've ever had in my whole life." He stops and thinks a little. "But I've got to be going. I promised to help my brother with a car he has in his auto shop. He asked me to check out the Slough bank. He's concerned that a flood could wipe out his business." And then it's like he wants to say something to me but can't find the words. Instead, he puts his hand on my back squeezes me from shoulder to shoulder. He always smells like garlic. "Come see us sometime, Bobby. We've been missing you too."

Jess walks off then turns, looks back at me, starts to wave me off again, comes back. "You're family," he says. And I see a real sad look in his eyes, like maybe there's something he's not saying. "We need to see more of you. Especially now that Leroy's gone. You're family."

I walk back over to Papa and Mr. Grissom. Keep my head down. They're talking about whether they'll have to pre-irrigate this year. It's beginning to rain more now. Drops streak through the air and ripple in the water where they hit. I'm family? Now what did Jess meant by that?

This time I think maybe Lenny's pistol won't be powerful enough and the bullet just goes in Charles' head but doesn't go through and maybe there's no blood at all so the police have trouble figuring out what Charles died from, just dropping dead like that.

I have mud all over the bottom of my good shoes. God, Papa could talk the neck off a giraffe.

★

I just spotted Charles. He's going into the Sierra Theater with this girl, only she looks like a woman. Could be thirty years old and with dark hair. I park my car in the vacant lot across the street, then high-step it through puddles to get to the outside box office. Have to keep my hand on the pistol in my coat pocket to keep it from jumping out. The thing is heavy and pulls my coat down on the right side. Just two blocks from here's the Danish Creamery, and on the other side of it is the Ash Slough where they're still trying to hold back the flood. In the distance I hear the workers shouts and the clang of machinery.

Phyllis Thompson is selling tickets. "Where's Bev, Bobby?" she asks.

I don't rightly know what to say for a second. I forgot about her. I think I was supposed to call her today. So that's what I say. "I don't know."

"Did you two break up?" And she smiles at me like I am her best friend.

"No." Why's she asking that? I'm wondering of maybe Bev's mad at me for something. Maybe I'm not taking her out enough for us to be going steady. But if she has a problem with how often we have been dating now, wait until after tonight.

"Did you hear that Thomas got expelled for a week?"

"Thomas Powers?"

"Yeah. Too many tardy slips. You could hear him screaming about it all over school. Wants to get Mr. Sonnett fired. His father's going to the board." She gives me my change.

"I saw Thomas last night. He didn't say anything about it."

"He's ashamed of it. Have you talked to Brenda lately?" she asks.

"No!" I say and it comes out a little more forceful than I wanted.

Phyllis jumps back like I hit her. "Well," she says, and she turns her head away from me, "you might think about it."

Why's stuff like this always happening to me? Here I am trying to kill someone, and I got all these girls I have to worry about. So I'm thinking about doing it and the first shot to the head doesn't kill him and he doesn't even know he's been shot. Just feels a sting and has to rub the back of his head a little, maybe sticks his finger in the bloody hole. His mind is confused like mine gets sometimes when I can't figure things out, so I have to shoot him again to be humane like he had to help me with the rabbit I gut shot.

Just off to the right of the lobby as you come through the door is this room called the Sweet Shop. I buy a bag of popcorn and a Coke from Phyllis Thompson, making sure to keep my right hand in my coat pocket. Phyllis is just so pretty. I like to watch her hands move. They're always so quick and sure of what they're doing. Then I find out that my eats and drink will take both hands, so I hold my pocket closed with my elbow as I walk out. I get almost out the door.

"Bobby," she says.

I jerk a little, thinking my gun's showing, turn around real slow.

"You forgot your change," she says. "Is some thing wrong with your arm?"

The lights are already dim and the movie's just starting. It is called "Tarantula." I can hear the rain falling on the roof. I see Melvin and Eugene on the other side of the theater. They're trying to get me to come sit next to them, but I wave 'em off. I bought a ticket for down stairs, which cost 75¢. I'd have bought a loge but they cost $1.25 and I'm trying to save a little money. But I can't smoke down here. That's where Charles and his woman will be sitting though. In a loge. I'll have to sneak up there after the movie starts. But this is it. I'll kill him here. After I eat my popcorn.

I turn to look up above and sure enough there's Charles and his woman sitting about three rows from the top. I could tell just before the lights faded that she has dark red hair, almost black it's so red. I see a couple of empty seats above them. Down front, shining in the dark, there's a red exit sign on each side of the theater and a little blue clock on the right wall that says 7:20. It's always fifteen minutes fast. The theater's crowded with kids for this movie. A bunch down front can't keep their mouth shut. Some are from high school. Oh, shit! There's Brenda. She jumps up, goes to talk to some girl sitting just across the aisle from me. They're talking about the flood. Look scared. She's squatting in the aisle to talk. Her light blond

240

hair hangs to her shoulders. She has dark eyebrows. Brenda always wears a blouse and a skirt. Never wears a one-piece dress. She looks at me, then laughs just as the lights go out.

"Bobby," and it's Brenda, right by my ear. She just scared the shit out of me because I thought she went back to her seat. "I'm still talking to Helen for you," she says, and she doesn't seem to be mad at me anymore. "But I'm concerned about her." Then she turns and looks up into the loges. "She's not acting right. She doesn't seem like Helen. There's something really bad going on. I don't know what to do about it. That's Helen up there with Charles. I need to talk to you, about a couple of things." And I'll be damned if she doesn't kiss me right quick on the cheek, then runs back to her seat, settles down for the movie next to Becky Wynsum, looks back at me. God, she sure runs hot and cold about me.

So Charles has Lenny's girl with him tonight. The night I'm going to kill him. And I'm still worried about not having Bev here with me, too. I bet she's sitting home wishing she could see the movie. I should have called her today. I wonder who all saw Brenda kiss me?

About halfway through the movie, while this scientist and a policeman are investigating these large white puddles of tarantula venom, I figure it's time to make my move. I walk up through the loges and as I pass Charles, either he doesn't notice me because he's saying something to Helen or he's just ignoring me. I take a seat on the right in the last row, where the seats end because of the projection room. The door to the room is just behind where I sit. I don't like that door being there. I don't know who might come out of it. I look down at Charles as he leans over and says something into Helen's ear that she's not too pleased with.

At the start of the movie that tarantula was about as big as a hand and in the middle of the movie, the size of a house. Now it's big enough to step over mountains, and I don't want to think how big the puddles of venom are. The scientist just said, it's "fiercer, more deadly and cruel than anything that ever walked the earth."

I get to wondering if I have any bullets left in the pistol. I haven't checked it since we shot up Fairmead. My hands have been sweating so much my whole pocket is wet, so I take my hand out, wipe it on my Levis. This is it, I keep saying, but my hand won't move. The thing that bothers me is that all these kids around here know me. What're they going to think? If I just stand up and shoot, they'll start screaming. They won't know why I'm doing it. And I have to do it. I just can't wait any longer. But what will Brenda think of me? I think maybe it's cowardly to shoot him in the back. Maybe I should go down and shoot him from the front. I guess using a gun on an unarmed man is being a coward anyway so it doesn't matter. Besides he's a lot older than me.

While I've been sitting here, I have been thinking about all the reasons I have for killing Charles and not able to work up the courage. Used to, I hated Charles for what I though he did to Lenny, but now my reasons are my own. Well, Prissy and the hog are part of it too. Maybe I'm not thinking enough of Lenny. So I pretend that I'm Lenny sitting in this seat looking down at Charles and Helen sitting there enjoying the movie, and I try to think the same thoughts Lenny must've had when he looked inside Charles' car and saw Helen on top of him. And Charles being the kind of guy he is. Lenny must have known a lot more about Charles than I do. Maybe Charles has changed some but, god, the stories I hear about what happened five years ago sound so much like what's going on now. I just wonder what kind of girl Helen is that she would go anywhere with Charles? Brenda seems to think a lot of her though.

And then I think about Papa. He wishes he'd killed Charles five years ago. Is that the real reason I think I should kill Charles? Is it just because I think Papa would kill him if he knew what I know? I should quit all this thinking and rethinking and just kill him. Just pull the pistol out and shoot him. If he just wasn't sitting with a girl. If I shoot him in the head, I might blow brains all over Helen. And all these kids in here. I'll scare the shit out of all these kids. What'll they think about me?

Here comes the Army, Navy, and the Marines. They have the tarantula caught in a fireball. Now the Air Force swoops in low. If I just had one other person that thought he deserved killing, I could do it. Anybody except Papa. Maybe that's what I should do. Find somebody else that agrees I should kill him. I could never tell them what Charles did to me though. I just need to be sure I'm doing the right thing. Maybe it's the right thing, but this is the wrong place. Maybe I should wait and get him when he goes home. Maybe I'm feeling this way because the place is just not right. Maybe I'm just a coward. But that's what I'll do. I'll follow him home, shoot him dead right out front of his little shack just as he gets out of his car.

★

242

Chapter 32: *Flood a Coming*

I kill the headlights, leave the park lights on and get out of my car with the windshield wipers still flapping. I feel the cold rain on my face. Charles has just crawled out of his car and I have my hand in my coat pocket on my pistol, but he still has Helen with him. That must be her car parked at his front door. He says something to her and she goes on in his shack. I'm cold and the wind drives the rain through my clothes. Damn. After the show, I thought he'd take her home. I followed him. But he went over to the Slough where there was a big commotion, flashlights, caterpillars and men stacking sandbags. A couple of police cars. Water was coming over the Slough bank washing a hole in it. They were piling old car bodies, tree stumps and sandbags in the hole but it just kept getting bigger. Looked like even the train track might go. Mr. Grissom came running over to my car, motioned for me to roll down the window. He still had the same cigar in his mouth. Told me I better get out of there because they just lost it. As I pulled out, the sirens went off and they were starting to evacuate the town.

Now I'm thinking that the reason I'm doing this is to keep Charles from killing someone else. Like maybe shooting a colored in Fairmead. Dogs and baby dogs is what he called them. And he shot a dog over there by the 99 just because it made a run at his jeep. He'd shoot one for laying in the shade if he had a chance. So as he's coming toward me in the rain, I have all my reasons lined up. I can imagine what kind of fear will run through him when he sees me pull this pistol on him, knowing he's about to die. He slapped me the other night too.

He stops a ways away and waits for me to say something.

I'm just cold and wet and can't think of anything.

"What are you following me for, Bobby. What is it this time?"

I just wish I hadn't thought about him being the only boy in the family, wish I hadn't thought of him having a family. And now he has Helen with him and if I shoot him, what's it going to do to her? She'd be in his little shack all alone and him laying out in the yard dead. If he didn't have all these connections with other people.

"I've got a girl with me. If you're looking for trouble, I don't want any."

We stand there for a while longer. Maybe what he did to me wasn't that bad. Who ever heard of a boy getting raped?

"You're losing it, Bobby. You know that? You're really losing it." Then he turns and walks off.

That's it. I'm not going to do it. What a worthless piece of shit I am.

The Escape of Bobby Ray Hammer

I've brought every bad thought I can find to this, and I still can't do it. What else does it take? I think again about that little baby dark boy I shot, pull out the pistol, take a look at my car all glistening with rain and the radio going. Kick in the side of my car. Put a bullet in my taillight. Red glass flies everywhere. Now the light shines bright. Everything is covered with rain.

CHAPTER 33: *Dog Rescue*

This morning, half the world is one big puddle. I have my Chevy parked crossways in the middle of Robertson Boulevard halfway to town. The rain's coming down in huge drops. I'm standing on the white line and the water starts at my feet and goes off in the distance as far as I can see. Off toward town, fence posts on each side of the road gradually disappear below water level. Palm trees still mark the road on both sides all the way into Chowchilla. Out in the open fields, only trees and houses stick up through the flat shiny surface. No bridge in the world is big enough to fit over all this water.

I've seen two rats, a rabbit and a snake trying to make it to high ground. Right now, I'm watching a dog, a scraggly looking sucker, try to make it to me. Looks like he thinks I'm going to save him. Guess he has some catching up to do on me.

I can't go out with Bev anymore because I might have a disease. What if I give it to her?

I couldn't sleep last night after I got home. Kept wondering why I couldn't kill Charles. Think maybe I'm a little glad I didn't this morning. I was dreading going to Texas. Then after I finally got to sleep I woke with a start. Decided I should go back to the police and tell them I killed Leroy. Somehow, in the middle of the night, it seemed so clear that I did. I kept trying to remember how it was when he let off the gas and I was coming up fast behind him. His car was making some strange moves, kind of a rocking motion, back and forth. And then I was on him. I think I heard something then. Was it a bang when I clipped him or was he off in the ditch and hit a chug hole? Last night, seems like I clipped him. This morning, I'm not so sure. Seems like maybe I should keep my mouth shut. Even if I did kill him, I'm not so sure I want to go to jail for it. Why can't I just leave well enough alone? Anybody else would be glad they'd been cleared. Me, I keep wanting to convince them I'm guilty. Sometimes I feel like I'm not even on my own side.

Then, laying there with dark all around me, I started worrying about my car. Got up at daybreak just to see how bad the dent was where I kicked it in. Maybe I can take off the door panel on the inside and push it out. My taillight looks really bad though. That pistol really took care of it.

The dog's not going to make it. So I'm a going out to get him. I walk the white line till it goes under water then I follow where I think it is. The water is cold and when it gets up to my waist, I start to freeze. Wish I'd left my wallet in my car. The old dog is making a turn and coming toward me and paddling like he has new hope. I remember when I learned to swim. I held my head above water just like him. I grab a hold of him and he's trying to climb up on me with his old stiff legs. He tries to shake off in my arms, feels like trying to hold a lawn sprinkler. I turn him over so he lies in my arms like a baby. He's just a small dog. And then he takes a swack at the side of my face with his tongue. He has a collar. Belongs to Mr. Grissom. He's tried to bite me before.

PART V

Chasing Down Lenny's Journal

CHAPTER 34: *A Little About Bridges*

"So why haven't you called me. Did I do something wrong?"

"No, Bev. I told you. I've just been busy cleaning up from the flood and all lately." Bev is the unhappiest person I have ever known.

"The flood didn't even reach your place, besides you went to the movies the other night and didn't take me."

"I know, and I feel bad about that, but I had other business that night."

We're walking between classes, just came from English, and my physics class that Mr. Wood teaches is next. Today's the day we start on bridges.

"Business at the Sierra Theater?"

"Oh, jees. You're not going to understand this."

"You've got that right," says Bev. We stop at the door of the physics class, and Bev turns toward me.

Thomas gives me a wave as he goes in the door. Brenda's with him, but she doesn't hang on him like she used to. She's the only girl in physics. She gives me a look out the corner of her eye as she cuts inside the door. If I don't get in there, I'm going to be late.

"But what you said about me not wanting to go steady is not true," I say. "I do want to go steady with you, and I still want you to keep my ring."

Whoa! I see Chelsey, Prissy's brother, standing with three more colored guys not ten feet away. I've been avoiding him lately. What a glare I'm getting now.

"But I heard you've been asking questions about Brenda again. Look at me, Bobby. God, you've had the attention span of a tree lately. Look at me when I talk to you!"

"I'm listening, but I haven't ever asked questions about Brenda. Can't we talk about this later? I've got to get in class."

"That's not what I heard."

"Yeah? Well, who'd you hear it from?"

"I can't tell you that."

Chelsey is coming toward me. I always notice his shoes. He wears these brown two-tone jobs that have the tongue missing.

"Okay, so how can I defend against it? Phyllis was asking me about Brenda the other night at the show."

"Why did you go to the show without me?"

Just about the time I get my hand on the doorknob, Chelsey has me by the arm, and his fingers are cutting into my meat. I don't much want to talk to him. God, he looks black today. I don't think he wants to talk to me either because, "You motherfuck," is what he calls me to start out with. So I'm trying to get inside the door, but the next thing I know he has me pushed up against the wall. I look around to see who's watching. Bev has stepped back a few paces and taking it all in.

"Where ya want it, huh, Bobby *Ray*? Where you want it?"

"Stay away from me, Chelsey. I don't need anything from you."

"Well, I want somethin from you. I want those fuckin lips that you suck on little nigger girls with. I'm goin to put them back on the other side of your teeth."

"Quit messing around. I need to get to class."

He just stuck his hand inside my shirt and has a handful of meat that he's about to pull off my body. I knew I should've buttoned my top button. He just grits his teeth and squeezes while he's trying to get me to look at him.

"Stop it. You're hurting me."

"Little white boys can hurt, same as little nigger girls. Prissy hurts, Bobby *Ray*."

I wish he'd quit using my middle name like that.

"You thank you know something about hurtin? I want you, motherfuck. I'm goin to teach you what hurtin is."

"I need to get to class."

"I do too, so I can't fuck you up now. School's not the right place. But we got to have it out. You know that? We got to."

"Chelsey," and it's Bev talking to him, "you leave Bobby alone. He belongs to me." And she has this forlorn look like she just scraped me out of the trash can, but I still belong to her. God I hate it when a girl takes up for me.

Whew! I finally make it inside, and just as my seat hits the chair, the bell rings. Bev knows something about what I've done now. How am I ever going to explain about Prissy? Leroy's lying technique is the only way out of this one. Now I've got to think about physics.

"Doesn't anyone have an idea? Did anyone bring their brain today?" asks Mr. Wood. "Thomas. Can you tell the class how the Roman arch stays up? Maybe make a guess?"

Mr. Wood is standing next to the sink that he uses once in a while to demonstrate something he's trying to get across to the class. He runs his hand along the long metal gooseneck spigot. Thomas is sitting next to me. He kind of hunkers down, but it's too late to hide, Thomas.

"Cause it can't fall down." That brings a laugh from the class.

"As silly as that may sound to those of you who think you are more astute than Thomas, there's some truth to it. The Roman arch is in a state of equilibrium. I think that's what Thomas is trying to tell us. That right, Thomas?"

"Yes." Thomas wasn't about to answer no to that one. He hasn't had the right answer to a question in this class all year. I snigger a little under my breath.

"Bobby." Oh shit! Here I go. "Can you tell us why the Roman arch is in a state of equilibrium?"

I have an idea, but I don't want to tell him. Read all about it in a library book the other day. I hope he'll just go on to someone else, but he's being real patient with me. "The forces all add up to zero," is what finally comes out of my mouth.

I hear Thomas snigger next to me.

"What forces, Bobby? Be more specific?"

"The internal forces," says Brenda right quick.

"Did I ask you, Brenda?" And he holds his hand up so she won't say anymore and looks at me.

Brenda hangs her head. I wish he hadn't said that to her. "All the forces have got to be zero," is all I can think to say.

"Which forces?" asks Mr. Wood.

"What Brenda said, the internal forces."

"And where does that principle come from?"

"It was one of the things we learned during the first week. One of Newton's laws."

"Newton's first law, as a matter of fact," says Mr. Wood. "*A body at rest will remain at rest and a body in motion will continue in motion with constant speed in a straight line, as long as no unbalanced force acts on it.* All the forces must add up to zero. So which part of this Roman arch does that apply to?"

"Every piece in it. None of them are going anywhere."

"Tell me more."

"Well, you can look at each brick. Look at the forces the other bricks exert on it, and when you add 'em up, they have to equal zero."

"How do you go about that?"

"You do it once for the horizontal and once for the vertical."

"And how do the vertical forces differ from the horizontal forces?"

"One of the vertical forces acting on the brick is due to gravity."

"And how large is this gravitational force?"

"It's equal to the weight of the brick." I've been looking at Mr. Wood while I talk, but I feel eyes on me, so I glance around the room. How come everybody's looking at me?

"So an arch only has to hold up its own weight. But how about a bridge?" Then he's looking around for someone else to call on. "Brenda. Can you answer that one?"

"It has to hold up its own weight plus that of whatever is going across. Like a horse or a car, maybe a train." Then she looks over at me, raises her eyebrows and smiles. I haven't had a whole lot of smiles from her since homecoming night.

Mr. Wood goes to the board, draws an arch with a white piece of chalk. That old board is so scratched, looks like it's been around a hundred years. "Bobby and Brenda must be hanging out together," says Mr. Wood with his back still to us, and damn if Thomas doesn't turn the brightest shade of red I've seen in a while. Then Mr. Wood turns back around. "So how do we make this arch into a bridge?"

I know the answer to that one. "I'd go get the tractor with a scraper on it, and spread enough dirt across the top to make it flat and put a road across it." I knew I should have kept my big mouth shut because now I have the whole class laughing at me.

★

"What came over you?" is what Thomas is asking me after class. "I've never seen you act like that in class." I think he's a little disappointed in me.

"I read a lot about bridges." I have Thomas on one side of me and

254

Brenda on the other. "I want to get to college someday. I've started studying some at home."

"You're the most unpredictable human being I know," says Thomas.

"The most undervalued," says Brenda. She keeps brushing her hot arm up against mine.

I keep looking out for Chelsey. I don't need to see Bev again right now either.

CHAPTER 35: *Papa's Problem with Delbert*

Here comes Papa out into the field where me, Curt and Delbert are working on the planter. I can tell he's mad because he's walking fast and has on a straight face. When Papa's mad, everything better be working right, or else. But we've been broke down all morning and now it's noon and we don't have anything done. Sometimes Papa's mad when he comes back from town and I always wonder if he's not feeling guilty for sloughing off like that. But he wanted us to finish this field here on the home place today, this being Saturday, so we can move on tomorrow to the forty acres we've rented from Mr. Grissom because he's been talking to Papa about how come we don't have it planted yet.

I feel guilty anyway because me and Delbert have been talking a lot about how I might get the money for college instead of putting my mind to getting the planter fixed. Curt's been talking about the County Fair that comes up next month. He's been kicked out of school for fighting and I think he's kind of happy about it. Guess Papa'll have some more help for a few days. All morning, Curt's been talking like he's Papa and then like he's talking to Papa, sometimes like I'm Papa. We've all been having fun about the way Papa is, but that has to stop. Delbert's pulled off his cowboy hat and set it on the planter and now he and Curt are between the planter and the tractor, trying to adjust the height of the wedge that separates the ground so the seeds can fall through. I guess Curt's so hard at it that he doesn't know Papa has come up and standing right above him, blocking the sun, and Curt thinks it's me, but he's still acting like I'm Papa.

"Get out of my goddamn light, Hershel," Curt says, then looks up with a smile expecting to see me.

"I've told you about that cussing, Curt," says Papa and when Papa has a reason to be mad it seems to calm him. So now he hardly seems mad anymore, just puts on his calm face and starts pulling off his belt.

Curt looks thunderstruck. That face of his goes from smiling to crying so quick, it's hard to believe it's the same face. He's looking for a way out from under the planter, but Delbert's on one side on his knees and he's starting to move back but not very fast. Papa's on the other side, and he can't help but smile a little at Curt's predicament.

Curt has on a long sleeve flannel shirt with a big collar, and Papa raises him clean off the ground with it before he turns him loose. Papa hits Curt once with the belt, jerking it so that it pops hard, before Curt can get away, then he falls in the soft dirt and Papa's on top of him, flailing with that doubled up leather belt like he's thrashing wheat. Curt scrambles away from him, but Papa gets a kick in on the seat of Curt's pants as he runs off toward the house crying. Papa starts to run after him then changes his mind.

I pick up the wrench Curt was using, thinking I'd like to have a try at fixing Papa with it.

"I'll give you more when I get home," Papa shouts at Curt. "I'm warning you. You leave us short handed out here in the field, I'll get you. Better come back and take your medicine." Then stands watching him run on off with his head down.

Meanwhile, me and Delbert are working extra hard on that wedge. Delbert's put his hat back on.

"You worthless farm hands have been screwing around with this goddamn piece-of-shit planter all afternoon and haven't got this field planted yet. I can't believe I pay out good money for help like this."

"I realize it sure doesn't look good, Mr. Hammer." Delbert doesn't ever call Papa by his last name.

I see Papa out of the corner of my eye, bent over scratching through the dirt to see if we've been getting the seed in the ground right. He straightens up and looks out across the field then back at us. I'm working fast with that wrench now, because I don't want him all over me.

"Maybe we could get that bolt tight enough if we both got our hands on that wrench, Bobby," says Delbert.

"Crookedest goddamn rows in the state of California. I'm ashamed for people to even see my field," is what Papa comes up with next.

"I was hoping myself we could do better than we have been," says Delbert

But I know there's nothing wrong with the rows we've planted.

"I don't see how you let these kids plant these seeds so deep. We're going to have to plow this field up and plant it over for sure."

"Well, maybe I'm wrong, Mr. Hammer, but I was thinking that maybe it should go a little deeper because of the wind we've been having. It might dry out too quick."

"You don't get paid to think, Delbert. I do the thinking. You do the working." I haven't ever heard Papa talk to Delbert like that. And he's been working for Papa for ten years. Delbert don't know what to say about that so he just turns back to helping me.

"Why don't you let me pull on the wrench with you, Bobby. Maybe both of us can get it tight," says Delbert, being about as helpful as he can.

But I'm straining real hard already and damn if I don't shear that bolt off.

"Delbert, you sonofabitch. You just coaxed him to breaking that goddamn bolt. I ought to fire you. No wonder this thing's not fixed. You're more harm than good."

I don't think Papa should be talking about firing Delbert. He might quit and we have to have his help to get all this seed in the ground. I'm thinking about saying something for Delbert and hoping he'll take up for himself, but neither of us say anything.

"You've been out here with these kids screwing around all morning like you're on welfare and getting paid for work you don't have to do." And then damn if Papa, and I can tell he's real mad but I don't expect this, he makes a run at Delbert. And Delbert is backing off fast. "Get off my land, you sonofabitch! Second thought, come back here. I want to whip your ass." And Papa gets close enough that he throws a punch at Delbert. "You're fired. You hear me? You're a fired son-of-a-bitch," Papa shouts, and he raises his chin like he's lofting the words to get more distance out of them. Delbert's just running on out of the field with his hand holding that Texas hat on his head.

Well, Papa's run both of them off. Now what has he got for me? That's what I'm wondering.

★

"I don't know, Bobby Ray, I hated to fire Delbert like that. But bygod, he had it coming. I don't know why he did it anyway. Shearing off that bolt like that. He's been around long enough to know he can only push me so far. He knew what he was doing. Sometimes I feel kind of sorry for him, him being no smarter than he is. But I can't keep the likes of him around. I'll go broke. This isn't a welfare organization."

Me and Papa are in the house just finishing lunch. Mama put the fried chicken and potato salad on the table and then got out. I haven't seen her since.

"I don't have any handouts to give to people. I've been broke once in my life. During the depression and the dust bowl. Back in the '30's. You study about that stuff in school now. I'm never going to see a time like that again if I can help it. And Delbert's sure as hell not dragging me down to that level again. It may be tough on you and me and Curt before I can find someone to take his place, but we'll make it. May not get to see as much of the Fair this year as we'd like. But you're not working up to snuff lately either, Bobby Ray. Your mind's wondering off work. I'm going to have to lean on you if you don't start taking up some slack. Damn Delbert. Why couldn't he have waited until after the Fair to pull a stunt like that anyway? I'll never understand the likes of him. Sometimes I think he's the meanest man I've ever met. Stripping that bolt off like he meant to do it. Leaving us shorthanded at a time like this."

"He didn't do it, Papa. I did. Let's get that straight."

"Well, he was coaxing you. I heard him. I might even go see him at home. And this wasn't the first time either. I've been watching him lately. I think maybe he just plays dumb, like maybe he's a lot smarter than he lets on. He never has cared for me much. Ever since he failed at farming and had to come work for me, he's been jealous of my success. I've heard him talking before that I had a lot of blind luck, particular with the weather. And I admit that I am good at guessing the weather, better than those goddamn weathermen. They ought to shoot a bunch of those bastards just on general principles. They're always getting the farmers to thinking they know a little something, and then when it gets important, like maybe planting time, they get it wrong every year. There's a reason for that I tell you. They can't be that wrong by accident. But I do feel bad about Delbert. That poor dumb sonofabitch getting himself fired like that, and him with six kids and two in high school. To tell you the truth, I don't know how they're going to make it. I don't see how he could get himself fired like that."

"Well, it's sure not anybody else's fault but yours," I tell him. "And it's your fault cause you fired him." I've had it with Papa. I don't mean to talk back to him, but some things just need saying.

Papa's through talking, after me saying that, and just doing a lot of swallowing, so we sit here quiet like for a while. I push back my plate because I'm through eating lunch. Then Curt comes in real slow, testing the water. But when Papa sees him, he remembers what he told Curt out in the field, so he gets up slow like maybe he's tired and like maybe he doesn't even want to do what he's about to do.

"Come on, Curt. You know what I promised you when you left us shorthanded out in the field."

"Oh, Papa, don't whip me, Papa. I don't want to be whipped again, Papa. It hurt so bad the last time," is the way Curt is taking it.

But Papa's coming on, pulling off his belt. Curt starts crying and asking for Papa to use his hand, because then Papa will hurt too, every time he hits and he won't hit so hard. Papa's just really mean with that belt. Curt's lost his courage this time for sure. He's had too much time to think about it.

I get flashes of the last time Papa whipped him. I remember Curt in the back room, taking that belt across one shoulder and then the other. I still can't stand to think about the welts he had. I start to breathe fast and my legs are getting weak because I'm following right behind Papa as he's following Curt into the far corner of the living room. It's like my legs made the decision by themselves and just got up and are carrying me after him.

"Papa," I say, and I can tell my voice is real calm even if I'm not on the inside, but he doesn't even notice.

"Papa!" and this time I have a little force behind my voice, so Papa turns part way round to see what I'm up to.

"You're not going to do it, Papa," but my voice starts to quiver.

"What did you say, son?"

"You're not whipping Curt." And now out of the corner of my eye, I see Trish standing in the doorway to the hall.

"You're my son, too. You're not telling me what I'm going to do to Curt."

"Yes I am, Papa. I don't want to. But this time I am. He's too big. You're not whipping him. Not now. Not ever again." I'm just afraid I'm going to cry before I can get this over with.

So Papa comes to me. "Well, I guess I've got some for you that I'll got to dish out before I can give Curt what I promised."

"No you're not, Papa, cause I'm not taking it anymore either." And now I'm standing my ground, looking down at him and he's right in front of me, looking me straight in the eyes. And I swear to God, I'm not afraid of him, but I'm still shaking. He doesn't take his eyes off mine, but he rears back the belt and whacks me once across the shoulder and I catch the folded leather belt in my hand, feeling that hot stripe down my back.

"Turn it loose, Bobby Ray," he says, almost like he's begging me, and I can see tears forming in his eyes.

"It's all over, Papa. I feel just as bad about this as you do, but if you can't quit by yourself, then I'm going to stop you."

And so he jerks at the belt once, but I still won't let go.

"So you want to run the house? What the hell's wrong with you? You're not a man yet."

"I just want you to quit whipping Curt. You whip him too hard."

Papa acts like he wants to hit me with his fist, but can't bring himself to do it. So he runs into me with his chest, pushes me backward.

"Stop it, Papa. I'm warning you. I'm not taking it off you anymore."

"You're warning me! Goddamn! Didn't you hear that? He's warning me!" And he turns loose of the belt, turns around and starts to flail into me when Trish steps into the room.

"We're all warning you, Papa," she says. "We're not putting up with you're temper tantrums anymore." And Trish doesn't look mad or even determined for that matter. It's just like she has stated a fact.

Papa's afraid of Trish. He walks toward the kitchen. "Louise!" he shouts. "You come in here and help me deal with this kid. I'm not putting up with him anymore. Louise! Get Loretta on the phone. Get her over here. I haven't had anybody treat me like this since Lenny died." He bites his lip to keep from crying but he's not quite making it. And then he turns on me, again with tears in his eyes, but it's like he found a mean place in him that he's been saving just for me.

"Get your things and get out!" he says. "You're turning the whole family against me. You don't belong in this house. I'm not your father anyway. So get out! Pack your goddamn bags and get the hell out of my house!" Then he walks on through the kitchen, and I hear the backdoor slam.

And now here's Trish, smelling like a woman, with her arms around my neck. She's all sweaty and crying real hard. God, I didn't know she's so

261

tall.

    I walk outside through the front door knowing that mistakes don't come any bigger than the one I just made and wondering how Papa can say that he's not my father anymore.

CHAPTER 36: *Helen's Ring*

I step outside and take a seat on the front porch wondering what came over me. And now Papa doesn't even like me enough to claim me as a son. The thing that hurt most was that he sounded like he really meant it, that I'm not his son. I'm just sitting here thinking about this when up drives a pickup that I have seen before, but never at our place. It's Mr. McCallum's pickup that he hauls wood in from the lumberyard to his work sites. And Brenda's driving it. Brenda with another girl. At first, I think the other girl must be Phyllis because they're always together, then I see that it isn't at all. Brenda comes out of that pickup walking toward me and she has the other girl following along behind. Brenda's beaming.

"Bobby," she says, "I want you to meet my cousin, Helen."

Helen won't look up at me. Sure enough. She's the same girl Charles had with him at the show.

Brenda's still standing there. First she looks at Helen then at me. "Come on, you guys, talk."

Helen seems a lot younger standing here in front of me than when I saw her with Charles. Seems a lot smaller too. Her hair's a darker red than I've ever seen before. Even in the bright sunshine, it's the color of wine. Her lips are plain purple and fat like a bruise. She has a line around her lips where they become skin that's like a ridge and sharp like it's been drawn in with a pencil except that she doesn't have any makeup on. I have to remember that she was with Charles the night I tried to kill him. It's hard to keep that in mind while I'm looking at her. Knowing she was Lenny's girl.

"Maybe we should take a walk," I say. I start down the lane into our field and she falls in beside me. Brenda walks behind. Brenda doesn't look mad at me at all now. There's an old junkyard in Mr. Grissom's field where it joins ours. Not much to it, just piles of old used lumber, tangles of bailing wire, broken sections of cement pipe, pieces of old buildings. Mr. Grissom used to sic his dogs on us when he'd see us out here playing, back when Lenny was alive. I used to come here hunting with him. Ground squirrels and owls everywhere. Owls that live in the ground. Not many people know some owls do that. They live in old squirrel and rabbit holes.

I tell Helen about the owls and she listens. "'Come on, Bobby Ray,' Lenny would say. 'Let's go nip some rabbits in the bud,' because that's what I really liked, to find baby rabbits. We'd catch one once in a while and bring it home. I'd try to feed it grass or leaves or even a bowl of milk. Try to feed it right up until it died. 'Another one died of loneliness,' is what Lenny would say. I knew better, though. I knew it died because it wouldn't eat. I stayed with it all the time so I knew it couldn't have been lonely. I was just a little kid then." I'm just talking, telling Helen all this, when she stops me.

"You still miss him, don't you?" she asks.

"Lately, more than ever," I say. Let out a big breath of air. "It's been worse than when he died."

"Can you keep a secret?"

"That's one of my problems. I can't keep my mouth shut about anything anymore."

"Do you think you could handle just one? Brenda and I've been talking about Lenny's death for the last five years. Lately she's been trying to get me to talk to you. Now that I've met you, I can see why she thinks so much of you."

Her eyes are the darkest eyes I've ever seen. They don't even have a pupil, or maybe they are all pupil. It's hard to say which. She has on this sleeveless dress that's cut kind of low in front, shows a little skin in back too. She has dark skin like a natural tan only it's a little red, like her hair. And black eyebrows.

"I was more than friends with Lenny," she says.

"I know. You were his girl."

"I was more than his girl. And I want you to know this because it casts a different light on what happened to me and Lenny. Because Lenny wasn't true to me, Bobby. He was running around on me. And I was trying to hurt him by running around with Charles. I don't know why but I couldn't stay away from Charles. But I'm going to tell you something that no one else knows. Not even my father and mother. No one knows this, Bobby." And she walks me away from Brenda a little ways.

Brenda looks nervous. I wonder what that is all about?

Helen keeps going. "Not your parents, not my parents, not Brenda, not Charles. No one." She has a full load of tears in each eye now. And it's the strangest thing. She takes my hand. And it's the coldest hand I've ever felt. It's like her body doesn't have any heat. It's as if she needs the heat from my body to be able to say this.

I'm wondering if I really want to hear it. I'm in enough trouble already, and I'm beginning to learn that knowing things means trouble.

"Lenny had a hard streak. He could be the sweetest boy in the world when he wanted, but he could be real hard when he felt cornered. That's what he told me I did to him. I cornered him. He had so much ambition. All he thought about was baseball. Me and baseball were his life. Oil and water, he called us." Then she stops. She looks at me for a second, then back down at the ground. "Did he ever talk about me?"

I don't know what to say. I can tell that she needs to know that he did. But the truth is, he didn't. I guess I'm going to have to let her down. "He never talked to me about anything but baseball. Cept he cussed Papa for making him work when he wanted to play ball some in the summer and Papa said he had to work. Lenny never said that he was serious about a girl. I was a lot younger than him. But I remember him bringing you over to the house once. I think it was you. Seems like a hundred years ago."

"It does seem like it's been a long time, doesn't it? When he brought me over, that was the day after we did it."

"Seems like a dream," I say. I can't imagine Lenny with this girl. I can't imagine him kissing anyone. She just looks so soft and smooth all over. And she looks so young. It's like, the longer I talk to her, the younger she gets. I always think of Lenny as being so old.

"Brenda's been telling me how grownup you are." Her hand feels a little warmer now. "She's been telling me that you're different from everyone else. That you're a fine young man. She thinks the world of you, so I'm going to take a chance on you too. Cause I have to tell someone."

I start to tell her to stop. I have all I can handle right now. I wish I'd never gotten involved in trying to figure out what happened to my brother. It's just causing me so much trouble.

"I'd just turned eighteen. We were both eighteen."

I'm leaning up against an old windmill. It's a tall building with a lot of missing sideboards, slim with sloping sides and a flat top. The wheel doesn't turn anymore but the vane still points it into the wind. It creaks in the breeze.

"I'm looking for a ring," she says. "Do you know anything, anything at all, about a ring?"

"They buried him with his class ring. I know that because they had his hands folded across his chest. I saw him in his casket. He had his ring on."

"It wasn't that ring. It was another. Maybe your mother has it. It means more to me than anything else in the world."

"I don't remember another ring. Mama could have it in her cedar chest."

"If things could have only been different. If I could have told someone after he died, maybe it would have helped me a little. But at the Cemetery, there was Gretta all blown up like a balloon. All the trouble then was over her and Lenny. I couldn't tell anybody without making a fool of myself and even worse out of Lenny. So I let our secret be buried with him. At least I thought I did. But now Charles is back in town. I can't get away from this. It's like a sickness. Don't run around with him, Bobby. I saw you following him when I was with him the other night, and I'm concerned about you. I hated to be with Charles, but I had to find out if he had my ring. You distracted him just long enough that I got a chance to do a quick search of his car and his house. Lenny's journal isn't in his car anymore. Neither is my ring. I'm convinced that Charles doesn't have it either. He'd know more than he does if he had Lenny's journal. There's something strange about that Hudson but don't know what. Seems different somehow. But at least I got back some old clothes back. That was embarrassing." She starts crying and her face gets that tore up look about it. She pulls her hand out of mine. "It's hard to say this. But Lenny and I did it two months before he got killed. We went over and back in one day. Had to cut school. Got back from Reno late so both our parents were mad at us." She covers her face with her hands. "I've just got to find my wedding ring. It's all I have left. We got married, Bobby. Lenny and I were married."

★

This thing about my birth certificate not being with the rest of the family's and now Papa claiming that I'm not his son, has me to thinking, thinking hard. I have to do something I've been putting off for a long time. After Helen and Brenda leave, I get in my Chevy and drive to Merced. I need to see some hospital records and the hospital in Chowchilla is new so the records wouldn't be there. I guess I've been rubbing shoulders with Bev too long. Maybe it's not shoulders we've been rubbing against each other, but we've been doing it too long anyway. The woman behind the records desk at Mercy Hospital in Merced tells me that they don't have anyone at the files desk on Saturdays and besides, all the files are confidential and they can't let anyone but a doctor see them. So I go back to Chowchilla and stop at Dr. Wade's home. His daughter Billie looks glad to see me at first, but when I ask where her father is, she just gets huffy and says that he's at the hospital and goes back inside. Grace Magdalena is sitting in the hospital waiting room, she turns her head, won't look at me. And Dr. Wade's in the same place where they had Leroy only now he's with Brother Hensen, at least I think that's the Preacher's voice I hear. He's in a chair with his back to me. Dr. Wade has just said that needing a penicillin shot is not an emergency. Brother Hensen says that in the shape he's in, it is. Dr. Wade comes out to the reception desk because I'm raising a ruckus about seeing him. I ask Dr. Wade what he knows about Aunt Loretta trying to commit suicide, but he tells me that I better talk to my family about that. He's not supposed to discuss private family matters.

So I go from his office to the police station. I'll go to the County Courthouse in Madera if I have to. But I catch Brock about to get in his police car. I walk up to him.

"I know just what you're after," he says. "And I'm not signing that ticket until you get the steel wool out of those mufflers, so you might as well go on home."

I feel real bad about that because I just had some new glasspacks put on the other day. No steel wool.

"You got me all wrong," I say. "Can anyone look at police records?"

"Sure. Our records are public."

"I need to go back a few years," I tell him.

★

I've never seen Mama afraid of me before. It's almost sundown by the time I get home. "I've come back to get my stuff like Papa told me," I say. She keeps her head down and won't look at me. "But I'm not leaving here without having some questions answered. I've been down at the police station looking over their eighteen-year-old records. And I'm going to the County Courthouse in Madera if you don't talk straight to me. I know a baby was born by the name of Joseph Hershel Hammer on June 6, 1939

267

and I know that he died on July 10, 1939. You tell me that I was born on May 17, 1939, but I couldn't find a record of me. I know Aunt Loretta tried to commit suicide on August 7, 1939. I need to know the truth about Joseph and her. I want to know the truth about me. And I'm not settling for any less."

So Mama starts crying.

"For starters, I want to know where my birth certificate is."

"There isn't one."

"Jees, Mama." And already, I don't want to know the rest.

"You were born at home."

"Well who was Joseph? I thought maybe that was really my name."

Then Mama smiles at me through tears. "Okay, Bobby Ray. I guess it's time to get this one settled. This will put things back in their natural order."

Mama takes me into her's and Papa's bedroom, closes the door. She raises the top on her big cedar chest, digs down past the box with Lenny's, Trish's, and Curt's birth certificates that I looked through the morning after I talked to Charles under the bridge, and she comes up with a pink-paper candy box, has to take Papa's black revolver off the top of it. His pistol looks bigger than I thought it did. The lid of the candy box has blue and red flowers on it and some words that say HOOPER'S MY SELECTION CHOCOLATES. When she opens the lid, the first thing I see is a pair of tiny white baby shoes. Mama quits crying and just looks real proud.

"I got to keep my box of chocolates," she says. "But I had to bury my baby. This is all I have left of my baby boy, Bobby Ray." She bends over with heavy heaving sobs and falls to one knee. She won't let me help her up though. "You've done enough for me, as it is, over this sadness. If it hadn't been for you I wouldn't have lived a week past my baby boy dying. You brought me back from the black pit, Bobby Ray. Four years before, when Lenny was a baby, he wouldn't nurse. I don't think I ever really got over that. When baby Joseph was born, he was everything I ever wanted. He took to me good, but he had a bad heart. You and Joseph were born within a couple of weeks of each other."

"You mean, you're really not my mama?"

"That's right. At least not the one that gave birth to you. And that's the reason you don't have a birth certificate. Your Aunt Loretta is the one that gave birth to you. She had you at home and we never told anyone."

"Oh, Mama. No."

"We even buried baby Joseph with a quiet family funeral. Mr. Hickman was one of the few who knew he died. Almost no one knew about you. Most people think the two of you were the same baby."

"But how come you raised me, if I belonged to Aunt Loretta?"

"She had her reasons for giving you up. But let me go on with my story. Lenny and your papa weren't enough after baby Joseph died. I started out just being your wet-nurse because Loretta didn't have any milk. You were the hungriest baby I'd ever seen."

Somehow, I just can't imagine me feeding off of Mama's body.

"You took to my breasts like a fox sucking eggs. You even got mad about it when my milk was too slow coming and would butt my breast like a calf does its mother's udder and then you'd just squall. You'd get too mad to eat. Dr. Wade said that it'd be good for both of us, you and me. So all this time, and I know this has been unfair to you, but you've been living the life of baby Joseph for me. And since Lenny died, you've been living Lenny's life for your papa. He won't admit it, but it's true. So you've been carrying the burden of those two lives on your shoulders. It's time we quit doing that to you. Don't be too hard on your papa, though. He just had a real bad need for you to be someone you're not. He needed to correct some mistakes he felt like he made with Lenny, some things he thinks cost Lenny his life. He was trying to make up for it through you, and finally he just gave up. Now it's time for you to live your own life."

"But why didn't Aunt Loretta just keep me if I was her baby?"

"Talk to her about that. I know she wants to tell you herself. Give her that chance. The way you took to me liked to have killed Loretta, though. She wanted to nurse you herself. But even then she was talking about giving you up."

I walk away from Mama. I can't believe this. I stand in the corner, beat my head on the wall till it hurts.

"Come back over here, Bobby Ray. And quit hurting yourself. There is no reason to be that upset."

"I'm why she tried to commit suicide?" And I can tell that I've just hurt Mama's feelings. "She wanted to kill herself because I came along? She didn't want me?"

"That's not true, Bobby Ray. Sit down on the bed over there. I want you to shut up and quit feeling sorry for yourself because I'm going to tell you something. What you said is just not true. There's never been a mother on the face of this earth that loved her baby as much as Loretta loved you. I was even ashamed of myself for the way I loved Lenny after watching her with you. Loretta is not all there. And she knows it. I don't know why the Lord couldn't have blessed her with just a little more ignorance. She knew she was in no shape to raise a kid, so she gave you to us. She knew her big brother, Hershel, would see to it that you got raised proper. She was just a teenager when you were born. Just fifteen. Think of it. Just a few months older than Trish. She made the supreme sacrifice. Made it for you. And she's stayed with that decision all these years because it was the right one. But it killed her. Everyday of her life since then's been lived without the one person she loves most. And she hated herself so much knowing that she was no good for you that she tried to kill herself. More than tried. She did kill herself. Her suicide wasn't any mute cry for help. When Hershel first got her to the hospital, the doctors wouldn't even work on her. They said that no one could lose that much blood and live. She had no pulse, no blood pressure. 'She's already dead,' is what Dr. Wade said. Hershel just wouldn't have it. 'Well, look at her then, Hershel,' Dr. Wade said. 'Just look at her arms. They're laid open to the bone. She's bled herself like a heifer at slaughter. It's only been two months since she gave birth, for christsake. She's no bigger than a ten-year-old kid. She doesn't even weigh ninety pounds. She just didn't have the strength left to survive this.' Hershel backed Dr. Wade into the corner of that hospital room and told him if he didn't go to work on her that they'd be burying both of them cause Hershel was going to kill him."

"You mean Papa threatened Dr. Wade?"

"He was desperate. Loretta was the only family he had left. So Dr. Wade didn't like it but they went to work on her anyway. After a while, Dr. Wade came to Hershel and asked if they could stop. Hershel said, 'No.' He'd given up both his parents to a twister in Norman, Oklahoma two years before, just given up baby Joseph, and he wasn't about to give up his sister too. So they went to work again. Dr. Wade asked him three more times. Finally, he said, 'She's dead, Hershel. She's dead. Give her up.' They didn't want to waste any more blood on her. And Dr. Wade was mad too, so I thought they were going to fist city. Hershel didn't like it but he said, 'Okay,' and then he just walked out. Didn't thank anybody for their effort. They prepared Loretta for the undertaker, but when Mr. Hickman got there to pick her up, he saw that she was still alive. Three weeks later, they finally said she'd live. For three weeks she hovered between life and death. Dr. Wade said he'd never seen anything like it. I tell you, there was a tug of war for that girl's soul going on between God and the devil, a war the likes of which we've never seen on this earth. Looks like neither side could get the upper hand so they sent her back to us. Why they both wanted her so much is hard to say. Why she's still here even against her own will is even tougher. But don't you ever again say that she didn't want you. You do, I'll slap your mouth shut."

"So who is my father? If Aunt Loretta is my mother, who is my papa?"

"You'll have to talk to Loretta about that. She should answer it."

"But why is my name Hammer. Or is it Hammer? Why isn't it something else?"

"Because Loretta wasn't married, Bobby Ray. She never has been. So her name, and yours, is Hammer."

★

I'm in what was my bedroom clearing out my stuff. I have the sniffles. I'm worrying about who the sorry sonofabitch is that is my father. Curt comes in. He flips on the light. I didn't realize it was so dark.

"What you crying about, Bobby Ray?"

"The bedroom is all yours, Curt. You're old enough, you shouldn't be sleeping with your brother anyway."

"You mean Papa really meant that you have to leave?"

"That's the look of it."

"Guess you should've let him whip me."

"No. That's not the answer. Not anymore."

Trish is standing in the doorway. "What you up to, Bobby Ray? What's that box for?" She looks really huffy. "Papa wasn't serious. You're not leaving."

"I crossed him one too many times."

"No. You've got it wrong," she says. And she takes my red corduroy coat off the bed and hangs it back in the closet. "He'll get over being mad, he always does."

"I've already talked to Mama about me leaving." I take my coat back out of the closet, take it off the hanger, put it on this time.

"Damn, you. You're going to let him kick you out, just like that?"

"I can't see that I have a choice."

"No choice! This house is as much yours as it is his. He's not God."

271

"There's more to it than that."

"You just did the first thing in your life, in any of our lives, to make things better. For the first time you showed some real courage and now you just turn your back, show your yellow streak and slink off."

"Come on, Trish," I can't stand to cry in front of a girl, "leaving isn't as easy as you think."

"I can't wait to hear where you're going."

"Aunt Loretta is the only other family we have. Guess I don't have much of a choice."

"That's really a match. The two of you together should be against the law."

So here I go. I'm not telling them the truth. Trish and Curt seem strange though. I feel different toward them. They're not my sister and brother anymore. They are my cousins. I don't know what to do. It's obvious that Mama hasn't told them the whole story yet, and she probably won't. So I feel like this time, right here, with me putting my clothes in an old cardboard box and Trish standing there looking like she might want to hit me and Curt feeling like he owes me something for standing up to Papa but still wanting to cuss me, this is a crossroads for me. I can play it the way Mama and Papa have all these years, or I can start spreading the truth. Can the truth do anymore damage than the silence that I've heard so loud all these years?

"Curt, come over here and sit down. Trish, I'm not going to tell you what to do because you wouldn't do it anyway. But I'm going to tell you something because I like both of you. I know we don't do a lot of talking about how we feel about each other, but you've been my sister and brother all these years and now things have changed. I need to tell you about it. I don't believe Mama and Papa will ever tell you. I don't want you to wonder for the next hundred years what this is all about."

I think Curt just about wet his pants because he didn't have anything to say back. He just finds a place to sit in the center of our bed, his bed now.

"You're not my brother, and Trish, this is true, you are not my sister, not by blood."

"Ah, what kind of shit is this?" Curt's found himself again. "You may not want to be, but you're my brother, that's for sure."

"I'm going to call Mama in here. She can straighten this out," is what

272

Trish says.

"Sit down and shutup," I tell Trish, then I go over to Curt, shake him by the shoulders. "I want to be. You'll never know how bad I wish I was." Then I turn back to Trish. "Listen to me. Cause I'm telling the truth. I just had a long talk with Mama. I'm not who you think I am. I'm not even who I thought I was. You're my cousins, not my sister and bother." Then I close the door so Mama won't hear me. My voice is getting a little loud. "I don't have much time, so I'd better make this fast. I've got to get out before Papa gets home. You had a baby brother named Joseph that was born a couple of weeks after me. He died. Aunt Loretta is really my mother. Papa and Mama raised me because Aunt Loretta couldn't. Quit looking at me like that, Curt. This is the truth, I tell you."

"You've gone crazy," says Curt, but I can tell he believes me now.

Trish just shakes her head no over and over.

"Listen to me. It's the truth, I tell you. I just keep finding out more and more about our family all the time. The reason I'm going to Aunt Loretta's place to stay is because she's the one that gave birth to me. I could lie and say that I'm going to her place because I have no place else to go. But that's not true. I'm going over there because she's my mother. This world's a strange place. I feel like I live on Mars."

I have both of them stumped this time.

"I hate to tell you all this and just leave, but I have to. I know you'll worry about it, but try not to worry anymore than you have to. And for christsake, don't tell Mama and Papa I told you. Not yet anyway. He'd probably come looking for me with a gun. Give me a little time. I still have more to tell you, but not right now. It's not about the two of you. You really belong to Mama and Papa, both of you. I've seen your birth certificates, so don't worry about that. The rest of it, I think, is about Lenny. But I don't know the full story yet myself, and there'll be some things that I can't tell you until you get older. But I will tell you. I promise you that. Eventually, I'll tell you everything."

CHAPTER 37: *Bobby Ray's New Mama*

I'm afraid. Two weeks ago, I moved in with my new mother, Aunt Loretta. To go along with my new mother, I have a new perspective. I've been thinking about how we're always blaming everything on Papa. Maybe Delbert is a little simpleminded. Maybe Papa feels the pressure of taking care of so many people. I wish I could've found a better way to stop him whipping Curt. Maybe I should've just talked to him after he did it the time before. And now I find out that Lenny's problems were worse than I ever imagined. Helen says she thinks she can't go on. Life just seems like it's not workable. I don't know anybody that's making it too good, now that I think about it. Curt told me Trish woke up screaming the other night. Took Mama a half hour to calm her.

I can't stay away from Papa's farm. Keep dreaming about it. Right now, I'm out on this piece of ground on the home place that we were planting when Delbert got fired, scratching at the old crusted earth to see if the cotton's going to come up. In places the ground's cracked and lifted a little. I take a broken twig from one of last years cotton stalks and lift the earth, and it's like finding a little green surprise underneath. Seems almost impossible that that's what's happening all over this sixty acre field, just beneath the surface.

I used to feel like this place was mine. I knew it belonged to Mama and Papa but still, it seemed like it was also mine. Now this place just belongs to Papa. I don't know why, but Mama doesn't even seem like part of the family. Life's so strange and I'm the strangest part of it. I don't belong to anybody. I don't belong anywhere. I feel like I'm living in a stranger's body. And I'm afraid to be by myself. When I walk into Aunt Loretta's kitchen, I'm afraid of the knives in the silverware drawer. I don't carry my pocketknife anymore. Put it in my dresser drawer. I don't know what I might do.

Now I'm a part of everything I've ever been ashamed of. Aunt Loretta's spare bedroom has always been locked. When she unlocked it for me, it was like someone had been living there all these years. The cleanest room I've ever seen. My things have always had a way of disappearing. Sometimes it was old worn out toys, other times old clothes. I always thought Mama threw them away. When I questioned her about things of mine that were missing, like maybe an old shirt I really liked, she'd say she probably threw it away, or when one of my favorite toys turned up missing, she'd say Papa took it off to the junkyard. Now they show up in Aunt Loretta's spare bedroom. When she opened the door, there was my little rocking chair I had when I was three sitting in a corner. My first tricycle, with a back wheel missing, was out in the middle of the floor. I've been thinking about fixing it. Papa never would. All my old shirts that got too small for me were on hangers in the closet, and on the shelf above them were all my old coloring books. I never knew I was so bad about not staying in the lines. My old B-B gun with the stock loose, the one I killed birds with, was standing in a corner. Before I could put my clothes in the chest of drawers, I had to take out all my old holey underwear and stacks of socks that weren't fit for a foot. Everything washed clean and smelling a little like lye soap. A cardboard box was in the floor of the closet filled with old baby diapers. I feel more at home here than I ever did at Mama's and Papa's. And that's the big problem. I feel comfortable in her house, more than I do with my life, if you catch my meaning, and I'm ashamed of her. She's crazy. Not only do I have my own bed, I have my own room. Aunt Loretta even bought a little radio for me with her own money because she knows how I like to listen to Stan's Private Line out of Fresno before I go to sleep. That first night I listened to "Butterfly" by Andy Williams, "Round and Round," by Perry Como, and "All Shook Up," by Elvis. But I like Fats Domino best, and I was just about to turn off the radio and go to sleep when Fats started singing, "I'm walkin', yes indeed, and I'm talkin', 'bout you and me..." The last song I heard was Gogi Grant's "The Wayward Wind." It's been around a few months, getting kind of old, but I don't know if I'll ever get tired of it.

I step from furrow to furrow scratching in the ground, then walk along a row into the middle of the field, stop, scratch some more, think about how close to it I was last night. Standing there in the kitchen by myself after Aunt Loretta had gone to bed, or at least after I thought she'd gone to bed, I felt like something had taken over control of me from the inside.

I've never been so afraid. I opened the refrigerator door and there on the bottom shelf was a piece of red meat sitting in a puddle of blood, a roast Aunt Loretta's cooking right now for lunch. I got out the butcher knife that she'll use when she cuts up the fresh cooked roast after she's pulls it out of the oven, and I ran the blade along my arm, just to see how it felt, ran it along my neck. Cut my finger a little on the sharp edge. Sucked the blood.

Later that night, I woke to what I thought was music, sounded way off in the distance. I peeked out my door and saw a thin column of light coming from a crack in Aunt Loretta's door, tiptoed down the hall and took a peek. I don't want to say anything bad about my new mother, but what I saw I wouldn't want to be known around town either. This is something I won't tell Curt. She was also dressed like a high school kid and dancing with a broom like it was a man. Every time I woke during the night, I heard the music. It's been that way night after night. I don't think the woman ever sleeps. Sometimes when I look in on her, she's coloring in a coloring book.

One morning, we were out in her turkey shed, where she keeps the little turkeys before they get big enough for her to put outside. Now I know why she's so strange. All the peeps out of those thousands of beaks is enough to put your mind away. I couldn't find the courage to ask her who my father is. She doesn't seem to be in a big hurry to tell me either. She put on her gloves, and I don't know why because there wasn't anything else that could stick to a human being's hands. We'd just finished painting her house red. She told me why Mama and Papa left Oklahoma and came to California. How Papa couldn't take going broke during the dust bowl. There was four of them then, Papa, Mama, baby Lenny and Aunt Loretta. She stayed with them after a twister killed their papa and mama. Now I understand Papa and don't feel too good about myself.

Only Papa's not my papa. He's my uncle. And Mama's my aunt, not even blood kin. So now when I look at my life, everything is turned around. The things I used to think they did to me now seem like things they did for me. Like Papa trying to get me to stay and farm with him. Even talked about buying me a little piece of ground. I'm not even his own kid and he put clothes on my back and fed me all those years. And when he told me he'd like for me to farm with him, I didn't even think that maybe it was because he cared for me. I was just thinking about myself, thinking about

276

getting out of here. Now since he's calmed down a little over me standing up to him, he says that he still wants me to work for him. Says he can pay me a decent wage. "I can always use good help," is what Papa said. God knows, Aunt Loretta doesn't have the money to give me all the stuff I need. And Papa let me keep my car. "It's yours," he said. "I gave it to you." Now who could be fairer than that?

And this thing about Papa's pistol. Aunt Loretta said that he bought it when they were still in Oklahoma, brought it home the day after they told him to get off his own land. Loretta caught him in the bedroom loading it and ran to tell Mama. Mama asked him what was he doing with a pistol? You should be ashamed of yourself buying a weapon of the devil like that, she told him. He didn't even own a rifle then, but Mama didn't mind rifles because you need them for hunting. The only thing a pistol is good for is killing people, is the way Mama looks at pistols. Papa was a member of the church then. Even used to do a little preaching himself. But losing his land broke his faith. Lost faith in himself. Aunt Loretta said he'd loaded the pistol with three bullets.

Papa was right about the way we planted this field. I can tell just where Delbert helped us plant and where he didn't. I can tell where me and Papa and Curt did it alone. Where Papa didn't help, the rows are not quite as straight and in places it's planted a little deep. I find a spot where the ground's not lifted and scrape aside some loose clods dried hard from the wind we had a few days ago, dig down in the moist earth. I find a few of the little black seeds with a small tuft of white cotton still attached, buried probably two inches. That's too deep. They haven't swelled any. The sun's warmth can't reach them. They may never make it, just stay buried and rot. Only once in a while, one of them has this pale green spike sticking out the end of the seed. Then I know that sprout'll turn downward and put out white roots and the little black husk will turn up, sprout two little green leaves that'll bend over like an umbrella and start pushing up the ground. They'll make it, but the rest won't.

I asked my new mother who it was Lenny wanted to kill just before he died. I asked her if it was Charles.

"Don't think so, Ray," she said. "Think it was a girl. He was talking some nonsense about people hurting so bad and killing things that hurt. Kept saying over and over again that he couldn't stand to see people suffer."

I had it all wrong about Lenny wanting to kill Charles. Not that he didn't want to kill Charles, he just wasn't the one Lenny talked to Loretta about. It was a girl. Lenny was a really confusing person. From what she and Charles both told me, it could only be Helen.

I didn't know that I was thinking about hurting myself. But after last night, I remember that the idea of not living sort of sits off on the side of my mind worrying me. I have this fear of tight places. I worry about getting buried and then waking up inside the casket. It's hot and stuffy in there, either that or cold and damp. I know that the undertaker is supposed to embalm all dead people, but let's just say that Wayne's father was real cramped for time or maybe that he was cutting a few corners to save a little money and that maybe I'm not completely dead yet. Aunt Loretta wasn't dead and they almost buried her. So I wake up under there, six feet down.

I think it might be better to have them burn me like they do some people. But then I'm thinking about what the *Bible* say about those that go to hell and how they burn for all eternity. And I know that I haven't been doing so good the way I've been living.

Who knows what happens after death? Fact is, I don't. So, what it comes down to is if I want to take the situation here and now or trade it for another situation that I don't know anything about. Except that Mama says there's some really bad shit coming down for people that commit suicide. Besides, someday I'm going to die anyway. I can put it off, do it later. I'll always have that way to go. Can't come back, but I guess my mother, Aunt Loretta, did come back. Maybe if I tough it out now, things won't be so bad later. But some times my arms do things on their own.

I know that I am capable of anything. When I was cutting hay and Tangi, my little orange dog, came bounding through it to see me, she didn't know the mower was off to the right side of the tractor. It was hidden in the falling hay. I didn't see Tangi until she yelped. I screamed at her, but it was too late. She already had her legs in it. She'd run a step and turn a yelping somersault. She dragged herself under an old trailer that was slumped over in the weeds and had a wheel off. Papa saw her too and came running with his pistol. I crawled under the trailer. It was just me and her. She'd whine like she wanted me to help then growl at me when I got close. She looked like she had a bone she was chewing on. She did. Her leg bone that was hanging by a flap of hide. I touched her and she bit me. She was just fine inside, just wasn't a whole dog on the outside. "Move back, let me see, Bobby Ray," Papa said. I could smell Papa because he'd been working hard and it was hot under that trailer. The sun'd been shining on it all day. "No, Papa," I said. "Give me the pistol." I was eleven. Papa used to let me target practice with his pistol. He always held my hands steady while I pulled the trigger. "Do you think it has to be done?" he asked, like it still might be possible to fix her. I had to use both hands to get the hammer back. All I'm saying is that it wasn't like I said before. Papa didn't shoot Tangi. I did.

None of this land will ever be mine. I feel a lump in my jacket. I thought I left that pair of pliers in the toolbox. I reach in my pocket and it's not the pliers. It's Lenny's pistol. I thought I hid this in the trunk of my Chevy. I pull it out, hold it off to the side. I'm not saying how. I'm seeing how it feels with me looking out toward the open field, but that doesn't do it. So I turn around and face the house. I see it all real clear now. I have them all right were I want 'em. I look across the rows of cotton to Mama's garden that hasn't been touched since last year. Then there's the lawn that they don't keep mowed anymore. Off in the corner of the lawn is the burn barrel. Now they use two and still they're over flowing because they won't take 'em to the junkyard. Then there's the house, sitting silent, as if nothing's really happening, sort of like a scream that won't come out. I feel the cold barrel of Lenny's pistol on my neck, just below my ear.

CHAPTER 38: *Gretta's Baby Girl*

Curt thinks Trish is pregnant. He overheard her and Mama arguing in the washroom this morning. He said it had to do with the laundry and what Mama found on Trish's underclothes.

It's afternoon. Bev and I are going to the fairgrounds because her little brother needs help with a sheep he's entered in the Fair.

"Look, Bobby, if you'd just talk to Mr. Watkins, I'm sure he'd help you with Civics. The class is just not that difficult."

"But, Bev. The last time I talked to him, he was acting like it's curtains for me unless I get all Bs from here on out. I just can't go from Fs to Bs."

The fairgrounds are still mostly empty, but the big wire gate's rolled back so people can get in. As we drive through, off to the left I see the Little Theater where they'll have the Miss Madera County beauty pageant Wednesday evening.

"I can't believe he would keep you from graduating. He's just trying to scare you into studying."

"Sometimes I think that it's not even worth keeping going. Maybe I should just drop out right now."

It was a shock to see in the Chowchilla News that Brenda has entered the pageant. Her picture was in the paper with six other girls and even her measurements, 37-24-36. When I was looking at her picture, it was like I had X-ray vision because I kept seeing through that swimsuit. I can't get rid of my memories of being on top of her. I feel that way about Brenda, even with Bev all scooted up against me. I haven't seen Brenda with Thomas a whole lot lately either.

"If you want to drop something," Bev tells me, "get out of that physics class. You spend so much time on it. You don't need it to graduate. I don't know what you think you'll do with that stuff anyway."

"That's the one class that means something to me. Civics is just a pain."

Before I veer off to the right to go to the livestock pens, Bev points to the Ferris wheel sticking up above the big auditorium. All the rides are going up now. I hope they have the tilt-a-whirl. That's my favorite and last year a gang of us rode it all day Saturday. I don't know about the Hammer. I couldn't bring myself to ride it last year. I never have. Every year, just before the Fair starts, I have dreams about it. Last night I dreamed a wild animal was chasing me, had me cornered there by the Hammer. I climbed inside that basket because it was the only way I had of escaping.

"So what if you don't pass civics, Bobby? It's just one class. You could take it next year to graduate. You'll still go through the ceremony with the rest of us. Besides, you're planning on being a farmer anyway. What about our plans."

"I don't know. I was still thinking a little about one of those junior colleges they have in some places. I just can't quit thinking about it. I really don't want to live the rest of my life in Chowchilla."

I think maybe I do see the Hammer going up. That guy that runs the Hammer—I never notice people that work the Fair, the carnival people—but that guy is different. Every year it's the same guy, a skuzzy sucker. He watches me all the time. Maybe someone else will run the Hammer this year.

"You're building a future," Bev tells me. "The rest of our lives will depend on the decisions we make in the next couple of months. This is our life together we're planning."

The livestock building is a long open shed with wood walls that only go part way up, about to my waist, and a galvanized roof. Inside they have all these little square pens for animals along each side with an aisle down the middle. We look through several rows of these sheds and find Steven in the middle of one on the far side, spreading straw from a block of oat hay. Their mother's leaning over the wall of the pen talking to Steven. She's a short little woman with dark rimmed glasses. The sheep's over in the corner, sitting up and looking around like this pen is the best thing ever happened to him.

"I was hoping you two would to get here in time to help," their mother says as we walk up. She's smiling and looks like she's having a good time even if Steven is not. "I'm trying to convince Steven that Lambchops 'll be okay here overnight."

Steven has this hard-looking face that didn't change even when he saw us.

"What's the matter?" asks Bev. "You're not concerned someone will take him, are you?"

"No," says Steven, "and I want you to stay out of this. You wouldn't understand. Lambchops is afraid. I can see it in his eyes. He's never been away from his mother."

"I don't know, Steven," I say. "Lambchops looks calm enough to me. I'd say if anything, he's enjoying being away from her. Maybe she gets on his case all the time."

Then Steven's face breaks. "You really think so?" and he's taking me serious, like maybe he thinks I'm an expert sheepherder. His mother laughs a little, and Steven takes a quick look at her and then back at me. "He's really a sensitive lamb," he says.

"Good lord, Steven, you act like that dumb sheep's a human being," says Bev.

"You wouldn't understand, Beverly."

"He's just an animal."

"He's a lamb," says Steven. He unlatches the little board gate, swings it open to come out of the pen and damn if that sheep doesn't look like that is just what he has been waiting for. He makes a break for it and beats Steven through the gate. So the sheep's running down the aisle, headed for open country, and we're all after him, Steven shouting, "Come back, Lambchops," but a woman with a little girl coming down the aisle heads him off.

The woman is kind of stocky with these thick legs and big arms and has on sandals and a plain blue dress with no sleeves. She looks familiar.

Steven has his sheep and is headed back to the pen with it, but I'm just standing and staring and I'm not staring at the woman or Bev or anybody else except that little girl who has moved in close to her mother and grabbed her leg through her dress and is peaking a look at me from behind that plain blue skirt.

"Well," she says. "I haven't seen this face in a while. It's you isn't it? Bobby Hammer?" She has this long blond hair pulled straight back with a rubber band around it.

I know I should be saying something back, but I'm just thinking that that little girl has this long brown stringy hair and a thin face like only one other face I've ever seen on a little kid in my life. And she's thin like she's never had enough to eat.

Chapter 38: *Gretta's Baby Girl*

I hear her mother's words without even looking up. And it's something I already know.

"You do remember me, don't you? I'm Charles Kunze's sister, Gretta. You do remember me, don't you?"

I'm looking at her now, and, god, do I remember her. She was at Lenny's funeral, and I remember all that blond hair and the black hat she had on. Maybe it was the hat that made her hair stand out so much. "Is this your little girl?" I ask, and I want to know the answer to that question real bad. I never made the connection between her looking fat at the funeral and what Charles said under the bridge until right now. All Charles' lies are coming true.

"This is my big girl," says Gretta, then she picks her up and sort of bounces the little girl on her left arm. "You've never seen her. She's four years old." Gretta uses her finger to push the little girl's hair out of her face and hooks it over her ear. Gretta is a little shorter and a little bigger than I remembered. But not so big around the middle. It has been a while.

"This is your Uncle Charles' friend, Samantha. His friend that he shoots rabbits with. Can you say hi to Bobby?"

"And you should be 'shamed," is what Samantha says to me. Didn't take her long to figure me out.

Gretta has to laugh. "Why do you say that, Sammy?" she asks.

"Cause he shoots bunny rabbits," she says, then adds, "That's why." Boy, she's sure not too pleased with me.

I'm thinking about Charles and trying to remember exactly what he told me under the bridge. I'm still looking at Gretta, and I know I've been staring at her for a long time but I can't quit. "Charles told me about something once and I didn't think it was true," is all I can come up with.

"You mean about Samantha."

"Well, about a baby."

"It is true, Bobby."

I feel my legs getting weak, and I have this burning in my throat that I can't seem to swallow, but I don't know for sure that Gretta's saying what I'm thinking. I'm trying to get myself to bring Lenny's name into this but I can't. "What's true?" I ask.

Gretta smiles. "Samantha," she orders, "tell Bobby about your father."

"He's gone to hea-ven."

"And can you tell Bobby what his name is?"

"It was Leonard, and he wan't post to drive fast." But she's not saying it to me anymore, she's talking like it's something she's memorized. She squirms to get down now and takes off running. As she goes by me, I reach out to grab her and she screams real loud so I jump back.

"Don't go too far," calls Gretta.

I turn my back on Gretta to watch Samantha running away and I guess with my back turned, Gretta's not afraid to say it out loud.

"She's Lenny's daughter, Bobby. And she reminds me so much of him. She's so wonderful."

And that hits me really hard, like I've never heard words as good as that from anybody before and that burning in my throat is coming up fast, but then Samantha turns around and runs straight at me, jumps into my arms.

I've never felt a little girl's body before and she's real hot and has all these arms and legs that are in a hurry no matter where they are, and she has on this little short dress with legs underneath that have this real smooth skin all over and her mouth has little white teeth and a tiny breath that puffs in my face every time she says something. And she's telling me about a hurt she has on her knee where she fell on the sidewalk and she's pointing at it with her finger but I can't see anything. So she wants down real bad and I can't get her down fast enough and she almost jumps out of my arms, then pulls at me for a little bit, and runs off screaming, "Hogs! Hogs!"

"She wants you to see the hogs her cousin has entered in the Fair. But we're on our way to her grandfather's. We're supposed to be there by three o'clock. If you're at the Fair on Saturday afternoon, we'll see you then. Just look for us on the Midway. We won't be hard to find."

★

I want to talk about this deep breath I just took. It felt like a drink of water I got once. I'd been out in the hot sun chopping cotton all day and I walked across the dirt lane to the irrigation ditch that was running full. I just laid down on my stomach, blew aside a little brown foam and a few floating sticks, stuck my face through my reflection in the cool water and drank until I thought I wouldn't be able to get up. And now I'm taking another deep breath, just like that.

CHAPTER 39: *Rumors of Chelsey*

Bev and I are over at Phyllis Thompson's house on Ventura Street. Phyllis is tall and thin and has a little girl's body even though she's a senior. You can really tell it in a bathing suit. But she has the prettiest face and is very nice. We're in Phyllis's heated swimming pool and I'm out in the middle, just treading water, and since I've been doing it for a while, I'm getting tired and wondering which bank to go to. They have these trees and bushes all over the backyard so that the neighbors can't peek in. I want a home like this and a job in town so I won't have to come home dirty all the time.

Bev's treading water just in front of me. "At least you could've helped. Good lord! That's why we went to the Fairgrounds in the first place. To help Steven." She's bobbing up and down, pushing pieces of hair under her swimming cap to keep it from getting wet. Her head looks too small without all that hair.

I have to spit a little water. "I thought I did help." And I start to the side because I can't tread water forever.

"Not much though. And you left me alone again. That's just the way it is so much of the time now. You're always leaving me alone."

"But I came back."

"I had to hunt you down. And all of this over that little girl that you think might be your dead brother's daughter. I know how much you think about Lenny, but you have to have some sense about it. I had to wait until even my mother was ready to leave. Honestly, Bobby."

"I thought you were interested in Lenny."

"I was, before I found out how obsessed you are with him." And then she swims off. Becky and Billie Wade, the doctor's daughter, are at the other end of the pool. Billie still seems a little peeved about me coming to their house the other day and not talking to her.

Phyllis walks along the deck to get to me. "How do you like the water?"

she asks. Phyllis' mother comes up and sits down not too far from us. She's with a guy that looks kind of young. But she is a widow. Guess that's her business. He is Corbin Smeal, the new barber in Olin Davis' barbershop.

"Better than swimming in an irrigation tank. A little warmer too."

She lays down flat on the cement so she's closer to me. "I like the pool best in July. Come visit then." She has her arms under her chin, and her face is up close to mine as I hang on to the edge.

"I overheard Bev say something about your niece."

"Sort of," I say, feeling uneasy talking about this. She's prying into my life. Here I go again, keeping secrets. I haven't told anyone about my new mother.

"You must have an older brother or sister. I always thought that you were the oldest."

"I have a dead brother."

"I'm sorry. Guess I shouldn't ask so many questions."

"He's been dead five years. But, turns out he wasn't my brother. He was my cousin."

"You mean, like your parents adopted him?"

"They adopted me, I just found out. The woman I thought was my aunt is actually my mother."

"Oh, god! Bobby. How can you stand it? I'd die if I found out I'd been adopted." She rolls over on her back and looks up at the clouds. "That's every kids nightmare. You seem to be taking it so well."

"Hard to get used to. You can believe me on that one."

"Your niece is really your dead cousin's daughter."

"That makes it sound like she doesn't mean anything to me."

"I'm sorry. Nothing ever happens to me. I'm just getting caught up in your family intrigue. You could look at it like you have two sets of parents, like having a fairy godmother."

"I don't quite see it like that."

"But now you know who your real mother and father are?"

"I'm not ready to talk about my father. Not yet."

"Okay. I'm sorry. I think I hurt your feelings again."

"Well, I just feel real strong about that."

"So who was your brother married to?"

"He wasn't. That's the other problem."

I hear the sliding glass door open and Phyllis turns around to see who it is. "Oh good," she says, "there's Brenda." Then she turns to me again. "Do you mind if I ask who the mother of your niece is? Or should I keep my big mouth shut?"

"Well, this is all kind of new to me because I didn't know I had a niece until today." And now I see Thomas coming through the sliding glass door and Brenda right behind him. She has on the same bathing suit she had on in the paper. "Bev'll tell anyway. It's Gretta Kunze."

"I know her. She's Charles' sister. She's smart, Bobby. Did you know she's graduating summa cum laude in mathematics from Stanford this year?"

"I don't even know what that means."

"Well, trust me. That means she's smart. I saw her picture in the Chowchilla News a few days ago. She's gorgeous too. God, what a mess of blond hair."

"Bev didn't think too much of her."

That brings a laugh out of Phyllis. "That's Bev alright." And now she turns back on her stomach to face me because she needs to whisper. "From the picture in the paper, Gretta reminded me of Brenda. Brenda's always had everything Bev wants. Blond hair and brains. Bev's always been smarter than she thinks, but she'll never be blond. With that Italian blood, her complexion's too dark to bleach her hair. All she'll ever be is a knockout brunette." I like to watch Phyllis's mouth when she talks. Her words come out through a smile.

"When I saw Gretta today," I say, "she didn't say anything about going to college."

"I'm sure that was her though. You don't get into Stanford unless you have brains and money. Are you going to college next year?"

"I wish I could. I definitely don't have the brains."

"Me neither. That's why I'm going to Fresno City College. It'll be less expensive there too."

"That's another thing I'm worried about. Money."

Now I see Melvin and that Mexican girlfriend of his coming through the sliding-glass door. Melvin has on dark sunglasses. I hear a ruckus over by where Bev and Brenda are standing. I didn't know Brenda was so much taller than Bev.

"Just shut up about Bobby and physics!" is what Bev is shouting. "I don't want to hear any more about physics."

Brenda says back, "But Bobby is doing great in physics. Mr. Wood is very proud of him. He thinks Bobby is good college material. Mr. Wood looked up his Iowa Test scores and got the shock of his life."

"Bobby!" and now Bev is shouting at me all the way from the other end of the swimming pool, "Tell them you're not going to college. Tell them about our plans."

I'm having a hard time finding the words. Think I'll just let my head sink down under the water.

"Say something, Bobby. Tell them."

"Well, Bev. Farming sounded like fun a few months ago, but a lot has happened since then." How come everybody is looking at me?

Bev comes walking over to where Phyllis and me are talking.

"Are you trying to make a fool out of me?"

"I'm sorry, Bev. But I'm backing up again on this one."

"Bobby," and Bev just won't shut up, "can we go now?"

"We just got here."

Bev takes me by the hand, pulls me up on deck, and we're heading for the sliding glass door. I'm still dripping water. I stop for a second to talk to Melvin, thinking I see something on the other side of those sunglasses. When he saw me coming, he turned his back on me.

"What do you have behind those sunglasses?" I ask.

He pulls them off for me.

"Whoa!" He has two big-time black eyes, and now I see a split lip. I thought that was a fever blister.

"Chelsey got me yesterday after school," is he says. "That nigger's got it in for us poor white folks. He's looking for everyone that's a friend of Bobby Hammer."

"I thought you wanted a piece of colored action," I say.

"He was mighty accommodating. I don't think I even got a punch in."

Thomas has walked up, smiling. "We had to pull Chelsey off him."

"Come on, Thomas," says Melvin, "it wasn't that bad." I see a dark red split in the gums between his upper teeth. He is lucky he didn't lose some teeth.

"It was worse. A whole lot worse," says Thomas.

"I guess he's someone to stay away from," I say. "He pushed me up against the wall the other day."

"You're next," says Melvin. "He just wanted to toughen up his fists a

288

little on me."

"Stay away from him, Bobby," says Thomas. "I don't know why he's so up in the air about you, but give him a chance to cool off. Melvin's right. You're the one he's really after, and he doesn't mind talking about it either."

CHAPTER 40: *Papa in Trouble with Mama*

It's late afternoon and I'm in the kitchen trying to find a way to talk to Mama about Samantha. I don't feel at home over here. I've been wanting to talk to Papa about what he's paying me because I hear it's less than other farm hands are getting. But Papa's been acting like he's not too pleased with my work since he started paying me for it. I ask Mama if she knows where Curt and Papa are?

"They went to town early this afternoon to get some pump oil, and I haven't seen 'em since." She answered real quick, like that's just what she's been wondering too. She's standing over the counter drying her hands on a dishtowel. I feel the heat from green beans and bacon she has cooking in this big pan on the stove with all this steam coming out of it. Every time she lifts the lid, the steam fills the kitchen again. But she's not thinking about me. She has something churning on that mind of hers, and I bet it's Papa and she's wondering if he's drinking again.

"I just don't know what I'm going to do with Trish," she says real quiet, as if she's talking to the wall.

"What's she done now," I ask, hoping she'll tell me about that argument over Trish's underclothes.

"None of your business," she says. "Don't concern you." Then she stops for a bit, but she's not finished. "If you ever see her with Eugene again, I want to know."

"What's wrong with Eugene?"

"That's not any of your business either, just if you see them together, I want to know."

I guess that's all of that. If she thinks Eugene's bad, as good of a kid as he is, wait till she finds out about Trish and Charles.

"Mama," I say, and now I'm trying to be real careful, "I was talking to some people downtown and you know what they're saying about Lenny?"

This gets her attention real fast. "People 'll say most anything. What've you heard this time," she says, just like I'm bringing a story to her every day.

"Well," and then I have to swallow some spit, "some people think Lenny has a daughter down there." And I don't know what "down there" means exactly, but it seems like I need that part of it. The same time I say that, I hear Papa and Curt come in the front door.

"There's not any truth to that story, Bobby Ray. Don't even think about it, and if you can't quit thinking about it," and now she's turned toward me and pointing a fork, "I can help you stop, that's for sure."

Wow, I think, that's a hornets nest that needs to be stirred a little, so I'm sorry Papa's coming in. He looks tired and dirty, not like he's been to town, and I can tell by the glare in his eyes that I've done something wrong again.

"Where've you been," is the way he starts with his little beady eyes glaring at me, and then his voice goes up, and he doesn't give me a chance to find an answer. "Don't you know we're short handed out in the field since Delbert up and quit on us? What do you think I'm paying you for?"

This is real strange, him still talking like that because he knows he fired Delbert, so I know there's going to be no talking sense to him. But I've got to try.

"I thought after what you said this morning about us being caught up, that we were. So I went to town."

"Yeah, well, not only are you lazy but you're stupid. Didn't take you long to start acting like a goddamn hired hand. Doesn't matter that I've raised you. You know farming can't all be forecast in the morning. Maybe that goddamn turkey farming is what suits you." Papa hasn't ever called me stupid before, and that hurts so bad I can't hardly stand it. If he's going to treat me like this, maybe I'll just get myself a job up town. Mama looks surprised too.

"Don't call him stupid, Hershel," she says, like it's an order, and Mama just doesn't put orders on Papa, she only asks questions. Then she adds, "He's not stupid," and she sounds mad. She's never been mad at him unless he's drunk.

"Oh! So you want to get in on it too, do you? Well let me tell you something, woman."

There's so many firsts going on in this house right now that I want to leave real bad because Papa doesn't call Mama "woman" and he's just being real sassy, so I don't know what either one of them might do.

"I've been... well let me get this straight now," he says. "Me and Curt

291

here, the only boy I've got that's worth a damn, at least I guess Curt is my kid if I have to believe you..."

Oh no, I think. I hope I've heard him wrong. What he just said about Curt, I hope he didn't mean something against Mama, because no one has ever questioned Mama's... Mama's... and I don't know what to call it, but they just don't question it.

Papa's still talking. "...have been out in the field working our butts off while this lazy other thing over there, I don't want to call a son but I guess I have to because I raised him, has been off to town messing around with the female trash of Chowchilla."

Doesn't seem like Mama's even heard him, because she's turned her back and working to get dinner ready. Papa's standing there like he's a little taken back by his own words, maybe a little sweat showing on his wrinkled brow, and maybe working up to the first apology I've ever heard come out of his mouth. If we're going to have a bunch of firsts, we might as well have one on this too. Mama's grabbed a paring knife and the biggest potato I've ever seen and cutting it as fast as she can, can't really say she's peeling it because it's coming apart in chunks.

Papa says, "Louise, now don't you go getting..." Then his voice just trails off and he turns to Curt like he is dying and needs some help bad, but Curt's on his way out of the kitchen, and Papa sure as hell knows he's not getting help from me on this one, and then out the corner of my eye I see a quick movement from Mama and something hits Papa with a thud and then something hits the floor. It flashes through my mind that Mama just threw the knife at Papa and maybe it chopped off his hand and maybe that hand just hit the floor. But that's not it at all. It's that big potato and it's followed by a drinking glass that misses him and takes out the kitchen window with a crash and Papa's moving on into the living room pretty fast and then a plate, and a part of a peanut butter sandwich left over from lunch, and then a Mason jar full of peaches that shatters and splatters just behind Curt and just ahead of Papa, so he knows that the front door is the right place for him.

Mama's puffing like a steam engine and I'm afraid of what she might do next but she just ignores me and grabs a broom, starts sweeping the already-clean floor, faster and harder than it's possible for a human being to sweep. And I'm even wishing Trish was here to see this power sweeping, but I'm just moseying on out the back door.

CHAPTER 41: *Papa Wants to Shake Hands*

I'm out back in the field of short green cotton. I closed the door behind me real quiet and grabbed a hoe that was standing up against the house, figuring I'd chop a row. If I could work up half the energy of Mama sweeping, I'd finish this twenty-acre field before sundown. But I see Papa coming around the corner of the house real fast. He stops to grab a hoe too, but he's still walking like he has important business, and I can tell he's not mad at me or anybody else because he's in bad trouble with Mama like I've never see before. He skips the first part of the row, starts in chopping beside me, chopping something close to the way Mama was sweeping and he starts talking to me, real serious like.

"You and me've got to talk. This isn't right."

I don't know. There's just something real funny the way he's talking about the two of us talking.

"Look," he says, and he has to catch a breath, "I know this is tough on you having to turkey farm and then come over here to help me. Maybe I was a little hasty about having you leave. Maybe you should move back in over here. It just doesn't seem right, you not living with us anymore."

I look up at him, and our eyes touch for a second. He's so serious. And I try, but I can't help it. I laugh. And he laughs too. A real quick, hurting laugh. And then he starts to cry. And he's talking about him and me being the men in the family, and how we've got to try to get along better and that he's willing, and that we have the future to think about and us farming together.

But I'm not talking. Papa just has so much to learn.

So he stops hoeing, takes a deep shuttering breath with his chin in the air so he can quit crying. And this is the damnedest sight I've ever seen. Papa wants to shake my hand. "What do you think?" he asks.

I take his hand because he's never offered it to me before, take his hand and give him a good firm shake. His hand is hard as a board. "No," I say. "I'm sorry, Papa, but I just can't do it. I'm going to stay with my new mother."

Then Papa wants to know if I'd be disappointed if he asked Delbert to come back to work with us.

★

Papa asked me to go with him to see Delbert, and now we're standing out front of Delbert's trailer house with the sun going down again. Papa is standing real casual like with his hands in his pockets and his chin in the air. Delbert's standing facing him with his head down. He clears his throat, then spits it on the ground in front of Papa. Both of them have hats on.

I'm standing off to the side. I don't wear a hat.

Papa has just said he's sorry for the way he acted the other day and wonders if Delbert would like to come back to work.

"I've got work, Hershel," Delbert says. "So, no thanks." But he winks at me just as he says it, and Papa sees him. Then Delbert turns his head a little, puts his finger to the side of his nose and blows a stream of snot on the ground.

CHAPTER 42: *The Fight Without End*

"What so interesting about Phyllis?"

"I'm not interested in Phyllis, Bev."

"Can't tell by looking."

It's lunchtime and I'm standing with Bev in the schoolyard over by the gym, eating a cheeseburger wrapped in wax paper that I just got from the little house across the street. Eugene and Trish are with us. "We enjoy talking. She's going to a junior college next year. One in Fresno."

"You like to talk to every girl but me."

These people on the corner of Humbolt and Tenth Street put a serving counter in their living room and made it into a stand for us kids to get hamburgers during lunch. Stays so crowded at noon the line extends out onto their lawn.

I spot Chelsey standing on the grass next to Humbolt Street and he's talking to another little colored kid, Stanley. It's not like two coloreds to be out here on the lawn at lunch. They're usually off by themselves. I don't know where they usually stay but they're out of sight. Something funny going on between them anyway because Stanley's backing up now and looking afraid. Chelsey's pointing at Melvin who's standing just a few feet away.

I punch Eugene with my elbow. "Look at that," I say. "What're those two coloreds up to with Melvin."

"Nigger stuff, I guess."

A couple more coloreds're standing just a ways away but they're staying out of it. One of them is Jim Broden. I've seen him lay people out cold on the football field. He wears those baggy khaki pants just like Papa. The other one's not quite as big but he's the blackest colored I've ever seen, and I don't know his name. Stanley has big fat cheeks on his baby face and is a little big around the middle. Melvin gives him a shove and he stumbles out into the street. But Melvin is after Stanley and has a hold of his shirt with one hand and hitting him in the back with the other. Then Chelsey steps in, pulls Melvin off him.

So I start to walk on over. No sense in a bunch of coloreds ganging up on Melvin.

"Where do you think you're going?" asks Trish.

"I want to see what this is about."

"Don't go, Bobby," says Bev. "I don't know why Chelsey's mad at you but he is."

"Stay here," is what Trish says again.

"Why's my little sister messing in my business?" That's what I want to know.

I going on over, a few white kids starting to gather. Eugene comes up from behind and puts his hand on my shoulder, tries to pull me back.

"Watch it, Eugene," I say. "I don't like that," and I can tell my temper's coming up a little.

"Bev's right," he says, backing off. "Chelsey's father's a professional boxer. Chelsey's had a few amateur fights himself. Don't screw with him."

Now the other two coloreds get mixed up in it. Jim Broden helps Stanley up and the big black one is trying to pull Melvin off him, and Chelsey is shouting something about "Uncle Tom" to Stanley, but here comes Thomas and he's no one to screw with either.

"Now just wait a minute here," says that black nigger, and he is acting like he just took over the world. And it looks like everybody thinks he has something worth listening to because they all stop. "We got two men here that want to work out a problem, so what do you say we all just stay out of it and let them hammer it out. Is that okay with you two?" he says turning to Jim Broden and Thomas Powers.

And I'm thinking someone could get killed here if those big guys get into it.

"Sounds good to me," says Broden.

Everybody stands back and I see a few more coloreds and I don't know where they came from, but they're really coming out of the grass I guess. Stanley's face is lank and his eyes are big like the crowd is starting to bother him.

Now here comes Sonnett striding across the lawn and into the road. It's not just that Clyde's face is red, it's his entire baldhead, so he must be mad as hell. We're not even on the school ground now, we're over by the dirt parking lot on Ninth Street. He doesn't have anything to say that means anything here, but his chin's up high like he is the boss. I wish somebody would take that sonofabitch out. I think maybe I want to be in on this, so I run a little, push past a few kids, crowd in, get just as close as I can to that asshole, stand behind Clyde, breathing hard and fast.

"Just look at you two," he says. And he's talking like they're in the third grade. "I know the both of you well and yet hardly recognize you. Two fine kids like you should be friends instead of enemies. You should know by now to settle your differences by talking. Violence settles nothing. It just leads to more violence..."

I'm wondering how much of that is sinking into Melvin's hard head, but Clyde just keeps going on about friendship and getting along and all of us being brothers under the skin.

All the time I'm standing right here behind Clyde looking down at his wing tip shoes and black wool slacks, up at the back of that white shirt, and I know that just in front under his chin is that bow tie, and that's what I want to get my hands on, just my left hand, feel my fingers go in through his collar and around that black bow tie so I can pull his face into my fist over and over and over. I didn't get to play football this year because of that sonofabitch. He's just screwed up my life.

Clyde finishes his speech, Stanley walks one way and Melvin another and the crowd starts to break up. Just as I start to leave, Sonnett turns to walk back to his office like he's the president of these United States, and has just solved the world's most pressing problem and bumps into me because I'm still right behind him. He's scared at first, then he sees it's just me and gives me a push like he's going to walk through me. It's like my arms are working on their own, and I feel my fingertips touch that bow tie when somebody spins me around by my right arm that I had drawn back to bust Sonnett's head open, and slings me down the road so hard that I have to run to keep from falling, and then he's right behind me pushing me so that I can't regain my balance and up the road I go into what's left of the crowd and onto the sidewalk. Finally I get a chance to stop and look back. There's Sonnett still standing in the middle of the road looking at me real confused, like maybe he's a little disappointed about something, but then he turns and walks on off.

"You're a stupid shit. You know that, Bobby?" It's Thomas Powers. "Don't you have any thought of the future?"

"Aw, Thomas," I say. "How could you stop me? I'll never have another chance like that. Chance of a lifetime."

I have my head down walking toward my car so I can sit and think if I should cut the rest of the day when I see some kids running toward Eighth Street. Then goddamn! Something hits me right in the back of the head so hard that I fall against my car, and I catch three more blows on the back and one in the side. So I bulldog that sonofabitch, and it's Chelsey, that stinking goddamn nigger, and I throw him off away from me. I remember the smell of that nigger stuff from Prissy now.

I have to get away from Chelsey, or he's going to kill me, so I run a ways down the sidewalk with him right after me. I hear a couple of shouts and some scuffling, so I stop, look back. It's Thomas, Melvin and Jim Broden, and it's taking all three of them to hold Chelsey off me.

"Goddamn, look what he did to me!" I say. "He already busted my nose." And I have blood all down my Levis. "This is my blood, man. Turn him loose."

"He'll kill you, Bobby," says Melvin.

"That's okay," I say. "I want him. He started this. Let's see what he's got." I just can't stand that sonofabitching nigger anymore.

"Bobby Ray! Stop it! Just stop it!" It's Trish screaming at me.

"Eugene? Where are you Eugene?" I shout.

"Here I am, Bobby," he says stepping out of the crowd of kids.

"Get her out of here. This ain't no place for a girl."

Then Chelsey is on me again. And I've never seen so many punches come from only two arms. So I just cover up and take the rain of blows, and he's beating me in the ribs and on the arms and shoulder, and I feel the knots coming all over my body.

But I dip down low, then I throw a punch, my first, and it's the one I have been saving ever since Lenny died. I throw the right hand that I wouldn't throw at Melvin or Thomas. I hear it crack like a gun going off. Goddamn if it doesn't put Chelsey down. There's a roar from the crowd.

"Kill that fucking nigger," someone says. "Whoopee, son-of-a-bitch."

So I have a little time now. I can't believe the crowd we've drawn. The entire school is here. There's little Becky Wynsum with front row standing room; I believe she's crying a little; Eugene has Trish by the arm, pulling on her, but she's not going anywhere. There's lots of freshmen with smiling faces like this is the biggest thing that ever happened to them, and a new crew of niggers is mixing in the crowd.

Chelsey can't figure what happened. He shakes his head a couple of times and takes his time about getting up.

"Take him, Bobby! Oh goddamn!" says Melvin. "You've got him. Don't let him up." He's dancing around like an Indian at a war party. "Hurt him, Bobby. Hurt him! Don't let him up."

I have all these knots. I feel like I have bee stings all over my body.

Here comes Chelsey again, and I see a little blood between his lips this time. He still has his machine gun fists going so I cover up, but it doesn't help this time. I put both fists over my eyes, but he's beating my ears off of my head, and when I move a fist he busts my lip, so I don't have any choice, I run. I run along the sidewalk with Chelsey right behind. He catches up with me and pounds a fist in my back. I stop in the intersection of Eighth Street and Humbolt, and we throw a few more punches standing in the middle of the blacktop. I hit him in the middle of that big black nose and he backs off. He's shedding a little blood through the snout now too.

Here comes the whole damn school running after us, and they look like a herd of stampeding cattle. I don't think Sonnett's got the guts to come into this crowd because they've come to see a fight. Kids are packed tight trying to get close enough to see. A couple bump into me. I shove them back.

Chelsey comes at me again. This time I listen for the sounds we make. I hear a thud or two. He likes to grunt when he throws a punch. Now some kids are cheering. I hear girls cheering. Every time he hits me, I start to swell. My left eye is almost closed now. I step under a right and swing my body, so that I have a little leverage, and pound my fist down into his ribs. That gets a grunt out of him, and then I bring in a sweeping left hook that I hear crack again and he goes down.

"Goddamn," says Melvin, "you can't let him up like this. He'll chop you to pieces, Bobby. Get him while he's down."

So I have some more time. I sneak a peek, see Becky, Phyllis, and now Brenda brushing past Thomas to get a look at me, pushing past him but not paying him any mind, and there's Bev, or at least it looks like the top of her head, coming through the crowd, and now she's right up front. So I run again, this time into the empty lot on the other side of Eighth Street. And Chelsey tackles me in the dirt. We roll around a little in what feels like six inches of dust. When we come up for air, there's blood-mud everywhere.

The crowd has followed us, like a flock of black birds flying in formation around us. Bev's on the other side of Chelsey, her tits heaving from the footrace. Broden's standing close by, and he puts both those big black arms out and backs into the crowd, pushing them back to get more room for Chelsey. His hand's pushing Bev back, and it's about as big as her entire chest. Thomas has a front row seat with Phyllis. She just looks shocked at what's happening. The fight's going to be finished here because we are both tired as hell.

"Come on, Bobby," shouts someone. "Take that goddamn nigger's head off."

We go at it again and I hear the pop and thud of fists against meat and bone, but I don't feel anything. We're kicking the dirt now, and it's powdery and boiling up, and the crowd's raising even more. We quit again and stand here puffing with dirt all over us. I have my head forward with blood dripping off my nose. I brush off some bloody mud.

"You want some more, sonofabitch?" I ask.

If Chelsey wants some more, he's not telling. He's just looking around like he wants to know if there's going to be a way out of this when it is finished. He looks over at Broden. Broden looks across at the big black nigger I don't know, then he nods to Chelsey. So we go at it again.

I hear Wayne shouting, "Hit him! Hit him! Get that sonofabitch, Chelsey, take that motherfucker, take him. Goddamnit! Goddamnit! Goddamnit! Kill that bastard, Chelsey. Kill him!" I guess there's no mistaking whose side he's on.

Off in the distance I hear a siren. A real one this time. Broden motions Chelsey off. Chelsey looks back at me. Starts to walk off. Turns toward me again. I go to meet him, but the siren's closer this time.

"Bobby! Bobby!" It's Thomas. "Follow me. We've got to get you out of here. The police, Bobby! The police!" I take one last look at Chelsey. He's still staring at me. Then he runs.

★

The sun's going down now and we're over at the Beacon gas station on Robertson and First Street. I'm with Melvin and Thomas in the bathroom. I have my Levis off, and Thomas is washing the blood off them in the sink. We just finished my shirt, wrung it out. No choice but to put it back on wet. Couldn't get all the blood out.

"Proud, so proud of you, Bobby," says Melvin. "Oh, god, am I proud of you. Be my brother. I know you keep saying you don't have one anymore since your papa run you off. My stepfather run me off again too. You and me'll always be nigger-fighting brothers."

This bathroom just has a sink and a stinking toilet. Little mirror over it. Not enough room for two people, much less three.

"I hate that nigger." I say. "I've never hated anyone before. But I hate him. I could fight him all day." I have my pants off but my shoes are still on. No sense in getting my feet nasty on the bathroom floor. My legs could stand a little suntan.

"Well, your face couldn't take it," says Thomas. "Put some more ice on his eye. That left one needs it most. And you should leave Bobby alone, Melvin. He needs to calm down. It's been three hours since the fight and he's still high. Get down off it, Bobby."

"But he was so good," says Melvin. "Goddamn, Bobby. I've never seen a right hook like that first one you put him down with. An absolute work of art. Chelsey's never been off his feet in a fight. Did you see that goddamn nigger's face, Thomas."

"Sure. I see his face all the time. Every school day."

"Na. Na. I mean when he hit the ground. Goddamn, when his ass hit the ground. Did you see his face?"

Then Thomas laughs a little. "Alright. All right. I saw his face. But, Bobby, you've got to calm down. I've never seen you wired like this. And leave him alone, Melvin. Shit! He doesn't need to hear about how great he was. I can still see that vein in his neck and his heart's beating two hundred a minute."

"Ah, but he's good. So goddamn good."

"Good at getting his face beat in. It stinks in here. Did you fart again, Melvin?"

"Smells like nigger," I say. "I got nigger on me, Thomas. Can't wash that off. Don't you like the smell of niggers?" I ask Melvin.

"See what I mean about fighting niggers?" Melvin says to me. "God! There's nothing on earth feels better. Fucking a girl can't hold a candle to fighting a nigger. Wow! What a fight! You knocked him down! I'd give a million dollars to have done that. Knocked him down twice. And here he thought he was champion of the world."

"You should just shut up, Melvin," says Thomas. "You know that? Just shut up. He didn't win that damn fight."

"No shit, Thomas! If I didn't know better, I'd think you were mad at me."

"I'm, goddamnit! I said, shut up! Can't you tell he's still pumped up? He's got to go home. He doesn't need you yanking his fighting chain again."

I hear a car pull up outside. I think I hear nigger voices. "Let me see," I say. "Who's that?" I crack the door a little. "Gimme my pants. My nigger's back."

"Stay in here, Bobby. Keep that door shut," he tells Melvin.

So now I have my wet shirt and my wet pants on. Feels like a wet tarp wrapped around my legs. "Let me out," I say. "My nigger's waiting."

"Listen to me," says Thomas. "I'll get rid of them. Just give me a couple of minutes."

"You don't understand," I tell him. "I want to fight him. I need him. Again."

"No, Bobby. Not now. Wait till tomorrow. If you still want him then, okay. But let it rest a day."

" Uh-uh. Not on your life."

When I throw the door back, there're four of them milling around this old beat up Studebaker that has the bumpers held on with baling wire. It's Jim Broden, Stanley and that black nigger I don't know the name of. Chelsey's standing behind them. I step out and catch a whiff of fresh air. I don't smell nigger anymore.

"You hiding, Chelsey, or you just real bashful? Maybe you came to kiss and make up?" I ask.

He comes running at me, almost knocks Stanley to the ground to get to me. I put my shoulder into him, throw him up against the side of the car, pound on those black bones. He kicks me off him.

I have blood dripping off my nose again, and he has a bruise on the side of his head that looks like a bunch of grapes under his brown skin. I'm learning to hit him in the ribs cause he can't take much of that. Backs him off every time. We fight between the two cars, bouncing off of them like they're ring ropes. I keep trying to break his ribs and take a few shots to the head for my trouble. Since I ripped his shirt off him, I have his red and blue ribs, where I've been beating him, to shoot at.

Then I take a big right hand, and suddenly, it's like I don't know where I am. I'm down on one knee, for some reason. Chelsey's backed off a little.

Chapter 42: *The Fight Without End*

I hear a buzz, off in the distance, think maybe I hear Mama call my name. Someone says, "He's coming to." Think maybe it was Thomas. I look off and see a crop duster in the distance, down low to the ground. Couldn't be though. The cotton is just barely tall enough for chopping now. I'm trying to stand when I hear the screech of rubber and a black car shines a red spotlight in my eyes. Brock and another policeman get out.

Thomas comes to me. Puts his hand on my shoulder, bends down to talk in my ear. "You okay?" he asks.

"I'm fine, but what's Brock doing here?"

"Bobby," Brock's talking now, "I want you in the backseat. Chelsey, you go home."

Brock gave me a good talking to. Something about my papa and mama. He knows about Aunt Loretta. Said he knows what I'm going through. He says I can only push the law so far.

★

It must be one o'clock in the morning. I'm with Chelsey again. We've been fighting for two hours. I haven't been home, been out with Melvin. I couldn't face Aunt Loretta looking like this. We're in the peach orchard that Brenda and I used after the football game when she had me between her legs. Thomas showed up a few minutes ago. He gave up on me after the police caught me. Went home. Someone went to get him again, I guess. He just watches us for a few minutes, shakes his head and walks off. You can't possibly bleed anymore, he told me. You couldn't have anymore blood. He won't look at us. I hear crickets off in the dark between trees. Even the mosquitoes won't leave me alone. It must be the car lights shining on me. Every time I knock Chelsey down, he gets up. Every time he gets up, he beats my face in. I've knocked him down several times, but now I'm afraid to. I've gone through several stages. There was a time when I wanted to kill Chelsey. I asked Melvin to get me a tire tool, a wrench or maybe a knife. I broke a limb off a tree and chased Chelsey with it. I wanted to kill him so bad. Chelsey just stood there while I tried to talk Melvin into getting me a sledge hammer. Then I got real calm. None of the blows to my face seemed to hurt. Even the one eye I can't see out of just seemed like it wasn't there. Like I never had a left eye. His blows to my body just went through me, like my body didn't even exist. But now, everything he does to me hurts. And I like it. It's like the first time in my life I've ever felt anything that happened to me. I feel my feet in the earth. I feel the wind

303

on my skin. I feel how sorry Thomas feels for me. I feel how much Melvin wants me to win this fight. I feel my clothes everywhere they touch me. And when Chelsey hits me, it's like a earthquake running through my body. I can tell all my teeth are loose in my gums. My old head is huge from my eyes up, and I don't have a voice anymore. All I can do is grunt. At times, I've thought that I could feel horns growing out my forehead. My hair feels like baling wire or maybe a mess of snakes.

We've stopped for a second, while Chelsey blows the blood clots out his nose, again. He has to stop and do that every once in a while. And now there's another car pulling up. Just another set of headlights. More light just means more pain for my one eye that still sees. I don't know who's here anymore. People come, some go. Some are niggers, some are white. All the same to me. But something has happened. Someone else is here now. And I feel so ashamed of myself. I hear a girl scream. Who is it? Who's that person? Who's that girl?

"Why doesn't someone stop them? Thomas! You son of a bitch! You could stop them. Why're you letting them do this to each other? Bobby Ray. Oh no, Bobby Ray. Why are you killing yourself? Thomas, why are you letting Chelsey hurt my brother? Oh God. Please stop them, God. Please don't let them keep doing this."

Chelsey's standing in front of me with his arms down. He has blood all the way to his knees.

I feel like I'm a hundred years old. Turning my head is like turning a house on a pivot. I only see out through one window. But that window sees Trish.

CHAPTER 43: *Now Jesse Has Something to Say*

"I can't get the smell off me, Jess."

"Get in the car. We can talk about the smell later."

It's three in the morning, and I'm standing in front of Farnesi's talking to Leroy's Uncle Jesse. He wants me to get in his car. I've been feeling like crying, and choking it back is harder when I have to talk. So I don't say much. Jess was in Farnesi's having a hamburger when Melvin took me into the bathroom to clean me up. Turned a few eyes when I walked inside. It's kind of strange, but Jess had been out looking for me. Aunt Loretta called him. Why would she do that? Mama and Papa always let me go about my business. I didn't recognize myself in the mirror. I looked like a Mongoloid idiot.

"I need my pistol, Jess. Can you take me to my car? I need my pistol. We better hurry, too, because my other eye's closing." Goddamn, won't my face ever quit swelling?

"Why do you want your pistol?"

"Two people need killing."

Jess shakes his head, but he takes me back to the high school anyway, and now I'm rumbling around under my seat trying to find my pistol. It'd help if I could see a little better. When I bend over, my eyes go completely shut.

Jess hasn't said a lot to me. He just looks real down hearted for some reason, seems to be thinking a lot. And Trish has gone crazy. She wouldn't let Eugene take her home. She was out with Eugene when she heard I was fighting Chelsey in that peach orchard. After she broke up the fight, she made Eugene leave, gave his ring back to him right there for some reason. She told him how sorry she was and hugged him. Told him good-by like she was leaving town. Then she started cussing Thomas and chasing him around the peach orchard. Threw clods at him. But Melvin told me that it was Thomas who took her home.

I finally find my pistol. It slid out from under the seat onto the floorboard in back. The metal's cold in my hand, and that feels good because my hands are still swelling too. Too fat to make a fist. I've told Jess that he can leave, but he's still standing around like he's waiting on a train.

"I thank you for bringing me to my car, Jess. But I'm leaving now, so you can go on home."

"Bobby..." Jess just has on a T-shirt, so I get to see his tattoos on his arms through this little slit in my right eye.

"You're holding me up," I tell him. "Can you make this quick?"

"I can't let you do it." His skin's so tan from working in the field that he looks almost like a nigger himself.

"This is my business. You don't have a say-so."

"Yes I do."

"How's that?"

"Maybe we should talk."

"Jesuschrist, Jess. I appreciate you helping me out by bringing me to my car, but now I've got to take care of my business."

"Who you going to kill?"

"First Chelsey, then Charles Kunze. If you really think it's any of your business."

"Why don't we talk first? Give you a chance to think it over."

"Goddamn you, Jess. Now see what you've done? You kept me out here talking like this, and now my other eye's closed. I can't see anything." And then I start to cry. "If it hadn't been for you, I'd a been alright."

"There's more truth in that than you know. Go with me to my place and we'll see if an ice pack and a cold shower won't stop the swelling."

"Do I have a choice?" I ask him.

★

I've been crying for the last twenty minutes. When I finally decide to do something about the way my life's going, seems like everything stands in my way. I don't have times like this very often where I know what to do. I'm sitting on the edge of an old cot they have in a shack out back of Leroy's house. That's where Jess and Jake stay. Jess is Leroy's father's brother and Jake's his mother's. When we came in, Jess woke Jake, told him to go in the house and sleep on the couch. Let me take Jake's bed. I asked Jess why he treated Jake like that? "Cause he's a freeloader," he said. "Don't work or nothing."

When I get out of the shower, Jess has a towel ready for me, and by the time I get dry, he has some underclothes, a pair of Levis and a shirt. "They're mine but should fit," he says. "We look to be about the same size."

So after I get dressed, he sits me on the edge of Jake's bed and hands me a handful of ice cubes wrapped in a towel.

"Let's see if we can't get that right eye down to where you can see something," he says. "This business of killing people does require a little eyesight even if it doesn't require foresight. There's no use working on the left one yet. It's going to be closed for a day or two."

"Why'd Aunt Loretta called you instead of Papa." I take an ice cube out of the towel and push it into my eyeball, put those in the towel on my left eye. Damn that shit's cold.

"Cause she was worried about you," he says, and he seems a little peeved.

"Worried? No, that's not what I mean. How come she called you?"

"Cause she's known me a long time. How do you feel after that cold shower?"

"I feel okay, but how come I can't get this nigger smell off me? Chelsey's a stinking nigger. That shower didn't seem to help the way I smell."

"That nigger you're smelling didn't come from Chelsey," he says.

"I know nigger when I smell it. I screwed me a nigger girl a while back. It's nigger alright."

"What're you doing messing around with colored girls? No wonder Chelsey was so mad at you. That girl must have been a friend of his."

"His little sister."

"Shame on you! How'd you like to see him with Trish?"

"Don't say shit like that. Damn you, Jess. Where's my pistol, anyway? I'm going to kill that sonofabitch. Look what he's done to me."

"Looks to me like he was giving you the benefit of the doubt by just using his fists on you. He must have a hell of a sense of fair play. But that isn't his smell on you, and that wasn't her smell on you either."

"Come on, Jess. I know nigger when I smell it. You got some more ice? I need some more ice. Thomas gave me some ice too and it helped the swelling a lot. But Thomas is mad at me. You know that Jess? Thomas is a friend of mine and he's mad at me."

"The whole damn town is mad at you. No reason Thomas shouldn't be."

"The whole town? You mean Chowchilla."

"The whole town and everybody in it."

"Why would Chowchilla be mad?"

"Cause the whole damn town likes you. And you beat yourself up."

"You mean Chelsey beat me up."

"No. I mean you beat yourself up. You could've stepped out of that fight anytime you wanted."

"A guy has to take up for hisself."

"Sure does. Particularly when he's wrong. There's nothing like being wrong to make a man feel like fighting."

"You don't know what you're talking about. I need some more ice, Jess. You got some more ice?"

"That's the pitiful part of it. I do know what I'm talking about. I've been there more times than you ever will."

"You still didn't tell me why Aunt Loretta called you instead of Papa."

"Loretta's your mother. She worries about you."

"She may be my mother, but she's crazy, Jess. She's a crazy woman."

"Don't talk like that. You watch that lip of yours. Your mother's a fine woman. Respect her. She's the finest woman I know."

"How do you know what she's like? How do you know her at all?"

"We go way back."

"Damn I wish I could quit crying. My eyes just keep running water. I told you I need some more ice. This stuff is melting fast."

He goes to the icebox again, works with an ice pick for a minute, comes back with another rag wrapped around a chunk of ice. I watch him through a slit that's starting to open in my right eye. I take out the ice, put it on my eye. He's pulled off his shirt so I get to see all those tattoos. He has these fantastic snake-like things that run up the insides of his forearms.

"I need to go, Jess. I've got to get my work done. Got to get my trouble over with. I can take some of this ice with me. I'm starting to see a little out of my right eye now."

"Sit back down. What you want to go off killing somebody for? You don't have a murdering streak in you."

"Yes I do. I tried to kill Charles a couple of months ago, but I couldn't do it. Couldn't get the job done. Tonight I can. And he needs killing. Both of them do. I'm serious, Jess, I would've killed Chelsey tonight. If I had my pistol I would've. Now I have my pistol. As soon as my eye can see, I'll kill him. And people won't mind, I tell you. I heard 'em while I was fighting. Some people were even laughing about it. One guy got me a tire tool for me to kill Chelsey with. But Thomas wouldn't let me have it."

"I've had my turn at that," he says, like I just told him I wanted to eat breakfast or something and he had already had his.

"Come off it. You haven't killed anyone. You're making fun of me."

"Sure I have. I killed Germans."

"You really did kill someone?"

"More than just someone. Killing people was my business."

"It must have been during a war or something. Not like you hated them."

"Double-U Double-U II was my excuse. Strange things happen to you when you're in hand-to-hand combat. I was with General Patton. That pistol of yours. Where'd you get it?"

"It's right here on the bed somewhere. I laid it right here. You must have seen it."

"Here it is. I found it. No need in you trying to look for it. You still can't see much of anything anyway."

"I can see a little through my slit. The pistol used to be Lenny's."

"And before that, it used to be mine."

"You gave it to Lenny? The pistol was yours?"

"That's right. Lenny just wouldn't let it go until I gave it to him."

"What did Lenny want it for? Did he say?"

"Same question I asked him. Said he just liked pistols. I told him I'd give him a rope if he wanted to hang himself. He just laughed at me. 'Give it to me,' he said. 'I'll give you five dollars for it.' I thought that was pretty good, to get rid of the pistol and get five dollars to boot. So I made a bargain with him. 'Lenny,' I said, 'I'll sell you the pistol, but you've got to promise me one thing.' 'No bargains,' he said. 'You want the pistol or not?' I said. 'Okay,' he said, 'one promise.' So I made him promise that he wouldn't kill himself with it. He laughed at me, but I could tell that it bothered him a little."

"So Lenny got the pistol from you."

"And before that it belonged to a German," he says.

"Lenny gave it to Charles just before he died. I took it from Charles. Can't say he really wanted to give it up."

"Why do you want to kill Charles, anyway. What's he done to you."

309

"He's rotten to the core, Jess. He doesn't deserve to live."

"Tell me what he did to you."

"He steals all the time. And he shoots roof tops out at Fairmead."

"The same stuff you've done? But you still won't tell me what he did to you."

"You don't know what he's like. He just deserves killing."

"Tell me. What did he do to you personally that you want to kill him for?"

"He did something once. Something I can't tell anybody about."

"You could tell me, Bobby. I might understand."

"But I'm not going to tell you. So don't push me."

"Suit yourself. But you took the pistol from a German, too. Charles is a German. Can't say the one I took it from wanted to give it up either. But he was dead, so he didn't have much choice."

"You killed him?"

"He had a wife and two kids. I killed him right out front of his home with his family watching."

"He wasn't a soldier?"

"He had a uniform on. But I worked for General Patton then. The good General loved to stand on top of an army truck and tell us we were going to take a hill if they had to haul the dog tags out by the truckload. He loved war. They always needed the trucks for the dog tags and we always took the hills."

"I would've killed Chelsey if they'd let me. I hate niggers. That's something I didn't know until lately. I always thought I kind of liked 'em. They seemed harmless enough. But now I know, there's nothing worse than a nigger."

"True enough. Nothing worse than nigger. It's a fact. But let me tell you something about colored people. And this is something I saw in Germany, France, Belgium, the Philippines. In Germany, it was the Jews. To a German there's nothing worse than a Jew. That's the way we felt about Japs. So now you hate colored people and you're right. There's nothing worse than a nigger. Once you've been with them, you know the truth about them. You learn to smell them. I've worked with them, even lived in colored camps. I've hopped trains, been a fruit tramp. Been a part time hobo after the war. Walked a few railroad tracks with a pack on my back. I've been with the coloreds and Mexicans until I forgot I was a white man.

But I'll tell you something, and it's God's truth. The colored man never knew he was a nigger until the white man told him he was a nigger. The nigger is what the white man carries around inside him."

"Come on, Jess. What're you talking about?"

"I'm talking about truth. I don't doubt that you recognize the smell of nigger. It's yourself you smell. The nigger is inside the white man."

"Come on, Jess. A nigger is a nigger. I know one when I see one."

Jess smiles at me. "Did you use soap when you showered?"

"What you talking about? I know how to get myself clean."

"What do you smell, Bobby?"

"How come you tell me all this stuff? It's always you and Loretta. But I always figured that was because she's crazy."

"That mother of yours is a fine woman, Bobby. She's spent all these years out on that turkey farm by herself. She's always done a man's work and made her own way. How many farm women you know that work the farm by themselves?"

"None, I don't guess."

"She's always been too trusting of people. Some have left her holding the bag from time to time."

"Like who?"

"Like me."

"What have you done to her?"

"See this tattoo here over my left titty? Can you see enough out of that slit of an eye to see this tattoo?"

"Ya. I see it."

"Tell me about it."

"You can see it. Why ask me?"

"Just tell me."

"It's a broken heart with "Loretta" written above it in blue letters."

"So what do you think of that? You've seen it before. You ever wonder about it?"

"I figured it was your business."

"You were afraid to ask me."

"Come on, Jess. Quit needling me. My head hearts, man. You got some aspirin?"

He gets up, goes to the cabinet above the sink. "I knew your mother before you were ever born. Before I went away to war. I knew her like

311

only a man can know a woman. You ever poke that little girl you go with? That one you and Leroy had a falling out over before he got killed?"

"Come on, Jess. Why you bringing Leroy and Bev into this? I'm asking why Aunt Loretta called you instead of Papa."

"And I'm trying to answer you, but you're not listening. I know it's hard for you to hear this, but it's hard for me to say too. That's the reason I joined the Army, went away to war. Hershel ran me off. He's mellowed about me some the last eighteen years. But I haven't pushed him on it either. I've been using Hershel as an excuse for me not living up to my obligations all these years."

"You're still not making sense."

"Let me try this then. You know my middle name?"

"God, Jess. No! I don't know your middle name!"

"It's Robert. Loretta always called me by my middle name."

"All I can say is, big goddamn deal, Jess. Anything else you need help with?"

"What does Loretta call you?"

"She calls me Ray. She won't call me Bobby."

"Because that's my name."

"Damn, I'm tired, Jess. My head hurts so bad. If you have something to say, why don't you just say it?"

"Okay, but don't be so hard on me." And now I think Jess' voice is about to crack, like he's going to cry on me. "It's just like you said. I'm like your Aunt Loretta. She's your mother. And I'm your old man."

"You're what?" I stand up on my feet and look down at him through my slit. A little light's coming in from the one window in this shack. Must be getting close to sunup. Jess looks little, like he's way off in the distance. Then he turns from me like he's afraid I am going to hit him.

"I'm your father."

★

I only get a couple hours sleep before Jess wakes me.

"Time to go home," he says.

"I'm tired," I say. "Leave me alone." I feel like I've been at his place for a week.

"So am I. But I want to get this over. No way out this time, nobody left to blame. Let's go see your mother."

★

Chapter 43: *Now Jesse Has Something to Say*

As Jess turns in Loretta's drive, I see my mother standing outside the turkey shed like she's expecting us, wiping her hands on a tow sack. Jess' hands are shaking on the steering wheel. There comes that German shepherd pup tagging along behind her with his tail wagging like he's just see his best buddy. Off by the turkey shed, I see a litter of baby kittens with their mama.

"Is she a working woman, or what?" asks Jess.

I feel like I've never been to her place before. But I still feel like I'm coming home. I feel ashamed of the way I look. I know it's going to hurt her to see my face. When I get out of the car, she comes running, just throws her arms around me.

"What have they done to you? My boy. My boy. My baby boy."

If she hadn't cried, I think I could've kept from it, but she doesn't have any shame when it comes to crying. Last night no one would look at my face, even today Jess keeps turning away, but my mother can't get enough. She has both hands with those red fingernails crawling around my face like she's soaking up all the pain. I'm wondering how much infection I'll get in my cuts.

Finally she takes me by the hand, says, "Come on in, Jess. Have a cup of coffee with me and Ray."

"I want to sleep," I say. "Don't need no coffee."

So my mother takes me by the hand and leads me into my bedroom like I don't know the way. She always makes my bed for me and already has the covers turned down. I just lean back on the bed because I'm so tired. She pulls my shoes and socks off, then starts unbuttoning my pants. I won't let her do that, so she stands beside me while I get my pants off, and when I slip in between the cold sheets, she pulls the covers up to my chin and kisses me on the forehead, leaves the door open a crack.

I sleep all day, wake a couple of times and hear the two of them talking in the kitchen and the clatter of dishes. Hear some water running. Some time in the afternoon, Mama and Papa show up. I hear them asking about me. They sound worried, but Loretta won't let them see me. Tells them I need my rest. I feel strange about laying here in bed, not being in school today, and I wonder about all the kids yelling and screaming at each other in PE, and cutting up in class, wonder what the principal, old Clyde Sonnett, is thinking about me right now. Probably planning what he's going to say when he gives me the boot. I may not give him the chance. What is the use of fighting for a lost cause?

I wake in the evening after dark. I'm about slept out. Loretta has my fighting clothes in the washing machine, so I put on some clean clothes and walk through the dark, out to the turkey shed. My teeth hurt. When I jerk open the shed door, the gobble-gobble runs from where I stand clear to the other end. It's bright as day in here. I smell feathers. The floor's littered with white feathers and sawdust. I don't see anybody at first, then spot Jess with Loretta down at the far end, bent over something. I start through the shed, and the turkeys nearest me pile up in the far corner, so I take my time. No sense in spooking the gobblers. Another gobble-gobble runs the length of the shed. As I walk along, I check the bins for feed. Looks like they just finished feeding. I see an empty tow sack now and then. The thing I hate the most about my eyes being all swelled is that my face feels like I'm grinning all the time.

"You come back to us from the sleeping dead?" asks Loretta.

They have a roll of chicken wire fencing off one corner of the shed, and Jess shoos a few turkey's into it. Then he catches one and holds it while Loretta clips off the top part of its beak with a big toenail clipper. I helped her do this last year. It keeps the turkeys from killing one another. If one of them gets a sore, the others will pick it to death for the blood.

"Your dinner's on a plate in the oven, Ray" she says. "And get some more ice on those eyes. Mr. Sonnett called this afternoon from the high school asking about you. He wants to see us before you start class. I want you looking decent when you go to school tomorrow."

I guess that settles that.

CHAPTER 44: *Confrontation with Mr. Sonnett*

I feel like an ogre, like some monster out of a Grimm's fairy tale. I'm standing just outside Mr. Sonnett's office at the high school and feeling a whole lot like I don't belong here. It's nine o'clock, just between first and second period, and kids are running around making this old hardwood floor squeak in a million places, trying to get to class before the next bell rings. No one's saying hi to me. Everybody staring. A couple of freshman even ran from me. I got a call from Bev at home this morning wanting to know if I was going to pick her up. She knew that I'm in bad trouble but was still mad about me not calling her yesterday. She's a little huffy about that Prissy episode, and me having this fight with Chelsey has set her off again.

We had to bring two cars. Loretta and Jess came with me in my car. Mama and Papa came in their pickup. Trish came with them. What a sour puss she is. Still won't talk to me. She's the one that called me an ogre, and if you want to talk about ogres, one's standing beside her right now and its name is Thomas Powers. I wish he'd leave her alone, or maybe it's her that should leave him alone. I don't know which. I just know I don't like them together a whole lot.

I feel someone grab my left hand and turn to see who it is just about the time Brenda kisses me on the cheek. "Good luck, Bobby," she whispers in my ear. "I miss you." And then she's gone.

And now here's Mr. Wood, my physics teacher, standing in front of me looking real serious. He has dark brown hair that he keeps in a flattop. "If he won't let you come to class, call me at home," he says. "I'll give you the homework assignments." He gives me a look of utmost seriousness. "Don't give up now, Bobby. Please. Don't quit on me." Then he goes in a room where only teachers are allowed.

I hear a door open and when I look up there's Chelsey and Mr. Sonnett standing in the doorway to his office. Chelsey's nose looks like a big brown cucumber. Two other colored people come out of the room, and I guess that's Chelsey's mama and papa. Chelsey's papa spots me, but I turn away, pick out a board in the floor to look at.

"Bobby," says Mr. Sonnett, "would you come in here for a moment please." He looks a little confused, eyes Mama and Papa and then Jess and Loretta. "I want to talk to you and Chelsey alone a moment, then we'll want to talk to your mother and father."

Chelsey sits on one side of the room and Mr. Sonnett motions for me to take a seat on the other just as the final bell rings.

"The first thing I want to know," is the way Mr. Sonnett starts in, "is why the fight? What's going on between you two."

Chelsey looks a dagger at me. I know he can't say anything without doing his sister wrong, so I figure it's up to me to answer the question.

"Let's just say, I made a mistake and Chelsey here was good enough to help me find a way to pay for it."

That gets a frown out of Chelsey.

"How about you, Chelsey?" asks Mr. Sonnett. "What's your side of it?"

"It's personal. I'm not saying."

"You two are going to have to help me out, or we're going to have a real problem with this." He looks from Chelsey to me. "Come on. Is it still going on between you or are you through with it?" He struggles for some words for a minute. "Is it racial?"

Whoa! I wish he hadn't asked that question. Now I'm in real trouble.

"No," says Chelsey, straight out. "With some of the other kids round here it'd be. But not Bobby. I don't get none of that from him. Never have."

Mr. Sonnett looks like he just got a stay of execution, maybe even lets a little smile creep across his lips. "But is it over? I've got to know that. Is it over between you?"

Chelsey pulls out a blood stained white handkerchief, blows some clots out of his cucumber, sneezes. "I'd like to get Bobby in a ring," he says, finally. "Put on the gloves with him. Let's just say that it's over, but not forgiven. I'll never forgive him for what he did to my little sister."

Mr. Sonnett turns to me.

"Since my head got bigger," I say, "I can think a little better. I don't want anymore of Chelsey. Not in a ring either. And I'm sorry about his sister. I don't think I'll ever forgive myself for that one either."

Chelsey has to laugh about that, then blows out more clots.

316

Mr. Sonnett stands up. "Good," he says, walking around to the front of his desk. "I'm glad to hear that. Now, Chelsey, you go on to the doctor and call me this afternoon. I'll give you the Board's decision."

Chelsey winks at me on the way out. He's walking like a boat that's taking on a little water.

★

"I'm not sure where I stand here," says Mr. Sonnett. "Bobby, who are all these people?"

When Mr. Sonnett invited my two sets of parents in, I thought Jess was going to chicken out. He walked in last like an old dog that'd just been beat with a whip.

"Well, these two," I say pointing to Mama and Papa, "are my Aunt Louise, that you met before when you kicked me out of school, and my Uncle Hershel. They raised me for eighteen years and were my parents up until a couple of months ago. And this is my mother that I used to think was my Aunt Loretta, that I'm living with now, and this is my dead friend Leroy's Uncle Jesse Korenski that I just found out yesterday is my father."

"I see," he says, and then drops his eyes and has to swallow real deep.

Mama's face just turned redder than a sunburned tomato and her lips are pursed tight like they have a drawstring in them.

Jess just dropped his head to get a good look at the hardwood floor.

"Ray's a good kid," and it's Loretta who has started off the discussion. "I won't let you do anything to hurt him. Will we, Jess? And anyone that lays a hand on him will have me to deal with."

Mr. Sonnett takes a deep breath like he's just about to dive into a waterhole swimming with cottonmouth rattlesnakes. "I understand your concern, Mrs... Mrs..."

"*Miss* Loretta Hammer," I say. I figure he needs a little help with that one.

"Thank you, Bobby," he says. "Miss Hammer, I think we all have Bobby's best interest at heart here. I know I do. I agree with you that he's one fine young man. And I can see that there's more going on in Bobby's life than his problems here at the high school and that maybe that should be taken into consideration. I appreciate all of you coming down here. This hasn't been easy for any of us. In light of the situation, I think I'll cut this short. I just want to say that the decision on Bobby staying in school for the rest of the year will not come exclusively from me. The School Board

317

will make the final decision. Whichever way it comes out, I hope you'll remember that we have to make a decision that's also in the best interest of the high school. And quite honestly, we have a touchy situation here right now." Then he turns to look at me again. "Bobby's sure had his share of adolescent behavior problems this year."

Mr. Sonnett stands up and so does everybody else. As my two sets of parents go out the door, Mr. Sonnett turns to me. "Stay for a few more minutes, Bobby," he says. "We need to talk some more."

★

"Why'd you take a swing at me," Mr. Sonnett wants to know. "When I broke up the fight between Stanley and Melvin, Thomas stopped you from hitting me. What made you want to do that?"

It's my turn to look at the hardwood floor. I'm thinking that I didn't just want to hit him. I wanted to kill him. We are both standing with his big wood desk between us, but he's looking just a little over my head.

"I thought you hated me," I say.

"Hate you? I don't hate you."

"Why did you kick me out of school, take football away from me?"

"Cause you were disrupting the whole school. I have to maintain discipline here, Bobby."

"So if a kid gets involved in a ruckus, even if it's not on the school grounds, you've got to take his future away from him. That's just the way it goes, huh?"

"I didn't take your future away from you."

"Maybe not completely, but you sure made a dent in it."

"I like to think I've done a reasonable job of maintaining discipline here at Chowchilla."

"Here at the CUHS prison."

"Now you stop that. You're just mad all the time. When you have a lot of anger, it sticks to everything. You can't think straight. It's kids like you that stand in the way of other kids getting a good education so they can go to college."

"Maybe so. But your attitude about me is showing through too. That's the reason you think I'm here. Just to keep other kids out of college. So keeping me out of school as much as you can is a good deal. Well let me tell you something. I've got plans too."

"Well, tell me about your plans, Bobby. I need to hear about them if

I'm going to talk to the Board."

"So you wanted me to stay in here with you so I could help you find an excuse to get rid of me for good. It's going to be a permanent expulsion this time. I can see it coming. Bet you already have the papers drawn up."

"No, Bobby. That's not why I have you in here. I've never, never had a student take a punch at me. I want to understand why."

"I've already told you. Cause you've ruined my future."

"What is this future you're so concerned about. What is it that I'm keeping you from doing? It's you that's getting low grades, not me."

"I wouldn't be in such bad shape if you hadn't kicked me out of school for a week. Me and half of the rest of the school."

"But what am I keeping you from?"

"How about, 'Going to college,' for an answer? Think you can handle that one? I want to go to college."

Mr. Sonnett looks like I just shot him. First he just stands there and I think maybe his face gets a little white. He swallows some air.

"College?" Then he stops like he's waiting for the world to start turning again. "But you're not even in college preparatory classes. And... you want to go to college?"

"Why do you think I'm in Mr. Wood's class?"

"So that's what's up. God! He told me the strangest story about you and bridges the other day. Everything is a secret with you, isn't it? Why didn't you tell me, Bobby."

I don't believe this, but I see tears in his eyes. Then he stops for a minute like he's thinking. "Maybe that's why I've been so hard on you. I had some trouble too getting where I am. I wasn't always a model student. And I don't believe I've seen all the sides of Bobby Hammer either. A couple of weeks ago, Mr. Wood was in here talking about you. He called my attention to your Iowa Test scores. You have excellent ability in several areas. You were close to the top of your class in mathematics and the sciences. A little low in some of the other areas, but overall, your test scores were excellent. And now maybe after seeing your family I can answer my own question about why you aren't performing better? Mr. Woods is right. You do have the interest, don't you?"

"I do. I have more than you could imagine. I'm disappointed too. I don't know why I can't do better." And now I can feel my eyes starting to wet up a little. "But I know what I want to do. And you can go to the

Board and talk to them behind my back about what a lousy kid I am. But I can tell you one thing. I'm not giving up on myself. You do what you have to with me. The thing is," and now I've started crying, so I turn my back on him. I don't want him to see my face anymore. And my voice is just this real loud whiny thing. "My older brother didn't make it through high school. I need something he didn't get, if I'm going to make it. But I don't need to be kicked out, beat up, scolded or sent to jail. I need help. My brother didn't get any help. I need it real bad. And I promise you this. I know I can't graduate without your help."

"I'm not going to tell the Board you're a lousy kid. I don't think that. For what it's worth," and he comes over and puts his hand on my shoulder and talks to my back, "I'm with you on this. I'll do my best for you when I talk to the Board. When I met your family just now, I started to wake up a little. I can't imagine what you've been going through. Most kids your age can't stand one set of parents, and you have two."

"One more thing," I say.

"What's that."

"I want to attend my classes until I find out from the Board if I can stay in school."

"You mean now?"

"Yes. I've got physics in fifteen minutes."

"Bobby..." He walks back over to his desk, looks through my folder. "God, you are persistent. I'll lose my job over this. But that's my problem. Okay. Okay. Go on to class, for christsake."

I turn around. He's still looking through my folder.

"But no Studyhall or PE, your last two classes. Make Civics your last class of the day. Then you come directly to my office. I'll have the verdict by then."

★

I've been sitting in Mr. Sonnett's office for an hour and a half. What could be taking him so long? My classes didn't go so good. More boring than usual. We had a pop quiz in Civics, and I think I flunked it. Everybody stared at me. I have this problem thinking people are staring at me, but today it was true. They weren't laughing either. I think they're worried about me.

All at once, here comes Mr. Sonnett, mumbling something about never having seen so many hardheaded people. He goes straight to his filing cabinet, jerks out a file, probably mine, then looks up at me.

"I feel like I've sold my soul to the devil on this one. But I got you one last chance. The rest is up to you."

CHAPTER 45: *Trip to the Junkyard*

I'm standing in front of my locker looking for my history book and some scratch paper. I wonder where I put that pencil? I'm here all alone because I'm late for class. I've been talking to my counselor about what I have to do to get graduated. Looks pretty bleak. I hear someone walking up the cement steps so I look around to see who else is late. It's Brenda so I smile at her, then turn my head back because she's made it plain we can't be any more than friends. I hear the sound of her footsteps coming closer and then they stop. I get uneasy with the silence knowing she's standing behind me so I turn to look, figuring she'll be getting into her locker on the other side of the walkway. I jump a little because there she is standing facing me about two feet away. I've never seen a girl look so afraid.

"Bobby, don't say anything, just let me talk for a minute." She hides her face in her hands and then peaks through her fingers at me and I see that her face is real red. "I'm ashamed, Bobby. I really am. I found out that when people were talking about me and what I'd been doing with some boy, that they weren't talking about you and me. They were talking about me and someone else. Someone I don't care about nearly as much as I do you. I brought all my problems on myself, Bobby. I wasn't very... discreet. Didn't have anything to do with you." She hides her face in her hands again and I don't hear any whimpering but tears run through her fingers. "I have a bad rep... a bad rep..u..ta..tion."

She snivels a little, catches a trembling breath. "It's my own fault. And you know something?" Then she sniffs and looks me straight in the eyes. "They still don't know anything about us. After me accusing you of causing my problem, you didn't tell anyone. You didn't even try to defend yourself against me, all the names I called you. Nobody knows anything about us, Bobby. And I have you to thank for that. They don't even remember that we went out together. Except for Mother and Daddy, of course. I told Mother it was you and she told Daddy. So they know for sure it was you.

Everybody else just thinks I don't like you. I've said some uncomplimentary things about you."

I nod my head, yes, because I know that's true.

"I've known this for months but couldn't bring myself to face you. I couldn't face myself. But now it's so close to the end of school, and after graduation we may never see each other again. I don't expect us to be friends after what I've done, but I just can't carry this around for the rest of my life. Helen's taught me that. I'm sorry I hurt you, Bobby, very sorry. And I do like you. We could've had a lot of fun together." And then she laughs. "I didn't mean it that way," and blushes again. "You really are a gentleman." She's still crying.

I can't stand anymore of this, so I reach for her and hug her for a minute.

"Ah," she whispers, then kisses me on the neck. "Thank you," she says, and walks off with her head down.

I stand there for a second with the cold feel of her little bits of sweat, tears and spit drying on my face and neck. Every time I touch her, she gets wet stuff all over me. Brenda always leaves juice. Bev leaves welts and bruises.

Then she turns back. "Helen tried to commit suicide," she says. "But she's okay now. Her parents have a psychiatrist working with her. I just thought you might want to know. She told me that she and Lenny were married. So you don't have to keep that secret anymore."

She walks a little further away from me. "Oops, almost forgot," she says. Guess she has a lot of stuff cooking today. "Helen said to tell you that Lenny used to keep his journal in his car. Up under the dashboard. She also said to tell you that Charles is wrong about having Lenny's car. It must be a different Hudson. The journal and her wedding ring are probably still in the car if you can find it."

"What?" I ask. "It's not Lenny's car?"

"The inside's not the same color. She knew something was different. She asked Charles. He said he didn't have to repaint the inside." And now Brenda has turned around and walking toward me again.

"So his car is still in the junkyard."

"You know where?" she asks.

"Yes. The Berenda Junkyard."

"That's not far. Take me with you, Bobby. Let's go get it."

I don't know if it's the thought of Lenny's journal or Brenda's body that has just taken my breath away. Since the weather has turned warm, she's gone to these sleeveless dresses and this one doesn't have shoulders, dips a little in front too.

"You mean right now?" I ask. "But we've got one more class before the day's over."

"You ever heard of a senior cutting class?"

"I can't do that. I promised Mr. Sonnett."

"A promise is a fact with you, isn't it?"

"I'll be at my car before the last bell quits ringing good." If Bev finds out about this, it's curtains for me.

★

"It's a '48 Hudson," I tell him one more time. I've been trying to talk to this sixteen-year-old kid for fifteen minutes about the Hudson, but he keeps arguing with me. I feel like grabbing him by the hair of the head and wringing the right answer out of him. Maybe the thing I'm mad about most is that when he talks to me he keeps looking at Brenda's tits.

"I think I remember it now. We sold it about a year ago."

"No that was a different one," I tell him.

He hollers at an old guy in the back. "Chet! We got another '48 Hudson?" He doesn't get an answer, so I figure the guy's hard hearing. The kid turns to another customer.

I turn to Brenda, whisper in her ear. "If your breasts could carry on a conversation, we'd a seen the Hudson fifteen minutes ago."

She starts laughing so hard she has to walk away from me.

"Chet'll be here in a second," the guy says with a grin. "He's not as old as he looks, but he's a lot slower. That your girlfriend with you?"

I look at him but don't give him an answer.

"A girl like that a'd be worth a couple of black eyes."

I watch Brenda with her back to me, window-shopping the junkyard.

"Who wants that Hudson?" booms a husky voice.

"I do," I say, turning back around.

"We got one over in the southeast corner. Been there five, maybe six year." The old man hasn't had a shave or a bath in five, maybe six day. His shirttail's out and the hair on his chest looks like black worms. "What you want off it?"

"Just want to look."

"You standing here wasting our time for a look?"

"My brother died in it. I just want to see it."

"Oh, shit," he says, real quiet like. "That be the case, be my guest. You want some help finding it?"

"That's okay. South-west corner?"

"Ya. Over in the corner of the fence. Don't take nothing off it though." He raises part of the counter to let me and Brenda through, so we can go out back. "Take your time," he says. "I had a little brother that died in a car wreck."

Lenny's Hudson has three flat tires. The brake drum, where the fourth tire used to be, rests on the ground. The driver-side door is wired almost shut with bailing wire. Someone's busted out all the windows, and the hood's propped open with a piece of angle iron. Seeing his car for the first time in five years, I have to look behind me to make sure Lenny isn't standing there.

Brenda takes my hand in hers, squeezes it, then hugs me for a second. "This is difficult, isn't it?"

"I just saw a ghost."

This is the first time I've seen the damage Lenny did to his car in the accident. The front bumper's all caved in and the front tires shoved up into the wheel wells. Hood's buckled a little. The top's caved in a little too, so it does look like it could've gone end over end. Even the trunk's sprung open a little. I go over to the trunk. That's what I want to see first. I look around the license plate a little bit. Rub off some scrub marks.

"Look at this," I tell Brenda.

"What?"

"It's where I shot it with my .22. The last time I saw Lenny alive, he came out of the house and drove off in this Hudson. I was mad at him, so I took aim and put a bullet in the back of his car. I've worried all these years that I wounded Lenny and that caused him to have his accident."

"So you can quit worrying now."

I rub the indentation with my finger. "My little .22 didn't have power to even penetrate the metal. Look. There's a little dimple, maybe even a crack in the metal. But the bullet just bounced off. I was trying to shoot out his license plate light. Only missed it by an inch. I was a crack shot with my old .22."

I go to the passenger-side door, pull it open, see a little mud still in the

325

floorboard from the last rain. A little puddle of water. I lay on my back on the front seat, look up under the dash. Can't see much.

"Did Helen say which side he kept it on?" I ask. I have my arm up in electrical wiring and spider webs. Must be a mess of black widows up there too. Then I feel something. And there ain't no doubt what it is.

★

I always thought Lenny's journal was a little blue notebook and was real nice. I can't tell what color it is, could be green. And it's just a steno pad with a wire spring through the top. We searched the Hudson for a half hour but couldn't find Helen's wedding ring. I took Brenda home after we left the junkyard. She said she understood that some things had to be done in private. Right now I'm sitting in my Chevy in the dip at the Berenda Slough, on the very spot where Lenny's car was found five years ago almost to the day with him lying on the ground outside it, dead. I start reading on the first page.

Jan 18, 1952, Saturday

Weight: 142. Got to gain some to hit the long ball this spring. The blooper base hits won't cut it in the pros either. Started sucking eggs at home. Mama's making milkshakes. Gretta says after we get married she'll out weigh me by the time she's twenty-five. She wants me to use a rubber but I tell her I'm good at jerking it. I've been kidding Charles about Johnny Swensen. I've never seen two guys buddy up to each other like that. I swear I caught them in Charles' hay barn the other day with their arms around each other's shoulders like we used to do in the sixth grade. Made Charles mad when I laughed at him.

Feb 1, 1952, Saturday

Papa saw me with Gretta today after school. If he tells Mama I'm in deep shit. Me and Gretta have been sneaking around for three years. Coach says he thinks if I do good in college I have a shot at the pros. Screw college, is what I told him. I'm no bookworm. I'm thinking about the minor leagues for starters. What's Coach mean, college? How's he think I get through high school so easy? I take bonehead classes. One of my teachers called me a con artist the other day, said I'm taking a free ride.

Feb 14, 1952, Friday – Valentine's Day

326

Chapter 45: *Trip to the Junkyard*

Mama chewed me out about Gretta this evening. Papa said it wasn't him that told. That bastard Charles did it, I bet. He always acts like it's great that I'm punching his sister but you can never tell what he's thinking to himself. Mama's been after me to stay away from Gretta since 8th grade. Started screaming at me tonight. Slapped me right in the face. Me and Gretta have always been a big bad thing with Mama. My ear's still ringing. Why does she hate Gretta so much? I really like that girl. Mama called Karl Kunze, told him to keep his girl away from me. What does she have against the Kunze's? Gretta's been telling me that we should fight Mama, bring it out in the open. But maybe Mama's right. I'm leaving here this summer and Gretta still has one year of high school left.

Feb 15, 1952, Saturday night
First week of baseball practice. Took Helen away from Charles tonight. They had a fight in Farnesi's so I took her home. She finally found out about Charles' nigger girl, Maggie, that lives out at Fairmead. Helen decided she likes Hudsons. I've never been with a girl that runs so hot. I had to keep cooling her off afterward. She can't stop. I'm young but I'm not Superman. I've known Helen all my life. No one told me she was hot like this. I'm in love again!

Feb 21, 1952, Friday night
First baseball game is next week. Went to see Helen babysitting for the McCallum's tonight. First time I've ever done it in a bed! Charles can have his sister back. Who cares about old backseat-Gretta anyway. I think Helen's 12-year-old cousin, Brenda, saw us in her parents' bed. Hope she learned something. Helen showed me around the McCallum's home. Started talking about a home of her own, marriage and kids. Whoa! is what I said. Charles has been after me to stay away from Helen. He had tears in his eyes.

Mar 1, 1952, Sunday
Mariposa, 3/4 = .750. Weight: 138. Drove in three runs. What the hell's happening to me? I'm wasting away! Caught Helen with Charles again. Goddamn him! She's out with me Fri and Sat night and sneaking out with him Sun. What a bitch! She said she was through with him. My batting average is three times Charles'. Ha Ha. One game into the season. Watch

out Yankees. Here I come! Turlock next week. Playing 3rd is the berries. I talked to Papa about a new glove. He said no.

Mar 6, 1952, Friday

Turlock, 4/5 (7/8 = .778). Helen wants to get married. I just turned 18. She's been 18 for a couple of months. I said, we need to get to know each other better, only been going together 3 weeks. She said, we've known each other for 12 years. How long does it take? She showed me what it would be like again. Every night, she said.

Mar 13, 1952, Friday

Los Banos, 2/4 (9/12 = .692). Johnny told Charles to stay away from his girl or he would kill them both. When I told Johnny about Charles, Helen and Maggie, Johnny said that he has a female German shepherd that he keeps on a chain when Charles is around. She's a purebred and Johnny doesn't want any mongrels.

Mar 18, 1952, Wednesday

Turlock, 1/3 (11/15 = .625). I struckout for the first time since I was a freshman. This old dog had his tail between his legs. Saw Gretta Monday night at the Tasty Freeze. She's had the stomach flu for two weeks. Missed a lot of classes. I feel real sad when I'm around her now. She told me that I sold out to Mama. She says I'm giving away my life.

Mar 20, 1952. Friday

Dos Palos, 1/5 (12/19 = .524). I dropped a pop fly at third. Coach about fainted. Glad to see you're human, he said. I bet he is. Gretta has a new boyfriend. At least I saw her walking and talking to this dipship junior that she has a lot of classes with. She wouldn't even look at me. But I took a good hard look at Mama this evening while she was fixing dinner. She thinks she's God. Told me again to say away from Gretta.

Mar 27, 1952, Wednesday

Washington, 1/5 (13/24 = .462). Me and Helen got married today. Don't tell nooo body! She said that marriage was the one thing that would keep her away from Charles. We'll see. So we cut school and I missed baseball practice. Coach is going to be pissed. Can't wait till I get old enough to play the slots in Reno. I felt sorry for Gretta tonight. She called me late. Said she thinks she has a problem. Another month will tell for sure. I told her, Don't call me anymore.

Apr 3, 1952, Friday

Central, 1/2 (14/25 = .464). Coach held me out of the game because of missing one day's practice. What an A–number one asshole. First game I ever missed. Put me in in the 7th inning (the last). I drove in the winning run. At least I kept my streak alive.

Apr 10, 1952, Friday

Edison. 0/5 (14/30 = .394). Batting average is a little low for this late in the season. Lost my hitting streak. Joe DiMaggio set the record at 54 for the majors. Mine just snapped at 51 for high school. First game I have ever played in my life that I didn't get at least one hit.

Apr 19, 1952, Monday

Dos Palos, 0/4 (14/33 = .351). Papa caught me screwing Helen last night. We were parked down the road a ways from the house. It was 1:00 in the morning. I never thought anyone would be out at that hour. But Papa, he gets up at all hours to check on the water in the hay. I looked up from Helen and there he was standing beside the car. He just let me see him and then he backed off into the dark. Papa's a pervert. He came to me this morning and told me she was trash, to leave her alone. First it's Mama telling me to stay away from Gretta, and now it's Papa telling me to stay away from Helen. I told him to mind his own goddamn business and he turned white as a sheet. He told me she wasn't anyone I could have a family with. I told him that we were married and to keep his fucking mouth shut. I told him if he told Mama I would kill everyone in the family. Helen's a Catholic, so her parents can't find out yet. We didn't get married in the church.

Apr 28, 1952, Wednesday

San Joaquin Memorial, 1/5 (15/38 = .333). Every base hit seems like a miracle. I don't know how I did it before. Measured myself this evening, 5' 7". Not tall enough for the pro's. One month past 18. Won't grow anymore. Caught Helen talking to Charles again at school. Still miss Gretta. Charles dropped the transmission in my car Saturday night. I told Papa I wasn't dragging. He'll help me put in a new one to save a little money. Charles was dragging my Hudson against Johnny Swensen's new Ford. Charles wouldn't shut up until I let him try it. Can't tell Papa that Charles was driving.

May 2, 1952, Saturday night

Washington, 0/2 (15/40 = .318). Coach says it can happen to anybody. I don't get into slumps. Goddamn! What a piece Helen is. Used a motel room in Fresno. Used Helen's car. Had to show our marriage certificate. I never knew there could be so much sex inside one girl. We did it and did it until my tool just spit and spit and then quit. I told her if I caught her with Charles again I'd kill her. When she gets started crying, she can't quit that either. I wish I hadn't said anything. I had to do it to her again to stop the crying. She says, "Oh, Daddy. Oh, Daddy," while we do it. Papa still thinks I was dragging when the transmission went. We were under the car and I told him he had shit for brains. He banged his head twice trying to hit me with a wrench. Bobby Ray ran in the house and wouldn't come back out. What a chickenshit he is.

May 3, 1952, Sunday night

Don't know if we should be doing some of the things that Helen wants to do. I don't feel like kissing her mouth afterward. I brush my teeth real often and real hard now. Need a new toothbrush. I don't have any rhythm at the plate. A grounder went between my legs at third. But DiMaggio retired. Maybe I could play the outfield in the pro's. Papa says it's all a pipe dream. I asked Helen where she learned how to do that but she's not talking.

May 4, 1952, Monday

Saw Gretta at school today. She's got more than a problem. She's got a baby inside her. My baby she said. She doesn't know I'm married and I'm not talking. Fuck her. I told her it's in her body so it's her baby. She was crying when Helen caught us talking. Each of them had two fists full of loose hair when me and Charles got 'em separated. Charles took Gretta home from school. I told Papa if he didn't get my car fixed I'm stealing another one. I'm tired of his excuses and all this slow-shit way he does things.

330

Chapter 45: *Trip to the Junkyard*

May 6, 1952, Wednesday night
Weight: 135. Where the hell is the weight going? I eat everything in sight. Even my body is against me. Mama's feeding me steak for every meal, even breakfast. Papa bought a new eating calf. Charles says Gretta vomits all the time now. Not just in the morning. So why does everyone feel so sorry for her? It's my life that's going down the tube. Every time I flush the toilet, I watch the old brown thing and say, that's my life and there it goes. I sat in a new Chevy with the motor running for ten minutes the other day in Merced before I decided not to steal it. Wish I'd brought it home. I'd like to see the look on old Hershel's face.

May 8. 1952, Friday
Central, 0/3 (15/43 = .311). Coach said I may set a new record for times at bat without a hit. I pushed him up against the goddamn lockers. Took three guys to pull me off him. Struckout twice today. I'm not dropping below .300. I'll never live it down. Six guys on the team are hitting higher than me. I've always hit leadoff, 3rd or cleanup. Now he has me hitting 7th. Next thing you know I'll be hitting 9th like a wimp-ass pitcher. I hear snickers in the locker room. And by the way, goddamn Charles is hitting cleanup. He's a .350 hitter but he carries a big stick and hits a lot of long balls according to Coach. Charles sucks the coach's big bat, is what I said back. Finally got the new transmission in my Hudson and I'm on the road again. So Mama knows that Gretta is pregnant. But believe it or not, Mama is on my side. It can't be your baby, Lenny, she said. It just can't be. The Lord wouldn't do that to me.

May 11, 1952, Monday
Mama and Karl Kunze are going to kill each other. Karl says I have to marry Gretta. Mama says, over her dead body. She told him to find another sucker to marry his whore daughter. She added that if he wanted to pimp for his daughter, don't bring her to our house. I told Mama to shut her mouth cause Gretta's a nice girl.

May 13, 1952, Wednesday
5:15 AM. I can't face the game Friday against Edison. If I go 0/4, my BA will be .268. I've never been scared of baseball before. It's early Thursday morning. The sun's not up yet but I see some light on the horizon. I'm

still parked in front of Helen's house watching it for signs of life. The lights haven't gone off since Helen went inside. Last night (this morning) Papa got me up at 2:00 AM. He never wakes me at night through the week. Get out to Beacon Road, he said. There's something going on out there that you should see. I took my pistol. I had a suspicion. Papa is a pervert. Helen was on top of Charles when I got out there. I thought the guy was always supposed to be on top. I jerked the door open and shot out the window on the other side of the car. Helen screamed when the dome light came on and Charles cussed. Remember, Lenny, she's just a whore, he said. I had Helen get out of the car, never mind your clothes, I said, and then I ran Charles off. I emptied my pistol in the back of his old man's car. Tried to put one in the back of Charles' head but guess I missed. Helen wanted to know why I was reloading. She didn't even have shoes on and the gravel hurt the bottoms of her feet. I knew I was going to kill her, the stupid quivering bitch. I just didn't know where I was going to put the bullets. I was thinking about blowing her tits off first. She kept saying, Forgive me, Lenny, forgive me! Stupid bitch. I was going to put one up the crack of her ass. But when I started shooting I couldn't get the bullets to go into her body. I kept shooting first to one side of her then the other. While I reloaded she turned her back on me. I thought I could kill her then. She was screaming, Oh, God, help me! Please, God! Oh, Mother Mary! The thing that stopped me, I guess, was the image I had of Papa peeking in on them. I just couldn't live with knowing that Papa had watched my wife screw another guy. Then I realized that my problem was with Papa. So I pulled off my shirt, draped it over Helen's shoulders and took her home. She peed in my seat when I slapped her. I've never hit a girl before but I had to to get her to let me take her wedding ring off her finger. I asked her why she didn't at least take her ring off while she was fucking Charles. I wanted to pound all the meat off her bones. I'm still sitting here in front of her house. The light in her bedroom has been on ever since she went inside. But I think I need to see Charles again before the sun comes up.

7:45 AM. I'm back in my car. The sun is up and high school classes will start soon. Looks like a good clear morning. Somebody's got to die today. That's for goddamn sure. Who is it going to be? Right now I still vote for Papa. That crummy sonofabitch. Why wouldn't he stay out of my business? I just left Charles' place. He was really afraid of what I might have done to

Helen. He hadn't gone to bed. I told him I am going to kill him before the days is over. He just screamed at me. She's just a woman, he said. Why can't you understand that? Helen's just a goddamn woman! He kept shouting at me as I walked away. So maybe I'll kill all three of them. I'm parked a ways away from Charles' house now but I'm close enough that I see a car pull out. It's Gretta. She's going to school. Christ! I'm going to be a papa. Maybe she'll have the good sense to get rid of it. Charles'll be coming out soon driving that jeep of his so I guess I'll be going. The Fair starts this evening. I sort of wanted to see the Miss Madera County Pageant.

2:30 PM. I didn't go back home this morning. Didn't go to school. I drove back to Helen's house and watched from a distance. I watched the front door for an hour after it was time for her to go to school but she never came out. Then I went to where Papa was working in the field. I watched him from a distance too. I felt like a ghost or maybe a drifter that had been gone from home for a long time and came back for a visit but for some reason wasn't welcome anymore. Papa was late getting the tractor in the field. Then I drove to the house and watched Mama through the kitchen window for a while. After that, I don't know what I did till noon. Then I went to Wilson School and watched for Bobby Ray. I knew a hoe was waiting for him when he got home. He has to chop for three hours everyday after school. God, he is a case. He has a real concerned look on his face all the time. And that kid, Leroy, always following along behind him. I call him Bobby Ray's puppy dog. Bobby Ray has Leroy trained so that he's always heeled. While I was watching, damn if Papa didn't drive up in the pickup and Bobby Ray got in with him. Now why would he be going home? Then I drove over to Stevens School where Trish is in the fifth grade. I had to cry a little there. I don't know why. Maybe it's because one day I overheard her tell another little girl that I am her favorite big brother. Little Curt is at Stevens School also. Can't say much about Curt. I hardly know him. Seems like I haven't seen him for the last month. It's like sometimes he doesn't even exist. I drove around in the country for a while, went up to Raymond to get a look at the foothills that have all turned green. Just playing hooky. But now I've got to talk to Mama.

4:30 PM. It's not Helen, Charles, or Papa that's got to die today. It's Gretta. I was going to tell Gretta that I'm married, so she'll have to work her problem out on her own. But that won't solve the problem now. I'm going to have to kill her. The trouble is. Gretta doesn't even know what we have done. Even getting rid of the baby won't fix this. We have committed an abomination. I've got to talk to somebody. Maybe Aunt Loretta can help. Mama hit me again. She just started screaming at me. Then Papa came in. He wouldn't listen to reason. So we had a fistfight. I can't believe it. I hit my own papa with my fist. But on top of all that, I can't believe what Bobby Ray just did. After I fought with Mama and Papa, I drove off in my car and Bobby Ray took a shot at me. My own brother tried to kill me.

5:30 PM. Aunt Loretta was no help. What a stammering idiot. But then I couldn't tell her what the real problem is. I'm thinking about checking out of here. I've got to unload this pistol. I don't want the devil to catch me with this thing. Jess should have never sold it to me. All I want to do is kill people with it ever since I got it. Maybe Charles can find a use for it.

6:00 PM. I just left Charles holding the bag. I would have liked to see Gretta and Helen one more time, but what's the use? What's done is done. I keep looking at Helen's wedding ring here on my little finger and wondering about her. With what she's done with Charles, she don't need an explanation. And as far as Gretta goes, if God has a problem with her condition, let Him work it out with her. This problem is too big for me. I'm checking out right now. I've always wondered what it would be like to take the dip at the Berenda Slough at 120 mph.

PART VI

Mama Shuts off the Water Pump

CHAPTER 46: *Trouble Following on the Heels of Trouble*

Lenny's journal continues to affect me. Every time I reread it, I feel like he's right here with me. When I put it down, it's as if he just died again. I went to the Cemetery and stared down at his tombstone. It only has his name, Leonard Hershel Hammer, and the years of his birth and death, 1935-1952. That's all. Even his tombstone refuses to talk. Now before I go to sleep, I read his journal like a bedtime story. I get this feeling that he was so afraid to live. He knew he was messing up his life and couldn't stop. I've felt like that so much myself. When I'm working with Loretta among the turkeys, walking that old sawdust-covered ground, I think about how different Lenny and I were, and yet, his life's so much a part of me. How can I ever get out of Chowchilla without knowing the truth about him? And now it's the whole truth I'm after. I know Lenny committed suicide but not why. Every answer leads to another question. Where does it all end?

I've been thinking a lot about Helen wanting her wedding ring back. Just before he died, Lenny wrote that he had Helen's wedding ring on his little finger. But I saw his hands when he was in the casket. He didn't have the ring on. Someone took it off his finger and didn't say anything about it. The people that drive ambulances don't do things like that. But Jess was the first one at the accident. He found Lenny. I tell you, these people changing places in my life become different people. I can't remember who Jess was before he became my father. He was the one who found Lenny and called Mama and Papa, and he sure wouldn't have taken the ring. I don't want to believe that about him. Someone at the hospital could have taken it. But the hospital in Chowchilla wasn't even built yet, so it would have been the one in Merced. But I don't think they even took Lenny to a hospital. He was already dead. They must've taken him to the Chowchilla undertaker, Mr. Hickman. I can't believe he would've taken the ring. Somebody did it to keep people from asking questions. Mama and Papa were at the scene of the accident. They saw Lenny dead, lying in the dirt. And Papa knew that Lenny was married. Lenny said in his journal that he told Papa he was married and said that if Papa told Mama, he'd kill all of us. That gives me a creepy feeling about Lenny. Papa was the only one who knew about Lenny and Helen being married. Papa could've taken the ring to keep Mama from finding out. He's known Lenny was married to Helen ever since Lenny died and told no one. And now I know Samantha really is Lenny's little girl. Why won't Mama believe it? She knew they were messing around together. That just doesn't sound like Mama. She would have wanted them to get married. I mean, Mama is just about the most religious person in the world.

I called Brenda the night I got home after reading Lenny's journal, told her not to say anything. The other end of the line got real quiet.

"Too late," she said. "Helen already knows."

"Oh," I said. "Did you tell her?"

"I'm sorry, Bobby. Yes I did."

"Why did you do that?"

"Because... I thought you'd want her to know. I was excited. I just can't seem to do anything right this year, Bobby."

"I know what you mean. Even if I *don't* do something, that's wrong too."

"Exactly. I'm sorry."

"Well, don't worry about it. She'd have found out anyway. I just wanted a little time."

"Anything important in it?"

"If there wasn't, I wouldn't be bothering you."

"You can bother me anytime. Helen probably told Charles. She's been out with him again."

★

It's Friday night and I have this knot right between the eyes where my class ring just hit me. Broke the skin a little. I keep touching it with my finger to see if it's still bleeding.

I'm standing on the Midway at the Fairgrounds again but this time I'm alone, at least I'm alone now because there goes Bev, and that little round butt of hers is working in those tight pants like it's late for something big. We just came back to the Fair after being parked in this grape vineyard out east of town where she was all over me. I was feeling a little uneasy about the whole thing. It was like she had something to prove. I just kind of stopped and she still had her tongue in my mouth. I was wondering what I was going to do with it, but then she stopped too.

I drove us back to the Fairgrounds; we got out and started walking the Midway. Bev kept coming at me with these half questions. She'd start out with, "Bobby, do you think that…" then she wouldn't finish, or she'd say "Bobby, can I ask you a question?" and I'd say, "Yes," and then she wouldn't ask it. She'd look at the ground and talk so soft I could hardly hear over the screaming, the clang and whir of rides. She wouldn't go any further with it. We hadn't said anything in a while, and my mind got to wandering. "There goes Brenda," I said.

That's when she bounced my class ring off my forehead. Sometimes it takes a blow to my head for me to understand what I'm thinking.

So I'm standing here watching Bev's little butt squiggle away from me through the crowd, watching the searchlights. I'm standing in the middle of the Midway. Up above my head, I make out faint stars among the clouds. I'm looking at that ride I've been worrying about, the Hammer. That scuzzy sucker who runs the Hammer stays back out of sight in the daytime, but at night he comes out of hiding. He's looking over at me now. He's hairy, like an animal. He turns his back on me, walks around to the far side of the Hammer. He walks humped over, like he has a big weight on his shoulders, but when he's back by his trailer, he's always down on all fours crawling around.

Merry-go-round lights flash, music rings, and two big searchlights scan the heavens. Insects crawl around on them, moths, mosquitoes, gnats, just silhouettes on the glowing surface. Some look like flying sticks. I follow the light beams up into the dark where they roam around on some small thunderheads.

So I'm just standing here, thinking about the Hammer, when Brenda walks into my line of sight, between me and the Hammer. She has all that golden hair falling on tan shoulders. Helen's with her, trouble just following on the heels of trouble. But Helen turns away from Brenda, comes over to me like she wants to talk.

"Brenda told me you found Lenny's journal. Can I read it?" she asks.

And now here comes Trish and Curt. They stand off to the side, but I'm afraid they've overheard Helen.

"No," I say and the word just pops out of my mouth. I've been wondering what my answer was going to be when she asked.

"That's not fair. Why not?"

"Why did Lenny take back your wedding ring?"

She closes her eyes and looks at the ground. I feel as if I hit her with my fist. I get this flash like I'm Lenny and just opening the car door and see Helen with her clothes off, on top of old naked Charles. She has tears in her eyes. "But the ring. Did he say anything in his journal about my wedding ring? It's my grandmother's."

I'm looking past Helen at Brenda, and Brenda is shaking that blond head of hair, telling me no, that Helen has just lied to me.

"I can't let you see it. Most of it doesn't concern you."

Helen comes up close to me. She just got her wine colored hair cut so that it looks like a boy's. Short and combed back on the sides. She starts talking real quiet, fat lips already pouting. "I have more right to his journal than you. What was his, is mine now." She smells like peach cobbler.

"Since he took back the ring, I don't think he'd have wanted you to have it."

So Helen gets huffy, turns her back on me. "Come on, Brenda. I've got to do something about this."

"Bobby Ray," and now it's Trish I have to contend with, "who's that girl?"

"Helen Hammer," I stammer a little getting the words out, "Brenda's cousin."

"Helen *Hammer*?" Trish says, but she's looking at Curt.

"Used to be McCallum," I say.

Trish looks up at me with that baby-bird-at-feeding-time look, eyes blue as robin eggs.

"Lenny and Helen got married a couple of months before he was killed," I tell her. "No one else knew but Papa. And Papa didn't tell anyone, not even Mama, I don't think."

"You mean that's Lenny's wife? That girl's his wife?"

"His widow. Trish," and I start to turn away from her, then turn back, "you sure that you want to know about all this?"

"Lenny used to talk to me even though I was a lot younger. He never said anything about getting married. I've talked to Charles. But he's closed mouthed about everything. I don't know anything about that last day. Helen said something about a journal. If Lenny left something, I want to read it."

"He did. He wrote about a lot of things. I just found it in his wrecked car."

"I want it."

"Trish, there's more to this mess than you think. I agree you should see it. But I'm warning you. You won't like what you read."

We're standing close to those searchlights, and the bugs are beginning to bother me, brush a couple off of my clothes and pull one out of Trish's hair.

"You'll let me see it?"

"Yes," I tell her, "both of you. He must've wanted the truth to come out or he would have burned it. Follow me to my car. I'll read it to you. Right now."

We pass the stockyards and first it's all the 4H-ers feeding their homegrown meat, hear the hogs squeal then the sheep bleat, the calves bawl. Just outside the gate we wait to cross the road, car lights shining in our eyes on one side and red taillights on the other and start through the parked cars in the open field on the other side in the dark. This field is a pasture, so we have to watch our step. I wonder where they put the cows? It's a little dusty.

Inside my car, I turn on the dash lights but still have to take my flashlight out of the glove box. Wish this ragtop had a dome light. Trish won't let me read it, so I shine the light for her. She's a better reader anyway. She folds back the cover to the steno pad and reads every word, even his weight and batting average. Curt sets in the backseat. When she starts reading, he stops her. "Lenny was just a little guy," he says. "I thought he was a giant."

But that's all that's said until she gets to the last day, finding Charles and Helen out in the boonies and almost killing both of them. Her voice cracks when he tells about her and then Curt. She hands the pad to me, and I read while she cries. Then, suddenly it seems, we're through. Lenny's told his story again, sad that it is. We just listen to the crickets outside the car in the grass for a while, hear kids hollering from the top of the Ferris wheel in the distance.

"That's how Lenny died," I say. And then tears start coming, old soap-opera me crying again. I don't know why I have to hug everyone lately, but I reach out for her. She puts her arms around me a little. I look in the backseat. "What do you think, Curt?" I ask.

343

"I thought he was bigger 'n that" he says.

I drive them back over to Mama's and Papa's. As they get out of the car, the glow of dash lights reflecting off their faces, I say, "Look for me tomorrow again on the Midway. I have someone else you should meet."

★

I'm sitting in the dark on Ventura Avenue just outside Brenda's house. My Chevy keeps creaking as it cools. I was hitting ninety on Robertson coming back into Chowchilla. I got to thinking about Brenda telling me that Helen was lying about the ring, that it wasn't Helen's grandmother's ring. So here I sit watching the yellow light coming from Brenda's bedroom window through the big trees that surround her house, wondering if it's safe to go peck on her window. Guess the answer is no, and no amount of waiting will make it safe, so I get out of my car and walk on over through the tall lawn grass. Guess Mr. McCallum's busy building houses. Wonder why he doesn't have Keith cut the grass? I'm standing in the flowerbed at the side of Brenda's house, and when I hit the windowsill with my knuckle, I hear a dog bark inside. Damn. I didn't know she had a dog. Maybe this isn't even her window. I don't know why I thought it was hers in the first place. Maybe it's her parent's window. I don't know why they would have the light on in their bedroom so late, but then I hear some people like to do it with the lights on. Someone pulls back the curtain and I see Brenda. She screams a small little scream at me. I back off, walk away from the window, think maybe I better get the hell out of here. Then I hear the window creek open a crack.

"Bobby," I hear this loud whispering voice. "Come back, Bobby."

So I go back but that damn dog wants to see me too, and he acts like I'm his best buddy that he hasn't seen in next to a lifetime. I have all this slobbering dog spit from my hand all the way to my elbow. He's a black cocker spaniel with fluffy bear-like paws.

"Get down, Shadow," she tells him. "Bobby's my friend, not yours. How come you're not home, Bobby? It's really late."

Just about the time I start to say something, there's a knock at her bedroom door and then it opens a crack.

"Mother, get away from my door," Brenda says.

I back off out of the light.

"Mother, I have been of-age for four months now. Besides, it's just Bobby Hammer."

Then I hear some muffled words from her mother that I can't make out, something about getting some more clothes on.

"You going to peek in my dorm room when I go to college?"

Then her door closes again, and Brenda turns out her bedroom light.

"Bobby? Come back. It's just my meddling mother. Come close so I can see you."

I wonder if I still have Bev's lipstick on my face? Maybe on my collar? "I want to talk about Helen," I say.

"Closer so I don't have to shout. So ask me about Helen." But when I put my hands on her windowsill, she runs her hands up my arms all the way to my shoulders, her fingers up my short shirtsleeves.

"If her wedding ring didn't belong to her grandmother, who did it belong to?"

First Brenda kisses me and just about pulls me through the window. "It's the ring she and Lenny used when they got married. She told Lenny it was her grandmother's but that was a lie. I know where the ring came from because she showed it to me when she first got it. It's a big, beautiful ring. A huge diamond. But it wasn't her grandmother's and it wasn't Lenny's. She got it from Charles."

"Charles? But that doesn't make any sense."

"Sure it does." She's whispering in my ear now. Tickles a little, and all that hot breath sends chills down the side of my neck. She kisses me again before she continues. Trading slobber must be her favorite thing. She's worse than her dog. "Helen and Charles were planning to get married, but something happened. Helen won't say what. It must have been bad because she really loved Charles. She dumped him overnight."

"They fought about Charles' colored girlfriend."

"Charles? With a Negro girl?"

"Still sees her. Maggie lived in Fairmead then, now lives outside Fresno." I roam my hands around all that smoothness beneath her underclothes. "Lenny had the ring on his little finger when he died, but not when they buried him."

After that it's just soft skin, hard nipples, and my feet growing into the soil of that flowerbed.

CHAPTER 47: *Trish and Curt Have a Niece*

"Bobby! Bobby! Bobby!" She runs through the crowd toward me, screaming. Jumps in my arms. "Fers wheel, Bobby! Fers wheel!"

"Can I take Sammy for a ride?" I ask Gretta.

Gretta's wearing sandals and Bermuda shorts, has big toes.

"Be careful with her. She squirms about so much. I'd take her myself but I'm afraid of high places. That Ferris wheel..." She shakes her head. "I can't handle a Ferris wheel."

We stand in line, walk slowly up the wood ramp. Samantha holds my finger and Gretta stands beside us.

Samantha wants me to hold her, then wants down. "Can I have some cotton candy?"

"After the ride," I tell her.

"And a snow cone."

"If you think you need it."

"See my new hurt, Bobby? See it? See it? Still hurts."

"That does look bad." I see a little scab on her elbow. "How did you get it?"

"Dogs, Bobby. Knock me down. Mean dogs. Don't like dogs. Do you like dogs?"

"She has a puppy," says Gretta. "Our neighbor's old bitch had a litter of mongrels, and Sammy just had to have one."

I pick her up when we walk under the big wheel, set her beside me in the wide seat. The wheel starts to turn, we rise above the single story buildings here at the fairgrounds and the entire countryside is spread out before us. I look back toward town, see the 99, even a train on the track that parallels it.

"I'm not afraid. Are you afraid, Bobby?"

"No. Not if you'll be still and quit flopping around."

When we finally get off, Samantha starts in again.

Chapter 47: *Trish and Curt Have a Niece*

"Fish! Bobby. Fish!"

So now we're standing before this booth and out in the middle is a square table with sides like a big box and with a big white cloth over it. On top of the box are all these round bowls with colored water inside, a goldfish in each one. Some are blue, some red, yellow, green.

"I want a red one, Uncle Bobby," says Samantha. "Get me a red one."

I think even I can do this one.

"Can you throw too?" Samantha asks.

I give the girl in the apron a dollar and she gives me four Ping-Pong balls then I pick up Samantha and give one of them to her.

"Throw it," I say

"How?" she asks. "You do it."

"Watch that kid over there," I tell her, pointing at Grant Pierson's ten year old that has already thrown away two dollars in balls. Grant's another of the barbers here in town.

She throws one but it doesn't even make the box. She tries again

"You do it, Uncle Bobby. You do it."

I set her down and lean into the box a little.

"Throw it, Uncle Bobby. Throw it hard."

I get the last two to bounce off the rims. So I pull out another dollar.

"Sammy, are you sure you want a fish?" asks Gretta. "They're a lot of trouble. You have to feed it and change the water all the time."

I have four more white balls, and I get a splash on the first one. But it's a blue one and when the girl tries to hand it to Samantha, she won't take it. Starts screaming.

"No! No! No! A red one. A red one."

The girl takes it back, gives me one with red water. I give it to Samantha.

"Eeeeeek! A fish! It's a fish, Uncle Bobby. Gi'me it. Gi'me it. Get your hands off. Get 'em off." She can't get a hold on the bowl because her hands are trembling so much. First she shakes both her hands like the bowl's hot, then she grabs it, holds it against her chest with both arms wrapped all the way around it. Then she is quiet. Real quiet. "I love him, Mommy. Do you love him? He's just the best fish in the whole world. He won't cause any trouble. And we won't eat him either."

"Hey Richard," I say, that's Grant's boy. "Catch." I throw the rest of the balls to him one at a time.

"At least uncles are good for something," says Samantha.

"When we were on the Ferris Wheel, I told her that I'm her uncle. Is that okay?"

"Sure Bobby. You are her uncle."

Trish and Curt have come up from behind me. Trish has overheard me and looks as if her brain is calculating by some long algebra equation. "On which side of the family, Bobby? Jess Korenski's or Aunt Loretta's?"

"The Hammer's."

"How come that don't make her my niece too," asks Curt.

"It does," I say but I'm looking at Trish.

"She's your niece?" Trish says. Trish's eyes look big enough to pop out of her head. "And she's not my baby and she's not Curt's. Is she Curt?"

"Shut up, Trish," he says.

"She belongs to me," says Gretta.

"Bobby," says Trish. "Who is this little girl? You better tell me what this means." And I think she is going to cry. Because she knows what it means. She turns her back, walks off a ways.

I walk after Trish, put my hand on her shoulder. "I don't know how to tell you this without it being a shock. Remember? In his journal Lenny said Gretta was pregnant. She's Lenny's daughter," I say her to her back.

She shakes her head, yes. She sniffs her nose a little and turns to face Gretta. Then she looks down at Samantha and back up at Gretta. "His journal seemed like a dream. I can't make the things that happened then connect with today." She looks at Gretta. "She's Lenny's daughter?"

Gretta nods and smiles.

"What's her name?"

"Samantha," says Gretta.

"She's so pretty," says Trish and she covers her face because she is crying again. Shoulders just shaking.

Then she looks up at Gretta. "You're Charles' sister, Gretta," she says.

"Mama and Papa already know about Samantha," I tell her. "They won't talk about her and if you mention her to them, they'll be mad. They don't believe Samantha is Lenny's daughter."

"Mommy, who are these people?" asks Samantha.

"Well Sammy, that's your Aunt Patricia and this is your Uncle Curt."

Curt looks at me like somebody just called him a bad name. "I'm not old enough to be an uncle," he says.

"She's just gorgeous," says Trish.

Chapter 47: *Trish and Curt Have a Niece*

"What can you do with her," asks Curt like she's a new toy somebody bought that he hasn't figured out yet.

"Well," says Gretta, "she's versatile. Likes to play a lot."

"I like to ride rides a lot too, Uncle Curt," says Samantha with her head down like she's real mad about it. She's catching on to this uncle business.

So while the three of them are on the tilt-a-whirl, Gretta and I stand in front of the Hammer and talk.

"Charles says Mama had something to do with your mother's death."

"Charles never recovered from it."

"How did she die?"

"Automobile accident on Highway 152. A very foggy night. She hit a tractor trailer."

"So why does Charles blame Mama?"

"He knows something but Daddy won't let him talk, says that she's dead. No use resurrecting her."

"Does Sammy know what Lenny looked like?" I ask.

"Has his senior picture on her wall and says a prayer for him every night before she goes to sleep. I got his picture directly from the photographer. You're mother wouldn't give me one."

"Mama can be hard. I know that."

"She makes the world to suit herself."

"She wouldn't tell me about my past until she had to."

"Family secrets?"

"Yes. Things like my Aunt Loretta being my real mother."

"Oh, god, Bobby."

"I keep opening the door wider and Mama keeps slamming it shut."

"You know more than the rest of us. Charles tells me you have Lenny's journal."

"Word gets around. I suppose you've heard by now, but if you haven't, it's time you were told. Helen and Lenny were married."

"Charles told me last night. Helen wouldn't tell it because they didn't get married in the church, and her parents don't recognize the marriage. My mother's death is another mystery."

"Wasn't it an accident?"

"Yes, but my mother and father had problems then."

"Charles told me something about my papa and your mother. Any truth to it?"

349

Gretta flinched a little when I said that. "I hope you're not repeating this gossip around town," she says. "I'm surprised Charles would talk to you about Mother. He must like you a lot."

I don't say anything for a minute. "He accused Mama of killing your mother. Charles was mad. It wasn't as if he confided in me. Charles is crazy. He's done some things to me that I can't even talk about."

"He's eccentric."

"He's a pervert."

She won't look at me now. "Can you tell me why Lenny acted so strange toward me the day before he died?"

Can't say anything about the abomination, so I don't say anything for a while. "No, I don't." And no way am I telling her was thinking of killing her. "Lenny still has some secrets he's keeping."

Trish and Curt are back with Samantha. She still has the goldfish, but the bowl is only half full, a little trash in it. She has this sour look. "Dumb old fish," she mutters.

We're still standing by the ride I don't like too much, the Hammer.

"Hey, Bobby." It's Thomas and Melvin. "Ride the Hammer with us. Room for three."

"Not today. I've had enough ups and downs."

"A Hammer should be able to ride the Hammer."

"By the way, Thomas, Papa's bringing in that harrow you sold us last year. The teeth are falling out."

"You guys been running it thirty miles an hour on blacktop again?"

"It's just falling apart with the air sitting on it. Can't take much of a load."

"We're busy. He better not expect it soon. Who's that little girl?"

"My niece."

"She's a cute little squirt."

As they get on, I watch this young guy who runs the Hammer, letting the kids on and off, engaging the motor. But the old man who owns the Hammer is standing back out of sight. I remember seeing him here last year, the year before. He has a different kid working for him, but he comes back every year. And the reason I remember him is that he looks so bad, as if his body's rotting. Some people who don't take regular baths look dirty, like maybe their skin is made out of grease, but he doesn't look like that. He looks like he's died and his body is rotting. Like the blood that runs in his veins is seeping out in places. I get the shivers just looking at him.

I turn back to Gretta. "Charles has been really upset about not being able to find a ring he gave Helen a few years ago. But Helen says it belonged to her grandmother. Brenda tells me that's just not true."

"Oh, no it wasn't hers." And Gretta seems really primed on this one. "The ring Charles gave Helen was an engagement ring we found hidden in my mother's personal things two years after she died. An engagement ring, not a wedding ring that our father gave her. We don't know where she got it. Mother was buried in her wedding ring. Charles wanted the engagement ring, but my older sister and me wouldn't let him have it. So he stole it from us and gave it to Helen when they were planning to get married. We've been mad at him for five years about that ring. We won't let him rest until he finds it. It represents another mystery, probably something about her life before she married Daddy."

I have an inspiration, just figured out something Charles has known all along. I know who has the ring. But I know something Charles doesn't: who can tell me why he took it off Lenny.

I take one more look at that sucker who owns the Hammer. Has his head down but he's looking out through the tops of his eyes. Looking at me. It's as if he knows I'm afraid of the Hammer. As if he's been coming to Chowchilla every year, just for me.

I walk away from Gretta, but Wayne steps in front of me, blocking my way. Stands there with his legs spread and his hands on his hips.

"Showdown, Hammer," he says. I see Eugene and Curt standing off to the right.

Showboat Wayne. I've had it with him. If he wants it that bad, I'll just have to give it to him. It'll be his problem after that. "Okay, Hopalong Cassidy. Let's go do it. Or is it Lash Larue? If it is, I don't see your whip."

*

Wayne and Eugene are walking twenty feet in front and I'm just following along behind. We pass the stockyards and first I hear the hogs squeal, then the sheep bleat, then the calves bawl.

Curt has followed me. "Think you can take him?" he asks as we pass through the South Gate. Lots of people coming in.

"You tell me. What do you think?"

"I don't know. I've always wanted to see you fight though." His voice is really shaking.

351

"You want to see me hurt him? Break his nose. How much blood do you want?"

"I just want to see you fight."

"Well, that's what I would like to do. I'd like to break his nose so that it peels back on both sides of his face, just squirting blood with a little raw flesh showing, and knock all his front teeth out, maybe even chip some back teeth. I'd like to see him standing with his head hung over, spitting blood and teeth and pieces of teeth out on the ground. Crying a little cause he knows his mouth and nose will never be the same. And then I'd go up and hit him in the side of the head with him all bent over and helpless. Knock him cold as a wagon tongue on a frosty winter morning."

We cross the road and start through the parked cars in the open field on the other side. This field's a pasture. I wonder where they put the cows? I wish it wasn't so dusty. A little too lumpy to walk easy on.

"Maybe you'd like to see him hurt me. Break my nose. Knock out a couple of teeth."

"Come on, Bobby Ray. Quit talking like this."

"All that could happen. Anything can happen, Curt. No matter what's been planned, nobody knows the future. Not even the next ten minutes. You don't even know yourself, how you feel about things. Watch how you feel about me during this fight. You might learn something about yourself."

Eugene looks like his best dog just died. He hasn't acted quite right toward me since Trish dumped him.

"You want to tell me what this is about first?" I ask Wayne.

"It's about Leroy. You were the cause of him dying. I'm going to make you pay for it."

"Well, there's no reason to fight then, cause what you're saying is a lie. He was my cousin. I didn't want to kill my own cousin."

"That's a lie, Hammer. You're not talking your way out of this one." He's pulling off his shirt and showing all that pale freckly skin, but he does look like he has muscled up a little lately. "Besides that, I just hate your guts," he says.

I think I will take him just like I am. This pulling shirts off and putting them back on is just a lot of trouble.

"I used to feel that way about you too, but since I found out your father saved my mother's life many years ago, I've changed my mind. Besides that, if my cousin Leroy liked you so much, you couldn't be all bad."

"It's no use, Hammer. Your ass is grass."

"Okay, Wayne. Have it your way. Come on. Let's see your stuff."

I walk over to him, shove him on both shoulders to get him going good. I'm afraid he may need a jump start at this point. He's looking kind of scared, like maybe he froze up on me now that the fight is about to start. I didn't realize that I'm so much bigger than him.

He takes a swing at me and hits me on the shoulder, so I back off.

"Come on, Bobby," somebody says, "break him open a little. Let's see what color he is on the inside."

He comes at me running this time and when he swings at my head I lower my shoulder, put it into his chest and hear the air go out of him just before his butt hits the ground.

"Goddamn it! Fight with your fists," he says after he gets his breath back.

"Okay," I say. "I'm real sorry, Wayne. Guess I forgot how to fight." I look over at Curt give him a wink. We're starting to draw a crowd.

Wayne comes at me again, takes a swing with his left. Then his right. I step back, let 'em go by. Now he's getting real red in the face. Freckles hardly even show.

"Damn you, Bobby. Come on. Fight." He doesn't seem nearly as mad as he was. But here he comes again. This time he gets down low and I think I can push him back with my hands, but I don't quite make it. He hits me in the mouth. Hurts real bad. So I step back. Check the corner of my mouth with my finger but don't have time to look at it because I have to run backward and circle a little to get away from him. I stick my finger in the corner of my mouth again and damn. There is a little blood.

"You're a coward, Hammer. You know that. Nothing but a goddamn coward. You going to fight or run?"

"You were the one that wanted to fight. Seemed real important to you. I hate to see you so disappointed." I hear a laugh from someone in the crowd. It's Tom Broden, that big colored guy who was at my fight with Chelsey.

"You're going to fight," says Wayne, "if I have to force you." And he makes another run at me. I don't have much room for maneuvering this time because he gets me up against a car. So I duck a blow and grab his arm. He throws the other one at me and I duck it too, but I still have his arm. And then, "Oh shit," he kicks me right in the shin and steps on my

353

foot. And I would have rather taken a blow to the head any day. So I'm hobbling around on one leg and when he makes his next run at me, I'm slow to move so he has me on the ground now. I think he's going to pull my face off. We roll a little in three inches of powdery dirt and when I finally get on top of him, I jump off.

"I'm whipped, Wayne." I tell him. "Can't take anymore." I hear another snicker from the crowd. "You're just one tough sonofabitch." He did manage to pull my grin off though. "I think you're ready to climb up a step, Tom Mix or maybe Gene Autry. Zorro may even have you on his list."

"What do you mean?" and he's screaming at me. "You can't quit now. We haven't even started. I've been waiting for this for two years. You can't be that big of a chickenshit."

"Some of us can take it and some can't. I guess I can't take it anymore." I look over at Curt. He's grinning and shaking his head. What a brother he has. It's going to be hard to live me down. "Look at how dirty you got my shirt," I say pulling it away from my chest. "And look at this." I stick my finger in my mouth again, hold it up to show him. "You done bloodied my mouth."

Wayne looks over at Eugene. "He's chickenshit," he says. "There's nothing I can do about it."

I start dusting myself off. Curt comes over to help me. As the crowd breaks up, this little kid walks by. "Gosh," he says. "I thought Bobby Hammer was suppose to be tough. I didn't know that he's such a wimp."

Now that hurts. That hurts a lot.

"I whipped your ass, Hammer," says Wayne. "You hear me? And that's what I'm going to be saying."

"I'll back it up," I tell him. "I'm just glad you let me off so easy." I can tell that some of my sassiness has gone out of my voice now.

"Good grief, Bobby," says Curt. "You look worse than Papa after a day on the tractor."

"What do you think? Isn't your big brother fighting a sight to see?"

Curt just keeps dusting on me. He is smiling a little, but I can tell it's not easy for him.

"Sometimes the toughest fights are not with your enemies," I tell him.

"Everybody in town will sure hear about this," he says.

"That's what I'm hoping," I say. "Come on, let's go get me cleaned up, if that's possible."

CHAPTER 48: *Loretta and the History of the Ring*

"Damn turkeys. Turkeys are a plague on the earth," is what Loretta has just said. She's on her knees crying and looking over four dead turkeys on the ground in front of her. "Turkeys are the dumbest creatures on the face of the earth," she says. "Just look how they turn on each other at the first sight of blood. They draw a little blood and then pick the bleeding turkey to death. Even clipping their beaks isn't enough to stop them."

But losing four turkeys is not a big deal. Loretta overreacts to everything. So I grab each turkey by a leg and carry them two in each hand out to the pit I dug for her a couple of months ago. Before I came to live with her, she just threw them off in the weeds and let them pile up and stink until a dog or maybe a stray coyote would drag them off to eat. Her old dog Twinkles use to like chewing on them before he died, but that new German shepherd won't have anything to do with them.

When I get back inside the shed, she's already broken into a sack of feed and pouring it into the bins. She has to dip a pail into the grain to get it to the bins because she's not strong enough with that bad hand of hers to carry a feed sack. I just pick up the sack by the front-and-back corners and string the feed along. I don't know how she's managed to get all these turkeys fed by herself through the years. She needs Jess. I wonder why he didn't show up this morning?

"Loretta," I say, and then I have to cough a couple of times because the dust these turkeys are stirring up makes it hard to breathe, "a ring is missing, one that Helen and Lenny got married with." She's just real quiet like maybe she's not going to answer my question. So I just keep on talking. "Lenny was wearing it just before he had the accident. But he didn't have it on when he was buried. Helen and Charles are upset about the ring being lost. It belonged to their mother. I wonder if you know something that would help me find it."

Loretta is not talking. She acts like I didn't even say anything, so we just go on feeding turkeys. I even think she's a little mad for me asking. I ask her a couple of times about when she plans to sell the turkeys, if she knows what the price is now, how much they're paying a pound. But she is not talking. We finish the feeding and we walk back to the house with her in front like she's mad, doesn't walk beside me like she usually does with her arm on my shoulder. When we get inside, she puts two plates and silverware out on the table. I'm not hungry with all the barbecue I ate at lunch, but then she puts some apricot cobbler in the oven to heat, makes a pot of hot coffee. I can't pass up a cobbler. We picked the apricots off of the tree by the side of the house last July and she canned them. I remember using a ladder but she was like a cat climbing inside the tree. Scared me the way she went to the top and was always hanging out on a thin limb that didn't look big enough to hold her weight.

"Is something wrong?" I ask. "Have I said something to make you mad at me?"

She puts on a little smile, one of the first smiles I've seen since Bev was over here with me that day of her birthday party when it thundered and lightninged so bad. "No, Ray. You didn't make me mad."

I'm getting used to the scars that run up the insides of her arms so I don't notice them much anymore, but I see them now. After we finish the cobbler and have a couple of cups of coffee, she lights a cigarette. I get Lenny's journal and ask her to read a couple of pages. She just turns real red and stares at me. I finally realize that Loretta can't read. That's why she colors in kids coloring books to pass the time at night. And now I have never seen her look so down hearted. I don't mean worried like when she's lost a bunch of turkeys or when the price of turkey meat has dropped a few cents. She's suffering a terrible pain.

"When Lenny came to me that day, the same day he died, he was desperate. Like I told you before, he was looking to kill someone. I noticed the ring on his hand then. I noticed the ring because I recognized it. I hadn't seen it in eighteen years, but no doubt that was it. That ring was the first diamond I'd ever laid eyes on. I was just a kid when I first saw it, no more than ten years old, and I had no idea such a thing as a diamond even existed. We didn't get out much in Oklahoma. We lived ten miles from a town of two hundred and didn't even get there but once a month if we were lucky. So when Hershel brought that ring home, I felt like he'd bought a miracle. He even let me put it on my finger. 'For just a minute,' he said, 'but only a minute because then it goes on my girl's finger forever.' Hershel was getting engaged to the one girl he'd loved all his life. She was the little Jorgensen girl that lived two miles from us. They went to school together and Hershel had been in love with her since the first grade. When Hershel turned eighteen he drove into Oklahoma City some fifty miles away and bought the biggest diamond ring he could find. You should've seen the roll of money that young man had in his pocket. Hershel had been farming his own land for three years. He didn't go to high school much during those years either. He had too much work to do. He thought he was grown ever since he turned thirteen and talked our Papa into giving him a piece of his own land and the little old tractor. He saved his money and he bought that ring for Heidi Jorgensen. Her family had come over from one of whose European countries, Switzerland, Holland, Austria. Some place like that. So the two of them got engaged, but they never got married. I don't know what happened but they had a falling out. That temper of Hershel's probably had something to do with it. So Heidi dumped Hershel just before they got married, but Hershel wouldn't take back the ring. Guess he figured if she kept the ring she'd change her mind sooner or later. But that's not the way it turned out. The next thing Hershel heard was that Heidi was gone. She'd married someone else, an older family friend is what we heard, and they'd already left Oklahoma for good and moved to California. The man she married was Karl Kunze, and the town they moved to was Chowchilla, California."

"You mean that wasn't Mama that Papa got engaged to?" And I get out of my chair and go to the stove to get another piece of that apricot cobbler and another cup of coffee. I have to have something to help wash down this story.

"Nope. It was the woman that Karl Kunze married. It was Charles' and Gretta's mother before she married Karl. And don't you go telling Louise this either. No sense in her knowing what Hershel did before they got married. Hershel liked to died over Heidi. He moped and lay around like an old dog on his last legs, and Hershel wasn't like that, always up and going. So your grandpa kicked him out of the house. They hooked the tractor to the outhouse that set out back and drug it over onto the little piece of land he'd given to Hershel, put a floor in it and told him that outhouse was his home from then on and that he couldn't come back on our property until he'd married and had a kid."

I have to laugh at that and she laughs with me. "You mean my papa, who's really my uncle, got his start living in an outhouse?"

"Well, it was big for an outhouse anyway. Even had enough room for an easy chair and the cot that Hershel stole from home during the night after we were all asleep. Your grandpappy was always going overboard. It's a shame you never got to know your grandmother and grandfather, Ray. You'd have loved them. When your grandfather built that outhouse, he said he wanted the best goddamn outhouse in the state of Oklahoma, so he built a five-holer. Why five holes, God only knows cause there was only four of us and us two kids were so big that we never used it but one at a time. I used to sit in it and laugh imagining all four of us, Mama and Papa, me and Hershel all four sitting in that outhouse at the same time, all lined up like birds on a perch, sitting and grunting and the fifth hole sitting empty. Then I thought that maybe Papa put in the fifth hole because he was expecting company. I just split my sides.

"Hershel was mad at the whole family. He lived in that outhouse and didn't set foot on our place for six months, but we'd see him out in field plowing, dust just boiling up around him like it was his anger. Then one day we saw fresh lumber sticking up above ground level, and there was more than one person living there. That's when Mama got the preacher to go see about Hershel and whoever it was living with him. But the preacher already knew because he'd married them. Brother Hensen told Mama..."

"Loretta," and I hate to interrupt this story but I just have to know, "is that the same Brother Hensen who preaches down here in Chowchilla?"

"One and the same. I wish he'd stayed in Oklahoma, but I don't get all my wishes. He came here a little after the rest of us. His life hasn't been easy either. His wife died in childbirth no more than two months after they got to Chowchilla. The baby died too. He never remarried."

"Okay, tell me some more about Papa. I just wanted to know a little about Brother Hensen."

"So Brother Hensen told them about the girl that Hershel had married. You know Louise doesn't have a family. No mama, no papa. She was a little orphan girl that the Hensen's brought home from an orphanage in Norman. Your mama that raised you was a orphan. She was a beautiful little girl, and I can understand why Hershel took to her right away. They had a baby nine months to the day after they got married. Hershel had trouble getting that house he was building finished in time for the baby. When Lenny was born, Hershel brought the baby and his new wife to see Mama and Papa. Your grandpapa was the happiest man I've ever seen. He kept slapping Hershel on the back. "A wife, a baby and a five-holer," is what Papa said. Hershel had converted the outhouse back into an outhouse after he finished his home. So everything went pretty good until the next spring, when the wind began to blow. And let me tell you something about the wind in Oklahoma. It never stops blowing. Twenty miles an hour, day and night. But then it was more like thirty to forty. And the rains never came that year. And the next year, they never came either. That next spring was when the twister came and killed your grandmother and grandfather, took them out of our lives forever. I was over at Hershel's helping Louise with baby Lenny when the twister came or I'd be dead too. Hershel was beside himself, lost all interest in life. He'd been working with Brother Hensen on a new church. Hershel had even taken to teaching Sunday school. Brother Hensen told him he thought Hershel had a natural calling for the pulpit. Brother Hensen was thinking of sharing that new church with Hershel. But the twister and drought changed all that, changed Hershel. Hershel got restless. That's when he bought that black pistol of his. Louise was real worried. 'You've always talked about moving to California ever since we've been married,' she said. 'Well, now we don't have anything to keep us here.' So when the other farmers got restless too, Hershel was ready to leave. They were talking about moving out west. All the talk was about oranges and California. No one knew where to go in California, but Hershel did. Evidently he'd been brooding about Heidi every since she left. Hershel never told anyone why he wanted to go to Chowchilla. Even I didn't know Heidi was in Chowchilla or I would've changed his mind. Hershel brought us all straight here. Karl had never met Hershel. And Hershel and Heidi never let on that they knew each other. When the four of them started getting together to play pinochle, I scolded Hershel, even though I was still a little girl. But Hershel wouldn't listen. The rest I've told you. Heidi and Hershel had a secret romance. When Louise found out, I thought it was the end of Hershel's and Louise's marriage but Louise wasn't a quitter. She fought hard for Hershel, and in the end, she had her way."

I look up at Loretta from my empty plate. I can only eat so much apricot cobbler. I used to think that I had a family background that sort of held my life in place. I never thought about it that way, never really realized it, I don't guess, but I know now that that was the way I felt. Everything I've found out about my family is letting my life slip away. I already feel like I don't have a home. Living here with Loretta just seems like a place to hang my hat. Mama's and Papa's place doesn't seem like home since Papa ran me off. I can't depend on anything anymore. Everything I learn about my family takes something else from me. I feel like I'm being forced to give up the only life I have known.

"So the ring," I say, "that Lenny had on his little finger when he died, was actually the ring Papa gave to Heidi Jorgensen who became Heidi Kunze when she married Karl."

"The very same, Ray. The ring Louise wears, the one that Hershel married her with, is the wedding ring matched with that engagement ring. Hershel bought the two at the same time. Came in the same box. He never gave Heidi the wedding ring because he was going to do that at their wedding ceremony. So he gave the wedding ring to Louise when Brother Hensen married them, and Heidi kept the engagement ring. Hershel's heart has been split between those two women ever since."

"So Heidi kept that ring, hid it from Karl and the rest of her family, until she died in an automobile accident. And then Gretta and her sister found the ring somewhere in her personal things. When Charles wanted to give Helen a ring, he gave her his mother's ring. And when Helen broke up with Charles, she kept the ring and told Lenny that it belong to her grandmother. She used it when she married Lenny."

"Every woman that has ever seen that ring, falls in love with it."

"It's easy to put together the rest of the puzzle. When Lenny had his accident and Mama and Papa were called to the scene, Papa must've seen the ring on Lenny's finger, and took it off to keep Mama from seeing it and asking questions because it matched her wedding ring. Papa knew Lenny had married Helen and didn't want anyone to know. He thought Helen was trash. And Papa probably also took the ring because it belonged to him. He'd probably wanted the ring back ever since Heidi died. Papa had lots of reasons for taking it. Papa must have the ring. Charles is not going to like this if he finds out. And Charles is not going to leave this alone. That's for sure. He knows Papa and Heidi had a fling. But he doesn't need to know the rest. And then there's this thing about Samantha. If Mama and Papa don't accept her as their granddaughter, the trouble will continue.

Lenny made some mistakes, and the only way to set things straight is to have them recognize Samantha. It can be cleared up if they'll just accept the truth."

"That may be," says Loretta, "but Hershel and Louise are set in their ways. You can talk to them if you want, but don't expect much."

"They might if we both talked to them. And I have the journal. They'll have to believe Lenny's own words. Will you go with me?"

She looks at me for a long time like I just asked her to help me commit a murder. "If you want me to, Ray. But let's don't do it now. Wait a few days, until the Fair's over. I'll talk to Louise with you, if you still think we should. Can't start with Hershel. He might explode on us. We'll feel her out. But not a word about the ring to either of them. No sense in stirring that pot."

CHAPTER 49: *Riding the Hammer*

It's Sunday evening and even though I'm tired from being out in the field all day helping Papa, I'm back at the fairgrounds. This is the last day of the Fair. This time I have come alone. Papa really has a problem with his crops. The nut grass has taken over one field. He couldn't cultivate it soon enough to get the dirt on the grass before it got almost as tall as the cotton. And one field has just started dying on him. We walked out a ways in the field together. He showed me. The roots are rotting off of the stalks. The plants just slip out of the ground like they don't have a hold of the earth.

The wind kicks up a little dust, trash blowing around. Hardly anyone here at the Fair anyway and some of the lights have been shutoff. Even turned off the searchlights. That's what I miss most, the searchlights. The tilt-a-whirl is still going. The guy who runs the Ferris wheel is using a wooden mallet to knock out the bars that hold the seats. All the fish bowls are gone and the stand empty. A man with a wife and baby, people I've never seen before, is throwing at the metal milk bottles.

I hear someone behind call my name, so I turn around and see Uncle Jess, my father, coming toward me. He's walking funny and I smell him from ten yards away. Why does he eat so much garlic? His shirttail is out and shirt unbuttoned up the front so his tattoos show. When he gets close he tries to talk but no words come out. He still has his arms going though, and it's as if he's letting his arms do the talking.

"Money, Bobby," is what he mumbles at me. "Just a little money. Maybe seventy-five cents for a bottle of wine." I don't see how he could be sweating so much with it so cold. I swear, he looks like he's shrunk six inches since I saw him last. I have to look down at him. "I have the shakes. A little wine 'll simmer me down."

So I stick my hand in my pocket, but I don't have any change. I reach for my wallet, pull out a five.

"No. Not that much," he says. "Don't trust myself with that much money till I get on the wagon again."

So I pull out a single.

"Ah, that's a good boy, Bobby. I hate for you to see me like this, but I'm in a pitiful state. You take care of yourself now, you hear?" And then he walks off, but he's limping.

I can't stand this, so I go after him. Grab him by the arm. "Jess? What's wrong with your leg? Are you hurt?"

"Na. It's an old injury. Bothers me at times like this."

"Do you need a ride? Can I take you home?"

"I'm okay, I tell you." And I think maybe he's a little peeved at me. "Now don't let me embarrass myself any more than I already have. Goodnight, Bobby. I'll see you in a couple of days."

I just stand here for a minute watching him walk away and letting what just happened sink in. Jess has always seemed sensible and upstanding. I'm not sure that was even him. Seemed so old.

I walk past this horse race booth where the little horses are made of wood and move in straight lines along the back wall. It's one of the few places still open. I pull my jacket around me a little tighter, zip it halfway.

The Hammer's at the back of the fairgrounds, where the rides end and the darkness starts. But the Hammer's lights are off too, so I guess I'm out of luck. I might as well go on home because the Hammer is the reason I came. I see a big dog, or at first I think I see a dog, round back eating something dead on the ground. See a tail wag. Then I see it's that scraggly sucker who operates the Hammer, picking through his tools. I figure, what've I got to lose, so I go on around back, stand off to the side waiting to get his attention. I don't. So I kick a little dirt, start to walk off.

"You wanting me?" he calls out.

"I need a ride," I tell him, looking back. I'm figuring it's going to cost me some money so I'm ready to go five, maybe ten bucks.

"Fresno? Bakersfield? Yuma's where we're headed. It ought to be hot enough for ya down there." He never has turned to look at me.

"No, I mean the Hammer here." And I walk a little closer.

"Well, you see," and he stands up wiping his hands on an old oily rag, walks toward me as he talks so that his words come in real clear, "I'm all shut down." The wind blows what's left of his hair all over to one side and shows his baldhead. I see some top teeth but all his bottom ones are gone. His bottom lip turns in a little.

"I was hoping you'd turn it over a few times for me."

"Were you, now? Glory be. That's optimism for you. I like that. Haven't had a whole lot to do with optimistic people lately." He looks like he sweats motor oil.

"Well, I didn't figure you'd be too excited about it, but thought I'd ask anyway. Thought maybe I could pay you a little something for your trouble."

He's looking me over real good like he's never seen a kid up close. Squints like the wind's blowing dust in his eyes.

"What's your name?" And I notice a cut above each of his eyebrows with fresh blood beading up, looks like they've been sewed together with coarse black thread out of a sewing machine.

"Bobby."

"Sure are a good looking kid. I could give you a nice ride over there in my trailer. Make you feel a whole lot better than the Hammer."

I'm confused, get an image of a rocking horse on springs like I used to ride when I was a kid.

"I can turn a real trick for you," he adds.

I think maybe he's also a magician. Then it hits me, what he is talking about, so I just get weak all over, stumble back a couple of steps.

"Now don't start running from me. I'm not going to hurt you. Not one to push people around. But you know, you sure look like my brother Paul's boy. How old are you?"

I don't even need the ride if I have to go through this. "Seventeen," I say, but I still keep my distance. I put my hands in my pockets because I'm starting to shiver.

"Same age my boy is, if he's still alive. Come on, what's your last name."

I look down at the ground, toe a clod, look up. "Hammer," I say.

"Say what?" And he jerks his head back a little.

"Bobby Hammer."

"You're shitting me." First he smiles, then he looks mad. "You're pulling my leg just so I'll give you a ride. That's right isn't it? You think I'm too dumb to know the difference. I got another hammer over here I'll give you some of, a claw hammer." And he digs through his toolbox again. It's hard even seeing him the way he melts into the dark.

"I can't help what my name is, mister." And since he's mad, I turn around and walk off. I didn't really want a ride anyway. Still a little afraid.

Chapter 49: *Riding the Hammer*

"Bobby Hammer wants to ride the Hammer," he says. "Everybody thinks they can con a carney." I leave him muttering to himself.

When I walk past the horse-race booth, I hear the trumpet and then the bell. "And they're off..," a loudspeaker says, and this woman starts calling the race.

But the Hammer operator hollers after me. "Hey, kid. Let me see your drivers license." Sounds more like a growl than a holler, his hoarse voice. Maybe a deep throated bark. The wind catches a piece of tarp around one of the booths, starts to shake it like it'll rip it off. Makes a popping noise.

I stop, but I really don't want to go back. Then I look up at the Hammer, the big stout arm with the pivot at the low end and the two sided basket at the top like a giant fist, notice how high up in the air it is, a cloud of billowing dust blowing past it. I remember last year when I was afraid just watching it rise and fall. That's what I'm after though, that falling feeling. And right now, I understand why Brenda was afraid to face me that day in front of my book locker. I get to thinking that there's a right time to do some things, and that we don't really ever get a second chance at the important stuff. It's like harvesting time. If I don't do it now, maybe do it later, tomorrow, next year, it'll be all spoiled. Right now, it looks like a bumper crop. This may even be a sign for the future. So I go back. Pull out my wallet, and I really don't want him to touch my driver's license, but I hand it to him anyway.

"Bobby Ray Hammer. And you're name's really Bobby too, not Robert."

I've never cared much for that. I have always blamed it on Mama, but now I don't know who to blame.

"My son'll be your age. Providing he's still alive. They took him from me when he was born, the sickly little thing. But I wouldn't have been any good with him. His mother died in childbirth. That was back in my younger days. My blacksmith days. I worked for a time with the Master Blacksmith."

I'm putting my license back in my wallet, listening to him jabber, and I can hardly see him because his skin is so dark, but damn if he doesn't reach out with two long greasy fingers, like he's going to pinch me on the hand, and just as I jerk back, he catches the tip of my only twenty dollar bill, plucks it from my wallet. I feel a chill sink through to my bones. It's as if I just recognized this guy. He's the only one who could give me a ride like this.

"That's not going to be too much, is it?" he cackles, crooking his head to the side and wrinkling his forehead. He switches on the lights, and I hear the creaking and clanging as the Hammer comes to life. "That won't be too much for the ride, will it?" he asks again, then winks at me, like we share a secret. Puts his hand on my shoulder like we are brothers. "Not for the ride you're getting."

CHAPTER 50: *Putting the Pressure on Mama*

Today is the day Lenny was buried on. My mother, Aunt Loretta, and me are over at my used-to-be home talking to my used-to-be mama. Mama has just pulled a pan of hot bread out of the oven.

"Can I have some?" I ask.

"Wait till it cools," she says. She used to always cut a piece for me. She knows how I like to eat it before it has a chance to cool.

Loretta has on that old duckbilled cap she wears half the time. I've been trying to talk her out of wearing it, but she won't give it up. At least I got her in a pair of woman's pants today instead of men's Levis. We didn't have to find an excuse to come here. Mama called Loretta and told us to come over but now she won't talk, acts like she's mad about something, and I'm afraid I know what it is. I was afraid Papa would be here, but I guess he's out in the field. I want to talk about Samantha, but I just don't know how to get started. Then I think about what day it is so I try that.

"Do you know what today is, Mama?"

Right away she looks like she has the biggest worry the world has ever seen. "Don't do this, Bobby Ray. Some things are just not supposed to be talked about." She won't look at me, except out the corner of her eye, and she's grabbed a bag of pinto beans, opened one corner and pours them a handful at a time on the counter.

"But me and Loretta are thinking about going to the Cemetery. Thought you might want to come with us."

She hangs her head with her eyes shut for a second, and I can tell now that I have hurt her real bad. "I can't face it. You two go on by yourselves, if you have to go." And she's already sniffling a little as she sorts through a handful of pinto beans. "Loretta, you know better. Why didn't you tell Bobby Ray?"

"I thought it might be good for all of us," Loretta says. She's sniffing and wiggling her nose back and forth like it itches inside. I think she has that duckbilled cap on to hide that rat nest of a head of hair. She picks a big scab on her arm that she got when she fell chasing a turkey. Her German shepherd is grown now. He caught the turkey for her. Killed it at the same time.

I get out of my chair, grab a handful of beans, and figure I can help Mama sift through them for rocks and clods. She used to have me help. Loretta has already started. Mama seems different now that I know she was an orphan. I never felt sorry for her before. I guess everyone gets their share of life's troubles.

"I was thinking about taking Samantha with me," I say.

"I told you once before to quit thinking about her. Nothing to talk about where she's concerned, and I don't want her messing around Lenny's grave." And then Mama turns on Loretta, again. "I'm holding you responsible for this kid. He's out of control. Ever since he moved out of this house, he's not been the same."

I'm afraid I'm standing a little close to Mama. "But, Mama, she looks just like Lenny."

"I bet you sicced Trish onto this, too, didn't you? You got Trish wound up on that little bastard girl, didn't you?"

"I took her to meet Samantha, but I let her make up her own mind."

"You let a fifteen year old girl decide? Trish is still a baby, Bobby Ray! I'll never forgive you for this. Never! You went against my wishes. I'm your mother."

"But, Mama, Samantha is really Lenny's daughter. She really is."

"I'm not talking to you about that little bastard, Bobby Ray. She's not Lenny's. They tried to say that before just to drag our good name into the gutter with them and I'm just not having it."

"Mama," and I take a look over at Loretta, because here I go, "you know I have Lenny's journal. I brought it with me." And I hold it up so she can see it. "It even has his name in his own handwriting."

So Mama turns her back on me, faces toward the laundry room. "Burn it, Bobby Ray, before it's too late."

"But, Mama, a lot of people know about Samantha."

And then Mama turns on me. It's as if she's changed into another human being. "Damn you! Bobby Ray," and I've never heard Mama use words like that. "Damn you to hell. God wouldn't do that to me. You don't know what you're saying."

Chapter 50: *Putting the Pressure on Mama*

"Don't you talk to my boy like that, Louise." I never thought about the two of them getting into it. "He's just trying to help, so don't you go cussing at him."

"The both of you, get out of here and shut your mouths. That Kunze girl wasn't fit to clean Lenny's boots. No telling who that baby belongs to. Even went to his funeral and her body swelling with sin. And now you've got Trish into it. This is all your fault."

"But, Mama, all I want to do is get all this about Lenny straightened out. And get some proper words said over Lenny's grave. The preacher never finished the words they say to put the dead to rest," I tell her.

"You're telling me? Shame on you. The Lord takes care of His own."

"That's not good enough for me." I don't think I've ever been mad at her like I am right now.

She doesn't have a comeback for that. "That little bastard girl is not Lenny's," she says. "The Kunze's live like a pack of dogs. They lived that way before Heidi died. She was another no-account piece of trash."

"All I'm saying, Mama," and then I have to pause to get some air, "is that Lenny wrote in his journal that he got Gretta pregnant, and I've seen Samantha and she looks like Lenny's pictures when he was her age."

"No!" and Mama has started shouting. "He couldn't have. Don't you even know human decency?" She starts crying again. "Here I've always tried to live a good Christian life and you making us all look like a pack of alley cats."

I hear the front door open and here comes Papa. Seems like every time Mama and me get into something, Papa comes in. This time I'm not stopping.

"But what's the truth, Mama? What is the truth?" And I'm shouting at her, but I can't help it.

"Loretta, get this kid out of here. I'm not having anymore to do with the likes of either of you." And she throws a handful of pinto beans at me, feels like buckshot all over my chest, then they scatter around on the floor.

But I'm not budging.

Papa throws his hat in the easy chair, comes on in the kitchen, real calm. Looks over at Loretta like what's she doing here? This is different though, him all calm and me and Mama mad.

"What you in a row over?" he wants to know.

"Bobby Ray is trying to get at Lenny beyond the grave."

369

"What?" Papa looks confused.

"I'm not either, Papa. Lenny has a daughter and Mama keeps denying it. It's true. Charles told me, and maybe I don't think much of Charles, but I've seen the little girl. She's Lenny's daughter, I tell you. Her mother says she is too. And I've read Lenny's journal, and he said that he got Gretta pregnant." I'm talking to Papa, but I'm looking straight at Mama. My voice just won't seem to quiet down at all.

Papa stands in the doorway with his mouth open.

Mama's given up on the beans, grabbed a knife and started slicing on the bread. "Charles filled you with lies while he had you out alone." Instead of using her finger, she's pointing that knife at me now. "You should have more sense than to run around with someone that much older than you. He's made you sick, Bobby Ray, sick in the head."

"No he hasn't either, Mama. I don't respect him at all. I know more about him than you do. I hate him. He was part of the reason Lenny got killed. He's even been messing around with Trish." There. I've finally said it, and said it in front of Papa. I don't know when I've ever felt so good about something.

"So Charles Kunze is behind Lenny dying." And he looks like the world's biggest puzzle has just been solved.

"Now I didn't say that, Papa. Don't you go putting words in my mouth. I know he didn't kill him. It says so right here in Lenny's journal." I'm sorry I said anything about Charles. "It's just that Charles has been asking questions about Lenny's journal. If we could get this thing about Samantha settled, we might be able get rid of a lot of the ill feelings between the Hammers and the Kunzes."

"But he's been messing around with Patricia? That cocksucker? Why didn't you tell me?"

"I didn't know what you would do, Papa. I didn't know what you would do."

"Damn, son, I would've killed him if you told me. You know that. That sonofabitch caused Lenny's death, for sure? And now this with Patricia?"

Once he gets something in his head, there's no getting it out. Now here comes Trish in the front door just as if she's been waiting outside for her name to be called.

Papa starts in on her. "What the hell are you doing messing around Charles Kunze?" And Papa has taken a couple of steps toward her like he could hit her for the first time in his life, and he's shouting at her. "Tell me, goddamnit. I'm waiting for an answer."

Mama jumps in the middle of Papa. "Now, Hershel, you back off of Trish. You're not talking to her like that."

"You just shut the hell up, woman. You don't run this household. I've had all the shit off of you during the last month I'm putting up with. Trish! Don't you start down that hall. Tell me about you and Charles Kunze."

Trish turns part way round, slings her words over her shoulder. "Charles is looking for a ring, Papa. He thinks you have a ring that belonged to his mother. He said some bad things about you and his mother." Trish always has known how to stop Papa cold when she really wants to. She doesn't mind hurting him either. And now the cat is all the way out of the bag.

"Well, what did you expect, Hershel?" And now it's Mama scolding again. "You and Heidi messing around together all those years. What did you expect?"

It's as if Papa didn't even hear what Mama has just said. "I'm going to kill that sonofabitch. Him messing around you." And now he's turned around, gone in the living room looking for his hat. He clumps down the hall with Trish right after him, the old boards creaking with the strain of his weight, turns in their bedroom. I don't hear anything for a little bit. Then I hear the cedar chest close with a thud. And then I know. Papa has his pistol.

I look over at Mama. She's breaking off a piece of bread and sticking it in her mouth. It looks dry and useless, like she can't swallow it. "You've pushed your papa too far this time," she says with her mouth full. "You should have stayed out of this. What was done, was done."

"I just want to get it straightened out, get the truth told so that there wouldn't be any hard feelings."

"You don't know the half of it. I felt the same way you do several years ago. So I found out the truth about Gretta. I found out beyond all doubt that Karl isn't Gretta's father. Hershel is. It took Heidi killing herself before I made up my mind. I confronted her with what I suspected about Gretta, that she was Hershel's baby. She killed herself because of me. After that I thought how heartless I'd been pursuing the truth with such vengeance. I decided to let people's mistakes be forgiven in silence. Well, you've gone me one better, Bobby Ray. You're not my blood kin, but all the nursing from my breasts must have left something of me inside you. You've proved that Samantha is the product of incest. Now you take that downtown and shout it aloud on the streets of Chowchilla. Spread your truth, Bobby Ray. And now look at the state you've got your papa worked into."

And here comes Papa, clomping back up the hall, then turns, headed for the door. But Trish stops him again. "Where's the ring, Papa? Charles says you have it. I want to see the ring."

Papa looks taken back for a minute, finally realizing he has to come clean about the ring. Suddenly, he just explodes. "All right, goddamn!" he shouts. And he runs toward the wall, puts his shoulder into it hard, so that the drywall cracks inward. Then he looks at it real close for a second, rubs on the wall with his finger like he has completely lost his mind and then draws back his fist and pounds it into the drywall, lets out a cry and a loud "god-do-mighty" like it hurt more than anything he's ever felt. The force of the blow shakes the whole house. I can tell that Papa just broke his fist but that doesn't even slow him down. He rears back again and this time drives his fist clean through the wall, comes out the other side with meat, bone and blood showing, shoving drywall into the kitchen. Then he starts jerking and slinging drywall all over the living room. Finally, he says, "All right. Charles wants the ring," and he's holding it up between two broken fingers, "he can have it. But I'm going to kill him first." He strides toward the front door, then stops to look at me, top to bottom, like I'm a piece of trash. "Maybe you don't care if someone murders your brother and is after your little sister," he says. "You don't have a sense of family anymore anyway. Maybe you don't even have balls in your pants, but I can tell you one thing for sure. Your old man's not sitting on this one." And he slams the door behind him.

Mama seems real calm now. Papa going berserk has calmed her. "Look what the truth has done to your papa, Bobby Ray. But if that's not enough truth for you, here's one I didn't have the courage to dig into. Karl Kunze's sterile. It's possible he's always been sterile. All the Kunze kids could belong to your papa. Even Charles."

I'm still standing in the kitchen listening to silence because Mama has finally quit talking. I hear the clock ticking. As I take a couple of fast steps toward the door, I look back at Mama. She has this blank look on her face.

CHAPTER 51: *Charles in Danger*

Papa's in his pickup doing seventy through a stop sign. I'm right behind in my Chevy with my front bumper almost touching his. He swerves from side to side to keep me from passing. I have to back off a couple of feet as we go through the dip at the Berenda Slough, where Lenny was killed, and I see the old pickup's wheels leave the ground just before mine do, then up the other side and they leave the ground again. At the left turn onto County Road, Papa's going too fast and has to swing wide, then loses it. I take the turn on the inside and have to go part way into the bar ditch but when I come out, I'm okay. Papa's pickup is looming big in my rearview mirror now and I hear the engine whining like he has it revved out in low gear.

I scatter a bunch of chickens and slide to a stop in the dirt yard in front of Charles' shack with his little barn off to the left and step out into the cloud of dust I've raised. I hear a calf bawl. Charles comes out of the shack quick, as if he's been expecting us, letting the screen door slam. I see Gretta and Samantha peek out the screen door.

"What the hell you doing coming in here? This is my place."

"Papa's come to kill you, Charles. Better make a run for it."

"He can't chase me off of my own place."

"He found out you've been messing around with Trish."

"Who told him? Tell me that."

Papa steps out of his pickup slinging the chamber to his pistol closed and Charles starts to go back inside, then knows it's too late.

"So this is it," Charles says. "You've come after me with your papa and with pistols."

I have no interest in Charles now. I turn my back on him, face Papa.

"Come on," Papa says to me, "let's kill him together, Bobby Ray. Just you and me."

I get an image of Charles lying on the ground, us beating off parts of his body with our fists, blood and flesh flying. I shake my head. "I won't, Papa." I feel the tears start to come.

"Stand back then," he says. "I aim to finish my business." He has his black pistol in his left hand because his right one is quivering and dripping blood.

"No, Papa, I can't let you."

"I'm warning you. I'll shoot through you to get him."

"I'm not thinking of Charles. I'm thinking of Lenny, Trish and Curt. I'm thinking about you, Papa. So I'm not backing off."

"Charles," says Papa, "here's a ring that belonged to your mother." But he throws the ring in the dirt over by the little milk barn. "I've got something for you that comes with the ring. I should have done this five years ago, but I thought I'd let Lenny deal with you in his own way. But you're messing with Trish now. So I'm stopping you my way this time." Papa keeps trying to see around me. "Bobby Ray, it's time for you to step aside." He raises the pistol, and points it right between my eyes. I hear a rooster crow. I try to imagine how it'll feel when the bullet goes in my head. I see the hammer move back, the cartridge turn. He fires a shot. I feel the sting of a powder dusting me. Smell the smoke. I hear a rustling behind me, think maybe Charles has moved. "Go get the ring, Charles," Papa says.

"Stay behind me," I say. "He'll kill you, Charles, if you move."

"Jesuschrist, when are you going to wake up? That man behind you is the devil himself."

"I don't want you behind bars, Papa. He's not worth it."

"I can't live any longer with him alive. Five years ago I saw him with Lenny's wife. I have lived with that long enough."

"Killing him won't solve the problem. It's not him, Papa. It's us. We're the problem."

Then Papa turns that pistol toward my car, shoots out the windshield, a couple of clean holes in the side. Just when I think maybe he's through, he turns that pistol on Charles' shack, dumps three shots into it. Gretta and Samantha are in there. I hope no one is hurt. Papa throws the black pistol into the side of my car. "He's all yours then," he says to me and walks to his pickup. He revs the motor when he starts it, slides a hooker with that old pickup peeling dirt all the way, and when he hits the black top, it squalls and leaves black smoke rising off the road.

"Your old man's crazy," says Charles.

" I don't blame him a bit for wanting you dead." I walk over to pickup Papa's pistol.

"Leave it," says Charles. "You owe me a pistol."

"Don't push me, Charles," I say. "Just don't goddamn well push me. You have the ring. Papa gave it to your mother years ago when they both lived in Oklahoma."

"You mean Hershel Hammer knew my mother in Oklahoma? You're a lying son of a bitch."

"They were engaged. I don't care if you believe me or not. But that's the reason Papa took it off of Lenny's finger. The ring belonged to Papa."

"You lying sack of shit."

"I may not let Papa kill you, but I have to keep telling myself that you didn't do anything with Trish. If I thought you did anything to her like you did to me, I'd kill you right now easier than a mosquito."

"You really talk tough with a pistol in your hand," he says.

I hop in my Chevy, I drive back to Papa's place in a hurry. No telling what he'll have done by the time I get there.

CHAPTER 52: *When Words Fail*

I slide to a stop in the dirt out front. Soon as I crack my car door, I hear Mama scream. When I open the front door, I hear a back bedroom door slam. Loretta comes into the living room hollering at me, "Ray! Hershel and Louise are having a fight. They've locked themselves in the bedroom and it sounds like they're tearing out the walls." Curt's sitting in the corner of the dining room with his head between his knees like he's afraid to even move.

That's when we hear the screech of tires out front like someone is braking real hard, then whatever it is takes off again followed by a crash like two cars have run together, and we run to the front window to take a look see. Charles has followed me home in his father's old '49 Ford pickup. Looks like he's rammed the side of my Chevy, backed up and just as I throw back the curtain to get a better look, he rams the corner of the house so that it feels like an earthquake. Stuff falls off Mama's cupboard onto the floor, plates, cups and saucers breaking, and I hear the house even shudder off in the back bedrooms. I feel the same quake go through me like something just broke open my chest, except nothing even touched me.

"Hey, you crazy sonofabitch," I yell through the window, then I'm out the door like a shot. But I have to run for it because Charles is about to back over me. Charles and that pickup disappear around the corner of the house, wheels spinning, just tearing the hell out of the lawn, and me running right after him. I get around the corner just in time to see Charles heading for the lawn mower, take out the two rusted fifty gallon drums used for burning trash, then on around to the other side of the house where he runs over Mama's garden which doesn't matter because it's just last years and everything dead, but I guess Charles wants it anyway, so he takes out a few dead sweet-corn stalks and then goes on around to the front of the house again, runs over the red water hose then back-ends Papa's pickup but this stops him because the two pickups lock bumpers and his motor dies. So here I am, huffing and puffing, right on top of him opening the door and dragging him out by the front of his shirt.

Charles' blood is everywhere. I don't have any trouble dragging him out of the pickup because he's out cold as a wedge with big gashes across his forehead and nose. Mama comes out the front door screaming. I think at first that it's about Charles but Loretta is right on Mama's heels telling me that her brother has taken the shotgun and headed toward the far side of the field. Mama screams. "Hershel's going to kill himself!"

So I dump Charles on the ground, pile in my Chevy, and Trish and Curt jump in the back. I try to stop them but the top is down and there's no keeping them out of a convertible if they really want in. We're bumping along the old lane that goes down the side of our pasture, doing about forty miles per hour, looking for Papa off in the hay field. Maybe Papa's cotton is failing but this is the best crop of hay he's ever had, stands about waist tall and just right for mowing. I think I see the top of Papa's head sticking out above the alfalfa in the far corner of the field.

"Hurry, Bobby Ray, hurry," is what Trish screams in my ear but there's no way I can go faster and keep from killing us all. I turn at the end of the field and head west for a ways, then stop because the lane ends and we can't get any closer to Papa in the car. Then we're high-stepping it through the hay and when we get close to Papa, I see something really strange, so I stop Trish and Curt.

"Listen, Trish," I tell them. "The two of you stay here. Papa's just real mad at me. I've done some really bad things to Papa lately, so let me talk to him. Maybe I can talk some sense into him."

Trish has already started crying. "Don't do it, Papa," she shouts. "We love you, Papa."

Her words just break my heart. Curt looks more afraid than I'd have thought it was possible for a human being to look. But the two of them stay put. I think they're more afraid of seeing Papa like this than just minding me, and I walk slow through the fresh alfalfa to where he's sitting. I look back toward the house, and standing in the backyard, I see Mama and Loretta staring across the hundreds of yards of alfalfa to where we are.

Papa's sitting with his knees on the ground, his head bent forward and his arms stretched out in front of him. If it wasn't for one more thing, I'd think he was preying. But the thing is, he has that shotgun with the butt buried a little in the earth and the end of both barrels stuck in his chest. He has a stick in his left hand resting on the triggers. His right hand is wrapped in a dishrag and is hanging at his side quivering because it's all broken to pieces. Just a little nudge from that stick and no more Papa. He could be praying too because as I walk up I hear him mumble something.

"Papa, don't do this, Papa. Everything's going to be all right," I tell him. But it's as if Papa hasn't even heard me. I'm standing off to the side, a little in front, looking back at him but I've never seen such concentration on anyone's face. His forehead is just a mass of large sweat drops, some running down the side of his face, some dripping off his nose. "I'm sorry, Papa," I say, "I didn't know what trouble I was causing everyone. I'll stop all this stuff about Lenny now, Papa. It's going to be okay."

I think maybe he heard me because he just let out a big breath of air. It's just then that I see all the alfalfa flowers Papa is sitting in. White ones and violet ones and yellow ones and bees just a humming all over this field. I think I even notice the fresh smell of honey. Then I hear the worst sound a human being ever heard. That shotgun goes off, the two barrels almost at the same time, and I catch a look on Papa's face as he's being forced backward, as if he just realized what he's done, that he's made a terrible mistake. I shut my eyes because I can't look at this and I hear a sudden noise, like wings flapping, and I turn toward the west to see a pheasant that jumped up right by my feet when the shotgun went off, the pheasant flying about shoulder high off across that alfalfa field, flying a beeline into that old blood red sun sinking down on the far side of the earth. I hear Trish screaming.

When I get the courage to look back, I hope that it will have changed, that Papa will still be sitting there with that shotgun in his chest and I'll have another chance to talk him out of it. But that's not the way it is. The words I used will be the words that plague me the rest of my life. Why weren't they enough? Papa, who looked so large in life, now looks so small in death. The hole in his chest is just a small one, I think. Maybe we can still save him. But then I see the red bits of Papa strung out across that alfalfa field toward Trish and Curt, and I know that Papa is not a whole person anymore. Papa is dead.

Trish and Curt are walking toward us, so I go stop them. "You don't want to see this, Trish," I tell her. She has some bloody stuff on her forehead that I wipe off. "You don't want to see Papa like that." I put my arm around her and I grab Curt who has the sniffles now, and pull him in with us, put all our sweaty heads together. I remember how it was when I told them about Lenny being dead. That night we drove home on the little Ford tractor, the three of us all alone, three kids doing the things that should be left for grownups. When the times get really rough, it seems like it has always been just the three of us. And here we are again trying to face something that it isn't possible to face.

I hear Mama and Loretta in the distance shouting for us and then screaming. The screams are getting closer because Mama is coming to see what has happened to her husband, to find out what she already knows. But I just want to hold Trish and Curt as close to me as I can for as long as I can. There isn't going to be any peace in this world for me after this. My papa is dead. How can I have a life beyond his?

"Hershel! You get up, Hershel." It's Mama scolding Papa for the last time. She walks around him talking to him like he was sitting at the kitchen table reading the Chowchilla News. Then she rants on about all the good things that he did, as if she's still trying to talk him out of doing it. "You're just a good man, Hershel," she says. "You were just one hell of a good man. You had your weaknesses, but you were much more than just weakness. This farm is testament to that. Just look around you, Hershel. Look at what you've done with this farm in the twenty years we've lived here. Look at the fine children we've raised. Think of all the people you fed with your crops. Think of all the clothes you've put on people's backs with the cotton you chopped by hand, irrigated and cultivated with the tractor. Don't tell me you were a mean man, Hershel. I won't have any part of talk like that."

So while Mama is still ranting, I pull off my shirt and cover Papa's face and chest. I put one arm around Trish and the other around Curt and we walk back to my car and go to the house where I'll call Mr. Hickman to come get the latest Hammer to die by his own hand. We'll let Mama and Papa be alone together for the last time.

CHAPTER 53: *Bonfire*

We buried Papa two days later. Word of him dying spread like bad news always does. But Mama kept the time of the funeral a secret, begged Mr. Hickman to work on Papa through the night, and we had Papa in the ground by noon. Just the six of us. Jess made it too. His being there sure helped me a lot. Plus Reverend Hensen and his new wife, the former Grace Magdalena. He said some real nice things about Papa. Plus, of course, Mr. Hickman and Wayne. Wayne asked me if it'd be okay for him to be there to help his father. I said, sure.

Loretta had already called the ambulance for Papa by the time me, Trish and Curt got to the house. So when the ambulance got there, it picked up Charles instead of Papa. Charles was still unconscious. I hear he had a concussion and needed a few stitches, spent the night in the hospital, but Charles will be okay, okay to rape and pillage another day. I called Mr. Hickman and asked him to come pick up Papa. And then there were the police. We told them the truth about how Papa died, but Mama asked them to list it as a farming accident. They let it go at that.

I'm still struggling toward graduation. It's hard to study for final exams now, and I'm trying to think of a way to clean up the rest of my unfinished business. It's been two weeks since Papa died. Already I can't remember what it was like to have him alive and with us. It just seems like the pain of his death has always been a part of my life. And I keep wondering about what I've done. Why did I bloodhound this thing about Lenny so hard? I blame myself for Papa committing suicide, but then, so does Mama. And Loretta cries all the time about the part she played in it. Trish wishes she could take back some of the things she said, and Curt, well, he feels guilty about everything all the time anyway.

Right now, I'm sitting beside a little fire I have going out back of our turkey shed. An old filled-in slough bed runs through the back of our place, and the only thing that will grow back here is a few cottonwood trees and scraggly bushes. I've broken up some dead limbs, piled them in a little depression and struck a fire. I always have enjoyed a fire at sunset. I take a stick and move a few coals around. Seems like the smoke always wants to blow in my face.

This thing about Lenny's journal just won't stop. Gretta has hounded me about it again. I would like to keep it, but it just weighs so hard on my mind. That's the reason I have built this bonfire. Maybe that's the thing. As long as I have that journal, I won't be able to turn loose of the past. Seems like the reason I had to find it was so I could destroy it. Maybe burning it will return the past to the past, and people will think more about the future. So I set that little spiral notebook of Lenny's on the fire, watch the edges turn brown and curl. The sun has been set long enough now that it's starting to get dark. The fire spreads its light all around me. Nothing I like better than the red glow of a fire.

CHAPTER 54: *Bobby Gets a Haircut*

I need a haircut. I'm in Loretta's pickup because Pistoresi's has my Chevy. I pull into a parking place here on Robertson Boulevard just down from the police station. In front of me is Davis' Barber Shop. It has a red and white striped barber pole outside, looks like a big stick of candy, and it's turning so that it corkscrews like it's going to drill right through the sky.

All three barbers are out of work when I hit the door, and they're each reading a different section of the Fresno Bee, sitting in their own barber chair. Olin Davis has the funnies. He's sitting in the middle chair because he owns the place. He's been here so long, claims to have cut Orlando Robertson's hair back in the late '20s. Corbin Smeal, sitting in the first chair, winks at me as I come through the door. He's still going with Phyllis' mother. I don't like him. He's young and fills the spot given to the new barbers that come and go. I smell aftershave.

"Who's it going to be this time, Bobby?" says Olin, looking up from the funnies. "You taking me again or feeling reckless. Want a good haircut from one of these young punks?" Olin looks a little sadder today than usual.

I stand here for a second smiling. Grant Pierson, on the far end, gives the best haircuts in town. I've always wanted him to cut my hair. I can see his bald spot in the mirror behind him. But maybe another time. "Oh get up, Olin, if you think you can cut it good enough for graduation," I tell him.

He's the only one ever cut my hair besides Papa. He always lets me choose my barber though. When I start to get in the chair, Olin puts the padded wood shelf he uses for little kids across the chair arms for me to sit on, like I'm a kid again. Then he laughs and takes it off. He hasn't pulled that on me in years. He gave me my first real haircut twelve years ago. Papa used to cut my hair before I started school.

"Sorry to hear about that papa of yours," says Olin.

Chapter 54: *Bobby Gets a Haircut*

"Thank you, Olin," I say. My voice is not quite up to saying anything more, so it's real quiet while he throws the sheet over me, straightens it.

Thomas walks in, sees me sitting in Olin's chair, points at me. "That sister of yours," he says but doesn't go any further with it. He sits down in Corbin's chair. "Give me another flattop," he says. If there's one haircut Corbin can give, I hear it's a good flattop.

"Want me to trim the freckles, Thomas?" asks Corbin. Thomas doesn't have much to say about that.

"Yeah, I know all about my sister," I say. "So why did you take up with her if you don't like her."

Olin always pins the sheet and toilet paper too tight. Makes my neck want to stretch and twist. He always clips my hair a little close too.

"Hell, she won't go out with me graduation night."

"Sounds like good judgment finally got the best of her."

"Talk to her for me, would you, Bobby. I can't make it through graduation night without a girl."

"I don't have a girl for graduation and you don't hear me complaining."

"If that's true, it's the first thing you haven't complained about."

"I'm not a complainer. I'm real easy going."

"Like hell."

"Bobby's never complained about a haircut," says Olin. Runs a light comb through my hair then beats it out on the sink.

"Well that's the first," says Thomas. "Bobby Hammer bought a haircut and didn't complain about it. Somebody give him a medal."

Now here comes Charles in, that sonofabitch, and he has Herman with him. Where's Gordy, I wonder? Charles nods at Olin, takes Grant's chair acting like I'm not even in the room. Herman takes a seat and frowns up at me. I've been waiting for a chance like this.

"What'll it be, Charles. Shave and a haircut?" asks Ted.

"Just a haircut," says Charles. He's all business. Looks like he just got the stitches out of his forehead and nose.

I see a policeman through the window. It's Brock. He peeks through the door. "How long to get a cut, Olin?" he asks.

"Ten, fifteen minutes. We can work you in sooner if you've got police business."

Brock studies his watch for a minute. "Oh, what the hell," he says. So he takes a seat in front of me. Must be at least ten empty seats along the

383

wall. "The world's gone to shit anyway. What's another half hour?"

I hear the hum as Olin starts his clippers. Sounded like they stripped a gear getting going. My locks start hitting the floor.

I'm starting to sweat. I've been thinking about what to do about Charles for a long time. Had something new all worked out in my head for a few days and told myself that I was just waiting for the right situation. Trying to figure out how to set it up. Now I feel like I have set up myself. And here comes the Korenski family.

"Looks like you started the gold rush on haircuts, Bobby," says Olin. "You sure are good for business."

It's Leon, Ken and Cletis, haven't seen them since Leroy died, and my father, their good old Uncle Jess, their Uncle Jake plus their daddy. Guess Jake wants a head shine. The littlest one doesn't get haircuts yet. He must be along for the ride. Jess slaps me on the foot, sits down in front of me, gives me a nod.

"Heard your wife had a baby the other day," Olin says to Leon.

"You betchy. A big boy too. Ten pounds, two ounces."

"What does old grandpa over there think about that?"

"It's the first grandchild. I hope it's the last," says Mr. Korenski. "The world doesn't need another mouth to feed, not a Korenski's anyway."

Olin's clippers always get hot, burn the back of my neck when he dips 'em down. Here comes Delbert and he has two of his little kids by his second wife with him. She's from Texas.

"Hello, Delbert," I say. "How you doing?"

He puts his hat on the rack and takes a seat. The top of his head is white like it hasn't seen the light of day in six months. His two kids sit at his feet, start playing in the loose hair on the floor. "Great, Bobby. Just great. Came in here to get a haircut cause I'm celebrating getting a new job."

"When you starting?"

"Start tomorrow morning. Bright and early. While the frost's still on the punkin."

"Who you working for," I want to know.

"Just talked to old man Grissom, and I'm going to work for him."

"What's he up to that he can afford a first-rate hand like you?"

"Well, your mama has rented her ground to him. So he needs all the help he can get."

"Well, he can use you. I'll tell you that."

"I was sure sorry to hear about your papa. I figure if there's a way I can help out, I'd like to do it. I can sure as hell use the work too."

"If there's anyone knows how to farm that home place, it's you."

Delbert looks over at Charles. "How you doing Charlie Koonzass."

Charles just grunts because he doesn't much care for that.

I have my courage back up after that piece of good news from Delbert. "Brock, I've been meaning to tell you something," but I still can't believe it's my voice I'm hearing. My palms are sweating enough for it to run down the barber chair, puddle up on the floor.

"What's that, Bobby, you got another car I need to sign a muffler ticket on?"

Olin snorts. "Bobby still stuffing steel wool in those glasspacks."

"Hell, it's worse than that," says Brock. "Him and Melvin Swensen switched cars on me the other day. I had to sign the ticket just to keep them out of the mental hospital. Anybody find out about that, they're sure to put them away."

Herman laughs like a sonofabitch. I can tell my face is turning red but I can't help that. You'd have thought Brock would've said something at the time if he known what we were doing.

"No, Brock," I say, and then I have to stop to catch my breath because I'm winded already. "It's about Charles Kunze, sitting here next to me."

Olin kills the clippers, starts the sharp point of the scissors around my ear. More locks hit the floor.

"I always figured Charles could speak for himself. Isn't that the way you figure it, Charlie?" says Brock.

"You won't get this story out of him," I say, "cause he's the biggest thief in the San Joaquin Valley. Thieves aren't noted for talking about their work."

I hear a grunt come from Charles. Brock shuffles his feet, leans forward, then back. He's still looking at Charles.

"I've run around with Charles since September, and we've done some things you should know about. Cause Charles, he has plans."

"What is this, Charles? You know anything about this?" asks Brock.

"Bobby has a troubled mind. Hasn't been all there since his brother died," says Charles. "When his papa did himself in, it was more than he could take."

"Back in September," I say, and now I figure I'm doing this for Papa,

385

"Charles and I broke into Duane Powers tool shack, shot all the windows out of it, and stole a water pump. Pulled the generator off his John Deere."

"The county sheriff gets a lot of vandalism reports," says Brock. "They could use some help closing some of them."

"A few months ago, me and Charles shot up Fairmead. Made two runs through town at night shooting rooftops. Charles shot on one pass, I shot on the other."

"Just a goddamn minute," says Charles. "You may do shit like that but not me. You want to send yourself to jail, go ahead. But leave me out of it. I don't do stuff like that, Brock."

"Don't remember any report coming in to the station," says Brock.

I think that I'm not doing so good on this. Don't sound too convincing. "Probably so," I say. "I don't know what the coloreds feel free to report and what they don't. But we did it anyway."

"He's a liar about me, Brock," says Charles. "But I don't doubt that he did what he says he did."

It's just real quiet, again. Snip, snip, snip go Olin's scissors.

Old crippled Ben from the Beacon station walks through the door, sits down in a chair. "Ben," says Olin like he's real disgusted. "I've told you no haircut until you take a bath." Ben jumps up and walks out like he's going to cry. Maybe he can't take baths with that bad leg of his.

I'm not letting up on Charles. "How much gas, hubcaps, fender skirts he's taken is anybody's guess. I've helped him take a few."

"Don't listen to him, Brock. It's all lies. Him and his old man came out to my place just before Hershel killed himself. Hershel came to kill me, but Bobby stopped him. He's feeling guilty about that. I tell you, Bobby's gone crazy with guilt, so he's out to get me."

Brock straightens the belt that holds his pistol to his side.

"Uh-oh," says Uncle Jake. Jess is looking a mite uncomfortable in his chair too, but he nods for me to go on. Gives me a wink.

"Can you prove any of this, Bobby?" asks Brock.

"That's just it. Most of it doesn't really amount to much. On the important stuff, it's just my word against his. But somebody needs to watch him. I'm counting on you."

I hear Olin start mixing the lather in that old shaving mug of his.

"Charles likes little girls. He'll screw a fourteen year old, if you let him near one."

I feel the warm wetness of the lather that Olin paints around my ears. When Olin puts the mug back on the counter top, it chatters.

"He keeps talking about things he's done with my little sister. If I find out that he has, I'm going to kill him."

"Ken," says Mr. Korenski, "you and Cletis wait out in the car. I'll come get you when it's your turn." They get up and walk out slow like they'd sure like to stay to see what happens.

"Now he's started messing around with my thirteen year old brother. I hear Charles has a queer streak in him, so you can't trust him with little boys either. And during the Fair, he bought hard liquor for eighth graders. A bunch of them passed out in the bathroom of the Little Theater."

Grant turns the chair so that Charles is facing away from us. He's talking to the wall. "Goddamn you, Bobby Hammer!" says Charles. "You can't talk about me like that. You hear me, Brock? He's provoking me. He better be ready to pay the consequences."

I don't know how I keep talking except that I'm focusing on that twisting barber pole outside, it winding tighter and tighter. "Heard any dynamite go off around town lately, Brock?" I ask him.

That gets his attention. "Not since Halloween night."

"That's cause me and Charles haven't set any off since then. Charles took Leroy to help him steal the dynamite."

"Bobby," says Mr. Korenski, "Leroy was my son. And he's dead. Don't you go dragging him into this. I won't stand for it."

"What me and Leroy got into is a sight more than you'll ever want to hear about, Mr. Korenski. But Leroy was a good kid. Let's just leave it at that. I don't mean to try to drag Leroy down. Charles is the one I'm after. I tell you, Charles is dangerous. He shouldn't be running loose."

"There's no truth in any of it, Brock," says Charles. "Bobby, I'm warning you. I'll fuck you up right here in the barbershop, police or no police, if you don't shut up."

Uncle Jake gets up, heads for the door too. "Goddamn!" he says. "I can get a haircut another time. Jesus Keerist."

Leon follows him out. Delbert picks up his youngest kid off the floor, brings the other one to stand by his leg. I feel the pressure of Olin's thumb stripping the soap from behind my ear, feel the tingle of the razor slicing along my hairline. Jess looks up at me, gives me another wink, nods his head for me to keep going.

Thomas clears his throat. Shuffles his feet on the flat metal footrest. "I know about shooting up Fairmead," says Thomas. "I'm not too proud of it, but I was there too. Believe me, Brock. Bobby's telling the truth. Word for word."

"How many dogs have been found shot dead lately, Brock?" I ask.

"Old man Wynsum, over on Defender Street, had one shot in his front yard a week ago. Before that, about one a month, sometimes two."

"Charles shoots dogs like Buffalo Bill shot buffalo. Shoots 'em, lets 'em lay. At least if he's been skinning 'em, I haven't seen him yet. Wants a colored man real bad, but he'll settle for a dog. Same thing according to him anyway. Now, every time a dog or a colored is missing, you have a suspect."

Olin has the hot steam towel on my neck cleaning off the soap.

"Siphon pipes are his specialty. He'll take an order for them if you're not too particular where they come from." I hear a ruckus. Out of the corner of my eye, I see Charles climbing out of Grant's barber chair, the sheet still around his neck.

"Goddamn, you, Hammer. I don't have to sit here listening to this shit." He pulls at the sheet until the pin pops loose, throws it at me with the big clumps of his hair still on it. Still has soap on his ears. "Let's go Herman." But when Charles gets even with me, he grabs the sheet Olin has covering me, jerks it, and since it's wrapped around my neck, he jerks me toward him.

"Hey, watch it," says Olin. "Bobby's a paying customer. Get out of here, if your leaving. I don't won't tolerate trouble."

Brock stands up out of his seat, puts his hands on his hips. "Not going to be any trouble, is there, Charles?"

Charles just keeps glaring at me with his pale blue eyes, but he can't say anything to me here in front of Brock. Finally, he lets go of the sheet. I lean back into the barber chair.

"Pay your money, and get out," says Olin, pointing a black comb at him.

"I didn't get a full haircut," Charles says, turning on Olin.

"Pay the man," says Brock. "He didn't ask you to leave before he was finished."

Charles reaches in his pocket, throws a fifty-cent piece on the floor. "That's all the haircut I got, that's all I'm paying for," and he heads for the door behind Herman.

I only have one more thing left to say, then I'm through, and I want to get it in before they get out the door. "Now Charles has imported Herman Nelson here, and Gordon Smith, both from Mountain View, and they've set up shop here in Chowchilla. The other night I followed them out by Dos Palos. Looked like they were stealing a tractor. They're moving into a big-time operation, Brock. Stop them, if you can."

Herman goes on out, but Charles turns back, holding open the glass door. Gives me the finger with his arm outstretched, shakes that stiff finger for me. They walk out, stand by Loretta's pickup, talking and looking back at me through the glass. Charles sees me looking at him, gives me the finger again.

That powdered brush of Olin's always makes me cough when he flicks it across my nose.

"Goddamn," says Mr. Korenski, letting out a big breath of air. "Fella could have a heart attack waiting to get a haircut from you, Olin."

"I'm sorry, Mr. Korenski," I say, "but I had to throw everything I had at him. Maybe that about Leroy was one I should've left out."

"By god, Bobby Hammer. You've got the nerve," says Olin.

"Think I made a mistake?"

"Why do you kids get into stuff like that anyway?"

Brock climbs into the chair Charles just left. "Bobby, you better watch your step around town for a while," he says. "Charles may not leave this one alone."

Olin pulls the sheet off me, shakes it hard enough to get a pop. Motions for Jess to hit the chair. I stand up and have to stretch a little while I search through my billfold for a dollar. Take a quick look in the mirror. Sure enough, skinned again.

"Put your wallet back in your pocket," says Olin. "Consider it a graduation present. As a matter of fact, let me shake your hand. You just bought yourself a lifetime haircut. As long as I'm alive, you've got a free haircut."

"What are you so happy about, Olin," Brock wants to know.

"Charles shot my German shepherd five years ago. Pulled up in the street out front of my house and waited for my dog to make a run at him. Shot him dead with me standing there watching him. Damn good watch dog too. Hadn't bit anybody but the postman."

"Come here, Bobby," says Brock. Grant has the sheet on him now.

I stand in front of him, look down at the old linoleum floor.

"How much of this stuff about Charles do you know to be the truth?"

"Bobby's the best boy in the town of Chowchilla," says Jess. "Charles is a scum bucket. Everybody knows that."

Delbert puts his two cents in. "Bobby doesn't lie about anything. If he says it, you can believe it."

Brock gives them both a shut up look.

"I might have guessed on a couple of things. Damn good guesses though," I say, looking up. "This is just the tip of his iceberg."

"Two cotton trailers were taken during the night a week ago from Grey's Gin here in town. And a cultivator stolen out at Redtop yesterday."

"So maybe it wasn't a tractor. I don't see very good in the dark."

"I doubt there's any way we can bring charges against Charles for any of this."

"If I thought there was, I would've come to the station."

"Most of it's in the County's jurisdiction anyway. Then he smiles, shakes his head. "You watch yourself."

Here come the rest of the Korenski's back in. I give Jess a nod and, as I walk out I hear Thomas say, "Corbin, you call that a flattop?"

CHAPTER 55: *Waylaid on Robertson Boulevard*

I'm on the Boulevard, a little past Highway 152, when it feels like I have a flat. I don't think Loretta keeps a jack in her pickup, so I pull over and get out to check. Sure enough. But I'm in luck, because here's a car pulling over to help. Then I see that it's Herman driving, Charles sitting in the passenger seat. Looks like that may be Gordy's head in the back. I jump the fence and take off running in a cotton field, but Charles is faster than me. Herman and Gordy each get an arm, and Herman just broke my left one. They have my knees on the ground, each in a furrow so I'm straddling a row, the green cotton stalks standing halfway to my belt buckle. Charles bends over me. Pulls my head up by my hair so I'm looking at him.

"I'm going to kill you, Bobby Hammer."

"Oh, no! Charles. No killing," says Gordy. "Please, Charles. No more killing."

I hear Herman snigger.

"Hang on, Gordy," say Charles. "You're going to have a bad heart if you keep taking things so seriously. I can't do it now because they'd have me behind bars before I got the knife through Bobby's throat good. But there'll be a time. The next one'll be the right time."

Herman really has me sweating about my left arm. I keep hearing it pop. I know it's broken, but Gordy's taking it easy with my other one.

Charles thinks a minute. "I can't believe you even had to tell them about the goddamn dogs. Just for that, I'm giving you something to convince you of my good intentions. Do you have any scars on you, Bobby?"

This seems important to him, and I'm afraid that no matter which answer I give him it's not going to be good for me. I have to think a little. "No," I say. "I don't."

"Good, Bobby. That's real good. You're still a virgin. I'll just make a little slit here just above your collarbone." He pulls out a switchblade with a bright red handle, flips it open.

"Oh no, Charles. Don't do it to him," say Gordy, and he almost lets go of my right arm.

"Down, Gordy. Down. You're a psycho." And then Charles turns back to me, bends over me so that I can smell his breath. "Poke a hole, here in the little hollow of your neck," he says, pushing my head to the side.

And I feel the sharp sting just below my neck, can't keep from flinching as I feel the blade poke through my skin, the cutting edge slice, then grate against my collar bone, the blood puddle, run down my chest.

"Well, that's enough for now," he says, like he just took a sip of whiskey from a fresh bottle and recorked it because he wanted to save the rest till later. He takes a deep, satisfying breath. "From now on, I'm going to stalk you. Every time you round a corner, I'll be there. Every time you're out in your car alone at night, or maybe with a girl parked on some lonesome road, I'll be there. When you're plowing a field for your mama all alone late at night, I'll be there too. Maybe you'll be in your own bed and I'll sneak in a window. But sometime I'll do it, Bobby Hammer. You can depend on it. Sometime I'll kill you for what you've done to me."

★

I don't know how I got home. Just seems like I appeared at the door. I didn't tell Loretta what happened. Told her I had a nosebleed. My left arm felt better after Herman turned it loose. But later I told Jess what Charles said to me. He just laughed. "Charles isn't going to mess with you anymore, Bobby. Don't you know that? He had you all by yourself, him with two of his buddies out in a field. He's afraid of you, Bobby. I tell you he's afraid of you."

"But why did I run from him?" I asked Jess. "Am I a coward?"

CHAPTER 56: *Graduation*

It all comes down to this. Either I graduate or I don't. And we're all sitting here at the fairgrounds grandstand where they had the rodeo three weeks ago, listening to Mr. Sonnett give us what-for. Can't keep from squiggling in my seat. We're really a strange looking crew with all these flat hats and tassels. But I know I'll make it out of here even if I don't graduate. I'd like to get that diploma, but I can make it without it. I'll find a job somewhere. Sure I will.

I hear Charles has left town. Some say for good. So I don't have to be on the lookout for him here in the graduation crowd. I'm looking at it like Charles has done me a favor by threatening to kill me. Now I'm looking at my life like it's more important. I look at each day as though it will be the last I get to be here on this earth. Everything and everybody just seems so important to me now. And I don't know that my situation is really that much different from anyone else's. Life hangs in the balance with every tick of the clock. Most people don't realize that. But that's the way life is, and either you put that ticking out of your mind or you recognize it and learn to live by it. Charles has forced me to recognize it. That time after I tried to kill Charles and couldn't, that day that I was afraid of myself, taught me a lot. I know now that something inside of me is more threatening than Charles or anything that exists outside of me. If I can learn to recognize that fear, live with the fear of what is inside me, I can live with anything. When I remember that, I'm not so afraid of Charles anymore. And if Charles really knew me, and what I'm capable of, he'd know better than to come around.

Papa has taught me the most important lesson of all. I know that Papa wished that he hadn't killed himself. I saw it in his face the instant after the shotgun went off. Papa didn't have the courage to keep living. He was afraid to face what he had done. As Jess put it, Papa found his nigger, but he couldn't face him. The same was true for Heidi Kunze and Lenny. They couldn't face the truth of their lives.

Brenda didn't get to be valedictorian. Billie Wade, the doctor's daughter, beat her out. "Thank God," Brenda said. "Now I can enjoy graduation." So Billie is up there giving her talk and she has a lot of important things to say, and while she's saying them, I'm listening close, but I'm also sitting here feeling how much I like Chowchilla and its people. I can't believe how much my opinion of this place has changed after all that has happened. But I still realize that this isn't my home anymore. Whether I graduate or not is not really the point.

This afternoon, before I got dressed for graduation, I walked to the far side of Mama's field in my old dirty Levis, work boots and an old T-shirt I've been wearing for four years. And I noticed how much I love the land. Not just the land that I've lived on here for the last eighteen years. It's not just Chowchilla. It's this whole valley, the San Joaquin Valley. I like flat country. I like the way the sun goes all the way to the horizon at sundown. I like the way the ice cracks in the mud puddles when I step in them of a morning in wintertime. I like the feel of fog closing in, the feel when it lifts and the sun comes out. I like heat in the summer that makes sweat pour out of my body. This Valley won't leave me alone. It never will. But it's not home anymore.

I'm thinking about all this when I hear somebody behind me. It's Brenda on her knees behind my chair. She's left her seat and whispering in my ear. "What are you doing after the ceremony?" she wants to know.

To tell the truth, I don't have anything planned beyond the time that I get that little red-leather folder from Mr. Sonnett. Maybe it'll have a diploma in it, and maybe it'll just have a blank sheet of paper. But regardless of what's in it, I don't know what my next step is. My car's in the junkyard, so I don't have a way around tonight either. Everybody I could go with wants to go get drunk. I'm not interested in drinking. Maybe I'll just go on home afterward. So this is what I tell Brenda, not in so many words, but she can see that I'm not up for much of anything. I may not have anything to celebrate anyway. I could go in my room and pullout some of those college catalogs, some that go back to 1941, that Loretta gave to me a couple of years ago. She said they were her dead dreams.

"Come with me, Bobby," says Brenda. "Please. It's just Phyllis, her new boyfriend from Merced and me. We'll go to dinner first, then to the dance. My mother's willing to fix a big breakfast for us at two o'clock in the morning. She's promised not to complain too much."

I think about it a second. Can't wait too long because somebody will get on her case for being out of her seat.

"I would have asked you sooner," she says. "But I thought you had plans with someone else."

Me and Bev did have plans. I don't want to think about who she will be with, but I know anyway. It's Melvin in his stinking milking boots.

"No drinking, I promise," Brenda says. "And we might even have some time for just the two of us. Just you and me."

How can I pass up an offer like that?

Now Brenda is back in her seat and Billie has finished the valedictorian speech and all the other speakers are finished too. So we start filing past the reviewing stand. Mr. Sonnett calls a name and whoever it is walks by, takes the red-leather folder, gets a handshake and passes on back to their seat.

I'm standing at the edge of the platform now and over the loudspeaker I hear, "Bobby Ray Hammer." So here I go.

Mr. Sonnett's head is shining in these floodlights like it has a new coat of floor wax. "Good job, son," he says to me. He tries hard to look me in the eyes, but he can't quite make it. Got his eyes down to about my eyebrows.

I wonder what he meant, "good job"? I take the folder from him and shake his hand. But as I walk off, he does something he hasn't done to anybody else. He slaps me on the back, up there between my shoulder blades where my neck starts. "Take care of yourself, Bobby," he says. Squeezes a little. And he didn't do that to anybody else. Just me.

So I walk off of that platform, and we all walk in single file back to our seats. I have my head down. Brenda is the first one to me. "Tell me, Bobby. Tell me. Did you graduate? I have to know." I think she is about to wet her pants.

"I don't have the courage to look," I tell her.

"Give it to me then," she says, and she jerks the folder out of my hand. She's just silent for a second and when she looks up, I think I see tears in her eyes and she looks stunned. "My god, Bobby, you made it!" she shouts. "You made it. You graduated!" I start smiling and everyone in Chowchilla now knows that I have just graduated from high school.

Mr. Wood, my physics teacher, comes to me after the ceremony, shakes my hand. "I want to tell you something, Bobby. And please don't be offended."

I take a step back from him when he says that.

"You are a smart young man, but you sell yourself as a dunce. And, like everything you do, you're very good at it. Not only have you sold it to the rest of the world, you've sold it to yourself. But you can't fool me, not anymore. I've seen what's underneath that false front. Stop it or it'll affect your future. Let it end here, Bobby. Let it end tonight."

Then Loretta finally finds me. She's with Jess again. Jess even has on a jacket and tie. And Loretta. It's the first time I have ever seen her look like a woman. I just grab her and hug her because I love her so much. But she has something for me, and she can't wait for me to get it open. It's just a card, but what the heck. It's from my mother. But when I get it open I find a tiny little leather book with gold writing on the front that says Bank of America. My eyes start to fill with tears over this because I know how she's scrimped and saved all these years. Sure enough it's a savings account in the name of Bobby Ray Hammer. She keeps pushing pages until we get to the last entry in it. And she stands back beaming. Jess just has his head down. But Loretta has saved three thousand dollars for my college education.

So now I'm standing in front of Trish and Curt. Trish wants to know what I'm crying about. "It's just a graduation," says Curt. Mama stands behind them, but she's not saying much. God, I wish Papa could see me.

Then Brenda grabs me and it's just, "Bobby, Bobby, Bobby. It's over, Bobby. It's all over. We're free for the rest of our lives!"

CHAPTER 57: *One More Stop at the Cemetery*

Strange how I feel about Chowchilla after being away at college for a while. I survived summer school and Loretta survived without me. Jess seems to like being with her more when I'm not around. And now the fall semester has started. Phyllis was right about going to a junior college. They are less expensive, and the teachers have more time for their students. By the time I finish my two years here, I'll be ready for a four-year college. I'm thinking about civil engineering, still planning to build bridges some day. This is the first time in my life I've been away from Chowchilla for more than a couple of days, and now late at night when I'm studying in my dorm room here on campus, after all the other guys have gone to sleep, I think that all the things that happened to me there seem like a dream.

Back in October I went back to Chowchilla for a couple of weeks to work for Loretta with the turkeys. I'd been thinking a lot and I had a plan. I gathered up all the guns I could find. I had Lenny's pistol that I almost killed Charles with, Papa's black pistol that he would have killed Charles with if I'd let him, my little twenty-two that I shot the back of Lenny's car with, and Papa's shotgun that he killed himself with, and I took them all with me to the far side of Mama's farm, back to the junkyard where Lenny and I used to hunt rabbits and where Helen first told me that she and Lenny had been married. I dug a hole with an old rusted shovel I found and buried all those guns three feet down. I hope no one ever finds them. It won't be long before they rust enough that they won't shoot anyway.

On the way back by the house, I had Trish steal Mama's big black Bible from her bedroom, and then we rounded up Curt. We went out to the Cemetery and as we drove through the gate, I saw Gretta standing still watching for us, and little Samantha jumping from gravestone to gravestone like she was playing hopscotch. And then, on that autumn day, with the sun on my head and gold maple leaves scattered about, I looked down at Lenny's tombstone with all the others gathered round. Papa's grave still looked fresh beside Lenny's. But we'd come for Lenny. We talked about what verse we wanted for a while and ended up with St. John 14:27.

"Lenny," I said, "we want you to listen to this because we have something important to say. We bring a message from Jesus." I started crying but I didn't care, and I didn't care what Mama had said about how Jesus felt about me. No one there would question who Samantha's father was either. The little red letters stood out clear in the bright sunlight, but they didn't come out of my mouth very well because my voice kept cracking.

> Peace I leave with you, my peace
> I give unto you: not as the world giveth,
> give I unto you. Let not your heart
> be troubled, neither let it be afraid.

"We still wish you were here, Lenny," I said aloud, "but we forgive you for taking yourself from us. We think that if you had it to do over again, you'd decide to stay with us." It took me three tries to get all the words out. I wished, more than anything that he could have answered back and forgiven me for the mean things I did to him. But that's something that just won't happen in my lifetime. Then we all came together, me, Trish and Curt, Gretta and Samantha, put our arms around each other and stood together around Lenny's grave for a long time.

"Why's everybody crying, Mommy?" asked Samantha.

"We're crying cause we still love your daddy so much and he can't be with us."

Then Samantha cried too.

Lenny didn't graduate from high school, and I was already in college. I wished so much that I could have told him all that I'd learned. I wished so much that he'd made it to that point. Then he wouldn't have killed himself. Somehow I just knew that. Standing there that fall day, something happened to me, happened inside me, while I was standing before those two graves. It was what Gretta had just told Samantha that got me. And then I remembered something. And I dropped to my knees again, buried them in the earth there on top of their graves, because I hurt so much I couldn't stand it. Papa spent eighteen years of his life raising me. And Lenny was my older brother that I followed around pestering all the time. And then, while I felt my tears run down my cheeks, drip off my chin into the soft grass, I knew that, just then, I had found inside of me what I had been looking for ever since me and Curt and Trish drove home on the tractor the night Lenny died. I knew that I had lost everything that night, but I could never figure out what I meant by *everything*. And I'd been worrying about the words I used out in that alfalfa field to convince Papa not to kill himself. The words didn't get the job done. But no wonder. Everything I said was unimportant. I didn't tell Papa that I loved him. I didn't even know that I loved him.

Bev called Phyllis the other day, said that she and Melvin are expecting their first kid in March. They've been married four months. And I've been seeing Phyllis some lately. We both go to Fresno City College. We have the same English class, and we like to go to movies together. She likes to just sit and talk about things as much as I do. She's as pretty as ever. Guess she'll always be skinny too. I have seen Brenda a couple of times since high school graduation, but she goes to Fresno State and is so busy she doesn't have much time for socializing.

I'm having bad dreams again. This time about Mama. I'm still carrying around some things I'd like to talk to her about, but she seems more distant than ever. Mama keeps one of Lenny's baby pictures with her all the time, and Dr. Wade has had her under sedation the last two months. She sleepwalks at night, and Trish has to follow her around the house because she might go outside. Two weeks ago Mama came up missing at two o'clock in the morning, and Curt found her just at daybreak lying in the old pump house fast asleep on the loose floorboards. Mama had shut off the pump for some reason.

THE END

www.ingramcontent.com/pod-product-compliance
Lightning Source LLC
Chambersburg PA
CBHW031132260626
47153CB00021B/25

9 780982 953402